© Jill Sutton

MAGGIE MITCHELL has published short fiction in a number of literary magazines, including the *New Ohio Review, American Literary Review,* and *Green Mountains Review.* Originally from upstate New York, she now lives in Georgia. *Pretty Is* is her first novel.

Additional Praise for *Pretty Is*

"[A] stunning, multilayered debut . . . with a great deal of intelligent, beautifully written panache. . . . What a satisfying novel, with its shifting perspectives and competing stories and notion that our relationship to the truth changes with time and distance."

—*The New York Times*

"Mitchell knows what she's doing. As she patiently parcels out details about the abduction, she explores the horrifying yet magnetic grip such traumas have on our lives and imaginations. . . . *Gone Girl* has primed us for female leads with dark pasts, but Mitchell's novel is an original and haunting page-turner about the emotional shocks that come with—literally—rewriting your history."

—O, *The Oprah Magazine*
("Page-Turners Too Addictive to Put Down")

"A magnificently complex, psychologically enthralling, and intelligently disturbing debut novel . . . *Pretty Is* reveals itself to be far more than a breathlessly entertaining read. It's a work of sly and seductive brilliance. . . . Mitchell gives us what every real thriller, mystery, and psychologically compelling work promises but few deliver: a searching look into our own worst fears about what we desire and what we need." —*Psychology Today*

"Maggie Mitchell's *Pretty Is* is an addictive read—Lois's and Carly May's alternating narrations keep the pace moving forward irresistibly—but it also kindles provocative ideas about our culture's obsession with real-life horror stories. Don't get too attached to your copy; you'll be lending it out to everyone you know this summer." —*Bustle*

"The novel *Pretty Is* not only baits, then switches, it ultimately forces readers to ask, 'What exactly are we afraid of here?' It's quite a piece of work from first-time novelist Maggie Mitchell, who uses the psychology of suspense to take us where we most definitely did not plan to go. . . . There is something to see here, something profoundly complex and deeply intriguing."

—*Daily News* (New York)

"What does it mean, the book asks, to have a traumatic experience whose limits aren't clear-cut, and might blur to include feelings of attachment, excitement, even pleasure? . . . An intriguing premise."

—*The New York Times Book Review*

"Mitchell's debut combines psychological suspense and literary fiction with well-drawn, believable protagonists who alternate as narrators. The story is strongest when we go inside the young women's minds as they grapple with their shared past. . . . Mitchell is on her way to a place at the femmes fatales fiction dais with Megan Abbott, Gillian Flynn, Tana French, and Sharon Bolton."

—*Library Journal*

"Mitchell's debut novel is both a skewering of America's JonBenét Ramsey–style fixation with little girls in peril and a fascinating glimpse at the intensity of female friendship. . . . Told in flashbacks from alternating points of view, the work is most interesting when Mitchell explores the girls' desires and neuroses. . . . Psychologically rich, with haunting detail, Mitchell's work is a disturbing, insightful look at our deep fears." —*Publishers Weekly*

"Mitchell carries readers through a thrilling, literary psychological adventure that examines how pivotal moments can echo throughout our lives." —*BookPage*

"Suspenseful, quick-paced, and action-driven, *Pretty Is* also wisely invests in character development. . . . Mitchell's greatest strength, however, is in the riveting, magnetic pull of her plot, as the stakes grow higher and *Pretty Is* rushes toward its finale."

—*Shelf Awareness*

"Stands out for its slick, subversive take on a trope that is showing no signs of going away . . . There are layers upon layers upon layers in *Pretty Is*. . . . Mitchell teases and dances, always one step ahead, never happier than when she's refusing to pin anything down." —*The Guardian* (London)

"If you prefer to add a dark edge to your sunny vacation, this debut work of literary suspense should keep you on the edge of your beach chair." —*The Huffington Post*
("15 Beach Reads to Bask in This Summer")

"An interesting and unexpected exploration of the aftermath of an abduction that left invisible scars . . . The voices of the two women are distinctive, each sharp and witty in her own way. A satisfying, unusual novel." —*Kirkus Reviews*

"The best book of its kind I've read since Lionel Shriver's *We Need to Talk About Kevin* . . . A powerful plot that keeps the tension bubbling and the reader's attention rapt, written by a natural-born storyteller blessed with emotional intelligence and sheer deftness of language. *Pretty Is* is a real thriller of a novel that will keep you up all night."

—Fay Weldon, author of *Habits of the House*

"Mitchell's fresh, spectacular, and bristly heroines illuminate this story of a crime survived. *Pretty Is* promises mountains of suspense, while offering a transfixing look at the urge to give voice, to make art." —Amity Gaige, author of *Schroder*

"Ram Dass says, 'We are all just walking each other home,' and while reading *Pretty Is*, I thought of that wisdom often. Kidnapped at age twelve, rescued six weeks later, Lois and Carly May head off into adulthoods as far from each other as possible. Yet they cannot help but walk back into each other's lives and relive the event, honestly, for the first time. Maggie Mitchell has a wonderful style, combining classic thriller techniques with those of literary fiction to create a novel that spools out like a ribbon. Readers of Tana French, Dennis Lehane, and James Lee Burke will recognize another writer with a surefire ability to tell a story."

—Jo-Ann Mapson, *Los Angeles Times* bestselling author of *Solomon's Oak, Finding Casey,* and *Owen's Daughter*

"Intriguing and suspenseful, surprising and smart . . . A riveting drama that stays with the reader long after the last page is turned."

—Jessica Treadway, author of *Lacy Eye*

"Mitchell writes with such a strong sense of character and voice that from the first sentence of *Pretty Is* I was entirely hooked. It's almost impossible to believe this is her first novel. You'll keep thinking about this suspenseful, brilliant debut long after you finish it. Ms. Mitchell makes many compelling observations about gender, desire, and fear. Extraordinary."

—Christine Sneed, author of *Little Known Facts* and *Paris, He Said*

"*Pretty Is* intrigues the reader with moral questions and ultimately alters these queries frame by frame. To answer the question of what pretty is is to ask what ugly is, and to accept challenging ethical ambiguities. This is a unique book, with lucid prose and compelling frankness about an emotional taboo few writers dare to give voice to." —Margaux Fragoso, author of *Tiger, Tiger*

"*Pretty Is* announces an exceptional new voice in fiction. By turns poignant, funny, and terrifying, *Pretty Is* mines the contradictions of the heart with fascinating skill. The relationships in this novel are ones you have not seen before."

—Leslie Daniels, author of *Cleaning Nabokov's House*

"A daring psychological thriller . . . I could not turn the pages fast enough. A wickedly good debut novel."

—Elin Hilderbrand, author of *The Rumor* and *Barefoot*

Pretty Is

Pretty Is

a novel

MAGGIE MITCHELL

Picador

Henry Holt and Company

New York

This is a work of fiction. All of the characters, organizations, and events portrayed in this novel are either products of the author's imagination or are used fictitiously.

Printed in the United States of America. For information, address Picador, 175 Fifth Avenue, New York, N.Y. 10010.

picadorusa.com • picadorbookroom.tumblr.com
twitter.com/picadorusa • facebook.com/picadorusa

Picador® is a U.S. registered trademark and is used by Henry Holt and Company under license from Pan Books Limited.

For book club information, please visit facebook.com/picadorbookclub or e-mail marketing@picadorusa.com.

Designed by Kelly S. Too

The Library of Congress has cataloged the Henry Holt edition as follows:

Mitchell, Maggie.
Pretty is : a novel / Maggie Mitchell.
p. cm.
ISBN 978-1-62779-148-9 (hardcover)
ISBN 978-1-62779-149-6 (e-book)
1. Kidnapping victims—Fiction. 2. Women college teachers—Fiction.
3. Actresses—Fiction. I. Title.
PS3613.I8585P84 2015
813'.6—dc23 2014044393

Picador Paperback ISBN 978-1-250-09362-2

Our books may be purchased in bulk for promotional, educational, or business use. Please contact your local bookseller or the Macmillan Corporate and Premium Sales Department at 1-800-221-7945, extension 5442, or by e-mail at MacmillanSpecialMarkets@macmillan.com.

First published by Henry Holt and Company, LLC

First Picador Edition: June 2016

D 10 9 8 7 6 5 4 3 2

For my father,
Homer Mitchell,

and in memory of my mother,
Susan Reid Mitchell

Part One

Lois

Everyone thought we were dead. We were missing for nearly two months; we were twelve. What else could they think?

They were glad to have us back, of course. But nothing was the same. It was as if we had returned from the dead, as if we were tainted somehow. Our unlikely survival made us guilty. We must have sold our souls, I could see them thinking—or worse. Undoubtedly, it had not been our fault (not altogether, anyway), but still. We were not the same.

And it was true, though not in the way they thought. What mattered to us was that we had been chosen. Singled out. We had always suspected we were different; at last it had been confirmed. There was no point in pretending otherwise; in fact, to our relief, pretense was no longer expected of us. The world acknowledged that we were extraordinary—and kept its distance, as if we might be rigged like bombs, might someday explode without warning.

Once I insist that we were chosen, it is only fair to admit that he chose me second. Carly May was first. I'd like to think this was pure chance, an accident of geography; that he wanted us equally but happened to be closer to Nebraska, at the time, than Connecticut. But I know nothing was an accident with him. I was second. Carly was first. Forever.

Our pictures were everywhere, though we never made it to a

milk carton. We had that already-doomed, by-now-I've-been-chopped-up-and-buried-in-the-woods look in our photographs. The TV stations and the newspapers often showed our school pictures, in which we smiled dreamily, tragically, against smoky-blue backdrops. But they also showed our press photos: Carly with sparkling tiaras perched on her golden ringlets, her lipsticked smile full of disturbing promises. I, Lois, more serious, posed with my spelling trophies, alluring in the way that a hostile kitten is. Or so it seems to me.

Carly May disappeared again when she was eighteen, this time on her own. She left a note: "Don't look for me, you won't find me," she scrawled on one of her portfolio shots. She had drawn a mustache on herself and blackened the whites of her eyes. I know this because her stepmother, Gail, called me two years later when she was working on her memoir. She thought I might know where Carly May was. I didn't; I hadn't heard from Carly for years. This is all in Gail's book, with an emphasis on her own suffering and her resourcefulness; she sent me a copy. I dropped that book off a bridge.

By the time Carly resurfaced in my world, she wasn't Carly May Smith anymore, and we were nearly thirty.

Carly May

It's always been hard to talk about what happened without sounding all melodramatic. And as soon as that happens, I feel dishonest, like I'm trying to pitch an idea for some made-for-TV movie. "Based on a true story," which isn't the same as being true. Actually, I haven't mentioned it for years, not to a goddamned person.

It wasn't really melodramatic at all. That's the shocking thing about it, if you ask me: how calmly we accepted what was happening. For me, getting abducted in broad daylight on the main street of a nowhere little farm town in Nebraska was far from the most fucked-up thing that could have happened that day.

I left my ballet class and took my time walking down the street to the House of Beauty, where stepmother Gail was having her nails done and God only knows what else. That woman took a lot of maintenance. I was wearing skin-tight biking shorts and an oversized T-shirt, dragging my twelve-year-old feet down the hot, wide sidewalk of Main Street, Arrow, Nebraska, with my dance bag slung over my shoulder. I was thinking about ways to make Gail miserable when the car pulled up beside me. Nondescript, gray. I didn't know anything about cars. What I did know was that the guy driving it was an actual stranger. In Arrow, that was pretty rare. The man leaned over and rolled down the passenger-side window. *He must be lost,* I was thinking. I figured he was going to ask how the hell to get back to somewhere civilized, so I stopped walking and waited, more or less willing to explain how to get to the highway. I'm sure I had that snotty twelve-year-old look on my face.

But he didn't want directions, and he'd seen enough pictures to know he had the right girl. "Get in," he said, smiling. "I'll give you a ride."

And so I did. Didn't think twice. God knows why. When I've tried to explain it, I always come back to the way he looked at me—as if he knew me perfectly, as if he could read my mind, as if I were the only person in the world who mattered. Doesn't everyone want to be looked at that way?

Later, I studied the photos of me that he had in his file. In some I had a big, toothy, fake smile. In others I looked a little sulky, imitating the pouty faces of models in magazines. I tried to figure out how he knew; how he could have been so sure, I mean, that all he would need to do is open his car door and I'd hop in. I looked for some telltale reckless gleam in my preteen eyes, some hint of latent depravity. I'm sure the police looked for it, too, later. I could never see it, though, not even with the benefit of hindsight. I had already mastered the vapid gaze that we expect from beautiful girls. As far as I could tell, it gave away nothing at all.

We drove and drove. I knew only that we were going east. He hardly said a word in those first hours, just flipped through the radio stations occasionally, though he never seemed to find anything he wanted to listen to. He winced at Mariah Carey, Nirvana, Beck—paused once on Johnny Cash, but even then jabbed at the dial after a few seconds. I couldn't help wondering what he hoped to find, and why he set himself up for disappointment if he already knew the radio had nothing to offer. When the radio was off, I could see out of the corner of my eye that his hands were relaxed on the steering wheel, and somehow that made me feel safe. Every now and then he would glance over at me and give me a little smile: an uncle smile, I thought, or maybe a teacher smile, although I had no uncles and my teachers had so far mostly been anxious young women with permed hair and sad, flowered blouses. He was more of a fantasy teacher, handsome and a little mysterious. I watched his eyes when he looked my way and noted that they rested on my face; they didn't stray to my tanned, skinny legs or the recent bumps in my pink T-shirt.

Reassured, I relaxed and watched Nebraska rush by outside the window as if it had nothing to do with me. I had never been out of the state. I was thrilled when we crossed into Iowa, although it looked pretty much the same; I liked the idea of leaving my world behind. At that point we left the interstate and stopped at a gas station, where he pulled a dark brown wig out of a duffel bag in the backseat. He handed it to me as if he were giving me a present, as if he knew already that I would get a kick out of a costume. He waited outside the strangely clean ladies' room studying a map while I stuffed my long hair under the wig and adjusted it until the bangs hung straight across my forehead. The wig must have been cheap—it was like doll's hair, with a stiff plasticky sheen. I had never worn a wig, but I took to it right away. I rubbed off the lip gloss and pale frosted eye shadow I'd been wearing at my ballet class and felt like a different girl. In the cloudy, cracked mirror, I tried out my new look. I'd be shy and innocent, I decided. Guileless, though I didn't know that word then. (The plan didn't last long.) I glanced up at my reflection through timidly lowered eyelids and basically flirted with my new self until the man knocked politely on the door. He gave me a nod of approval when I finally emerged.

He bought us charred gas station hot dogs and we headed east on a rural highway, carving through endless cornfields. I couldn't have been happier.

Lois

It would have been easy to miss her. In the bottom-left corner of the screen, a shadowy woman in dark glasses flung herself to the sidewalk to avoid a bullet. Her action wasn't important in itself, or necessary to the plot; it only contributed to the general chaos—she wasn't a main character or even a secondary one. Her fate seemed irrelevant to the larger story. "Is she one of the gangsters?" I asked Brad, squinting at her blurry, half-hidden face.

"The chick down there in the corner, you mean? Gangster's floozy, more likely. Or moll? Isn't *moll* the word? She's hot. In that sort of dominatrix-Barbie way."

"She's got her own gun," I pointed out, keeping my voice light. "She's no mere floozy." I noted that she held it in her left hand. As I watched her long, narrow fingers curl around the gun—getting ready to make a run for it, it looked like—I knew I was right. I knew that hand. It was older, longer, more elegant. But I would have known it anywhere.

I had finished my PhD and landed a teaching job at a small SUNY school in upstate New York, where I was teaching British lit to young students whose brains, I was discovering, were attuned almost exclusively to electronic stimuli. They weren't all that much younger than I was, but they seemed to be from a different century. I lived in a spacious apartment on the top floor of a turn-of-the-century Victorian with more charm than insulation. (In upstate New York, *spacious* is a rental agent's code word for *cold*.) I spotted Carly May in the corner of my TV screen on a Thursday night in late January. Outside, it was below zero and had been for days. An English department colleague and I were huddled under afghans in front of my TV, watching a movie and eating take-out pizza. When I say *huddled*, I mean *separately* huddled. We weren't touching. Brad Drake and I were the youngest assistant profs in the department. The next tier, the thirtysomethings, had kids, yards, lives. They had dinner parties from which all the guests departed by ten o'clock, yawning and murmuring about the babysitter. I'd been to a few, when I first arrived. Watching-bad-movies-ironically was not a pastime that amused them any longer. Perfectly good colleagues; I knew they'd never be my friends. Which was fine. I didn't need many friends: Brad sufficed.

"Go to the credits," I ordered Brad, who was clutching the remote as usual.

"Can't we just wait till the end?"

"I know that girl," I said. "I swear I do. I have to check."

"How could you know her? You can hardly see her face. And if you *do* know her, why do you have to check? If you're so sure, I mean. And—"

"Why do you have to argue with everything I say?" A pointless question; this was what Brad did. It was an endearing form of perversity, usually, and one of the many traits that justified, at least to me, the decidedly nonromantic basis of our relationship. I seized the remote.

I scrolled quickly past the characters with actual names, then lingered over the ones identified more cryptically: first dead girl, second dead girl, girl in diner, girl with gun. In this last group I saw a name that was not the one I was looking for, but caught my attention nevertheless: Chloe Savage. The initials were right. And something else: a ghostly echo, beyond logic; a sort of thud in the pit of my stomach. I knew, simply.

"It's not her," I told Brad, feigning disappointment, sinking back into the couch. Subterfuge was instinctive; I didn't for a moment consider telling Brad the truth.

It made perfect sense that she would have changed her name.

After Brad left, dragging his sleepy self reluctantly out into the snow with a wistful look that suggested he was hoping for an invitation to sleep on the couch, I went straight to the computer. I found enough photos of Chloe Savage to confirm what I already half knew. The bios available were disappointingly sketchy, not to mention full of lies. Only one detail linked her to Carly May: competed in beauty pageants as a child. The bios didn't say she was Miss Pre-Teen Nebraska. They said, in fact, that she was from Connecticut. *Like me,* I thought. She was borrowing that from me. In an obscure way, that, too, counted as evidence.

I printed everything I could find: bios, filmographies, photos. I placed them neatly in a folder and labeled it *Carly/Chloe*. Then, for no reason, I slid it into the bottom of a drawer, as if to conceal it from—what? Prying eyes? I could have kept top-secret government documents on my bedside table at that point, and they would have been perfectly safe.

Nevertheless, I hid the folder. It felt like the right thing to do.

Chloe

I was cute as hell. Tall for my age, willowy, with pale gold curls and sapphire-blue eyes. Like a little fairy. A sexy little fairy, I should add, once they started dolling me up. That was after Gail showed up. By the time Daddy brought her home to meet me, it was already pretty much a done deal: she had agreed to marry him. She had dyed red hair and violet contacts and long pink nails. Nature had made her a drab, mousy little person, but she had done everything in her power to color herself in. It was like Technicolor, though: unconvincing. She had a high, nasal voice. To me, at seven, she seemed like a cartoon. Why sad, quiet Daddy would want to marry a cartoon just two years after my mother's death was something I would never understand. He must have thought I needed a replacement mother; maybe he assumed I would welcome siblings, which Gail was quick to produce, in the form of two little half brothers. Wrong on both counts, but he never bothered to ask.

"Doll" is what Gail called me the first time we met. "Oh, Carly May, you're such a little doll!" she gushed. "Hugh, you never told me what a doll she was!" My father just kept unloading grocery bags from the trunk of the car. I noticed right away that he tended to let Gail do the talking.

After I left the second time, Gail published a book. Notice I didn't say *wrote* a book. I swear she never wrote more than a grocery list in her life. No, it was ghostwritten by Liz Caldwell, whose name is in small print in the lower-right-hand corner, like an artist's signature—you only see it if you're looking. "With Liz Caldwell," it says. I can picture what *with* meant: Gail sitting in the living room, wearing enough makeup for the frigging Oscars, with a cigarette in one hand and every ring she owned smashed onto her chubby fingers, wallowing in self-pity and a pathetic vision of her own importance. Liz Caldwell across from her, pretending to be impressed by Gail's wisdom and strength of character, consulting her notes and offering an occasional gentle prod, tape recorder whirring away beside her. How do I know Liz was pretending? I know Gail, is all. In fact, Liz might not have had to bother hiding her contempt; Gail would've been too caught up in her own drama to notice. Sensitivity to other people's emotions was never her strong point.

Even the book's title is a lie: *Losing My Daughter Twice*. It would be nauseating even if it were true, granted. But I am not—was never, in any sense of the word—Gail's goddamned daughter. And you can't lose what was never yours.

I was smart, believe it or not. Am smart. People don't expect it. My mother, who died in a car accident when I was five, was a schoolteacher. My father liked to read. He would come in from the barn and collapse into his recliner and pick up a book. Nonfiction, mostly, but novels, too. They read to me when I was little, talked to me like I was an intelligent life-form. I got good grades in school, if I bothered, though under the Gail regime there didn't seem much point in trying.

She must have researched the pageants on her own. This was pre-Internet, so it would have been harder then than it is now. She would have had to send away for information. Anyway, when she brought home the brochures that started everything, it was the first we'd heard of it; I mean, Daddy and I. "I didn't know they had these things for such young girls," Daddy said, flipping through glossy pamphlets with his big rough farmer's hands like he was holding something he'd rather not touch—a dead animal, maybe. "I guess I would've thought they'd be older."

"Look at those girls," Gail said, tracing their round, smiling faces with the hot-pink talon of her index finger. "You have to tell me Carly May is cuter than every one of them. No question she could win these things without hardly even trying."

"Now why would she want to do that?" said Daddy, handing the brochures back to her and tugging one of my pigtails. "Carly

May has a good head on her shoulders." I was in second grade. "These girls look like a bunch of airheads. Just pretty faces, that's all."

"There's worse things to have," said Gail.

"Pretty is as pretty does," Daddy said.

I stared at the glittery, ruffled dresses the little girls were wearing—maybe airheads, maybe not; how could you tell?—and thought about what Gail had said. God, how do kids know the things they know? I remember very clearly understanding two things: one, that Gail was right when she said I was prettier than the other girls. I was only eight, but I knew this like I knew that hens laid eggs. And I sure as hell knew that, since I gathered them from the coop. I'm tempted to say no one told me, but the world must have told me, somehow.

I also knew that Gail—much as I hated her, even then—was probably right when she said how much it mattered. Being pretty, I mean. And I knew that there was something I wanted, something big, something I couldn't name. Something outside my present world. So I let her find me later, flipping through the brochures on my own at the kitchen table. Daddy was out.

That was all she needed to start planning.

Lois

I don't hide my past, exactly. My story did not follow me from high school to college, and I chose not to revive it. I wanted to try being a different Lois, at least publicly. Even when I wrote my dissertation on the trope of abduction in the British novel, no one but my parents and my dissertation director made the obvious connection. I have grown up, it seems, to be respectably anonymous: Lois Lonsdale, assistant professor of English, specialist in very long novels in which, according to my students, nothing happens. Stickler for the proper deployment of semicolons. Until recently, no one remembered the abduction, much less the names of the miraculously rescued girls. There have been too many girls in the news, most not so lucky; as spectators, we allow our imaginations to skitter from one tragedy to the next. Carly May and I essentially ceased to exist once our pictures disappeared from the papers; the reporters abandoned my doorstep long ago.

Now, though, I have a new secret: I am Lucy Ledger, author of the modestly selling thriller *Deep in the Woods*, which is, however improbably, soon to be made into a major motion picture. The novel is loosely based on the abduction. My life has become complicated again.

I have always liked secrets.

I've been teaching Samuel Richardson's *Pamela* in my class on the British novel. My plan is to get it out of the way early in the semester and then move on to the fun stuff. More fun, I mean; I admit that it's relative. I am trying to persuade my skeptical students that *Pamela* is, in fact, fun. It's an epistolary novel, of course, a novel in letters, though in a rather perverse way, as most letters in the novel never get to their intended recipients. But you could argue that it's also a kind of horror novel, spun as a marriage plot. When Mr. B's none-too-subtle efforts to seduce (or ravish) his young (very young!) servant fail, he abducts her, ships her off to another of his houses, and places her in the custody of his ally and conspirator, the sadistic Mrs. Jewkes. The fact that Pamela gets to marry her "master" in the end does little to mitigate the fact that she spends half of the novel imprisoned, warding off his attempts to rape her, and frequently unconscious from fear.

But then, it's a love story, too.

My students tend not to buy the love story part.

So when Sean McDougal darkens my office door one early February afternoon, I assume he is one of the disgruntled, and steel myself to deliver my speech about the importance of *Pamela* to this looming, cigarette-scented specter.

But he surprises me. "I Googled you." Sean is tall, pale, thin but also somehow soft around the edges. Sparse, wispy facial hair contributes to the effect: he is blurry. Would he be handsome if he were more kempt, less skulking? I think he might be. It's hard to say. I have a vague sense that he reminds me of someone, though I search my memory and can't find the source of the echo.

He's sitting altogether too comfortably on the other side of my desk, snow from his heavy coat melting onto my floor, a faintly malicious gleam in his pale, no-color eyes. He looks pleased with himself.

Damn.

Originally, I had thought adopting a pseudonym would magically secure me a double life; I had thought I could establish and defend a sharp border between Lois Lonsdale and Lucy Ledger, and shuffle between them as I pleased. My editor, Amelia Winter, swiftly disabused me of this fantasy. The first time she asked me about the backstory of my novel, I told her confidently that there was none. It's pure invention, I said. She extended a sinewy arm, selected one of the dozens of brand-new books stacked high on her desk, and flipped through it. Glittering skyscrapers crowded the twenty-fifth-story window behind her; I still couldn't believe my luck. My manuscript was taking on a life of its own. "The thing is," Amelia said, scanning the pages, "it's important for us to know. Because if there is anything—*anything*—it'll come out. The Internet makes sure of that. If we know ahead of publication, we can make it work to our advantage. Otherwise, if you've been less than forthcoming with us, it'll be hard for us to control the damage." She snapped the book shut, as if she had found whatever she was looking for. "Something to think about," she said.

I didn't want to think about it, but I did it anyway.

Sean sniffles loudly, and I thrust my box of Kleenex in his

direction. He ignores it. Beneath the desk I uncross my legs, bracing each flat-soled suede boot firmly against the floor. It's my defensive stance, undetectable from the waist up. "Oh really?" Needlessly, I straighten a stack of papers on my desk. "The wonders of modern technology, yes? If only Pamela could have Googled Mr. B, that whole scandal with his pregnant mistress would have come to light much sooner, and Pamela might not have been so sympathetic." I say this lightly, since I don't really consider it an acceptable way of talking about the novel. I am breaking one of my own rules: there are no what-ifs in fiction, no alternate universes in which the characters might have done something other than what is on the page, where everything would have turned out differently, had they only been half as wise as we. It makes no sense, for instance, to insist that Pamela shouldn't have agreed to marry Mr. B; Pamela matters only because that is precisely what she always does, has always done, must always do. There would be no novel, otherwise. No Pamela.

"We didn't get to that part of the book yet," Sean says, his voice devoid of humor. "Don't you want to know what I found? On the Internet?"

I know all too well what he has probably found. When I finally came clean with Amelia, I suspected that I was only confirming what she had already discovered; apparently it didn't require Holmesian sleuthing to trace Lucy Ledger back to Lois Lonsdale. Sean's hands rest on my desk, red and raw, nails gnawed and not as clean as they could be. I wish he would stuff them back in his pockets; they make me queasy. Sean is no Sherlock, but it seems he's about to prove Amelia's point.

I prevaricate. "If I wanted to know, I suppose I would have Googled myself." Which I have done, of course. Doesn't everyone? What I know is that you used to have to scroll through nine pages of obscure singers bearing my name, census data and death records, someone who still has a Myspace account, and a doggy day-care owner in Ohio, not to mention my own faculty profile and syllabi, before you came across a brief, dry item cataloging child abductions by decade. My kidnapping is listed as one of many from the midnineties. Now you need only click through four pages to discover that Lois Lonsdale is also Lucy Ledger, and from there it's a short virtual leap to the rest of the story.

I smile at Sean in a way that I hope is both teacherly and winning, hoping to divert him from whatever unpleasant course he is set on. There's still time to turn back, time to rethink whatever he's about to do. His plot is still flexible, unlike Pamela's.

But he is not to be won. He wrote a terrible first essay, I remember. Did I give him an F or a D? Probably an F. I am trying to make sure no one thinks I am a lightweight, a pushover. I flip open my grade book. Yes, an F. Too bad.

"It was when you were talking about Pamela and how she could marry Mr. B after what he did. I just thought there was something funny about how you talked about it." His voice is curiously uninflected. Creepy, I begin to think. Unnerving. "Sometimes that happens to me. I get these feelings about people. So I checked you out. Do you want to guess what I found?"

"I can just imagine," I say drily. "I don't suppose it was my third-place finish in the national spelling bee."

For the most part, I have managed to keep Lucy Ledger out of Lois Lonsdale's everyday life. In her author photo, Lucy Ledger is smoky-eyed and edgily glamorous. She sports a leather jacket and assertive earrings. Lois Lonsdale, on the faculty Web site, peers sternly through forward-falling hair, face framed by a crisp collar emerging from her prim suit. You wouldn't see a resemblance unless you were looking for it. We didn't broadcast my real name when the book was published, though a handful of intrepid reviewers figured it out. My parents received a few calls from people interested in reviving the old story, and Miranda and Stephen's disapproval of my literary venture deepened the faint chill between us. I told my department chair about the book when he hired me, but did not mention its roots in my history; he seemed to find the fact that I had written a popular novel scandalous enough and all too gladly agreed to keep it under wraps to the extent that it was possible. That part was easier than I had expected: there was minimal intersection between my worlds. I never saw a familiar face at a reading. I tried to handle most publicity long-distance; I became adept at the e-mail interview, the phone chat.

Sean McDougal is the first real threat I have had to confront.

After scrabbling for a moment in his backpack, he withdraws a battered paperback. It's swollen and darkened, as if it's been rescued from drowning—or dropped in a bathtub, more likely. "Got it used on Amazon," Sean says. "Basically free, except for shipping."

It's *Deep in the Woods.*

The thought of this grubby, ill-mannered student poking around in my life—and even in my sentences—chills me. Surely it's hardly disastrous, though. I think quickly, trying to anticipate how this terribly unappealing young man could use his discovery to hurt me.

I really cannot imagine.

For a fiction writer, that's a failure, I suppose.

Chloe

I belong on the stage. Zed told me so (that was what we called him—like the British letter *Z;* we never knew his name until afterward), and I knew right away it was true. But I've ended up in movies. They say my face is better suited to the screen. You need a speaking face for the stage. Big eyes, a wide, expressive mouth, shadowy cheekbones, a well-defined, even prominent nose. In a way, says my agent, you're too pretty. He doesn't mean it as a compliment. He doesn't even say *beautiful*. He says fucking *pretty*. And fucking pretty is perfect for certain kinds of parts in certain kinds of movies.

The thing to understand about your character, a director once said to me, is that she's beautiful, but she's completely unaware of how beautiful she is. That's why everyone falls in love with her. There's this innocence at the core of her beauty.

You mean stupidity? I said, laughing. He didn't know what I meant, and proceeded to explain the whole concept to me again, as if I hadn't been hearing it since high school, at least. *She's really pretty, but it's like she doesn't even know it!* people would say admiringly of certain girls.

Only then can you forgive a girl for being pretty: if she's an idiot or a liar.

There's no way you can grow up in this world and not be able to look in a mirror and gauge how much you look (or don't look) like the girls in magazines or on TV. Even if you somehow manage not to figure it out for yourself—because you're so terribly modest or whatever—the world will tell you, just like the world will be sure to let you know if you're ugly, or fat, or ridiculous in any way. I don't mean people will come out and say it, necessarily (though someone will, sooner or later), just that they have ways of letting you know. You can see it in the way their eyes react to you, the way they interact with you physically.

Unless, as I said, you're stupid, or totally delusional. I'm sure that's sometimes the case.

It's not a question of vanity, I argued with that director, knowing already that I would lose. I'm just talking about calling a spade a spade.

He thought I was playing my character as too knowing, too self-aware. People would lose sympathy with her, he said.

Sometimes I think we're a whole country of hypocrites.

And I'm one of them: I played it like he said, in the end. My character became some kind of cheesy male fantasy instead of a real person.

And I still didn't get famous.

I settle myself in a sunny window with a cup of tea, still in my robe, determined to read the script Martin has been nagging me about. He has told me it's good, told me I'll be excited, but I don't believe him. His enthusiasm makes me nervous. I know his hopes for me are different from what they used to be, and I'm a little scared to learn what he thinks is a "great role" for me these days—a pain-in-the-ass mom in a teen comedy, maybe, or the clingy, shopaholic ex-wife in a romantic comedy about other people. Caricatures. I'm almost thirty. In actress terms, since I haven't managed to become Nicole Kidman or Julia Roberts, that's what I'm fit for: caricatures.

The screenplay begins with a standoff between police and a lone gunman who has staked out a house in the woods. Two pretty preteen girls work on a jigsaw puzzle in the main room of a rustic cabin, their gazes turning anxiously to the windows. On the porch sits a man, gun in hand, gazing calmly out at the woods. The house is surrounded. As the police close in, the man ignores repeated commands from a loudspeaker outside, makes no move to come out with his hands up. The girls are frozen with fear. They are neat and clean, but oddly dressed: they wear plain, dark cotton dresses, and their long hair is long, loose, old-fashioned. They look vaguely cultish.

There is a sudden commotion—we hear it, rather than see it—as the police descend upon the back of the house. The man lifts the gun.

I read ten pages before I get up, go to the kitchen, and trade my tea for a bloody Mary. What I'd really like is something stiffer, but it's technically still morning, so I compromise. Then I go back and reread the opening scene. I need to make sure I haven't lost my mind.

Martin is out of his office and not answering his cell. I leave him five messages. I need to know if this is some kind of joke. I don't see how it could be; then again, I don't see how it could be anything else. There are differences: We were upstairs when it happened, not in the main room. There was no jigsaw puzzle; we were making costume decisions about a play we were working on. But the clothes, the hair. The cabin. The man in the Adirondack chair. *My fucking story.*

It takes a lot longer than it should to realize that I would not be playing one of the kidnapped girls. No, I would be the female detective who gets too involved in the case, helps to track the girls down, becomes obsessed with the kidnapper, must confront disturbing truths from her own past, blah blah blah. That would be me. Although I should find it comforting that I have no idea who the hell this woman is and can only assume she's totally fictional, like the jigsaw puzzle, I find it aggravating, instead. So much of the story is familiar that the discrepancies are weirdly jarring.

The beginning is the end. The rest of the script tells the story of everything leading up to that point. Everything from the moment the first little girl gets in the man's car, with some more lies thrown in.

Here's my story. The story that Lois has stolen. (It has to be Lois; who else could it be?) We never stopped at motels, the man and I. We slept in the car. I dozed on and off all the time, in a sort of lazy, pleasant way. He took quick catnaps in empty parking lots, on dead-end roads, in little parks. The first time we did this, he strung a sturdy rope through my belt loop and tied it to his own wrist; if I moved, he said matter-of-factly, he'd wake up. He didn't make it sound like a threat, though I guess on some level it was. By then I knew that he had a gun in the glove compartment. In Nebraska, everyone had guns—but this was different, a little handgun. *A TV gun,* I thought. I'd never before seen anything but hunting rifles.

You never know who's out there, or what crazy things they'll do, he said when I saw the gun, as if he wanted to make sure I understood that the gun was not intended for me but for troublesome strangers we might meet on the road. He sounded apologetic, a little embarrassed.

We didn't meet anyone, though. People must have assumed we were father and daughter, if they thought about us at all, though he would have been pretty young to have a twelve-year-old. One of the things that struck me on that trip was that most people seemed awfully preoccupied. They had their own shit to deal with. I was used to the small-town busybody-ness of Arrow, and it fascinated me to see that out on the road we could drift through town after town like ghosts, and no one paid any attention to us at all.

Glad as I was to be leaving Nebraska, I wasn't exactly in a hurry to get anywhere else in particular. I liked watching the world flow past my rolled-down window, farmland blending into small, dusty towns, the hot wind stirring my ugly-Barbie wig. Partly I remember the trip as a succession of smells: cowshit, chicken farms, fast food, charcoal grills, freshly mowed grass, doughnut shops. Once we got stuck in a town that was having a parade, for no apparent reason, and since we couldn't get through anyway we got out and watched, as if we belonged there. I can still smell the thick haze of cotton candy and sausage sandwiches and fried dough that made the atmosphere in the village seem like something you could eat, though you'd be sorry later.

He bought me cotton candy on the way back to the car, and I twirled sticky strands of it around my tongue for miles and miles, glad not to be the blond Dairy Princess who had ridden through town in a white convertible, swiveling her hand and wrist at the crowds like a useless flipper. The frozen smile fixed on her pink face could have been mine. *Thank God,* I thought when we were back on the road.

You could have yelled, people said later. You could have run, you could have gone for help. Sounds like he gave you plenty of chances.

Lois Lonsdale is the only other person in the world who knows this story.

Lois

"Have you ever had Sean McDougal in a class?" I ask Kate LeBlanc. I know she has; I looked at his transcript: he took a survey course with her last semester. She's an early-Americanist, and it occurs to me now that there's something fittingly puritanical in the creases that descend from the base of her nose to the corners of her narrow mouth, creating the illusion of a frown even when her face is neutral. I wonder if I am making a mistake. I don't ask for help, as a rule. Kate and I sit in a corner of a downtown café, well away from the door, which keeps opening to admit blasts of winter. It's a comfortable enough café, and the coffee isn't bad. It's about as cosmopolitan as this town gets. The local art on the walls is poignantly overpriced, and it never moves.

"Once. Last semester." Kate sips her tea, having recently eliminated coffee from her diet, as she seems eager to explain. Such arbitrary gestures of self-denial make me nervous, and so do her next words. "Why? Are you having trouble with him?" If she had said "Is he giving you trouble," it would have been fine. But her sentence, whether consciously or not, attributes the problem to me.

I press on, because I have to know: has Sean singled me out—which is what it feels like, and clearly what he wants me to think—or is this simply what he does? "Just a slightly creepy vibe," I say, making it sound as casual as possible. The problem, I mean to convey, is entirely his; I am not the one who's creepy. Nor am I the sort of paranoiac who sees creepiness everywhere, who spins the mundane into personal drama.

"Really!" Kate widens her eyes. Her long beaded earrings tremble and shimmer, echoing her surprise. "Odd. He's a smart kid. Quiet, certainly, but I wouldn't have said creepy. What does he do, exactly? If you don't mind my asking?"

Smart? Interesting. "Well, in class, not much. I just feel his eyes sort of fixed on me; it's unnerving. He comes to my office pretty often. Weirdly often."

"Yes, he's a big fan of office hours," says Kate. "Probably because he's so shy about speaking in class, I always assumed. He's more comfortable one-on-one." *Which a good teacher would understand and even encourage*, she doesn't say aloud; but it hangs in the air, all the same.

Why is she refusing to entertain even the possibility that I'm right? What's at stake for her? I should stop, at this point, I realize; I should change the subject to spring break, or local shopping options. I don't. The shy, smart student she describes is not the Sean I know, and my misgivings deepen. "Yes, but—there's something too *personal* about it, if you know what I mean. That's what I meant by *creepy*. He seems a little too interested in my life, as opposed to my insights about eighteenth-century literature. Did you ever get that?"

A look of something like distaste flits across Kate's face, and she cuts me off with a sharply dismissive wave of her hand. "Oh, Lois. I wouldn't think anything of it if I were you. Keep in mind he's a very socially awkward kid; I don't think he has much control over the signals he seems to be giving off. I don't think you want to jump to conclusions, or attach too much meaning to your first impressions. You're a new professor; this is a small school. Naturally they're curious about you, the students. They don't always know where the boundaries are. But I wouldn't mistake curiosity for obsession."

I never said *obsession*; that's her word, and it's hostile. Appalled, I see in her eyes what she really means: *Of course you assume young men are obsessed with you just because you're pretty. What's worse, you are vain enough to want me to admit it. You are waiting for me to say:* Oh, Lois, you must know, boys will always be like that with you. *Have you thought about putting your hair up, dressing more plainly? You are the sort of sick, ego-driven person who always demands praise . . .*

I tuck my hands around my coffee cup for warmth, though it's rapidly cooling. Kate is wrong. I don't care about flattery, not from my students, and certainly not from her. I do want information, even of the haziest kind; I want to know whether my suspicions are justified and whether I should be worried. But I can see from the tight lines that have formed around her mouth and the impatient tap of her foot that she'll be no help; what's more, I've turned her against me. You can't really afford enemies in such a small department. I think of my mother, suddenly. Why don't kids like me? I asked her once, after some elementary school social incident involving rejection. Oh, they're probably just jealous, she said vaguely, clipping a dead rose from a bush, failing to convince me that she understood my world well enough to make such a pronouncement. Later I asked one of my therapists the same thing, and by then I really wanted an answer. What do you think? she asked, in her usual helpful way, head tilted quizzically.

Finishing my coffee, I change the subject: I mention the snow that's predicted for the weekend, and we sidestep into a spirited discussion of the weather. After all, I have found out what I needed to know: Sean's behavior is specific to me; this isn't simply his usual routine. It's personal, and he wants something.

The part of my mind not actively engaged in the weather conversation slips nervously into an old game from my spelling days. It's been happening more often lately. *Kate,* I think. *Words with a* K: *kaleidoscope, keratin, kamikaze. Krypton, kosher, kirtle.* There are fewer than you'd think. *K* words are harsh and angular. *They suit her,* I think, draping them about her neck, fastening them to her ankles like anchors. I festoon Kate with *K* words. It soothes me.

Yes, third place in the national spelling bee, as I mentioned to Sean; it's one secret not worth keeping. It was before anyone cared: before the spelling bee movies, the television coverage, the geeky chic spelling acquired in the early 2000s. When I was ten, I saw an article in the kids' section of the newspaper about a boy who had won a local bee. Intrigued, I read carefully through the list of words he had spelled correctly in order to win: *gallantry, parsimonious, feckless, infallible, anemone, risible, psoriasis.* I knew most of them; they were book words, as opposed to words people actually used in conversation. I couldn't have pronounced half of them, but I recognized them, all the same. The others, the unfamiliar ones, imprinted themselves instantly upon my brain. I felt them do it.

I could do that, I thought. I plunged immediately into a fantasy of victory. I was convinced, then, that I was destined for great things; it seemed unjust that my life as a fifth grader afforded so few opportunities to demonstrate this. Spelling would be a start.

I began compiling dictionary lists, testing myself on them. I enlisted the help of my parents, who thought my pursuit odd but harmless, and of an English teacher seeking vicarious glory. I entered a regional bee and qualified for the final rounds as one of the youngest contestants. I didn't win that year, but I did the next. By the time I was twelve, I had qualified for the national bee in Washington, D.C.

In the end I retired early from the spelling circuit. For one thing, by the time I returned from that summer with Chloe in the Adirondacks, publicity no longer appealed to me; seeing my picture in the newspaper was no longer a thrill.

But the words in my head were there for good.

As I leave the café and trudge along the snowy sidewalk, I move on to the *Ls*.

Lagniappe. Lachrymose. Lugubrious.

Even to me, my childhood looks picturesque. The rambling New England inn, the horses, the roaring fireplaces and fifteen-foot Christmas trees—you can't deny their charm. But war-torn villages on the news, where ragged, ill-nourished children play in the beautiful bombed ruins of old stone buildings, can also be picturesque. That doesn't mean you want to live there. I don't mean to exaggerate the hardships of my childhood; my point is that I know it is possible to be desperately unhappy in surroundings that other people might admire on a postcard.

My parents ran an inn. The house had been in my mother's family for generations. At its core was a squarish colonial manor, flanked by long wings that had been added later. Another addition straggled out of the back like a spare tentacle, leading out to what my mother still calls the kitchen garden. That's where she had spent her early childhood—in the aesthetically dubious appendage at the back of the house, invisible from the road, not marring the grandeur or symmetry of the house's lines. It was not the nicest part of the house, but it was the most practical; the small, low-ceilinged rooms were easier to heat, for one thing, and the rooms did not dwarf or disdain the comfortable modern furniture my grandparents filled it with. The rest of the house was shuttered then—unused, unheated. But my mother says that as a little girl she found passages to the long forbidden hallways, the shrouded rooms, and played there as, no doubt, two centuries of children had before her.

Then my grandfather began to make money. Lots of money.

He managed to ride the cresting wave of Hartford's insurance industry. And the house, my mother says, eventually swarmed with men hired to restore it to its original state, until at last the whole place stood open, windows brilliant in the sunlight. The family took up residence in the main house, amid the graceful furnishings and chandeliers of another era.

My mother inherited the house, but not enough money to maintain it; the restoration had already consumed a great deal of my grandfather's wealth, and his increasingly extravagant habits hadn't helped. (There was talk, my mother said, of secret card games, horse racing, expensive mistresses in the city.) She had been raised to assume that she would marry well enough to serve the house's needs—which sounds improbably Victorian, I know. She went to Mount Holyoke; she was talented; she was groomed for more than husband-catching. But the family was prominent in local society; they mixed with other wealthy families; she dated boys who were destined to be bankers and surgeons and insurance magnates. There were expensive dresses and furs and cars and trips to the city. Horses, tennis.

But Miranda Sheridan did not marry into that world. She married my father, who had hazily grand ambitions and no money. Like her, Stephen Lonsdale was a painter, or so he thought then. He gave it up soon after they married; my mother, on the other hand, still retreats to her studio, though she seldom shows or sells her work. Her large abstract canvases lend the living areas of the inn a museum-like quality; they are too overwhelming, my father insists, for the guest rooms. According to my mother, Stephen was seduced by the glamour of the Sheridans' life and at the same time despised it, a sentiment he did not manage to conceal from my grandfather, who was, to all appearances, graying and stiffly respectable.

Upon my grandfather's death, my penniless and casually bohemian parents saw that the house would have to earn its own keep. Which it still does, admirably. They relegated themselves (and, eventually, me) to one of the wings and transformed the rest into a handsome New England inn, featured later in countless travel magazines, glossy photographs of upscale country grandeur that never look like home.

What an amazing place to grow up! I can't count the people who have said this to me. But imagine: The house was always full, my parents eternally occupied with the guests. From the guests streamed endless needs and desires, and it was my parents' mission to satisfy them. I saw little of my mother and father during the day; we generally had dinner together, but though we dined late in hopes that the guests would mostly have settled in for the night, it was common to be interrupted by the bell that connected our modest quarters to the rest of the house. My parents would sigh and meet each other's eyes across the table, mutely deciding who should go—or who had had the least to drink.

On weekends I spent as little time at home as possible. It was then that the guests seemed most present: they lingered after their breakfast, flipped through the pages of books on the shelves, read the newspaper on the porch. They paid well for these privileges, and in theory I did not begrudge them; I was well aware that our living depended upon these well-heeled, generally mild-mannered vacationers. Yet I couldn't help feeling displaced. Technically, the wing my family occupied was separate from the inn. But sometimes guests wandered accidentally into our kitchen, which adjoined the large main kitchen where my mother prepared gourmet country breakfasts each morning; occasionally, intrepid explorers would venture farther and find themselves in our small living room if someone had forgotten to latch the door. One small back porch, an architectural afterthought, was supposed to be exclusively ours. The guests had the wide, beautiful veranda that ran the length of the front of the house, as well as the patio out back; but sometimes, forgetting or seeking privacy, they found their way onto our porch. When people stumbled upon me, it embarrassed us both—as if they had been exposed to a mop, or a pile of dirty sheets in the middle of a hallway: something meant to remain behind the scenes. From the guests' perspective, my parents were creators of exquisite crab and goat cheese crepes and spinners of delightful local yarns, there to supply their every need or whim. I was a prop, prettily dressed and extravagantly well behaved. This, at any rate, was my conviction, and I fueled it with the kinds of books that confirmed my childish suspicion that I was alone and misunderstood.

I especially dreaded the guests who brought children. Young kids weren't allowed, as a rule, but we permitted children ten and up. They were even more likely than the adults to wander into my world, to express uncensored curiosity about my status. If they were bored enough—and sometimes they were—they'd even try to pick fights, in the hope that a good round of childish insults would save them from a dull vacation of books and board games and country rambles. The children weren't all monsters; once in a while I even formed a fleeting friendship with some lonely girl. For the most part, though, I cultivated a growing awareness that I was not entirely welcome in my own home. My parents' hope was that eventually profits would soar and they would be able to pay people to attend to the day-to-day management and upkeep of the inn, but they hadn't yet gotten much further than a couple of chambermaids and a groundskeeper. Like my parents—or at least my mother—I longed for the day when we would be restored to our rightful position as lords of the manor. By the time I got in the man's car, I had begun to realize that this rosy future was more a fantasy than a solid business plan.

If I had noticed that it had begun to rain, I might have stayed at the library that day; we lived on the outskirts of town, and it was a long walk home. As it was, a gray car pulled up to the curb just as I stepped off the stone steps of the library into a steady drizzle. I noticed that it had New York State license plates, but I thought nothing of it; those are common enough in Connecticut. I do remember feeling a vague sense of alarm as the driver rolled down his window. I think it was simply shyness, though; I was skittish at the prospect of talking to strangers, not because this stranger seemed particularly alarming. Quite the opposite, in fact: the man was pleasant looking, nicely dressed. Younger than my father, though I couldn't have gauged by how much; he was one of those people who manage to look simultaneously old and young. As I approached the car, the girl sitting in the front seat beside the man leaned forward to see me—or perhaps to allow me to see her. I noticed immediately that she was extremely pretty. Her hair was strange, a coarse, uniformly gleaming brown, but it had the effect of making her look even more like a doll than she would have otherwise. I tried not to stare at her in fascination; she stared frankly at me.

"We're looking for the junior high," said the man, his voice low and resonant, polite but with a friendly undercurrent of humor. "I wonder if you could point us in the right direction? We seem to have gotten turned around."

"I'll be starting seventh grade here in the fall," the girl added.

"So will I," I found myself saying. What was it about them that made me immediately comfortable, that so thoroughly disarmed me? "I'm pretty awful at giving directions," I said apologetically, looking down the street and trying to visualize the turns they would need to take. "Okay—keep on going down this street. You see the church at the end?" I raised my arm to point, hoisting my backpack into a more secure position with my other arm as I gestured. It was raining harder; I could feel my hair getting heavier, and raindrops clung briefly to my eyelashes before trickling down my face like tears.

"Listen," the man interrupted. "You're getting soaked. Why don't you hop in. You can show us where the school is, and then we'll take you home."

"Otherwise your library books will get wet," the girl chimed in.

I knew I could guide them to the school more easily in the car than I could explain how to get there. And I lived fairly close to school; they wouldn't have to go too far out of their way to bring me home.

If the man had been alone, I wouldn't have gotten in. I'm sure of it, or as sure as it's possible to be. I knew as well as any American child in the midnineties that it was ill-advised to accept rides from strangers. It was the presence of the girl that overcame my doubts. Her absurdly pretty face spoke to me somehow; it reassured me. *This is a girl I might be friends with,* I found myself thinking.

I slipped into the backseat, settling my dripping backpack beside me, perching in the middle and leaning forward between the two front seats.

"Okay. Go up there and turn right," I said. For a few turns he followed my directions perfectly, arousing no suspicion. Then, quite suddenly, he didn't: he took a left instead of a right, and without warning we were on a back road, heading out of town. I was so surprised, and he was so calm, that I said nothing at all. This is the part I could never explain to anyone's satisfaction. I didn't want to let the strangers down. I wanted to ride in that musty backseat forever; I wanted to belong to them. I could feel the girl watching me. I wondered if the man was her father, but I didn't think so. Age aside, that wasn't quite how they spoke to each other. I couldn't have described how they *did* speak to each other. Words rose to my throat countless times, but somehow it had already become too late to say anything that would matter. Weirdly, I was reluctant to seem rude. They were so sure of themselves, and so pleasant.

No one spoke for the first hour or so, and then it was Carly May who filled me in on what little she thought I needed to know. We stopped once for gas, and Carly and I stayed in the car. "You don't have to go to the bathroom, do you?" she asked me, and since "no" was clearly the right answer, that's what I said. "You should stay down," she explained, tucking herself lower into the front seat. "It's best if no one sees us." She sounded more like an accomplice than a victim of a kidnapping—if that's what she was, if that's what I was; *kidnapped* was a word that had drifted around my head a bit, but it carried little conviction. I did as she said. "There's no point in running away or anything like that," she added. She twisted around in her seat, fixed her blue eyes on me—darker than before, with only the lights from the gas station picking out specks of iris. "Are you scared?"

The car smelled of fast food and people who hadn't showered for a couple of days. I was hungry; I *did* have to go to the bathroom. Of course I was scared, though that wasn't all I was. How often had I imagined ways of leaving my world behind, woven elaborate fantasies of escape, of transformation? And now, in one confused, rain-soaked moment, my world had been snatched away. My feelings were—mixed.

"He picked us, you know," she said. "It wasn't just random that we found you. He knows all about us." I could tell that she thought this would please me, and sure enough, it did. A sense of importance touched up against my fear; I felt the fear take a step back.

"Why?" I asked. It was the obvious question, but I could tell she didn't like it. She turned back around in her seat and checked the rearview mirror. "Here he comes," she said, and fell silent.

"Not much farther now," he said when he returned to the car. Carly turned her full smile on him. The beauty pageant smile, as I learned later, but more real. And he smiled back.

That's how it was from the start: them smiling at each other in the front seat, me in the back, watchful, secondary.

Chloe

"It's perfect for you," Martin says. "It's an action role, in the sense that you play a cop, handle a gun, that kind of thing, but it has serious dramatic potential. You're an *emotional* cop. Maternal, conflicted, sympathetic. It's the best of both worlds! It could open new doors for you."

"Who wrote it?" I ask for the second time. The name on the screenplay is Adam Gitner, but this doesn't fool me. I repeat: "Where did the fucking story come from? Give me an answer, and we'll talk."

We're in Martin's office, which I have never liked; it reminds me that I am C-list and clinging to the third tier like a cat that's lost its balance. The neutral-toned office is not exactly seedy, just a little too five-years-ago. It feels *almost* seedy, like you would only need to scrape away the earth-toned veneer to get to the sordid underbelly of this godawful world. We're here because he wouldn't meet me for a drink. Do you think that would be wise? he had asked, almost gently, but right now I'm too single-minded to risk getting pissed off by his paternal bullshit.

"Who," I say. "Wrote. This. Fucking. Story. Not the screenplay. Who wrote the book?"

I realize that I'm freaking him out, that he can't possibly understand my urgency. I'll worry about it later.

"No one whose name would mean anything to you, I'm afraid," Martin says. I can hear the surprise in his voice. "Several writers have worked on the screenplay, I believe. As I said, it's based on a novel that came out a couple of years ago. Sort of a domestic thriller. I confess I haven't read it. Again, no one you would have heard of, I imagine, unless your literary tastes are less discriminating than I would have thought." He smiles. He's used to tossing out bits of flattery like dog biscuits. He knows I like to have my intelligence acknowledged.

Ordinarily I like flattery as much as the next desperate actress, but today I respond by grabbing a heavy paperweight from his desk. Dark, moody colors swirl beneath the smooth surface. I shift it from hand to hand, enjoying its cool heft. I wonder how far I could throw it. I bet I could dent the fucking wall.

"Lucy something," Martin says quickly. "Lucy-something-alliterative. Ledger. Lucy Ledger. Happy now? See? No one. Not involved with the screenplay at all."

Lucy Ledger, Lois Lonsdale. *Please.*

"They want you to read for the part," Martin says. "If you do that, I might be able to get you in touch with the writer. These things are touchy. Writers are touchy."

"Yes, Martin."

"And one more thing." Martin looks out the window, so I do too. Palm trees, a bit of a breeze. Aimless tourists, eyes peeled for celebrities. "This is an extremely big deal for you, I don't have to tell you."

Bastard. Also approximately the only person on the planet who gives a flying shit about me.

Five minutes later I am headed for the nearest Barnes & Noble.

I tell myself I won't have a drink when I get home, just to prove Martin's not-so-gentle hints unnecessary. But if anything calls for a drink, this is it. I make a martini, very dirty.

It takes me a few hours, with bartending breaks, to finish the book. I've always been a fast reader; teachers used to accuse me of not having finished. And this isn't exactly Tolstoy, as Martin had pointed out. The publisher had marketed *Deep in the Woods* as a sort of chick-lit/thriller hybrid of the more literary variety. The cover shows a trail of pinkish blood through the snowy woods leading to a fairy-tale cottage, a scenario that doesn't appear in the novel. The book, I notice, is more interested in what goes on in the characters' minds than the screenplay is; it tries to give a sense of their messed-up worldviews. My character—the Carly

May girl, I mean—is surprisingly complicated: she's arrogant, sure, but she's also vulnerable and lonely and confused. *Thanks, Lois.* I'm touched. Martinis can make a person sentimental. Lois has not been so kind to herself: the Lois girl is too self-involved to be very likable. Too jealous, too needy. I feel protective of her. I want to defend her young self to her clearly judgmental older self: *You weren't that bad.*

Then again, maybe she was, my martini whispers.

Lois has also taken some serious liberties with the truth. With certain truths, I mean. I'm partly relieved and partly—something else. I don't know yet. Betrayed?

Lois

Sean sits across the desk from me clutching his five-page paper on *Pamela*. My neat comments in polite purple ink spill out of the margins. The document has seen better days; it's rolled into a soiled, ragged scroll, begrimed with God knows what, and smells like cigarettes even from here. I am loath to touch it. I wish for the thousandth time I could have brought myself to scrawl a C on the paper and let it go at that. But that seemed unfair to other students, some of whom worked hard for their Cs.

"Tell me. What do you see as your thesis here?" I say. "Look at your introductory paragraph, and why don't you underline your thesis."

"I don't have a pen," he says. His ability to make things difficult is truly astonishing. I hand him a pen—not my own; one of the cheap Bics supplied by the department. He will probably take it with him, intentionally or not. He takes the pen and carves a dark line under a short sentence.

"Read it, please," I say.

"In reality," he reads, his voice exaggeratedly serious, "Pamela is a slut."

His answer is beyond inappropriate; it's aggressive. I could kick him out, and I am tempted to. I could report him, and he would get a probing follow-up call from a health services counselor. But I don't; I want to get to the bottom of this on my own. It feels too personal to make public.

Besides, however offensive his "thesis" might be, the truth is that eighteenth-century readers shared Sean's doubts about young Pamela, who eventually gets to marry her lecherous master after all his attempts to seduce her—or ravish her—have been thwarted by her indomitable virtue. In various spoofs and parodies, of which Fielding's *Shamela* is the most famous, Pamela becomes, in fact, a slut. A strumpet, a trollop. Or at least a conniving little wench. Which is not the same as saying that Richardson's Pamela *is* a slut: simply that she would have been a far more plausible character if she *had* been.

"Let's talk about how you might begin to complicate that argument," I say blandly, as if Sean were any other student and not a prying, ghoulish invader of my secrets.

Half an hour later he is stuffing his papers and—yes—the pen into his grungy backpack when he suddenly raises his head and smiles, exposing teeth that would have benefitted from braces. This should be preferable to his sullen sneer, but I find that it is not.

"I found the other lady, by the way," he says. "You know, the girl that was kidnapped with you? I tracked her down."

A flash of fury sends blood to my face and threatens to derail my determination to appear calm. Carly was capable of impressive rages; sometimes I envied her. For me, this surge of anger feels closer to the surface than usual—like a fish that flits through shallow water, looking out for vulnerable insects. I want to fling insults, drag a pen across Sean's smug face. A drop of sweat emerges from beneath my bra strap, curves down my lower back. He has sullied Carly May by searching for her, by tapping out her name on his grubby laptop—almost as if he had grabbed her shirt, torn it, left dirty fingerprints, exposed her skin. *Imbecile.*

I slide open my top desk drawer, extract a mint from its box, tuck it alongside my back teeth. When I speak, my voice is level: "You understand what I mean by *substantial* rewrite. I mean *unrecognizable.* New thesis, new everything. Or your grade will stand. You have one week." *Imbecile: Ichneumous, inimical, inquisiturient. Intermure, insidiate, imprecate.* The words aren't helping. I stand, signaling that the conversation is over. He looms; I wish I were taller. Carly-sized.

"Did you guys get along?" he asks, slouching toward the door. "Did you, like, keep in touch after?"

I wondered at first if Sean had some sort of handicap, some physical condition that affected his posture: something that would oblige me to dredge up more sympathy for him than I was inclined to feel. Since then I've decided that his awkward, crooked gait is an affectation of sorts. I cannot fathom what it is intended to signify. I find myself thinking of lisping aristocratic gentlemen in the eighteenth century. I am acquainted with this historical phenomenon in a scholarly way, but it has never made sense to me on a human level. Why lisp? Why limp, unless you have to? I wonder if this association is instructive in any way, and remind myself to consider it later.

Illision. Ignescent. Indign. I force myself to meet his gaze, but I make my eyes go blank.

What is it that I fear? I feel as if Sean is slinking through my mind, poking into dark and dusty corners.

One of the many unspoken expectations of new faculty members is that they accept all invitations from student organizations. I have already attended a number of excruciating breakfasts, movie nights, faculty mixers, and—most improbably—a 5K walk-run for some charity. This evening I have agreed to attend a sorority fundraiser for the local rape crisis center.

Which is why, several hours after meeting with Sean, I arrive at a rather imposing brick house on Main Street, wearing a not-especially-professorial red sweater dress and high-heeled black boots that are treacherous in the snow. I don't want to please the Kate LeBlancs of the world by looking dowdy and professorial; I don't want the young women to tower over me. I make my way through a small crowd, carrying a cup of tea, pretty cookies balanced in the saucer. I attend politely to an extremely earnest state senator, a prized special guest, who regales me with details about a controversial planned development on the outside of town that should interest me more than it does. From that conversation I ricochet across the room to the corner inhabited by a tall, dark-haired woman who turns out to be the director of the rape crisis center. I find her entertainingly caustic. "Nice life, right?" she says at one point, surveying the room, with its soft lighting, delicately upholstered chairs, and self-conscious air of civilization.

I am flattered by her assumption that I share her attitude toward this studied atmosphere of privilege. But I'm not sure she's right about the students; you never know what darkness lurks behind clear, bright undergraduate faces. We all know the statistics about rape on college campuses. Throwing me a quick, sharp glance, the rape crisis center director reads my mind. "Of course you never know," she adds quickly. "Violence against women is hardly limited to certain social spheres. It's just my own prejudices speaking. I can't stand this kind of thing." She sips her tea with manifest irony. "I bet tomorrow night they'll be at some fraternity mixer wearing lingerie and togas, drumming up clients for the center. They had to beg to get me to this little shindig." She's wearing a chunky black sweater over a flowing, flowery skirt and far more practical boots than mine. Delia, her name is. Impulsively, I suggest having a drink sometime, thinking she seems refreshingly different from my female colleagues. The murky aura of a darker world hovers around her, glowers in her critical, sideways glances. She has seen what people can do to each other. I want to claim her as an ally; I feel the need for one.

"I don't drink," Delia says. "Coffee, maybe?" I accept her politely proffered card, say I'll call. She places her china teacup carefully on a spindly end table and announces that it's time for her to mingle. She sounds like someone facing a firing squad. Guiltily, I acknowledge that I, too, should leave the safety of my corner.

I scan the room for students I recognize, or even the senator. Glossy-haired young women in demure dresses—all in muted colors, as if by agreement—stand in loose clusters, chatting with glassy animation. Such clusters are more structurally impenetrable than they look, I have learned; standing on their peripheries does not guarantee acceptance. A shred of chemistry comes back to me: something about noble gases, unable to react with other elements.

I wonder what is noble about such gases. *Noble: nasturtium, nadir, nescience.*

No one comes to my rescue.

Carly would know what to do. She always did. She was the opposite of noble, in the atomic sense.

My editor is excited about the sequel; this is why I got a two-book deal. "I'd love to see you confront the aftermath," she'd said at lunch in Manhattan. "Not the immediate aftermath, I mean, but the lives of these girls—after they've been returned to their families, their small towns, tried to reassimilate, et cetera. What becomes of them? What kind of connection do they have? Wouldn't they always have a kind of bond? What could bring them back together?" She had pressed on with questions like these, as apparently a whole novel unfolded itself in her excitable (but also practical) imagination.

Back at home I exchange my red dress for warm layers, including the knitted fingerless gloves I have taken to wearing in the evening. I pour myself a glass of wine and settle at my computer. My fingers arrange themselves on the keyboard. I will need to enter a more purely fictional realm than I have inhabited as yet. The kidnapper's son will serve as the mechanism that brings them back together, and he'll provide a fresh menace. He will want to destroy them, of course. But first he will need to lure them to him. Outside my window, thick snowflakes have begun to drift down; every now and then a gust of wind sends them whirling madly past.

Yes, a jealous son. I'll give the kidnapper a son, and I'll make him jealous. Our abductor *did* have a son, according to the papers, so it isn't much of a stretch. All his life this son has envied the two little girls his father abducted and adored, the girls he preferred to his own child. The girls with whom his father shared his final days—who, afterward, were on TV, in the papers, everywhere, while he was forgotten, living in his grandparents' trailer, not even sharing his father's last name. The girls who stole his father. He's always wanted to make them pay.

The sorority fund-raiser settles obediently into the background, along with Delia and the faint strains of the landlady's television in the room below mine.

I will start with snow. The jealous son. In a trailer. In the snow.

When Brad texts me later that week on a gloomy February afternoon, inviting me to the local pool hall, I agree to tear myself from my computer and go. In addition to the sequel, I have been working on the final revisions of my scholarly book. It's basically my dissertation. To have had it accepted by a major university press so swiftly on the heels of landing my first job is wildly impressive in this field. It's good enough for tenure, which is years away. It's the Oscar of academe, practically; it makes me a rising star. This is not a secret, though I am quiet about it and self-deprecating.

The department is officially enthusiastic, but I detect more complicated emotions in some quarters. I have a not-altogether-paranoid suspicion that Kate LeBlanc is rallying her forces against me. That's to be expected. You're supposed to pay your dues in this world, and I have not. No doubt there is concern that I will make demands, expect preferential treatment. Or that I will leave for a more prestigious job.

I might do any of these things. I like being a rising star.

Only Brad seems truly happy for me. We spent an inordinate amount of time at the pool hall our first semester, but we haven't been back since we returned from Christmas break. I have missed our excursions. Brad doesn't *truly* know me; I've kept many secrets from him. He knows the basic outline of my childhood, but he thinks I've put the abduction behind me; he knows about the book but not the movie. He knows me better than anyone else, though, that's for sure, and he is the only person in my life capable of reflecting back at me a recognizable Lois; or, at least, a Lois I would like to be.

As I shut down the computer and tidy my desk, I come across Sean's latest offering. He has been slipping photocopies under my office door: press from my abductee days. The first one sent me reeling. It was from the *Hartford Courant:* "Local Girl Returned Home, Apparently Unharmed," reads the front-page headline. There's a grainy picture of me walking with my parents, face in shadow. My mother looks regal and defiant and warlike; my father looks folded inward, absent. I am blurry; you really couldn't say anything about me at all, based on this photo. The most recent one is earlier, and it's from the local *Gazette:* "Community Rallies in Search for Missing Girl."

I've seen the clippings before, but it's been a while. They're as jarring as ever, referring to a world in which I was central but absent. My parents never spoke much about those weeks. "We were terrified," they said, but I have never been able to grasp their terror, to imagine Miranda and Stephen Lonsdale stricken by fear and loss. It's not that I don't believe it; I simply cannot see it. "We looked everywhere," they said. Where? I have tried to picture them in sturdy shoes and jeans, sleepless and haggard, searching the woods, circling the pond, roaming the village—while I, miles away, settled all too readily into a new life. I resent Sean for reviving this fruitless speculation, this belated guilt—but the precise nature of his offense is difficult to define: I have not been harmed; he hasn't even threatened me. Not in so many words.

Chloe

They gave me the part. I knew they would. I'm not religious; I don't think things are meant to be or not meant to be. But lately it feels like things are coming together in a way I'm not completely in control of.

It's not that I believe in shit like that, because I don't.

So I know it sounds crazy. But I *knew* the part was mine. I still went and read the hell out of a couple of scenes and did my best to make a good impression; I didn't go wandering in after a couple of martinis and leave myself in fate's hands. But I knew. I couldn't imagine anyone else playing Lois's detective. If this movie had to get made, I had to be in it. Obviously.

When the phone rang, just two days after my audition, it was all I could do not to say yes before they made the offer.

What I don't know is what to do until then. We shoot this summer in British Columbia. I have months to fill. Martinis to resist, bridges not to burn. And while I'm not broke, things aren't exactly rosy. My last film flopped. Which was too bad; I actually thought it was a pretty decent movie. A little indie neo-noir-type picture, not the kind of thing I usually get asked to do, but I thought some artsy cred would be a good career move. And maybe it would have been if anybody had seen the goddamned film. I played a woman who finds out that her fiancé killed a girl, among other sordid activities, and covered it up pretty successfully—until suddenly someone's snooping around, putting the pieces together, blah, blah, blah. But it was good and dark, with no cheeseball happy ending. And it was set in the seventies: great hair and costumes and a general willingness on the part of the cast and crew to get high on a regular basis.

But it was badly marketed, no one saw it, and I got paid shit. If I have to hang out in LA till the end of June, I really will be broke.

I used to like LA—back when I was new on the scene, and everything seemed to be coming together, and I was half convinced that I was one step away from being the Next Big Thing. I had an outrageously pure faith in my looks and my talent. I felt like the world owed me something, and I thought that what I felt mattered. I'd had a couple of very lucky breaks, and based on those I assumed that the world was planning to make good on its debts. I had a good part in *Destiny Wars*, a space movie with a modest budget that became a surprise summer blockbuster. I wasn't one of the leads, but I was one of the small group of astronauts who were at the center of the plot, and I was one of the few characters that got to live all the way through the movie, dressed in one of those tight shiny jumpsuits that filmmakers seem to have unanimously decided are what we will be wearing in the Future. I was invited to the MTV Viewer's Choice Awards; I did the red carpet thing. I was featured in magazines—no covers, but a few full inside pages—got some modeling jobs, more scripts to look at. One magazine even tagged me as the next It Girl. I thought I had made it. A few years of this, I thought, and I could return to New York in triumph: the stage would be waiting for me.

In *Destiny Wars 2: Ascension*, they killed me off in the first five minutes. I barely made it past the opening credits before a treacherous crew member launched me into space in my sleek silver astronaut nightie, a lethal futuristic space particle bullet through my head.

I wanted to do a romantic comedy, but my destiny, it seemed, was to be an action sidekick. Sub-sidekick, really. Not the ass-kicking, wise-cracking, all-important main sidekick. The expendable sub-sidekick. It turned out that people liked to watch me die. I came across an unauthorized fan site once that had put together a montage of all my deaths.

In the indie flick, not only did I actually get to act, but I was allowed to wear normal clothes—jeans and turtlenecks—instead of black pleather and stilettos. And I got to live. I was in the first scene and the last scene. I suffered, I learned, I grew.

No one saw.

My faith wavered. My faith in Chloe Savage. The only faith I have.

Still, I haven't yet sunk to sitting around my Silver Lake bungalow drinking my face off and moping about the past every night. This is LA, after all. Tonight, for instance, I have a date. A good old-fashioned pick-you-up-at-eight kind of date. The guy isn't even an actor. He's a writer, which for all I know might be worse, but at least it'll be different. I've sworn off actors. They're always looking at themselves through your eyes.

Lois

It's late afternoon, and Ivan's pool hall is crowded. It is also hazy with smoke, despite the statewide smoking ban. Brad and I claim the only open table, with faded felt and old-fashioned leather pockets; we order beers and select our cues. Ivan appears out of nowhere to rack the balls.

Brad is good. I am not that good, but I'm generally considered "pretty good for a girl," which is good enough at Ivan's.

I actually play better than usual today, though not well enough to win. But winning isn't the point. The point is that Brad is happy, shooting expertly, giving me occasional pointers. My willingness to play pool is a peace offering, which Brad accepts by attempting more difficult shots than he needs to in order to keep me in the game. Brad is excellent at this kind of communication, and I almost love him for it.

Brad and I like the pool hall because it seems worlds away from school; we never see other faculty there. The only danger is students. Because it's a liquor-serving establishment, someone is always stationed at the door to make a show of checking IDs, but some undergrads manage to get in anyway—mostly, I imagine, local kids who have been going there for years. Until now I have never seen a student of mine here. I'm startled, then, when I'm crouching low to make a long tricky shot across the table and I see Sean leaning against the opposite wall, watching me. I swing my hair out of my eyes, adjust my focus, measure the angle with my eyes again, and flub the shot anyway. Brad sinks his last ball then double-banks the eight ball into a corner pocket, and as I lean forward to give him a mock handshake, I say in a low voice, "My student is here. The one I told you about—the 'Pamela is a slut' one. Don't look—but behind you, by the wall, torn jeans and Docs and a ratty trench coat."

"Sounds original." By the time Brad turns around, Sean is right in front of him, sticking his hand out.

"Dr. Drake," says Sean, practically bowing over Brad's hand. "Nice to meet you. I haven't had a chance to take a class with you yet, but everybody says I should. I hope to. I'm extremely interested in the American modernist poets."

Brad nods a bit goofily, clearly caught off guard, trying to shift gears to professor mode. I tap my pool cue on the floor.

"I saw you make some sweet shots, Dr. Drake," Sean says, eyeing the table. "Not bad for a teacher. You want to shoot a game? My buddy over there, he can play, too. Students against teachers. What do you say?" Sean has a "buddy"? I'm surprised. I have pictured him skulking through the world alone; when I try to imagine him holding an ordinary college-guy conversation, maybe chugging a beer, I fail. And the Sean kissing up to Brad is not the menacing young man who frequents my office. Sean is complicated, apparently.

There are plenty of graceful ways to decline his proposal; I wait for Brad to think of one. Pointedly, I stand my cue against the paneled wall. "Sorry, but that's about it for me."

"Just one quick game of nine-ball with us, then," Sean says quickly to Brad, and I know my hopelessly amenable friend won't be able to refuse. I turn my back on them and retreat. From the safety of my crooked-legged wooden table, on which decades of sticky beer and ashes clog the jagged contours of sad old carved declarations of love and hate, I take stock of the crowd. I am strongly tempted to walk out.

Just then I see Delia, the director of the rape crisis center, at the far end of the room with a group of women—a rare sight at Ivan's. She's wearing jeans and a black leather jacket, and looks effortlessly bad-assed. She folds over the table and breaks; with a satisfying smack, the balls scatter around the table. Two rattle into pockets. I have never mastered the break.

I had said I would call Delia, and then I didn't. I completely forgot about it. Seeing her again, though, I feel the same urge to connect, or try to. It's as if I'm once again a lonely little girl on the playground, friendless. I check on Brad, who is neatly arranging nine balls in a tight diamond; Sean hovers nearby. That settles it. I start toward Delia, leaving my beer behind.

She demolishes her opponent in no time and then, spotting me among the spectators, separates herself from her cluster of companions. "Not exactly a faculty hangout," she greets me.

"That's what I like about it. I come here with a colleague sometimes." I nod in Brad's direction. "At the moment, though, I need to get away from the kid he's playing with."

"I can see how you might," she says, after a mere glance at Sean. I'm grateful that she's so quick to pick up on the fact that there's something *off* about him, something palpably wrong. I allow myself to feel vindicated. And then her eyes dart back in his direction and linger for a second, narrowing. She's just remembered him from somewhere, and the association is not a pleasant one. Considering her line of work, this seems like cause for concern.

"Do you know him?" I demand. "Where do you know him from? Because I have a bad feeling—"

She cuts me off. "It's nothing," she says. "Never mind. I shouldn't have said anything." I'm not reassured, not in the least. It seems less likely that she isn't sure of her memory than that some scruple prevents her from telling me what she knows. A confidentiality agreement? My mind begins to construct scenarios in which Delia could have encountered Sean, producing an impromptu series of brief horror movies. "If you know something, I really wish you'd tell me," I press, my voice low.

Delia raises a hand to her friends, waves her index finger to indicate that she just needs a minute. It isn't rude, exactly, but I feel dismissed. "No," she says. "Really. It's nothing."

Her friends are eyeing me askance. They look to me like women from the center—volunteers or victims, it's hard to tell. Definitely not sorority girls. What do I look like in their eyes? Hapless, dowdy movie professors flicker across my mind. Pop culture isn't kind to academics.

I take the hint. "Anyway, I just came over to say hi. Listen, do you still want to have coffee sometime?" I hear the note of urgency that has crept into my voice. She knows something about Sean. She is someone in whom I might confide, at least in a limited and strictly unofficial way—someone who might even have useful advice.

"You have my number, right? Call me, if you're serious." She turns away, and I cross the room to rejoin Brad. As a child I used to imagine that there was some sort of force field around me, deflecting people; that feeling returns as I make my way through the crowded room with peculiar ease.

I reach Brad and slip my elbow through his. "Let's go," I say.

What was Delia thinking when she looked at Sean?

"But I'm winning." Brad waves his cue in the direction of the table.

"Of course you are." I retrieve my abandoned beer and down the last swallow. "I'll take you out for pizza." I let him go make his excuses to Sean and catch the dark look my student sends my way. Brad is still pulling his gloves on and trying to zip his coat as I drag him out the door, steering him to the left, down the snowy street to Nicolletti's. Outside he stops me, his puffy sleeve bracing itself momentarily against my own. "Lois," he says. "What is it?"

I feel as if I am being blamed for something that is not my fault. This is perhaps irrational, since the only reason Brad doesn't know the whole story is that I have withheld it. Still, I have tried to offer meaningful fragments of the truth, and no one has taken me seriously: not Kate, not Delia, not even Brad, who obviously thinks I'm overreacting. "It's nothing," I say. I push his arm away and start walking, leaving him no choice but to follow.

Nicolletti's is one of this town's chief charms. It's a little mom-

and-pop Italian joint, the kind that's practically extinct: good pizza, good spaghetti, cheap wine, dark and candlelit. It almost always improves my mood.

So it might be the influence of Nicolletti's, of the familiar candle glowing through dimpled red glass. But as Brad and I settle into our booth, my anger is replaced by a strange and sudden warmth when I read in Brad's face that he is genuinely concerned. Ordinarily, genuine concern disconcerts me, but I find myself tempted to tell him—not just about Sean, and about Chloe, but about everything; all the parts I have left out. Beneath my resistance to telling—a habit of years—I have an intimation of the dizzying wave of relief that might follow. I have only to release the words, organize the unwieldy fragments. Or not. One more bottle of Chianti, and out they would tumble.

And then? What would be left of me? How would I anchor myself to the past?

No. Mine is not a story to be given away or traded for fleeting emotional gratification. What are your plans for the summer? I ask Brad, and that is what we talk about. He doesn't reach for my hand, as he might have; I don't have to slide it gently away. My secrets will not be tested today. I won't thrust them into the light and see what happens to them. Would they take a healthy gulp of sun and air? Or shrivel up like ancient tomb-dwelling vampires?

I'm sure it's better that I do not know.

Chloe

I think my parents had a good marriage. I think they loved each other. My early memories support this belief, and this was the sense I got when Daddy talked about my mother. I could also see their happiness in the old photographs I found in a shoebox in the back of his closet. But it was *her* relationship with my father that I grew up with. No wonder I don't have much faith in romance. I could never figure out exactly what they got from each other, Daddy and Gail, but it sure as hell wasn't healthy. Maybe Daddy wanted to be punished for my mother's death, not that it was his fault. Maybe Gail wanted to rule the fucking world, or at least Arrow, starting with my father.

Maybe that's why I don't go out hoping to fall in love or find happily-ever-after or even happily-for-a-while. It never even crosses my mind. What I hope for is to have a reasonably enjoyable time, with good food and good drinks and a moderately interesting conversation. As a bonus, at least if I'm in LA or New York, I hope that someone will recognize me and that I will impress them with my dazzling looks or sparkling wit, which could always lead to something, you never know. At *best* I hope for a spark of attraction that will lead to a little fling. Really, I don't even waste much time looking for the spark; I'm just glad when it happens.

So I'm not expecting a hell of a lot from my writer date, William. I like that he's not a goddamned actor, and I like that I met him at the grocery store in front of the asparagus.

If my life were a romantic comedy, which it most definitely isn't, you would now be expecting that William will, in fact, turn out to be my soul mate, after the obligatory rocky start. But my life sure as hell isn't a rom-com, so it would be a mistake to get your hopes up.

As for meeting William in the produce section, there's an explanation, and it has nothing to do with an impromptu, heart-warming debate between strangers over the merits of, I don't know, ugli fruit or something. What happened was that I was sort of half-consciously exercising my powers—like flexing a muscle, only what I was doing was sweeping my eyelashes upward, casting my eyes sideways at the stranger inspecting the white asparagus while I checked out the green. You can like me less for this if you want. But power is power; we all use what we've got. Or if we don't, we should. I don't know what beauty is—I mean I don't know how to define it—but I know that it's power. I've known for as long as I can remember that something about my face can not only get attention but hold it. It can arouse curiosity, desire, half-dead dreams. I actually think my knowledge of this has nothing to do with vanity. It's just the truth: the thing we call beauty is power. Sometimes it flashes out without warning, but you can also learn to control it. It's like having a special ability, like telekinesis or something; when you first develop it, you accidentally fling shit all over the place, breaking things and hurting people whenever you're the slightest bit riled up—and then gradually you learn to manage it, direct it at specific objects. You know what I mean. You see this process in movies from *Carrie* to *Firestarter* (thank you, Stephen King) to, I don't know, *X-Men*. Or *Star Wars*, I guess: beauty is like the force. Which also means that, like any halfway decent special power, you can use it for good or for evil. (And when you're young, of course, it's hard to know the difference. Hence: collateral damage.)

I recently read an interview with a model in a magazine. I won't say who, but you would know her. She said that she had never done anything she wasn't proud of. *Ever.* Nothing even remotely morally sketchy or ambiguous. She had her standards, and she stuck to them. This would be a pretty huge claim for anyone to make, but for one of the most beautiful women in the world, it was shocking. Could it possibly be true? She was "discovered," as they always say, when she was fourteen. Fourteen, then, would be the age when she learned that she could stop people dead in their tracks, drive men mad with the slightest flicker of her almond eyes.

What fourteen-year-old girl wouldn't try these tricks once or twice, just to see?

A saint, that's who. *Please.*

Anyway . . . although I've always thought telekinesis would be nice, what I got instead was my face. Not a supermodel face, but a good-enough face, attached to a good-enough body. Last week I flexed it in the grocery store and ended up with a date. Worse things have happened.

Lois

By the time we hit spring break, Sean has scraped through his British Novel midterm with a respectable C+, while continuing to torment me with old headlines: "Spelling Bee Champ Disappears." "No New Clues in Search for Local Honors Student." "Disappearance Remains Mystery; Parents Cling to Hope." If spring break delivers nothing more than a vacation from Sean, I'll be happy. Aside from the clippings, he's left me alone recently, but his very quietness is worrisome. What is he waiting for? Why haunt me with my own past? I can't imagine what he wants. I've considered calling his bluff, going public with my history—and why not? I have nothing to be ashamed of—but increasingly I feel as if disclosure is the least of his concerns.

I add the clippings to a folder that I keep in the same drawer as my growing *Carly/Chloe* file, though I'm not sure what I am saving them for.

Meanwhile, Brad and I have watched every movie in which Chloe Savage has ever appeared, however fleetingly; I finally told him she was a girl I had met at summer camp, to account for my apparent obsession. He has developed—or perhaps cultivated—a mild crush on her, which is actually convenient. I have an uneasy sense that he would like me to be jealous. I am not.

My sequel, meanwhile, has ground to a halt. It's not writer's block. My character—the kidnapper's son—has gone silent. I can't hear his thoughts, if he has any; I can't hear his conversations, spare as I imagine they are. I can't get him to do anything more interesting than drive his pickup down to the tavern for a beer or go out back to chop wood. As a result, he does these things too frequently. I craft lovely descriptions of the bleak snowy landscape in which he is stranded, and begin to wonder what kind of novel I am actually writing. But the kidnapper's son remains obscure to me. Gary, I am calling him. Gary will not act; he refuses to be diabolical.

Well, surprise, surprise, I hear someone mocking. It's called *fiction*, Lucy Ledger. Unlike thinly disguised autobiography, you actually have to *make it up*. Blame Gary if you like, but keep in mind—*Gary isn't real*.

The snow is melting. Streams of muddy brown runoff rush along streets, sidewalks, any groove they can carve, sparkling in the still-chilly sun. The students have gone home for the week, or they've flown off to Cancun or other sites of tropical debauchery; they'll return with peeling tans and faux-ethnic braids in their hair and monumental hangovers, tired of school and ready for summer. Brad and I stroll around town in the mud; it's nice to be outside after the long winter. We play pool (without running into Sean or even Delia); we have cheap dinners at Nicolletti's; we watch movies. The rest of the department thinks we are—well, a couple, obviously. They don't come out and say it; they are too polite. But I see them thinking it. Combating this mistaken impression seems like more trouble than it's worth.

We, however, like things the way they are. Or I do, anyway, which seems to be what matters. There were boys in college who swore it was okay to be just friends but whose hands were always straying where they didn't belong, whose faces brushed mine in accidental kisses, who eventually implored me to tell them what was wrong, why I didn't like them *that way.* Or who simply turned on me, in the end. I am truly grateful for Brad.

I considered visiting my parents over break; I didn't go at Christmas, and it's time. It's not that far: a morning's drive. But I told my mother I had to finish my revisions to *Kidnapped: Child Abduction in the Eighteenth- and Nineteenth-Century British Novel* in time for a January deadline, which wasn't true: I already submitted the revisions; the book is in production or will be soon. I didn't go because I didn't want to. "We'll miss you," my mother said on the phone, but I didn't believe her in the least. At such moments I always feel as if she is speaking from a mother-script, merely saying what she thinks she ought to say.

Just before I hung up, I thought I heard something at the other end—a little catch, maybe of breath, maybe not even anything that tangible. For a second only, I entertained the possibility that my mother had been about to say something else; something that veered from the script.

But by then she was gone, and upon further reflection, it seemed unlikely.

After I was returned to them, my parents actually became more distant. You might expect the opposite—that, suddenly conscious of years of benign neglect, they clung to me, found true joy in my presence. But no. They seemed a little afraid of me, in ways I couldn't understand then and have been trying to forgive ever since. When I find myself avoiding them, I remind myself of this.

My parents and Carly May's had little in common, but one thing they agreed upon was that she and I should have as little contact as possible. We would remind each other of what had happened, they insisted; we would encourage each other to dwell in the past. Whatever damage we had sustained would somehow increase exponentially if they permitted us to communicate. My mother was especially adamant about this, and Gail and the fathers were easily persuaded. My first therapist gently suggested to my mother that carefully regulated correspondence might actually help us work through what she called our "trauma," but Miranda rejected such advice. "Lois needs to move on," she said firmly, as if it were that easy. I think she meant that *she* needed to move on. The very idea of Carly May upset her; I think my mother even blamed her a little. Perhaps Carly's parents felt the same about me. I can imagine the appeal of making the *other* girl the complicit one, the one who thwarted escape, the one who was dangerously susceptible to the kidnapper's spell. In any case, geographically, our estrangement was easy enough to enforce; we could hardly sneak out our back doors and meet covertly in the woods, and cell phones had not yet made distance irrelevant. But putting the past behind you isn't like stuffing something in the back of a drawer or trimming a loose thread. The past has a life of its own. I think if they could have cut us off from it entirely, we would not have survived. That sounds a bit overwrought, I know, but I believe it is true. What had happened was part of us. We couldn't just lop it off like a gangrenous limb. We needed to acknowledge it, examine it, turn it over and let it catch the light at different angles. We had no idea what it meant—and yet we, and everyone else, seemed to take for granted that it *did* mean something. They just didn't want to talk about it.

So in the beginning we surreptitiously posted a few awkward letters; we snuck a couple of phone calls. We did our best to narrate to each other something true about those few strange weeks, after which we were not quite the same people as we had been, or would have been. I am still not the person I would have been, although I sense that person like a shadow. I'm not sure what she would have been like. There is no knowing. I suppose it's possible that Carly wrote more letters than I received, and vice versa; it would have been simple enough for vigilant parents to intercept letters with telltale postmarks. Phone calls showed up on bills and led to recriminations. The few stilted words we did manage to exchange weren't nearly enough. We needed more space and time to even begin to figure out what to say—what could be said, what needed saying. Could we have met in person, it might have been different; we might have preserved our connection, some trace of our cabin in the woods. But disembodied words were insufficient, perhaps even worse than nothing. After a while there was silence, and I only talked to Carly May inside my head.

It was when my parents came to pick me up that I knew how irrevocably I had changed. Carly and I had been swept from the lodge—the crime scene—and deposited at a tiny jail, where no one seemed entirely sure what to do with us except offer us food and assure us that our parents were on their way. Carly May had blood on her clothes, and a young policeman who seemed shy in our presence brought her some adult-sized jeans and a T-shirt that made her look like a scarecrow. (Later the police claimed my dress, too. It was evidence, they said.) I was struck by how pale we were, compared to everyone else. We had not been out in the sun for weeks. We looked like a slightly different species—related to normal humans but distinctly different. A man who identified himself as a detective asked us a few questions—What are your names? Are you hurt?—but my father insisted to the police on the phone that I not be questioned further until he arrived, and consulted a lawyer about my rights. We were numb, anyway; we had little to say. We were whisked away to a nearby hospital and subjected to extremely thorough medical exams—as if the truth might be found inside us; as if we might contain evidence that needed to be excavated; as if we were hiding something. That experience remains unspeakable. Eventually the policewoman who had accompanied us to the examination room took us home to her apartment, where we sat on her couch and watched TV. We hadn't seen TV for a month and a half, of course, but something about its familiar irrelevance calmed us like a drug. We stared vacantly at the absurd figures on the screen until we fell asleep, side by side on the couch, collapsed against each other.

The nice cop woke me when my parents arrived, and I still remember the few beautifully blank seconds before the gunshot went off in my head again, and I understood where I was and where I wasn't; the day rushed back in. My parents' faces loomed over me—Mom's somehow scattered, as if it had been taken apart and then haphazardly patched back together; Dad's angry and hard but with fear showing through the cracks. They could not sit on the couch because Carly was sprawled out beside me; instead, awkwardly, they reached their thin, tanned arms out to me, inviting me to stand and be embraced. Which I did, automatically; but I found no comfort. Their arms felt insubstantial, their eyes held too many questions I knew they'd never be able to ask, their fear was wordless and stiff. "I'm fine," I heard myself reassuring them. "I'm fine, I am, really I'm fine." And a dark space opened up between us as they searched me for clues, their faces imploring, and I could only look implacably, impenetrably back.

"Oh Lois," they kept saying. "Little Lois." My mother even whispered "my baby" at one point, with uncharacteristic sentiment. I did not think she had ever called me her baby before, except perhaps when I truly was one. But I was not their baby. I was not even Lois, exactly. My parents looked like kindly, helpless strangers. I don't know what I looked like to them, but whatever I saw on their faces didn't look like recognition.

After that they took me to a motel, where I stayed with my mother while my father talked to the police. I told my mother I was too tired to talk, and persuaded her to let me lie on one of the double beds and watch more TV. I asked her to close the curtains so I couldn't see the jagged mountains that surrounded us. She sat in a puffy orange vinyl chair by the window and watched me while I drifted off to sleep again, television voices chattering in the background. Sleep seemed the only comfort available. I tried to will myself to dream of nights at the lodge, playing hide-and-seek in the dewy grass, surrounded by fireflies and stars, but I did not dream at all.

What a strange situation, though surely it's not uncommon: a serious crime had been committed, perhaps multiple crimes, but the perpetrator of the crimes had been removed from the equation. There was no one to try, convict, punish. My parents wanted simply to take me home, but apparently there were procedures that had to be followed, steps that required our presence. We were evidence, after all. We were what remained. And I was not ready to leave Carly, though her father and Gail were also anxious to get her out of there. Reporters clustered outside the police station and flung questions at us as we hurried to and from our parents' rental cars; they hovered outside our motel rooms, desperate for a glimpse of our well-known faces, a word or two to spice up the news. Gail and Carly appeared on a local talk show, much to my parents' disgust; I wasn't allowed to watch it. After that her father put his foot down, and Gail sulked. Her defense was that other girls needed to hear our story in order to protect themselves from danger. "I won't have my daughter exploited by these vultures," Carly May's father said, taking what Carly May assured me was a rare stand, and that was that. I must have received similar offers, but my parents never mentioned it. "That woman is unspeakable," my mother said of Gail, and my father patted her tanned knee in mute agreement. They would have liked to have nothing at all to do with Gail, but complete avoidance was out of the question. We crossed paths with the Smiths at the police station often enough—at least in passing; generally, Carly and I were questioned separately.

She and I tried to plot seemingly chance encounters. Once we even persuaded our families to have dinner together; we went to an outdoor hot dog stand that claimed to be famous, where I watched my mother shrinking from the crowds of vacationers as if she had developed a fear of strangers. My parents and Carly

May's settled down at a picnic table. I can still feel the hot, splintery wood pressing into the backs of my thighs; I can see the wasp that wanted to drown in my lemonade. Carly sat across from me wearing a Whiteface Mountain T-shirt, tight and cropped, revealing a strip of untanned skin, her hair in a ponytail, a touch of lip gloss making her shiny and a little distant. The world was already reclaiming her, I realized, panicking, afraid of being left alone.

But then Gail made a stupid remark about Officer Hilton, the woman who had taken us in on the first day. "It's not just the short hair," she insisted. "It's something about her, you know? I think you can just tell, personally. I have to say I'm a little surprised they let the girls go home with her." My mother gazed stonily at Gail while our fathers, embarrassed, looked toward the sharp mountain peaks. Under the table, Carly gave me a sharp kick in the shin with her pointed bare foot. It was a characteristic Carly-message, familiar from the cabin, and I knew I hadn't lost her yet.

The dinner did not improve relations between our families. My father and Carly's might have done all right together, but Gail was too loud, too anxious to assert control, too eager to name what she didn't understand in order to diminish its power. Beneath her chatter I detected an edge, though, a sharp blade she was ready to wield, and I saw—with the strange clairvoyance I seemed to have possessed since our rescue—that it would be a mistake to underestimate her. In response to Gail, my own mother retreated to the Waspy, New Englandy hoity-toityness that was her all-but-abandoned birthright. She looked down her long, narrow, makeup-free nose at garish, babbling Gail and chilled us all. The fathers ate many hot dogs, commenting occasionally upon the weather or the beauty of the mountains. Carly's father kept tugging her ponytail—but gently, as if it might come off in his hand. Every now and then she offered him a half smile, one side of her mouth twitching briefly upward, and he visibly relaxed.

I wasn't ignoring my parents, exactly; that would imply that

I was aware of them and pretending otherwise. No, I was trying to register their presence in some emotionally appropriate way. I just couldn't feel that they were really there.

At last it was settled to everyone's satisfaction that Carly May and I had told all we could. There were no accomplices to our abduction and no additional victims. We had said this from the beginning; at last they accepted our story. According to the news reports, we had been rescued "just in time"—as if our kidnapper had been brandishing a weapon at us just as the cop cars pulled up.

Finally, the police let us go. Carly and I insisted on being permitted to say good-bye, though our parents wouldn't leave us alone. We hugged awkwardly, neither of us really being the hugging type, and we tried to think of things we could say in front of our parents that would mean something. We glared at each other, eyes full of secrets and promises.

And so she went back to the farm and back to her pageants, and I returned to the inn. The touched-by-(near-)tragedy inn. A house full of strangers. Home.

My parents sent me to a psychiatrist, of course. It made them feel as if they were doing something, and allowed them to believe that I was on my way to being fixed. At least that's what I assume they thought: naturally we did not discuss it, or not in those terms. They asked me guarded questions about my sessions, my sense of my progress. Usually I told them what they seemed to want to hear. Sometimes I wished I could be more like Carly, who would, I imagined, have been unafraid to tell the truth, to lash out, to make demands.

I always wished I could be more like Carly May.

Chloe

I didn't have to do as much work on the farm when I got back. I saw that I probably had a pretty brief window where I could bargain, and I totally milked it. I'd go out in the truck with Daddy sometimes to round up cattle or whatever, but my daily chores were lifted, passed on to my little half brothers. I spent a lot of my time in my room. Sometimes I practiced ballet; I was seriously out of shape after a summer with no lessons, and my legs needed to be retrained to turn out properly. Daddy had mounted a barre along one side of my room and a big mirror along the other, and I did endless pliés until I was strong again. Sometimes I actually did my homework. Otherwise I read trashy novels or scrawled stupid stuff in my diary, mostly about what I planned to do when I finally got the hell out. The diary felt like a Lois thing, although as far as I knew she didn't even keep one. She was the word girl, though. Scrawling my ugly thoughts on blank pages felt like a way of tapping into Lois's way of thinking and being.

And, as always, there were the pageants, an endless circuit of freak shows. Half the time, I was on the road with Gail. Now I wasn't just Carly May Smith from Arrow; I was Carly May Smith the abducted girl, the miraculously rescued girl. I was a freaking sensation. Reporters always wanted comments from me. The judges knew who I was. The other parents steered clear of me; the other girls seemed shy.

I could have quit, obviously. I had told Zed I would quit; he had hated my pageants. I think I really meant to at first, but then somehow it felt more rebellious to keep it up. Who was he to tell me how to spend my life, anyway? A criminal. A loser. A dead man. Someone who couldn't help me now, that was for goddamned sure. It made sense that the world would treat me differently now, since I sure as hell *felt* different. The truth was, too, that at least the pageants got me out of Arrow. And for that alone they were worth it—worth the trouble, worth spending hours with Gail. Worth the guilt of breaking my word to Zed, especially since the guilt faded a little more every day.

Gail was always a little pissed off. I had changed, she said, like it was a crime. You used to look sweeter. That was true, no doubt about it; I also used to *be* sweeter, but of course Gail couldn't care less about that. She was right, though; the appearance of a certain kind of sweetness mattered, at least to the judges. On stages across the Midwest I would stand in a line with the other girls, shoulder to shoulder. Most of us were pretty much the same height, although at the hick local pageants you always got a few shorter girls—bigger girls, too. Usually, though, I'd be sandwiched between two girls whose shoulders were level with mine, whose arms and legs I might almost mistake for my own if they somehow got mixed up. In a police lineup, I don't think anyone but our mothers (or coaches, as in my case—I was always careful to make it clear that Gail was *not* my mother) could have told us apart. We stood angled to the right, left knees crooked gently in front of right knees. This was supposed to be slimming. It also made us look like one of those strips of accordioned paper dolls I remembered from when I was little. Connected at the elbows, each one exactly like the next.

When it was your turn to step out of line, you were suddenly supposed to be an individual, not to blend into a lineup but to demonstrate how different you were. Suddenly you had to be the one with the brightest smile, the most graceful walk, the most wholesome air. The sweetest, in other words. But that was also the tricky part: Sweetness alone wasn't enough. You had to simultaneously pull off blushing-farm-girl-next-door and potential pinup. Really, whatever they said, you had to be both, once you got past the local Dairy Queen contests. And sometimes even then.

I didn't win as easily as I had as a preteen—as easily as I had preabduction, you might say. Gail made this connection and, through some twist of Gail-logic, managed to hold it against me.

At the Midwestern Cornhusker Teen Queen pageant, I failed even to place, and I thought Gail might actually smack me afterward, she seemed so pissed off. I was slightly disappointed when she didn't; I was always looking for things to use against her. A reporter approached her about doing a story on my struggles—"Teen Beauty Queen Haunted by Kidnapping," something like that. Gail actually said no, turning down a chance at publicity for the first time ever. But there were still triumphs: When I was fifteen, I became Miss Nebraska Teen USA. And I learned Gail's dirty secret. It was a turning point, that weekend, in more ways than one.

Like the other pageant families, we were staying at a hotel in downtown Omaha. Just Gail and me. Daddy would come down for the competition, he had promised, although he made it clear that he would rather spend his weekend some other way—mending fences in the west pasture, maybe. I wouldn't have minded if he hadn't come; his presence made the pageants harder for me. When I saw him sitting in the audience, my mind split in two: half of me saw the competition the way I wanted to see it, as a perfectly valid way to win prizes, praise, attention, whatever. But the other half saw it though Daddy's eyes, and then it was suddenly gross, a little sleazy, exploitative, degrading—nothing to be proud of. Then I'd remember *his* contempt for pageants—Zed's—and his disapproval would get mixed up with Daddy's, and their contempt would seem to become my own, and before I knew it the whole scene would seem cheap and disgusting to me, too. I'd feel ashamed and pissed off at myself for feeling ashamed. The contests were less complicated for me when he stayed away.

But before Daddy showed up in Omaha, it was just me and Gail. We didn't like each other any more than we ever had, but over the last couple of years we had figured out how to deal with each other. It helped that we wanted the same thing, though for different reasons; in fact I couldn't quite understand why the hell Gail was so anxious for my success. Maybe if she'd had a daughter of her own, I would have been spared. She obsessed over the details: the dresses, the hair, the makeup, the smile, the attitude. She was an expert on mascara. It all comes down to the eyelashes, was one of her favorite theories. Like my teachers at school—and later Martin, of course—she saw attitude as my biggest problem. "Don't smile like you've already won," she would say. "And don't smirk like you're laughing at some private joke with yourself. You have to look sweet. You want to be an actress, right? Act."

This was my second year trying for Miss Nebraska Teen and the first year I'd really had any kind of chance, though at fifteen I was still a little on the young side. Also a little on the *flat* side. The maximum age was eighteen, and the seventeen- and eighteen-year-olds had obvious advantages over most of the younger girls. Familiar as I was with Gail's big, loose, freckly bosom, I was in no hurry to grow large fleshy appendages on my chest. But I worried that my failure in that department had become a drawback. You could do things with tape and strategically designed bodices, but you could only do so much.

Anyway . . . Gail's deep dark secret. I was returning late in the morning from a rehearsal for our opening song-and-dance number. We were pretty strictly chaperoned as a rule, but our guardian for the morning had decided it was safe to let us off the elevator on our own floors without actually walking each of us to our rooms. Most of the girls had a mother with them, anyway. But Gail had stayed behind, much to my delight, complaining that she had a headache.

I got off the elevator on the ninth floor of the Sheraton and took my time strolling down the hall. In general I liked hotels because they made life seem clean and simple and uncluttered—as if you could just open the door, walk in, hang up your coat, and start fresh. But I knew our room that day would be stuffy and overheated, with some stupid soap opera blathering in the background. That was Gail's headache routine. Feeling in my pocket for change, I stopped at the vending machine in an alcove off the hallway. I bought a Coke, which I wasn't supposed to have. (Bad for the skin *and* the figure, said Gail the expert.)

As I turned away from the machine, popping my soda open, a man suddenly rounded the corner. I almost ran right into him. Most of the pageant girls were pretty paranoid; we had to listen to constant lectures about the dangers of strange men. I felt weirdly superior to the other girls in this respect; I'd already had my strange-man experience. Sort of like lightning not striking twice: I was immune. What was most disturbing initially about this man was that he seemed so unsurprised to see *me*, which made me suspect he had been watching me and had deliberately engineered the near collision. He had the kind of face I've always hated: full, wet lips and a sinister mustache, pale narrow eyes, flushed cheeks. He looked sort of hot and *damp*, like he had just gotten out of the shower, only not as clean.

"You must be one of those beauty queen girls," he said. Which was harmless enough because it was true and also obvious; the hotel was totally overrun with us, and I was carrying a dance costume over my arm. But maybe it was just his stating of the obvious that gave me the creeps. *Act normal*, I thought, and took a sip of my Coke.

"Think you've got a chance?"

I shrugged. "You never know." Which was true; you never did. The judges had issues of their own.

"Modest, too!" he leered, pretending to be impressed. And he knew that I knew that he was pretending, which meant that he knew that I knew that this was a weird encounter, not actually normal at all. Which made it all the more messed up.

The man stood between me and the hallway; I was basically trapped in the vending nook. "Well, wish me luck then," I said, mustering all the poise I had. I was very well trained, after all. "I've got to get back to my mom." *You have no idea who you're fucking with*, I thought. I reviewed self-defense techniques: Knee to the groin. Go for the eyeballs. I watched him carefully, waiting.

He didn't move. In some way I couldn't explain, he seemed to widen, to fill the space more completely. To try slipping past him would be to admit that I knew I was trapped. "Tell you what," he said. "You let me have a sip of that Coke, I'll wish you luck."

This caught me off guard. I stared at him in horror for about a second too long. It was like he had asked me for a kiss. His lips would be where mine had been. I couldn't imagine anything more disgusting. "You worried I got cooties?" Behind his wet smile he seemed to be laughing at me.

"No, here," I said, coming to my senses and thrusting the can at him. He kept his eyes on mine as he lifted it to his lips. As he swallowed, I darted past him, unable to avoid brushing against him. "Keep it, asshole!" I called over my shoulder. He was raising my Coke to me in a mock toast when I turned and ran.

When I got to room 914 I pounded on the door, not willing to waste time digging in my bag for my room key. Gail didn't answer right away. When she did, she looked pissed. She was still in her robe. "You're back earlier than I thought," she said. As if I could control the rehearsal schedule.

"Sorry," I said, only bothering with the faintest hint of sarcasm. I tried to edge past her, wanting a closed door between me and Mr. Spittle-mouth.

"What do you think you're looking at?" Gail said. She sounded weirdly suspicious, and I was perceptive enough to be able to tell that it was the kind of suspicion that's caused by fear; a sign of guilt. I looked past her and took in the tumbled bed, the silent television, the room service tray with two bottles of beer and two empty plates on it. Gail's crazy hair, her blurred lips. And the smell: like sweat, but worse.

It was him, I thought, too dumbfounded to say anything. The wet-mouthed man. I felt like I was looking down at her from a very high perch; like looking at a chicken from the top of a silo, say. She looked small, stupid, lost. Pecking frantically.

I had her. We both knew it.

• • •

I saw him at the pageant the next day. He was the father of Miss Teen Kearney, who was plumpish and unpleasant and not one of the girls who worried me. Gail saw me looking and gave me a glare—illogically, since she couldn't have known that I would recognize him as her visitor—but not before he had noticed me and sent a moistly conspiratorial smile.

Two days later, I won the state title. All along I felt like I was moving in a dream; I had this weird, calm confidence at each stage of the competition. I chattered eloquently through my interview, whirled through my ballet piece, strutted across the stage like I had been born in high heels and an evening gown. I felt so sure that I would win that when I did, I had to pretend to be overwhelmed and surprised and overcome when they fitted the rhinestone tiara on my head and everyone hugged me and the cameras flashed. I was good at pretending.

What I was really thinking was *What's next?* This crown had been my goal (not to mention Gail's) for a long, long time, but instead of feeling triumphant, I was impatient, anxious. *What's next? Now what?* The national competition was the obvious answer; Gail was already talking about it. Plotting mascara strategies. But suddenly a bigger pageant win wasn't enough; I wanted something not just bigger but *different*.

I rode home with Daddy in his truck, despite Gail's transparently fake pleas to keep her company. All my dresses and crap were packed into Gail's car with her frosty face. The truck smelled like the farm, and the radio wasn't working; Daddy and I rode in silence most of the way. He kept his eyes on the straight dark highway; I closed mine, mostly, and looked at the lights inside my head. At some point, though, something changed in the space between us, and I knew that we had established a truce. It didn't matter if we understood each other's choices or thought they were stupid. What mattered lay deeper, safe from Gail or crowns or whatever else the world had in store for us. Or so I thought then. We didn't exactly toss the word *love* around in my family, but I knew it was there. I've hung onto that moment for a long, long time.

Gail drove behind us the whole way home, as if unwilling to trust us out of her sight; her headlights flickered pissily in the rear-view mirror. "Woman ought to know better than to tailgate some-one for a hundred miles," Daddy muttered at one point—coming as close as I'd ever heard him to directly criticizing Gail. But I knew exactly why her headlights were probing the cab of the truck so insistently. She was wondering whether I would tell him about the bed, the man, the fake headache. Whether I would tell him, and what.

It was tempting as hell, that's for sure. But some instinct told me to bite my tongue. *Wait and see*, said a voice in my head. And because "wait and see" was more Daddy's phrase than Gail's, I decided that I would. I knew this wasn't a card I could afford to throw away.

Lois

I returned to a sweltering early August, the tail end of summer. It seemed like another world. The inn itself was air-conditioned, but our quarters were not. I retreated to the shady back porch and read in the hammock, day after day. I walked sometimes in the woods behind the house; I had grown unaccustomed to the free-dom to roam as I pleased in the daytime and felt a pressing need to stretch my long-confined body, but I couldn't stand to go into town, where I was convinced that people stared at me. Probably they did; I was a curiosity, a story everyone told, a cautionary tale for young girls. I would have been a media heroine of sorts, had we allowed this to happen, but we did not. When reporters turned up at the inn, my parents drove them away; they screened calls with a fierce vigilance that betrayed the depth of their fear and anger. I wanted only to be left alone, and my parents wanted to pretend nothing had happened.

What I dreaded was returning to school: facing rooms and hallways and auditoriums and locker rooms full of people who *knew*, or thought they did, what had happened to me, and wouldn't be able to talk to me—or even *not* talk to me—without somehow alluding to it. People I had known for years who had never shown the slightest interest in me would suddenly be overcome by transparent, prurient curiosity. I might as well stick a headline on my forehead, I foresaw, and despaired.

And then one afternoon my mother made a rare visit to my porch, where she found me reading *Jane Eyre* and indulging in lazy fantasies of escape, of power.

"Here you are," she said needlessly, as if I might have been anywhere else. She lowered herself into a chair and wiped the sweat from her brow with a gesture both graceful and weary. We were short a maid, and she had been cleaning all day. I sniffed inconspicuously, trying to detect the faint sharp scent of gin, but there was nothing yet. I raised my eyebrows in half-greeting and waited for her to speak. Her visit had to have a purpose; she had lost the ability to be casual with me.

"Your father and I have been talking," she began at last. This meant that she had been talking, and my father had been listening and agreeing. Her eyes seemed fixed on some distant point across the lawn where the trees began—where deer sometimes emerged from the woods and cautiously surveyed the grounds.

"We've been talking about private school," she continued. "Boarding school. Academically, of course, it would be an excellent opportunity for you. But mostly, you would have . . . a fresh start. People who don't know you. Does that appeal to you?" As an afterthought, she added, "We would miss you," though it was too late to convince me that missing me was part of the equation. It didn't matter. Private school *did* appeal to me. It appealed to me more than I could politely admit. From the parking lot came the sound of tinkling laughter, the gentle slam of an expensive car door. We had a wedding party that weekend. "I have to go." My mother heaved herself out of the chair and smoothed her skirt. Once or twice her eyes had skittered across mine. She had not once looked at me directly. She seldom did anymore. "Think about it, Lois."

But there was no need to think.

Three weeks later my parents deposited me, my bike, and a few suitcases at a white-pillared, redbrick dormitory that looked like part of a movie set. It was only two hours from home, but it felt like another world. "Rich kids," remarked my father, eyeing my fellow students. "Don't let them intimidate you, honey." My mother glanced at him sharply; she hated it when he suggested that he was not really at home in this world, her world. "You just be yourself. And remember"—he ducked and spoke into my ear—"you can spell their pants off, every one of them." His voice shook with what I took to be emotion. Curious, I searched his face for clues—how *did* he feel about me, anyway? But as usual, his body seemed like an awkward placeholder for a mind that had wandered elsewhere. My father had always been something of a mystery to me; since my abduction, he seemed almost a stranger, kind but befuddled.

I hadn't yet told my parents that I was giving up spelling. Not so much giving it up as cutting it loose. It was no longer going to be a part of who I was. I couldn't have explained my decision without at least alluding to Zed, who had taught me to see the spelling bees as an empty display of a meaningless skill. I knew they wouldn't want to hear that, and I felt no real need to make them understand.

My mother gave me a brittle Miranda-hug: our boniest protrusions glanced off each other. A strand of my hair caught on one of her rings and snapped. She was wearing a sharp navy-and-white linen dress and looked perfectly at home in this environment. These impeccably green sloping lawns, the tasteful flowerbeds, the subdued tones of the other parents—this was her world, the preppy New England world to which she had been born. She bent down and brushed cool, dry lips across my forehead, rested a steadying hand momentarily on my shoulder. For the first time I noticed the delicate lines etched at the corners of her eyes. I did not think they had been there in the spring.

"You'll be fine," she said, almost brusquely, and I knew she was right.

I had finished unpacking by the time my roommate arrived. This pleased me: I had already established my presence in the room, claimed my space. I was sitting on my bed reading when she entered. She was very tall, very blond. She dropped her suitcase as soon as she saw me and held out her hand, a gesture that struck me as very adult but somehow not forced or ridiculous. "I'm Jessica," she said, smiling. "I'm so glad to meet you." I put my book down and returned her greeting, relieved that she seemed pleasant without being effusive. "You look familiar," she said a while later, as she arranged her clothes neatly in dresser drawers. "It's funny. Like I've seen you just recently. Were you at the Vineyard this summer?" Even as she said it, though, she furrowed her smooth brow doubtfully; she knew that wasn't the answer.

I was prepared for this moment and glad that it had wasted no time before presenting itself. "No," I said slowly, as if hesitating to speak too frankly. "I guess you might recognize me from . . ." I allowed a shadow of pain to cross my face. "Well, it doesn't matter, really," I said brightly, jumping up from the bed. "Let's not talk about that. Are you hungry? Do you want to go get something to eat?" I saw her curiosity intensify, but her manners prevented her from pressing me. Every now and then I caught her inspecting me, though, trying to place me.

It mustn't have taken her long to figure it out. By the next day it was widely known that I was Lois, the abducted girl. But as I had neither broadcast this fact nor flat-out denied it, it was not held against me; some unfamiliar instinct had told me that this would be the case. I acquired a certain easy celebrity without putting myself forward. Had I stayed at home, it would have been different: I couldn't have controlled how people saw the story; history would have dragged me down. But here, among strangers, was a sort of frame within which I was free to construct a Lois I could enjoy being: a Lois who was clever, bookish, quick with words; a Lois who was not shy or awkward, just a little mysterious. A Lois who knew something of life: something dark, something that demanded respect.

A Lois who had something you didn't. A Lois you did not mess with.

Chloe

God knows what would have happened if I'd stayed in Nebraska. I could be divorced by now, with a couple of kids who spent weekends with their useless father while I sat at home on my widening ass watching crappy TV and drinking cheap wine from a box. I could be the hottest mom in Arrow, putting on lipstick and heels to pick my brats up from school. Those are the happy endings. I could also be in prison. I could be dead. You think that's melodramatic? Here are some ways I could have died: I could have been killed in a car crash with some drunken asshole at the wheel. Killed in a snowmobile accident, ditto. Dead of a drug overdose in somebody's skanky trailer. Dead of anorexia, trying too hard to disappear. I knew kids who died in all of these ways. It could just as easily have been me; I was as stupid and reckless as anybody. Anybody who thinks small-town America is a safe, sheltered place to grow up hasn't spent much time there.

By the time I was a sophomore in high school—the same year I was crowned Miss Nebraska Teen—nobody mentioned the abduction anymore. Kidnapping. Whatever. Which doesn't mean they didn't think about it; there just didn't seem to be anything else to say. I hardly ever brought it up unless I needed Gail to feel bad. (The fact that she'd been having her eyebrows waxed when I rode off with a stranger hadn't played very well in the press, as you can imagine, though it was actually one of the few things I didn't blame her for.) But even if it was buried as far as everyone else was concerned, it was never very far from my mind.

Daddy was always out on the farm; it seemed like he came in later and later all the time. I didn't blame him. The house had gradually been taken over by Gail and her kids, and by then they practically had full control. It was their world—not mine, not Daddy's. She'd had two boys pretty much one after the other, bam bam, after Daddy married her. My half brothers, technically. But from the start I didn't feel any real connection to them. They looked nothing like me, nothing like Daddy. The first one, Braden, was a boy version of Gail, a pale lumpy little thing. Jaden was different—taller, dark-haired, even handsome—but if he didn't look like a little boy-Gail, he sure as hell didn't look like my father, either. Which, after the Miss Nebraska Teen pageant, I had a definite theory about, as you might imagine. Still, if my half brothers had just left me alone, it would have been okay. I would have been happy to pretend they didn't exist. Stupidly, they made this impossible.

They tormented me, for one thing.

Which is no fucking excuse for maiming anyone, obviously, though that's what damn near happened. And although it could have ruined everything, my outburst of violence actually got me one step closer to gone. Maybe I should have suffered more; it's easy to feel guilty, looking back. If I'm completely honest, I have to admit that I even felt guilty at the time. And scared as hell; it was terrifying, frankly, to realize what I was capable of.

It happened one weekend morning when the boys and I were alone in the house. I was locked in my tiny bedroom as usual. We lived in an old farmhouse, with small, odd-shaped rooms, slanting ceilings, and narrow hallways. No right angles. It always felt crowded, like the walls were closing in. I was scribbling in the diary I'd kept since my return from the cabin when one of them started pounding on my door. "Carly May, look, Carly May, you have to see!" It was Jaden, yelling.

I jumped up from my bed and flung my door open, half hoping he would fall through it. Usually I made them wait longer. I had no interest in whatever he wanted to show me. I just wanted to scare him away.

Jaden, with a dirt-smeared face, had balanced one of my tiaras on his head, a stupid grin stretching his mouth wide. He would have been about seven then, I guess.

"Take that off, you little shit," I said. "You look like a retard."

"We're not supposed to say *retard*, retard."

"Take it off, or I'll kick your skinny little ass. Gail isn't home to stop me. You know I'll do it." This is how I spoke to them. Nice, isn't it? I'm not defending myself. Anyway, I was half-serious and genuinely pissed off. Like I said, I would have been glad to ignore them completely, if only they had been willing to cooperate. But I really hated it when they messed with my stuff. "One last chance," I warned Jaden. "Take it off, or I'm gonna smack you into next week."

He knew I meant it; it wouldn't have been the first time. But he was a fearless little bastard. "You'll have to catch me, snot-breath," he said, and then he turned and ran, my tiara crooked on his head. He looked totally demented.

I took off down the brown-carpeted hallway after him, whipped around the corner, and flew down the creaking stairs while he laughed like a little maniac. I caught him at the bottom. I had just gathered his overgrown hair into a pullable rope when I heard Braden call from the top of the stairs.

"Hey, Carly May," he said. "Look." He held my diary up for me to see. "You sneaky little bastard," I said, giving Jaden's hair a hard yank. I grabbed the tiara and looked up at Braden. "Give me that book," I hissed, "or I'm gonna poke your brother's eye out." I brought the tiara close to Jaden's face, aiming one of the pointy ends at his left eye. He stopped laughing, and I saw fear register on his face. I actually *saw* it; one minute it wasn't there, and then it was, changing the color of his eyes and the texture of his skin and the rhythm of his little-boy breath. Later I would think back to that expression when I was acting and had to do fear—I used it as sort of an emotional shortcut, a way to access a feeling I didn't really understand very well. But in the moment what got me most was how easy it had been to reduce my little brother to a shivering puddle of dread. *He really thinks I'll do it,* I thought, sort of amazed. For a second I felt like the biggest asshole in the world. I almost let him go—and then Braden started reading from the top of the stairs. "Sometimes I feel like he's standing in the doorway watching me sleep. Sometimes I pretend he is. I can't believe I'm even writing this down." He read haltingly—reading wasn't exactly his strong point. The clumsy sentences seemed to burn themselves into my mind, and without even knowing it I jerked the tiara closer to Jaden's eye. I would like to believe that I miscalculated. But there was no thought involved. I saw myself jab the thing in his eye. He screamed. I let go of him and took off after Braden.

Now if you actually try to picture this, you have to admit that it's partly comical. If it was in a movie, you would want to laugh, even if you were trying to tell yourself it really wasn't funny. I was using a *tiara* as a weapon. But Jaden howled for Daddy, who happened to be coming in from the barn. He showed up just as I caught up with Braden—I was wrestling him to the floor while he kicked me in the knees, the shins, wherever his thick little legs could reach. I'd managed to grab the diary out of his hand, and I punched him in the stomach with it as he went down.

That's what Daddy saw, that and then Jaden's red, swollen eye. He didn't think it was funny at all.

I felt awful, of course. I felt awful when I saw the disappointment in Daddy's face, and I felt awful when I saw little Jaden's angry, temporarily sightless eye. At the same time I was sort of relieved to notice that I felt awful, since it seemed to prove that I was not an absolutely heartless person, which I did occasionally worry about. I fully agreed that I should be punished, though I felt strangely removed from the endless conversations about what should be done with me. I felt more curious than afraid. What could they do to me, after all?

Gail was all for sending me away to some kind of home for problem children. This seemed like an awfully risky proposal to make, given my hold over her. *God, she must really hate me,* I remember thinking. "No more road trips, no more nice hotels and room service?" I said nastily. I saw her face flush as her eyes shot sideways to see if Daddy had picked up on anything. He hadn't.

"I'm sure we could work something out," she said, because of course she had never intended to give up her stake in me. She was fine with the idea of picking me up from some juvie home, my fellow delinquents waving good-bye-for-the-weekend as I got into the car with my gowns slung over my arm.

Ha.

"Don't forget what she's been through," Daddy said, though he didn't say—no one ever did—what that was, exactly.

"She can't use that as an excuse forever." Gail squirted a big blob of ketchup into the meatloaf she was mixing. I could tell from her voice that she would give in—she had no choice, really. I did

an obnoxious pirouette and then struck a graceful pose. I studied the long dark hairs on Gail's stirring arm, wondering why she didn't bleach them. It seemed like the kind of thing she would do.

"She isn't," Daddy said. "I am." He used his firmest voice, the one even Gail gave in to. He folded his newspaper, set it aside, and settled his fists on the table, knuckles touching, giving the question of my fate his full attention.

Daddy suggested, of course, that it was the pageants that should go. There was a logic to this, I had to agree. I would have fought it, but I also would have accepted it. The whole lipstick and-lace scene had gotten pretty old, and there were other ways to get where I wanted to go. Gail, however, would have none of it. She said pageants were the most positive thing in my life, what kept me grounded, gave me self-esteem. I watched her curiously while she spewed this crap. Then, against his better judgment, Daddy talked himself into believing her. I watched that too, my faith in him fading fast; I was disappointed but hardly surprised. The most interesting question, as far as I was concerned, was this: how the hell were they going to get me away from the boys?

In the end they decided I would go and live with Grandma Mabel for a while. Daddy's mother. She had moved into a small house in town when Grandpa Luke died, and she'd been there on her own ever since. We didn't visit Grandma Mabel much. She came to the farm for dinner every couple of weeks, but her house was too small and tidy, I guess, for all of us to invade. Or, I don't know, maybe she just wasn't Gail's biggest fan. I liked it at Grandma Mabel's. It was orderly and calm, a place where you could think straight. It smelled a little like old people, true, and Grandma Mabel watched horrible stuff on TV. But: no farm, no little brothers, no Gail. Getting off the farm would be the first step. From there I would find a way to get out of Nebraska.

Of course I'd be leaving Daddy, too. I would like to say that part of what I felt was sad; it would make me sound like a better person. Maybe I was sad; maybe I've just forgotten. What I remember, though, is that I was ecstatic. I sulked for all I was worth so they wouldn't catch on.

Lois

I can't get out of bed. I clutch my snowy white comforter beneath my chin. Under the covers, I lock one hand around my phone. My curtains are closed, but they don't altogether block the light; I am well aware that it is daytime. Spring sun, cold and bare, streaks my walls.

It's Friday. I don't teach today, and I have no meetings scheduled. No one will know if I get up or not.

I have lain here for an hour or more. My agent woke me, calling from New York with news: that the major parts in the movie adaptation of *Deep in the Woods* had finally been cast. She told me the names. I have been curious, but I have tried to divorce myself from that project as much as possible, to protect myself from disappointment—and self-reproach; I sold my right to care about the movie long ago. (The film, my agent, Erin, calls it loftily.) If Hollywood makes a mess of the story—which happens more often than not, I would venture to guess, at least from the author's point of view—it would be hypocritical of me to complain. My pretty antique sleigh bed, my expensive silk nightgown, my zillion-thread-count sheets, the lovely espresso maker that awaits me in my cold kitchen—all of these pleasant luxuries serve as reminders that I received a tidy little check in exchange for signing away any say whatsoever in the making of the movie.

What I had learned is that most books that are optioned never become movies; someone buys the rights and then sits on them forever. Before the novel's success, I had half convinced myself that the fate of *Deep in the Woods* would be no different—or that even if it was, I might somehow preserve my comfortable cocoon of anonymity, appearing to the world as Lucy Ledger only when it suited me, and keeping Lois Lonsdale safely out of the public eye. Once I revealed my history to my editor, I realized that this would be far trickier than I had imagined, and when I heard that a movie was actually going forward—and quickly—I suffered my first serious qualm. It finally occurred to me that I might end up seeing some wretchedly botched version of my childhood trauma on the screen, and that this might be—well—a little disturbing, to say the least; and that I had no one to blame but myself.

If I had reason to fear—if the early reviews were bad, for instance—I simply wouldn't go to see it, I told myself: *if* it even got a screen run, *if* it played anywhere within a hundred miles, *if* it stayed in theaters for more than a week, *if* any of this happened before I was old and stooped and gray.

And if it was a success? If success led to exposure? A secret almost-hope had glimmered into being, unexamined, barely acknowledged: *if success led to exposure, maybe it would lead me back to* Carly May, *wherever she was, whoever she had become.*

In the meantime, my discovery of Chloe Savage had explained why Google searches produced no traces of Carly May Smith's existence past the year 2000.

And now this.

A shaft of sunlight hits my slightly angled full-length mirror and reflects sharply across the room, falling on my face. With it comes a flash of realization: *she has to know.*

Chloe Savage has read the script. She will have recognized the story. She knows that no one else could have written it. She has sought out the novel from which the screenplay is adapted. Her expensively manicured hands have turned each page. They would have been shaking. With anger? Or simply with emotion? She would have been on the alert for misrepresentation, dissimulation, all forms of narrative misdirection or injustice. She would have found them. She would have tried to enter my mind, to imagine what I had been thinking—just as I am now trying to enter her mind. We are trapped in a telepathic loop: but without him, we're doomed, I think. He who could read our minds, who could lay them bare to us and to each other.

She took the part.

This is what finally gets me out of bed.

I stumble down the chilly hall and into the kitchen, wrapped tightly in my heavy robe, stiff from oversleep. I am making cappuccino when my phone rings again. I'm tempted not to answer it; my life is already complicated enough, and I don't want to dilute Carly May's influence with other voices.

But I do answer my phone, after all, because suddenly I wonder if I have become a bit unbalanced, and refusing to answer the phone strikes me as supporting that possibility. I do want to be sane. "Hello?" I say it with a bit of impatience, in my most businesslike voice—as if I am very, very busy; not at all as if I have slept until practically noon.

No one is there. Or, I should say, no one answers; there's a peculiar quality to the silence that suggests that someone *is* there, someone who has chosen not to speak. I think I hear breathing, ever so faintly. I think I hear something rustle. I try to discern whether the silence is male or female, hostile or—or what? Something else. Before I draw any conclusions, the silent person hangs up.

Who could it be but Sean? How did he acquire my cell phone number? I try to consider whether I should be afraid, and of what, but realize that—reason aside—I *am* afraid. *Fear: fescennine, furciferous, farraginous, fardel.* I picture Delia's card, tucked in my wallet; I try to imagine calling her. Could I trust her? Could she tell me anything I don't know? I push aside the thought of calling Delia, push Sean aside, stow my fear in a little box and stash it at the very back of my mind. I have more important things to think about: the sequel, my contract, my deadline. Yesterday's message from Amelia, wondering how the book is going.

A little while later I settle at my computer to write. A steaming mug warms my hands. Across the street, the neighbor's gray cat chases squirrels. Clouds hang heavy and low. All color has been washed from the world. I shift my eyes to the screen and begin typing.

After I have pounded madly at the keyboard for an hour or so, I get up, stretch, and return to the kitchen. I rinse my mug in the sink and toss a bag of popcorn in the microwave. (One must eat.) While it pops I retrieve from my bedside table the file in which I have stashed all the newspaper clippings Sean has left in my faculty mailbox. I flip through them until I find the one I'm looking for. "Kidnapper's Past Yields Few Clues":

In the weeks since the recovery of two preteen abductees from kidnapper John Whitlow's isolated Adirondack hideaway, police have tried to piece together information about the man's life. A hazy picture has begun to emerge of a painfully shy young man of considerable promise who, in his mid-20s, suddenly changed his name, retreated from the world, and cut all ties with family and friends. Whitlow left little trace in the years that followed until he resurfaced this month as the perpetrator of one of the most highly publicized kidnappings in recent years. Born on May 3, 1965, in Utica, New York, he was christened Randy McDougal but changed his name legally at the age of 21.

Mr. Whitlow's mother, Tina McDougal, is currently living in Boonville, New York, a small upstate town north of Utica, but claims that it has been a year or more since she has spoken to her only son. With her lives a young boy, two years old, a thin, solemn child with lanky brown hair. The boy, she says, is Whitlow's son, though she has no records to prove it, and claims not to know the whereabouts of the child's mother. He doesn't seem to take after his father, she adds, watching the boy throw a stick for a large dog of uncertain breed.

Though it begins as a routine enough story, the piece reveals its "human interest" leanings more blatantly with each paragraph. It's the same old angle: how could *this* person become *that* person? How could this ordinary community, this unremarkable woman, this redbrick school, produce *this man?* This monster? Were there signs? His high IQ, his shyness, his obsession with books? His failure to attend the prom?

The article has sparse facts with which to work. His neighboring Uticans aren't chatty. The mother's memory seems imperfect. (The article implies that she drinks and even hints at drug use, but stops short of specific assertions about her vices.) His yearbook picture is even more inscrutable than yearbook pictures generally are. One detail has always interested me: Tina McDougal also had a daughter, Zed's sister, three years younger. She ran away to New York City at sixteen. "Too pretty for her own good," Tina is quoted as saying. "I always knew she'd end up in trouble." The girl—Roxanne—had never reappeared. One thing I had forgotten: "Mrs. McDougal says that her son was devastated by his sister's disappearance. Just out of high school himself, he boarded a bus for New York with the intention of finding her. He claimed upon his return to have been unsuccessful, but his mother has doubts. 'He didn't talk much after that trip,' she says. 'But in my opinion he did find her, and whatever he found out messed him up so bad he never got over it. That's what I think.' She shrugs her thin shoulders. 'But what do I know?' "

The article does not come out and say that Roxanne became a hooker, but it invites readers to arrive at that conclusion. Carly May had asked him once if he had a sister. His anger had flared.

Roxanne is an important piece of the puzzle, no doubt. But

right now, another detail demands my attention, something to which I've never given much thought.

It's the two-year-old boy. Thin, solemn, lanky-haired. He would be—I add swiftly—about twenty.

I forget to listen to the popcorn. The charred bag collapses when I open the microwave door. Dark smoke pours into the room. It smells vile. I toss the bag in the garbage and return to my computer, promising myself vaguely that I'll go out later for something to eat.

It has begun to rain. Most of the snow has melted, and now it rains almost constantly, washing away the sand and slush, along with whatever else isn't tied down. The small fierce drops batter my window. I've become accustomed to working to a snare drum–like rat-a-tat-tat. Earlier this week I managed to wrench my disgruntled character from his trailer and set him on the road, but his movements still didn't feel natural to me. I knew, deep down, that I was forcing him. It's like trying to position a doll whose limbs are supposed to be flexible but actually have a limited range of motion; there's only so much you can do without resorting to violence—jamming their rubbery joints out of alignment and twisting limbs in their anatomically incorrect sockets.

At which point they tend to break.

Now, though, something settles into place. The young man moves freely and logically through his world. He's no longer at a loss for words. He is younger than I thought; there's much that I'll have to go back and change. Still, he leaves the trailer and his doting but useless grandmother. He heads off to a state university, with the help of financial aid. He's not the brilliant student they say his father was, but he is not without potential.

I am thinking this over when a figure comes into view on the other side of the street, carved into fragments by my many-paned window: all in black, slightly hunched over, umbrellaless. I can't see his face, but I know. It's Sean's gait, his coat. He's blurred by the rain, but I see him raise his face to my house as he passes. For a second it seems he is looking directly at me. Quickly I reassure myself that, given the distance, the rain, and the warped old glass, this isn't possible. But he raises a hand in a possible greeting, something like a salute. I get up to boil water for tea; I'm thoroughly chilled.

When I return to my desk he has vanished. What I mean, of course, is that he has walked away, but it feels as if he has simply disappeared—as if he could rematerialize anywhere, any time. *What does he want?*

I nibble on the end of a pen, letting my eyes go out of focus as I stare out at the rain. My novel's plot unfolds with startling momentum.

Chloe

The writer's name is Stephen, and he takes me to RapScallion. This means he wants to be seen with me, which I appreciate. (Unless it means that he wants me to *think* that he wants to be seen with me, which would obviously be a little less gratifying.) He's nice-looking—just a little shorter than I am, looks like he goes to the gym regularly but not obsessively, good (but not too good) hair. You never know with writers. I fear the paunchy and unwashed. Call me superficial.

On the other hand, he went to Harvard and mentions this within the first ten minutes or so. It's a potential strike against him.

We decide to start with champagne, for no apparent reason, and I begin to feel festive. I'm wearing a great dress and haven't been eating much, so I'm happy with my appearance. I see eyes wander my way as people wonder if they should recognize me. Stephen sees this, too, and it's obvious that he likes it.

He raises his glass and offers a toast to the success of our next projects. We clink glasses overenthusiastically, and both burst out laughing.

The food is great. I order whimsically and am pleased with everything. We get more champagne. Our knees bump under the table. I want to sail out into the starry night on a champagne wave and land in Stephen's bed, wherever that is. I glow encouragingly at him.

And then, as the waiter clears our last plates and discreetly sweeps crumbs from the tablecloth, Stephen starts quizzing me about the movie. The plot, the cast, the ending. "I can't really talk too much about it," I say coyly, which happens to be true. "You'll have to wait and see it."

"Oh, you can tell me a little," he says, with a big winning smile. His eyes crease ever so slightly at the corners when he smiles, making him look just a little older, a little more worldly, a little more devastating, at least if you've drunk a bottle of champagne on top of a predate cocktail (or two). I even let myself imagine that I see a hint of Zed in his face. His tanned hand glances against mine. I'm entranced by our picturesquely candlelit fingers resting on the white tablecloth. "Well," I concede. "There are a few things I can tell you."

I give him a rough sketch of the plot. I notice after a minute or two that he's frowning, but I tell myself maybe that's what he looks like when he's thinking. When I finish, though, he's still frowning. Our knees aren't touching. Through my sparkly champagne happiness I see dimly that I've made a mistake.

"I don't get it," he says abruptly. "What's the guy's motivation? If it isn't sexual, then what is it? And what about the girls? Why wouldn't they try to escape earlier? I mean, it sounds like a sort of basic male fantasy, doesn't it—falling in love with their captor? But if that's all it is, then why the insistence on chastity? Is it just for the PG-13 rating? And the policewoman is problematic, too. Why does she identify with these girls? Why are we, as the audience, even interested in her story? I mean really, I don't quite see the point. The plot doesn't work for me."

I should brush it off. "You'll just have to wait and see" is what I should say, lightly, while laughing. I sure as hell shouldn't be offended—he isn't attacking me, after all. His attack on the movie is tactless, definitely, but that's all. I feel attacked, though. Blindsided. "I don't think too many men would admit to that particular fantasy," I say nastily, still smiling. "Maybe you have some personal issues I should know about?" I know, this doesn't make an awful lot of sense, but at the moment it feels both witty and cutting. I no longer want to float into Stephen's bed; I want to carve him up in little pieces. "Honestly, I like writers who don't insist on spelling everything out, who leave some room for interpretation. I like movies that make you think. That show you that people are, you know, complicated."

"Well, I like movies that make sense," he says, and there's no handsome eye-crease now. "What I *don't* like are scripts that disguise laziness as ambiguity. That's a cop-out, and the worst kind of pretension." For a long moment we look right at each other. I feel a hell of a lot more sober than I should, and I have a feeling he does, too. I see things in his eyes I hadn't even noticed before, things that make me wonder why I'm even here. The hint of Zed vanishes. (Or maybe it doesn't—he disapproved of me, too, after all.)

And, maybe because my champagne brain has been reckless enough to allow Zed-thoughts to enter the equation, I make my biggest, stupidest mistake yet. What I should be doing is escaping to the ladies' and raising an eyebrow at the waiter so that the check will arrive in my absence. Instead I open my mouth.

"But sometimes things don't make sense, do they?" I sound a little belligerent in my own ears. "Because, actually, it's based on a true story. So whether you think it makes sense isn't the point. The point is that it *happened*. The point is that life *is* fucked-up."

"I thought you said it was based on a novel."

"Well, yeah. But the novel is partly based on a true story, I happen to know." Why the hell am I doing this?

He rolls his eyes and gestures—pretty rudely, it seems to me—for the check. "Actually, that doesn't surprise me in the least," he says. A snooty note has definitely entered his voice. Harvard counts against him. *Bastard*. "People working with nonfictional material can be the laziest of all. They think it's enough to say, 'this incredible thing happened,' without bothering to offer motives, reasons, basic explanations. They count on the material to be so shocking that you won't notice what's missing. That actually explains a lot about my problems with your movie. No offense." Now he flashes the smile again, but it doesn't work on me anymore. "I'm not saying it won't still be a really good comeback vehicle for you." *Comeback? Vehicle?* Obviously there are crazily deep insecurities at work here. It occurs to me that he hasn't said anything very specific about his own recent work. I'll never know, because I'm certainly not going to ask.

We're standing now, and he actually places his hand on the small of my back as we move toward the door. I sidestep (gracefully, I think) just enough that his arm doesn't reach, and his hand falls back to his side. Outside, he hands his ticket to the valet. "Where to?" he asks, as if our conversation isn't still hanging over us like a funnel cloud. "Do you want to go out? I have some friends at Plafond. Or . . . do you want to go to my place for a drink?" He has moved close again, and I realize suddenly that he is about to bite my ear.

We sure as hell aren't on ear-biting terms. "You go ahead," I say. "I'll just get a cab." I raise my arm, and immediately, thank God, for once in my LA life, a cab appears. One of the valets seems to have wrangled it and it's probably someone else's and God knows what it will cost me, but there it is. The universe is cooperating with my drama. I leave him standing there looking confused. "Thanks for dinner," I say breezily. "Hope you'll enjoy the movie!" I actually blow him a kiss, overdoing it a bit.

In the cab, though, I cry. I cry and cry, and laugh, and realize that I'm fucking lonely. The driver ignores me. It's nothing he hasn't seen before.

Lois

Sean settles into the chair across from my desk. A cloud of smoke and dampness accompanies him, as usual, although it isn't raining for once. Dressed in his customary musty black layers, he seems to have his own private climate.

I ask him to remove his iPod headphones. "I'm not listening to anything," he objects.

"It's my rule. I can't talk to people who are wired."

He yanks the buds from his ears.

Sean was disruptive in class today—sighing theatrically, slumping back in his chair as if in pain, loudly crinkling the bag of some vile snack he was ingesting. I got the distinct impression that he hadn't done his reading. I get the distinct impression that he has not come to my office to discuss *Tristram Shandy*.

Before break, week after week I kept resolving to kick Sean out of class if he continued to make my life unpleasant. I considered reporting him. I debated whether I had more to gain or lose by exposing my past to get rid of Sean. The answer should have been obvious, but I clung to the secret that was my story. New developments have inspired me to change tack.

As always, I battle physical revulsion in his presence. His hair badly needs washing. Acne blossoms behind the greasy veil of his bangs. I make a conscious effort to sit up straight, aware of my desire to conceal as much of myself as possible behind my woodgrain-finished fortress of a desk. At the same time, knowing what I think I now know, I also feel an unaccustomed flutter of excitement: Sean represents new possibilities. There are things I can learn from him. Under the desk my left foot taps wildly to some frantic beat of its own.

"Well?" I finally say. He has come to see me, after all; I didn't ask him to stop by. I must not reveal that I am, for once, glad to see him.

"I want to know what it was like," he says. He seems to be picking intently at a hole in his jeans. *Solemn, dark, lanky?* Well, yes. Among other things.

"What what was like?" I think I know, but I want to be sure. Could this be what he wants? Is he finally playing his hand? My heart feels skittish, uneven. I breathe slowly. I give nothing away.

"Being kidnapped. Like, held prisoner. It was a pretty long time, wasn't it? Everyone wondered why you two didn't escape, or at least try. My theory is you didn't want to. That's what I want to hear about."

"Your interest in my past is inappropriate, to say the least," I retort primly. Is there something familiar in the curve of his nostrils? I try to picture his face cleared of acne, enlivened by charm, touched by sun and time. "I don't understand why you want to know."

"You're always telling us we should be intellectually curious. Maybe this is just me being curious."

"You forgot the 'intellectual' part." I study him while waiting for him to stop posturing and say something interesting. His clothes are secondhand, I decide. He's affecting a sort of slacker style as a way of disguising poverty, but you can tell that this is a kid who has no money for extras. I know he lives in a ramshackle apartment complex off campus; cheaper than the dorms but seedier, too. Site of drug busts and late-night fire alarms and probably not much sleep. It occurs to me that his life has not been easy.

He shifts in his chair, and that slight motion releases another wave of stale ashtray and musty closet. "Whatever," he says. "I've done a lot of research. I guess I pretty much have what I really need already. I can always just make up the stuff I don't know for sure, right? But it would definitely be better if I could get your side of the story."

I have been waiting for months for a reference to his motives; this is as close as he's come. I am gripping my pen tightly; before I allow myself to speak, I deliberately relax each finger. "Why? What do you need it for? I am mystified, I confess."

"Material." He paws at his backpack in the way he always does when he is preparing to leave. "For this book I'm writing."

Sean? A book? I don't know what would have surprised me more. I rearrange my face into blankness. "A *book*? You're writing a book? Okay, but what does that have to do with me?" *A book about his father? Which would be, in part, a book about Carly May and me?* It would explain a lot.

"You figure it out," he says, beginning to slouch out of the room. "If you won't answer my questions, I don't really see why I should answer yours."

Because I'm the teacher, I want to say, but I don't. I simply let him go. I have seldom felt less teacherly, and Sean has become something other than a student.

Chloe

I keep having conversations in my head with that writer bastard. Thanks to him I'm now hung up on the question of motivation:

why *did* he do it, anyway? Lois and I never knew. That summer, we talked about it whenever we had a chance. We had theories, but we never knew for sure, and the cops never figured it out. The ending didn't really seem to give us a clear answer. In a way—and believe me, I seriously hate to say this—Stephen-the-asshole-writer was at least partly right: it's not a question the movie tackles. Or the book, either, to tell you the truth. I mean they give an explanation, but it's sort of the obvious one. I avoid his word, *cop-out*, but now I have a damned voice in my head saying: *But isn't it kind of lame to say he's just crazy? Just your regular old garden-variety movie psycho?* It occurs to me suddenly that movie logic is usually backward: they make the villain a maniac because he has to be a maniac in order to commit whatever the crime is, because without the crime there wouldn't be any fucking story. The crime *is* the story, and what we really care about isn't *why* he does it but what he does, and how. Maybe we get a cheap little psychological hint—he's not just randomly crazy, say, he's crazy because he was poor and his mother was mean to him. It's always something like that. Or maybe he was rich and his father was mean to him. Whatever. Either way, though, the same logic applies: the bad guy was poor and his mother was mean to him *so* he would be crazy *so* he would commit the crime, which gets us back to the story, which is where we needed to end up. The crime comes first; the motive is an afterthought.

But in real life, obviously, the motive has to come first. The default story is no story at all, right? Most people don't go crazy, or not that kind of crazy, and therefore don't commit some sort of horrible crime—so there is no story, and we never hear of them. They just work and maybe have a family and play golf or something, and then they die. *Most people's lives aren't stories.* This should have been obvious to me before now, but in my current state of mind it hits me pretty hard. My life became a story not because I did anything very interesting but because a crime was committed against me. Anything I do—everything I will ever do—refers back to that event, somehow. It's my story. I can't get away from it. I think I've always known this, though I've never really spelled it out for myself this way.

Which is getting away from the question of motivation, which I still can't answer, and which also calls for a martini. To hell with Martin. He doesn't know the whole account, that's all: I was kidnapped by a charming maniac for six weeks when I was twelve. *That's* my story. Of course I drink.

For a while after the tiara incident it almost looked like my life could become a different kind of story, a boring and potentially depressing one. To someone else it might have looked that way, I mean; *I* was never in doubt. Not long after I settled in at Grandma Mabel's, I called Gail and arranged to meet her at the Arrow Diner on a Saturday morning. I wanted this conversation to take place in public, so that she would have to more or less behave herself, and away from my father. I was cashing in.

"I need photos," I said. "Good ones. I need a portfolio. For modeling."

"You have—"

"The pageant photos aren't good enough." I looked past Gail at the cheap oil painting on the wall behind her—a weird still life with bananas, grapes, something that looks like a doughnut. Diner art. Next to it, a black-and-white print of the Eiffel Tower. "I'm not talking about headshots for cowtown pageants. I'm talking about trying to get an agent."

Gail looked more surprised than I had expected; I had caught her off guard. *Good,* I thought.

I was growing quickly, at that point, and I was already half a head taller than Gail. And I was very skinny. It gave me a mean kind of pleasure, sitting across from her in that red vinyl booth with carefully mended seats, to see how uncomfortable the contrast between us made her. I was wearing tight jeans and a dark flannel shirt—my uniform in those days. I had on only the most discreet touch of makeup, my nails were unpolished, my long hair casually (but carefully) pulled back, with the exception of a curl or two around my face. Next to me Gail was all swelling flesh and excess flowing fabric and bright clashing colors. With cruel adolescent insight, I knew she felt it. I knew she had noticed that all the old men at the counter slid their eyes sideways to look at me when we came in, and never glanced at her. I didn't give a shit about the gossipy, leathery old farmers, slurping their coffee and trading what passed for news, but I knew Gail expected to be appreciated.

To make matters worse, I had let her order first, and now she had a heaping plate of eggs and bacon in front of her. I had black coffee and toast. I knew that would make her feel like the pig she was.

I pressed my point while she chewed. "Obviously I can't use a local photographer. No one can do what I need. We have to go to Omaha. Even that's not really good enough, but it'll have to do. And I need you to make up something convincing to tell Daddy. There's no point in making him worry until something actually happens."

She raised her too-sculpted eyebrows and made a desperate grab for the upper hand. "So you expect me to lie to your father for you? And you think I have nothing better to do than run you around Omaha, is that it, missy? Anything else?"

"That'll do for now," I said, taking a sip of my coffee. I didn't even like coffee then; I just liked the idea of it. I watched Gail thinking. You could practically see the gears grinding. "We can have separate hotel rooms if we have to stay overnight," I said nicely.

She put down her fork and tossed her crumpled napkin on the table. She forced a fake smile and kept her voice quiet. "You little bitch," she said. I smiled back. She grabbed her big purse and began to scrabble for her wallet.

"Oh, don't worry," I said. "It's on me," I said. Which I had taken care of pretty smoothly, I thought, slipping Ada Watson a ten-dollar bill as we made our way to the table, letting her think I was taking my stepmom out for a treat. *Please.* As if. "I'll make arrangements and let you know when we need to do this," I added as Gail awkwardly wiggled herself out of the booth, knocking her napkin onto the floor and slamming into poor Ada, who was returning with my change. Gail lost her control then and stormed out, muttering audibly. Heads followed her, if only for a second; *now* she had their attention.

I finished my toast and coffee, in case anyone was watching, and left Ada a big tip.

So I had set things in motion, and before long Gail and I did make our trip to Omaha. After that, it was a matter of waiting.

You have to understand how small Arrow is: when I say *town*, picture a wide main street, just a few blocks long, crisscrossed by three dead end roads. Even in the middle of town, houses weren't all that close together; space was one thing we had plenty of. The businesses on Main Street occupied low-lying, featureless modern buildings: dingy white and gray and beige rectangles. Years ago a tornado had swept through town, and Arrow had rebuilt with tornadoes in mind: hunkering down, safe from the elements. Even the churches huddled against the ground. Everything looked just as bleak in the hot dusty summer as it did weighed down by snow in the winter. We had a tiny bank, a couple of shops, a bar, a diner. A school. We played six-man football because we didn't have enough kids to field a normal team. (Of course you couldn't just do away with football altogether. Not in Nebraska.) For gas you had to drive down the road a ways, back to the state highway. Just outside the town center was the grain elevator. You could see it from miles away, the same way we could see the one the next town over.

All the same, moving off the farm and into town was a pretty dramatic change. The town kids—maybe a couple dozen of us, altogether, from little kids to older teens—were into loitering. The kids I hung out with were mostly a year or two older than I was. There wasn't much to do in Arrow after dark, but they did their best: getting high on the school playground, climbing the water tower, lounging on the sidewalk outside closed businesses on Main Street like they were posing for some gritty teen movie that nobody ever came to see. Before long I had attached myself to a guy named Scott, who was more or less the leader of this little group. I didn't even realize how official this was until another guy was teasing me one night, calling me a virgin (which was considered the worst of all possible insults), when Scott grabbed me and pulled me toward him, all of us shadowy in the widely spaced streetlights, and said, "Fuck off, asshole. You're talking to my fucking girlfriend." The other kid backed off, and I didn't say anything. There didn't seem to be any need to. It wasn't exactly romantic, but I had already noticed that it was good to be claimed in that crowd; otherwise everyone was always jostling for your favor. If you were a girl, I mean. The town kids were considered cooler and tougher than the farm kids: They stayed up later at night. They didn't have to go to the barn in the morning or after school. They had more leisure. They smoked cigarettes and wore black and listened to punk or heavy metal instead of country or classic rock. The girls wore lots of black eyeliner; one or two of the boys even pierced their ears. People figured that this behavior did not bode well for their futures. *Our* futures. Soon I was considered one of them, more or less.

I knew perfectly well I was only biding my time and trying to amuse myself in the meantime.

Yeah, I took advantage of Grandma Mabel. I was nice to her, though; don't think my treatment of Gail was typical. I was really only a monster to Gail. My monster self scared the hell out of me, to tell you the truth. I felt sick that day I made my deal with Gail—literally sick. I checked out the other people in the diner, wondering if they had monster selves too, or if I was different somehow. Even now I don't know for sure. But I think Grandma Mabel actually enjoyed my company, for the most part, and although you could say I got away with a lot while I was there, you could also say that I protected her from knowledge that would only have freaked her out.

I didn't tell Grandma Mabel about Scott—it seemed like the kind of thing she was better off not knowing—but she saw us together one day. It was a Saturday and we were hanging out downtown with some of the other kids, wearing jean jackets although it was freezing out, trying to scrape enough snow off the ground to form snowballs. Grandma pulled up in front of the House of Beauty in her ancient Town Car—she drove everywhere, even two blocks away—and I didn't see her in time to make sure I looked innocent. She didn't say anything then, just gave me a look, but she was waiting for me in her rocking chair when I got home, her old crocheted afghan wrapped around her shoulders. Her steely gray hair was freshly permed, the tight curls lined up in neat rows. "That boy's too old for you, Carly May," she said—not judgmental, just matter-of-fact. "You'll get into trouble with that crowd." She said it like trouble was a done deal, like it was on its way and there was no stopping it. And then, as she neatly refolded her afghan and draped it across the back of her chair before heading into the kitchen, she added, for good measure, her favorite warning: "Pretty is as pretty does. Don't you forget that, Carly May." I always figured Grandma Mabel was just bitter; whatever pretty was had nothing to do with her after a few decades on the farm. But I also used to wonder what the hell that was really supposed to mean. What was it, after all, that pretty *did*?

For one thing, Grandma Mabel said darkly, pretty gets you in trouble.

I told her not to worry.

Then later that winter I got a call from an agent in Chicago—

Shelley Silver, Martin's predecessor. That's how things finally got started. The threat of Arrow and all the awful fates it had to offer faded into the background and seemed to disappear.

Lois

I discovered a Chloe Savage fan site, and I've developed a habit of visiting it regularly. It's updated more frequently than you might expect. It's a rather sad affair, run and designed by someone who declares himself Chloe's biggest fan and seems to favor pictures of her in which her clothes are half off, or she is pouting with overpainted lips, or languishing convincingly in bed with a costar. In other words, it's not necessarily her talent of which he is a fan.

I study these pictures as I have the other Chloe-images I have found. I think what I am looking for is some trace of our shared history. I'd like to say that I have picked up on some minute but revelatory detail, some almost imperceptible sign that only I could read. But her eyes seem cold—mercenary, even—and her flesh perfect and forbidding. She might as well be a stranger. I wonder about her life, and inevitably my imagination butts up against the walls of her presumably glamorous world. My assumptions all come from movies and magazines: I picture an endless succession of sulkily handsome actor boyfriends, parties where everyone is doing expensive, fashionable drugs, occasional stints in exclusive rehab centers, thousand-dollar shoes, exotic facials. Perhaps some of it is accurate; perhaps none of it. The only sense that I *do* get from the photos is that she is sad. And I don't trust it. She is an actress, after all. Publicity shots aren't exactly windows into anyone's soul.

Maybe—I barely force myself to acknowledge this possibility before it scuttles away again—maybe I want her to be sad.

• • •

I remember one winter, home for Christmas from my private school, creeping out to the formal living room in the middle of the night and sitting beneath the Christmas tree: not the modest family tree but the impressive, towering guests' tree, tasteful and elegant but also, somehow, so beautiful in the dark that it hurt to look at it. And that's why I ventured out in my nightgown at two in the morning, knowing no guests would still be up: so that the tree could inflict that strange pain on the part of me we refer to as the heart. What is it, I wonder, that pain? Some combination of magic and melancholy, hope and disillusionment. Or perhaps I am generalizing from my own experience, assuming that what is true for me must be true for others. But who knows what other people feel? In any case, I suppose I went out and sat under the tree because I wanted to cry. It worked; I *did* cry. But what I could not dispel was the sense that some part of my self stood off to the side, not crying, merely watching, as if at a play. I saw myself in my red flannel nightgown, the soft colored lights gently illuminating my face, the contrast between my dark, tousled hair and my pale, sad skin—a sad girl, a tragic girl, even, against such a lovely backdrop. But even as I reveled in the release of hot tears, my outside self suggested mockingly that if I were crying for an audience, even if that audience consisted only of me, I couldn't be crying for real—that my feelings were false. At that I only cried harder, and—startled into a flash of real, unstaged feeling—wished quite fervently to be someone whose emotions were more straightforwardly channeled; someone whose passions flowed more freely and naturally. Someone like Carly May.

I did not notice my mother glide up behind me. I noticed her presence only when she placed a hand on my shaking knee, then smoothed my hair in a rare motherly gesture of comfort. She, too, wore a long flannel nightgown, hers in a Christmassy plaid; her hair, too, tumbled loosely down her back. I caught a faint whiff of gin, not strong enough to worry me; I saw smudges of paint on her fingers. She'd been out in her studio, then. I wondered if she did that often, made time for her art in the middle of the night. There were a few short hours before she would have to get up and prepare an elaborate breakfast for the guests. I found myself in the uncomfortable position of imagining, for just a moment, what it must be like to be my mother—and then the sensation of her hand on my hair, unfamiliar as it was, brought me back to myself.

"What's the matter, little Lois?" she asked, so softly that her voice barely rippled the surface of the room's dense atmosphere.

I didn't know how to tell the truth, even had I been sure I wanted to. What *was* the matter? Everything was the matter—the world—magic, melancholy, the lovely tree—hope and the lack thereof. There are no words for what was the matter; I've felt it since then, though not as powerfully as I did at sixteen, when everything seemed so monumental. "I'm just sad" is what I settled for, looking not at my mother but at the tree, feeling suddenly very small beneath it, crying still more for the sad girl and her distant, enigmatic mother, as if we were characters in some Christmas story I was reading.

"I know," said my mother, and she, too, turned her greenish-gray eyes, sparkling with reflected electric lights, toward the tree. Her hand moved gently on my head. "You're like me. We're loners, you and I."

The familiar furnishings retreated into the shadows: curving antique sofas, spindly-legged end tables, plush footstools. A gilt-framed mirror at the far end of the room caught the light of thousands of tiny bulbs, flung it back, made everything strange, disorienting. I tried to absorb my mother's statement, to test it for the feel of truth.

"It doesn't have to be sad, though." She leaned forward to drop a light kiss on the top of my head and, rising to her feet, said, "I don't think you have to worry." With that she moved away as noiselessly as she had come, leaving behind her a trail of alcohol scent and a strange chill.

We're loners, you and I. Was this true? Pronouncements like that have considerable power. It was as if my mother had opened the door to a clean, orderly, pleasing room—sunlight streaming through pretty curtains, shelves well stocked with books. Small and plain, but comfortable. She had offered me an alluring idea to inhabit, an idea with a specific shape and precise dimensions. A definition.

The tree, with its mercilessly beautiful twinkling lights, offered no answers.

If I am a loner now, perhaps it's my mother's doing. Her magic: she gave me the word, and it became true.

Chloe

From *Deep in the Woods*, the screenplay:

```
INT.
A car, parked. It's very clean and impersonal,
with dark seats, fogged-up windows. A cup of
coffee sits in the cup holder. The driver
is wearing light-khaki pants, a white shirt,
sensible shoes. A pair of binoculars is slung
around her neck. She is not glamorous, though she
looks pleasant enough, and as though she might—in
other circumstances—be attractive.
```

This part intrigues me. I have never played dowdy before—or if not quite dowdy, then uptight lady-cop with potential to be sexy, sort of the modern version of the secretly sexy librarian. Later in the movie I'll be softly pretty, sexy enough to win the heart of a nosy, hostile-at-first newspaper reporter. According to the script, he will win me over—save me from my unhealthy attraction to the kidnapper—and I will allow him to kiss me at the end of the film. Just one kiss, but the kind that implies a whole future, the kind that, as far as I know, doesn't actually exist in real life. Anyway, my looks will never be the point.

For me, the key to understanding my character is that she's obsessed with the kidnapper. She sees him once before she knows who he is. He's shopping in a nearby town, and she is struck by him: his good looks, his seriousness, the intelligence in his eyes, an odd sense that he is different, set apart. There but not there. Only later does she realize who he was, how close she'd been. She keeps it to herself—it wouldn't help the investigation, she tells herself. What's more interesting, though, is that she feels that sharing this detail would be a kind of betrayal. She had smiled at him that day, tried to catch his eye. Now she carries old pictures of him around with her (in the movie, they figure out who the kidnapper is before they actually track him down), studies the photographs, tries to imagine her way into his head. She's grateful when the newspaper reporter digs up some information about his childhood—casual neglect, a tragic runaway sister—humanizing him just enough that we feel a little sad when he dies. But I think what she feels is darker and more powerful than sympathy.

```
EXT.
A wooded road, with jagged mountains rising up
on one side, a deep chasm opening up on the
other. No houses are visible; no cars pass. The
woods are dense; the road is shaded. The sun is
shining. It's very quiet. The car is parked in
a little pull-off area, as if for a trailhead,
although there is no trail marker.
```

I can see it so clearly! I keep reminding myself that we'll be shooting in Canada, that it'll be similar but definitely not the same. I can face the idea of reenacting this plot. I even get a kind of kick out of it, for some reason—like an inside joke, though it isn't exactly funny. But the idea of being back in that place, smelling the mountain air, hearing the birds, always the distant growl of thunder—that terrifies me. I don't want my memory jarred *too* violently, thank you very much. Objects may have shifted during flight? Exactly.

I've been reading the screenplay over and over. This is what I would normally do, up to a point, with a new project. But this time there's something compulsive about it. Something that raises the red flag for *crazy.* I feel like I'm trying to find something I've lost—something that has to be there but so far seems to be pretty well hidden.

I haven't tried to contact Lois. I don't feel ready—I don't know what I want to say. I honestly can't tell whether I'm thrilled by all of this or outrageously pissed off. Maybe a little of both? I'm pretty sure I need to figure this out before I confront her. Otherwise she'll be in total control of the situation. Lois likes to be in control.

Liked.

In fact, maybe that's what writing the damned book was about: control. A way for her to decide who we were, what the whole thing meant. It makes a lot of sense that this would appeal to her.

She's a college English professor in New York State; it was easy to learn that much from the Internet. The photo on the department Web site doesn't give much away; she looks severe and unsmiling, very scholarly, not necessarily someone you would want to have a drink with. But I think she's striking, with her sharply angled dark hair and her huge green eyes. Unlike me, she kept her old name. Lucy Ledger doesn't appear anywhere in

Dr. Lois Lonsdale's online materials—no line in her curriculum vitae, no author page, no reviews, no nothing.

So she keeps her novel-writing career a secret. She has a double life. Why?

I have way too much time, these days, to wonder about things.

During this drifting period I get a phone call from an old friend of mine from my modeling days. Erica was once one of the most sought-after black models in the business. I was just a clothes hanger, as they say, but she had real style. She wore clothes like she was driving a really fast car; there was something reckless and maybe even violent about it. It's hard to explain, but it worked. Erica still models, though less than she used to—she must be at least thirty, I calculate. She's in town briefly and suggests going out—"out" like old times. I agree, though I have my doubts: "out" isn't exactly my scene these days. But I'm starting to feel isolated—dangerously isolated, even. I've noticed before that if you go too long without anyone seeing you—really seeing you—it's easy to start wondering if you're really there. How have I gotten so disconnected from everyone?

On the other hand, going to clubs is maybe not the best possible way to confirm your existence if you have doubts. The morning after "going out," I wake up draped across my bed, still wearing my dress and knee-high boots from the night before, hair tangled, sheets smeared with makeup, head too painful to move. For a few seconds I don't remember a damn thing—and then my luck runs out, and my memory starts presenting me with little tidbits of the evening: depressing little short films, basically, with serious chronological gaps. In one I'm doing shots in a crowded bar with Erica and her friends. In the rest I'm very drunk. I dance, I stumble, I generally make an ass of myself. I run into Stephen the bastard writer, of all people, and spew insults at him. The girl in this short film obviously thinks she is very witty, but it's clear to the audience that she makes no sense at all. Her friends, if that's what they are, steer her away. She staggers, falls. Later she's back on the dance floor, dancing like she thinks she is beautiful, when the sad truth is that she looks like hell. Someone drags her to the bathroom. One of the most depressing little vignettes takes place in a toilet stall, where she is indulging in a temper tantrum and trying, pathetically, to reapply her lipstick. This goes badly. Much later someone is putting her in a cab—a very blurry friend or maybe a stranger, it's hard to tell—and the cab takes her home, where she sits for a while outside her door before she finds the strength to locate her key and turn it in the lock and haul her sorry, ugly ass to bed.

The phone rings a few times. I don't answer it. I think I've come up with a plan, a plan that might save me, though my head still hurts too much to be sure. It involves getting the hell out of here, the sooner the better.

I like to drive. Not so much in LA, where it's hell to get anywhere, but on the open road. If the highway is empty enough, the landscape deserted enough, I can almost feel like that little girl with the ugly wig and no idea where she's going but damned glad to be going there. This is my brilliant idea: I could drive north, instead of flying. I could take all the time I want and just drift toward Canada, staying in cheap motels, having adventures, the star of my own road-trip movie. I keep thinking there must be a good reason not to do this, but I can't figure out what it is.

I stumble into the kitchen, make a bloody Mary—which sounds awful but might just do the trick—and collapse on my soft gray couch with an old atlas. With a shaky finger I trace a rough northward route.

Head north. Stick to the coast. Why not.

Meanwhile, I settle down with Lois's damned book. Again. It's not the part about the lady cop that interests me most. It's the parts about us. When I read the chapters that focus on the kidnapped girls, not the investigation, I hear Lois's voice. I feel like she's here in the room with me. I read these parts over and over, like I'm looking for clues. God knows, maybe I am. And I find one or two—mostly about Lois. It seems she knows something I wish she didn't, something involving a very broken promise. A secret I thought was mine to drown. Eventually I start scribbling a chart. I try to break the book down—the plot, the characters, everything—into three categories: true, false, and somewhere in between.

In long, crooked columns, my chart looks something like this:

TRUE	FALSE	?????
He liked me (Callie) better.	*Hannah (Lois) was more perceptive than Callie.*	*He loved us.*
He took us swimming once.	*We made an escape rope out of old sheets.*	*We were happy.*

It's harder than you would think. The trickiest part is the ending. She hasn't changed the basic facts, I'll give her that. But it's a long goddamned way from the whole truth and nothing but.

Part Two

FROM

DEEP IN THE WOODS

by Lucy Ledger

"Here we are." The kidnapper spoke, his voice low and sonorous. It made the girls feel sleepy and safe. Shouldn't have, but it did. The car had left the main road an hour or so ago. Since then they had been curving through mountains, and now, as they jounced down a long unpaved driveway, the headlights carved out of the darkness a neat log cabin. A fairy-tale cabin. Midnight on the nose, according to the dashboard: the witching hour, the pumpkin hour. He cut the engine, and all went dark—car, cabin, woods, mountains. Still they were not afraid. They slid across vinyl seats and tumbled stiff-legged from the car, shuffled across soft pine needles in the direction of the little house they could no longer see. The sky was moonless, starless. Perhaps they could have run, but they did not think of running.

The two girls, pretty as princesses—one dark and one fair—were neither deprived of food nor cast into a dungeon. The kidnapper prepared hot chocolate on the old stove while they perched on the edges of their chairs at the long wooden kitchen table, legs swinging. He served it in chipped ceramic mugs with chocolate chip cookies straight out of a box. They ate and drank ravenously. Hannah let her chin-length dark hair fall forward to prevent the others from reading her face. She had no idea what it might tell them; her emotions were obscure to her, as if they belonged to someone else. She kept her eye on Callie, who seemed to be taking everything in stride; it made sense to take her cue from the girl who had been with the man two days longer than she had and seemed none the worse for it. As soon as they had entered the slightly musty, low-ceilinged cabin, Callie had removed her stiff dark wig to reveal the most impossibly perfect blond curls Hannah had ever seen. Right away Callie had felt lighter, more free; the wig had grown heavy and itchy. She felt herself expand to fill the room. She didn't mind that the kidnapper and the other girl, Hannah, were looking at her. Callie never minded being looked at. Hannah, wiping a cookie crumb from her lower lip, thought about this. Wondered what it meant, that she and Callie were so different. Did it mean anything at all?

The man seldom met their eyes, but Hannah felt him watching them when he didn't think they were looking. Attempting to gauge his expression, she decided that he looked contented. Peaceful. Pleased with himself; pleased with them. She didn't think he looked dangerous—but then, how was she to judge?

What did he want with them?

During this time the kidnapper spoke little. He paced the long main room of the cabin, adjusting the blinds, peering into the darkness, taking stock of the cupboards. When the girls finished their snack he cleared the table and led them upstairs to a little room under the eaves. There were twin beds and on each a neatly folded white nightgown. He showed them the bathroom, where matching bags of toiletries had been set out. After they got ready for bed—brushing their teeth side by side at the sink like small children, an intimacy both forced and welcome—he came in and took their old clothes away. They didn't ask why. They had not yet begun to ask questions, though they had plenty. That was the last they saw of their shorts and T-shirts. He watched them fold down their sheets and climb into their beds and then drew the door gently shut behind him. "You can keep the light on or turn it off," he said, in his low, pleasant voice. "It's up to you." Hannah would have been inclined to choose light, but Callie promptly switched off the dusty lamp on the nightstand between them, and Hannah did not object. She didn't want Callie to think she was afraid.

After he withdrew from the room, they heard a key turn in the lock, a bolt slide neatly into place.

Callie leaped up and flew to the window, pushing aside the plain white curtains and posing transfixed in the faint moonlight that slipped through a narrow breach in the clouds. After a minute Hannah followed. They stood together, their nightgowns merging into a single white blur. The darkness made the strange landscape otherworldly; their surroundings were a mystery. (Not until the next day would they catch their first glimpse of the dense woods, the jagged mountains.) Callie pushed the window open and leaned out into the night, gulping in the chilly mountain air, her long, golden beauty-pageant curls falling forward. "Rapunzel, Rapunzel!" Hannah said in a whisper, laughing, because she had been thinking of fairy tales since their arrival at the isolated lodge, and also because it was a relief to laugh, a sharp and surprising pleasure. But Callie scowled. "Spare me," she said, her voice full of scorn—for what? All things childish or whimsical, Hannah guessed. Hannah *was* childish, Callie thought, feeling superior. Framed by the window, they whispered in the dark, offered up wisps of their lives back home, their impressions; kept their fears to themselves.

Downstairs, the kidnapper paced. Unseeing. He listened for their breath, thought he could feel it, like waves on a rocky shore.

The girls slept better than they should have, and in the morning they found that the kidnapper had unobtrusively liberated them: the door was unlocked. Their steps were quiet on the sturdy wooden stairs, and the man didn't seem to hear them until they had crossed the big room to the kitchen area, sparsely but neatly furnished, stopping just a few feet behind him. They stood like storybook children in their long white nightgowns. Hannah registered once again how pleasant-looking he was—and how handsome, though it made her feel strange to catch herself thinking this. Tall, with dark hair waving neatly back from a sculpted face. Old, of course, from the girls' perspective—but in that movie-star way that made age almost irrelevant. Kidnappers, in Hannah's imagination, had been scruffy, unkempt, unwashed, faded-flannel-wearing, with blunt features and cruel wet lips. Like men she had glimpsed at truck stops. This kidnapper looked like the perfect English teacher might, had he walked straight out of a television set. She felt shy; she knew shyness wasn't necessarily the most appropriate reaction to the situation. As if to compensate, she quickly inspected the room for weapons: no TV-style gun tucked into the waistband of his jeans; no cruel knives resting suggestively on countertops; no chains, no handcuffs. Hannah felt herself blush when she saw that he had caught her inspecting the room for the paraphernalia of danger. The flicker of amusement she discerned seemed to imply that he knew exactly what she was thinking.

If so, he said nothing, and with the same sense of inappropriateness, she found herself appreciating his tact. Callie did not share Hannah's appreciation; she would have preferred candor, cards on the table. "Girls! Good morning," the kidnapper said cheerfully, sounding more paternal than criminal. "Help yourselves." There was a box of Rice Krispies on the worn wooden table. A carton of milk, a bottle of juice. He had set out bowls and spoons and glasses, indicating the girls' places. They sat.

The sun shone as brightly and purely as it ever had. The air that drifted in through the open windows smelled sweet and mossy. Hannah and Callie asked no questions, and the man offered nothing but light, pleasant banter; no explanations, no threats, no apologies. "I hope you were comfortable upstairs," he remarked rather formally, no dark undercurrents in his voice. "I love the sound of the wind in the trees, myself, and the smell of the woods. If you were city girls, of course, it might be a bit of an adjustment, but you're both accustomed to isolation. If you listen hard, you can hear all sorts of animals in the woods—you should try it tonight," he added, flashing them a quick grin. His teeth were white and even, his nails neat and immaculately clean. Everything about him vouched for his harmlessness. The girls listened and ate their Rice Krispies. How easily charmed they were, the kidnapper thought, almost happily.

Later that summer, when they had not only the courage and presence of mind but also pressing reasons to ask the obvious questions (What do you want with us? What are you planning to do with us? Why us?), it was somehow too late. Much later, Hannah would wonder what might have been different had they given voice to their curiosity that morning, had they resisted the seductions of sun-warmed pine and breakfast. Might *everything* have been different? (And how different would they have wanted it to be?—that was the question doomed to lurk wordlessly beneath the surface, unconfessed.)

But for the moment it did not seem urgent to press him. After breakfast he presented them with new clothes: plain dresses of stretchy cotton jersey, matching hooded sweatshirts, packages of Hanes underwear, white canvas sneakers. (In the weeks to come they would go barefoot, mostly; later, when it was over, their sneakers would look practically new. Callie would want to keep hers, but the shoes would be taken from the girls, required as evidence.) The dresses had short sleeves and fell just below the knee; Hannah's was dark green, and Callie's navy blue. Callie enjoyed all costumes and took to this one willingly; she was well aware that this prim garment flattered her blue eyes, hung gracefully on her lengthening frame. Hannah noticed that sometimes Callie even adopted a slightly revised way of moving, better suited to her new attire—a little more demure, almost somber. Hannah examined the dresses closely to determine whether Callie's was nicer in any way or more flattering, but she had to admit that they were identical; each the correct size, and each color chosen to complement their respective hair and complexions. (Eventually they would try switching them, just for a change, and he would insist that they trade back.) That first morning, when they traipsed downstairs to display themselves, he regarded them with satisfaction, as if they represented an accomplishment, a minor victory.

It was Hannah who asked, that first day, what they should do. What he wanted them to do. He was sitting on the cracked brown leather couch, reading a book. Callie glared at Hannah, as if the question were somehow beneath their collective dignity. But if there were rules, Hannah wanted to know what they were; that was the kind of child she was.

The kidnapper looked up. The question took him by surprise. He waved his hand toward a tall bookcase on the other side of the room. "Play," he said. "You'll find lots of books and games and puzzles and things over there. I'm sure you can find something to amuse yourselves." *Play.* Later that would remind Hannah of the scene in Charles Dickens's *Great Expectations* in which Miss Havisham instructs poor bewildered Pip to play with the supercilious Estella. At the time, the command seemed perverse: how do you *play* with someone you hardly know, with someone else you hardly know as an audience? *We need something with rules*, Hannah thought. She went obediently to the bookcase and began rummaging through the shelves. When she found three worn old decks of cards, she sat down and began to count them, making sure each deck was complete. After a minute Callie sauntered over as if she might have other places to go, and lowered herself rather provisionally onto the braided rug facing Hannah.

Callie didn't know any decent games, to Hannah's secret delight, so Hannah taught her Crazy Eights and Gin Rummy, games she had learned from her mother on rainy Saturday afternoons. That's what they did on the first day. They played cards. The man continued to read his book, but they could tell that he was also listening to them. After a while he got up and strode out to the porch, where he sat in one of the Adirondack chairs. Callie was facing the door and could see a sliver of him through the crack between the blinds and the window frame. His sweet pipe smoke crept in under the door. They were glad when he left the room, or so they believed, but there was also a sharp absence. An edge. They missed the sense of someone to please, someone who might offer praise. They noticed that they missed it, and wondered at themselves. They wondered, uneasily, if they had been boring him.

Hannah beat Callie effortlessly at first, but Callie learned fast. This interested Hannah: if you kidnapped a beauty queen and a spelling bee champion, it might make sense to assume that you had decided to acquire a pretty girl and a smart girl. But there was no denying Callie's cleverness.

They were exceptional: exceptionally pretty, exceptionally smart. Both of them. And old enough to know it.

Once he had them, he didn't seem to know what to do with them. Identifying them, tracking them down, rounding them up, getting them to the middle of the Adirondacks—that had been the meticulously planned part. So Hannah speculated, at first, and confirmed, later in the first week, when she found the files he had assembled on each of them. Two dust-free manila folders wedged between Edgar Allan Poe and an illustrated book about northeastern wildflowers. *He must have meant them to be found,* she thought—meant *her* to find them, even, since she was more likely than Callie to explore the bookcase. Still, Hannah was furtive, not wanting to be caught. Knowledge is always powerful; knowledge no one knows you have is even better. Callie was upstairs; he was sitting on the porch. She could see a strip of his shirt through the crack in the blinds; if he got up suddenly, she would have enough warning. She laid the folders on the floor and flipped them open.

He had all of their press clippings, Callie's glossy pageant smiles alongside shots of Hannah brandishing her spelling trophies with a curious combination of smugness and reserve. "Local Girl Sweeps Regional Pageants, Aims for the National Stage." "Sixth Grader Nails 'Vichyssoise' to Claim State Title." Quotes from parents and teachers about their promise, their talent, their preternatural poise: "She's an exceptional young lady," Hannah's sixth-grade English teacher had told the local paper. "We expect Hannah to go far." "We're all very proud of Callie," the principal of Callie's school had said. "She's the whole package." *Who are these girls?* Unreal, far away: Callie and Hannah dolls.

More disturbingly, there were snapshots. Even as Hannah studied them, trying to identify what he had seen in each of them, she began to feel as if she were being watched: Callie in a heavy winter coat, sulky, emerging from a grocery store with a grim-looking woman (surely the despised stepmother); Callie stepping onto a school bus, her back to the camera, recognizable from her long blond curls and a hint of her perfect profile. Hannah on the front steps of the library, arms full of books, her face strangely closed off, hair falling forward; Hannah trudging in the direction of home, her left foot angled forward as if she had just kicked a snowball along the sidewalk; Hannah entering a shoe store with her mother, looking back, almost as though she suspected someone was watching her.

Which someone had been. How long? How often? These were winter pictures. He had cryptic notes on each of them: "Leaves for school 8 am. Walks. Same route every day, always alone. Arrives

8:15." And worse: "No sign of friends." Had there been other girls in the running? Had he winnowed down a longer list? She tried to imagine him prowling through Glastonbury, Connecticut, snapping pictures, unnoticed, alarming no one. Maybe she had even seen him, or perhaps her parents had.

This was what Callie had meant when she told Hannah, during a quick gas station stop when they were still on the road, that he had chosen them. Did Callie know about the files? About the scouting missions?

A shadow crossed the floorboards in front of her, and a hand brushed her shoulder. She jumped, scattering the photos, wrenching her head around, wondering how he could have gotten behind her, busily spinning explanations, apologies. But it was Callie, not the man.

"I saw those already," Callie said, rather loftily, poking at the files with her pointed toe. She had startled Hannah deliberately; Callie envied the other girl's poise, liked to prove it could be shaken. "In the car, before we picked you up. He had them with him." Callie often found ways to remind Hannah that she had been first. "See? I told you he picked us. He *researched* us. We were the ones he wanted." Hannah followed Callie's gaze to the photo of the girl with the blond curls boarding the bus.

The files didn't change anything, exactly. But Hannah didn't forget them. They stayed with her, like a soundtrack, sometimes ominous, often soothing. Rising and falling, setting a mood.

After five days he stopped locking the girls in their room while they slept, or when he went out. And he did go out, usually once a day. They didn't always know where. Sometimes to the store. Later, the laundromat, though he took only his own clothes, not theirs, for obvious reasons. (They washed theirs by hand, playing *Little House on the Prairie*, a TV show they had seen in reruns when they were younger. They imagined bonnets, lace-up boots, a fire to tend.) People had to be searching for them, desperately trying to trace them, but they had no way of knowing: no TV, no newspapers. They didn't know what "town" was or how far away it might be. *How could there be a town?* Hannah wondered when he returned one day with groceries. The world had shrunk to this cabin, these woods.

Sometimes they quizzed him as they became more at ease. "Did you go to a diner?" one would ask. "A bar?" the other would chime in. "The dentist?" "A chiropractor?" "A taxidermist!" Until finally he said no, no, and the sadness in his eyes disappeared for a moment. When he seemed happy, it was impossible to be afraid. "Where would you go?" he asked once. "If you could drive into town." He watched them, searching, and they knew that their answers mattered. "The movies," said Callie. "Of course!" he said. "Naturally the future actress would go to the movies. Well, trust me, Callie, there's nothing worth seeing at the moment, so you're not missing anything. And you?" He turned to Hannah, who had been waiting for the question and dreading it, trying to come up with an answer. Not a real answer—the truth was that she couldn't think of anywhere in the hypothetical town that she would want to go. What she sought, as usual, was the perfect answer, the answer that would please. But her mind was blank. "Well?" he pressed, and she could tell that he saw too much, read her too clearly, knew perfectly well that there was nothing she wanted. "Ice cream," she said lamely. "I would go out for ice cream." He tossed his keys in the air, caught them neatly, tucked them in his pocket. "Really?" He didn't believe her; she could see it. She didn't even want him to. She knew it was a childish answer, and common. She had let him down.

"It's okay," he said, sorry to have embarrassed her. It was so easy with Hannah. "You have everything you need right here." For a moment she thought he might ruffle her hair, squeeze her neck, pat her shoulder. Her flesh tensed, hoped. Nothing.

All the same, the next time he went out he came back with ice cream. An offering. "What about my movie?" Callie demanded, then laughed and pirouetted across the floor to disguise her jealousy.

They did not discuss running away. Not in those early days. The first time he left their bedroom door unlocked at night, Callie had positioned herself between Hannah's bed and the door, arms spread wide, challenging. "You wouldn't do it, would you." It was not a question. "Do what?" Hannah had said—noncommittal, aggravating. Hannah had imagined leaving; it was impossible not to. What else was there to think about at night when she tried to fall asleep and lay for hours staring at the dark place where she knew the window was? She had seen him watching her and knew that he could sense what she was thinking, that he didn't even hold it against her. She had pictured herself slinking down the stairs, out the front door, into the dark, the woods, searching for a road that had traffic. Trudging along in her canvas sneakers, shivering in her nightgown, her sweatshirt hastily thrown over it while Callie thrashed and muttered in her sleep. Waiting for a car to come along, not knowing whom to trust. Not knowing if an approaching car was his. Walking for miles, maybe, before coming across anyone. Or being found by someone worse—a cruel bearded man and his zit-faced sons, for instance. Dragged into their foul-smelling pickup truck, country music jangling on the radio. She pictured the man following her, rescuing her from the rednecks, driving her back to the cabin in gentle, forgiving silence.

She knew she wouldn't go. She was waiting to find out what he had chosen them for.

In years past they had seen stories on the news: little girls who disappeared, never to be seen again. Not in one piece, anyway. They paid close attention to his moods and studied how to please him. He liked their hair loose and plain, though sometimes when it was especially hot they tied it back anyway. He abhorred makeup, and had confiscated Callie's. He disliked anything that smacked of worldliness; at night in the dark they sometimes spoke to each other of their real lives, their crushes, their ambitions, their petty rebellions, but never to him.

He wanted them to be pure, Hannah decided. He had this crazy idea that purity was possible. He wanted them to be those storybook girls she had imagined on the first morning—gentle and untainted, in love with wildflowers and the moon. Even when he spoke of their distant futures, he encouraged lofty and improbable dreams: Callie would be a legendary actress on Broadway; Hannah would be an acclaimed yet mysterious writer; they would be impervious to their fame, untainted by success.

Where did the gun fit into this picture?

It was to protect them. To make them possible.

One night after they had finished the dishes he swung the front door open and stepped onto the porch, pulling his pipe from his pocket. He left the door wide open behind him, and night air drifted into the cabin, swirling around the girls' bare legs, stirring their hair, reminding them of their captivity. Two enormous moths dove clumsily across the room, hurled themselves at the lantern.

"Well," he said, his back to them, "are you coming? Hurry up, the bugs are getting in."

As if under a spell, they edged forward, shoulders touching; they had one will, one mind. They stepped onto the porch as though it might conceal quicksand. But the floor was firm and comfortingly familiar beneath their feet. Callie seized the doorknob, pulled the heavy door shut, imagining for a moment that it locked behind them, shut them out. Felt a whisper of fear, rejected it; strode down the steps, planted her bare feet in the cool grass. Hannah followed, less certain.

He remained on the porch, puffing on his pipe.

Hannah and Callie veered to the right, away from the driveway, toward the stretch of clearing their bedroom window overlooked. The grass was thicker and longer there, tickling their ankles. A sliver of moon revealed the edge of the woods, dense and black, forbidding. After a few exploratory steps they broke into a run, feet kicking up, dresses climbing their legs, arms wide. When they reached the trees they stopped. Peered between trunks, saw nothing beyond. *We could keep running,* thought Hannah. *Never stop until we got somewhere. A road, a house. We could crash right through those trees,* Callie echoed. *Keep running. He wouldn't catch us.* They hovered, listening to each other breathe. Deep in the woods, something screeched—once, then again. Hunter or prey? They grabbed each other's hands, turned, raced back to the front of the house, the grass slick under their feet.

There he was, the bowl of his pipe glowing reddish, smoke curling away from him, rising skyward.

Nothing had changed.

After that he often allowed them to go outside at night once the last glimmer of sunset had been snuffed out behind the mountains. Their days acquired a new shape, a welcome layer of anticipation. During the sun-dappled afternoons they found ways to occupy themselves, but always now they were thinking of what night would bring, of the strange dewy glamour of pipe smoke and darkness.

They didn't know what to call the kidnapper. He steadfastly refused to tell them his name, for reasons they couldn't fathom. It wasn't as if they could report him, after all. When they suggested that he make something up, he wouldn't do that, either. "We have to call you *something,*" they kept insisting, but he was not persuaded.

"Why?" he asked wearily, as if the topic bored him. "Why do

you have to call people something? There are only three of us here. If you're not talking to each other, you must be talking to me, right?"

But they needed something to call him, even in their heads. They couldn't go on referring to him as "him," or "the man"; it was too awkward, too impersonal. So they began calling him something different every day. Every morning they named him—names that struck them as silly, impossible, names he wouldn't like: *Harry. Doug. Mort.* They hoped to annoy him into telling them something real. *Marvin.*

It was the day they picked *Eugene* that he finally broke. "Nope," he said, slamming his cereal spoon down. "Not that. You want to call me something? Call me . . . call me *Zed,* if you must. And that's the end of that." He carried his bowl to the sink. He never failed to clean up after himself.

"That's not a name," Callie objected.

"It's what the British say instead of *zee*. I like it. It means nothing, but you can make it mean whatever you want. That should entertain you for a while."

Zed. It worked, somehow. And he was right; they did try to make it mean things. *The end. The last word.* Nothing too cheerful, really.

One day when he was out somewhere, they took an inventory of the food in the cupboards. They tallied fifty-two cans of soup, thirty of tuna. Eighteen of beans. Fifteen jars of spaghetti sauce. Thirty-six boxes of pasta, ten of Minute Rice. Thirty-two boxes of cereal. Not to mention sacks of potatoes and onions, a freezer full of bread, gallons of juice. Nothing fancy. Just a long-term supply of inexpensive, easy-to-prepare basics.

"I guess we're staying for a while," Callie said. It was the most concrete evidence they had yet come across that they didn't need to be afraid. Whatever plans he had for them, murder didn't seem to be at the top of the list. Not for a while, anyway. Not unless he had a long winter of chicken noodle soup and canned tuna ahead of him.

They were, after all, aware that what men like Zed do to little girls is murder them. They had grown up in the eighties, and were accustomed to the lurid headlines. Children abducted, assaulted, tortured, sexually abused, found in the woods, strangled, dismembered, or, as often as not, simply gone. For days, weeks, they waited for the touch that would change everything. The hand in the wrong place. They knew what men like him really *want* to do to little girls. Murder is more of an afterthought. Destroying the evidence, essentially.

But he didn't touch them.

And he kept on not touching them.

And with every day that passed, they were more curious. Curious about what he *wasn't* doing to them. It wasn't that they wanted him to. But after a while what he *wasn't* doing was pretty much all they could think about.

Once a hunting lodge, the cabin retained traces of its grisly former purpose. Aside from what he called the mud room, there was just one big, long room downstairs, with a kitchen at one end. You could see marks on the walls where hunting trophies must once have hung—unstained splotches that had been protected by taxidermied torsos from the wood smoke that had darkened the rest of the walls over the years.

There were three small rooms upstairs, with slanted ceilings that made them seem even smaller. One was Callie and Hannah's bedroom. One was his, though he usually slept in a hammock on the porch or on the couch. The third was closed, at first, like his bedroom. A mystery. "What's in there?" Callie had asked once. "Nothing that need concern you," he had said.

It was near the beginning of the second week when he first left them alone. They emerged from their room in the morning and there he was, waiting. Too close: if the door had opened outward, it would have hit him. "Can I trust you?" he asked, looking from one of them to the other. "You're good girls, aren't you? I can count on you."

Hannah looked down at her feet and got distracted by his. Low boots, brown leather, well worn. Her father had a similar pair. "Obviously," said Callie, with her usual scorn. Hannah wondered why this should be obvious. Because they hadn't run away?

"Hannah?" He was different that morning; even his movements had a different rhythm: staccato. Jarring. Hannah could smell his shampoo, his toothpaste. She took a step back without knowing she was going to. His night-blue eyes narrowed, too close. "Hannah? I want you to read while I'm gone. I'll ask you about it when I come back." She hadn't finished her Connecticut library books yet, to Callie's annoyance; Callie resented being excluded. He turned and headed down the stairs, a surprising spring in his step, almost jaunty. It wasn't until he had his hand on the doorknob that he glanced back one last time. "Don't open any closed doors," he tossed over his shoulder. Wondering how long it would take them.

The cabin seemed colder when he was gone.

Fairy tales, again. "Do you know Bluebeard?" Hannah asked Callie. Callie executed a quick jeté, crossing the threshold into the hallway. She didn't like not knowing things.

Hannah took this as a no. "Never mind," she said, as if it would be too much trouble to explain. But the truth was that she didn't feel like telling that story: the dead wives, the instruments of torture. The door that was supposed to stay closed. She already knew what she and Callie were going to do, what they wouldn't be able to help doing.

They inspected his bedroom first. They snuck in, as if there might be a surveillance camera, or maybe he had special powers that would allow him to sense what they were up to. They could not have said precisely what they expected to find. Something he didn't want them to see, presumably. Family photographs? Love letters? Newspaper clippings related to some previous crime? Chains, blindfolds? Poison? At any rate, there was nothing. A high double bed with an old-fashioned iron frame dominated the room, neatly made, a faded patchwork quilt smoothed across it. Clothes were folded precisely in the dresser drawers: jeans, T-shirts, boxers, socks. Button-down shirts hung in the closet. No clock, no papers, no receipts, no loose change, no scribbled notes or shopping lists. No mess. A room that knew how to keep its secrets.

The mystery room turned out to be a storage room. A disappointment and a relief. They knew that whatever was in there wasn't his; it had been there forever. Still, they thought it might have something to tell them. Perhaps the hunting lodge had been in his family for generations; perhaps he had been there a hundred times before. "Ancestral secrets?" Hannah whispered when Callie wrinkled her nose at the musty smell. "Ancestral mildew," said Callie.

Mostly it was haphazardly stacked furniture: broken lamps, chairs missing legs, a sagging old sofa, stained, battered end tables. A big cracked mirror with a fancy frame. ("Mirror, mirror . . ." whispered Hannah. "Oh, knock it off," said Callie.) The boxes were stuffed with the kind of outdoor gear you probably needed at a hunting lodge: long slick raincoats, waterproof boots, hats, gloves, camouflage vests. A few faintly musty old clothes looked as if they had costume potential, but most of what they found was irredeemably ugly and way too big.

There were, however, books. Four boxes of old paperbacks, pages falling out, covers worn and stained. Mysteries, Hannah saw at a glance; her mother had bookcases full of them. She grabbed the one on top. The faded cover showed a woman's body sprawled on the floor of an elegantly appointed room. She was lying in a puddle of bright red blood and had fingernails to match, long and sharp. One of her high-heeled shoes had come off. She looked very pretty, for an obviously dead person. "Look!" Hannah said, thrusting it at Callie.

"Gross." Callie backed away, refusing to be excited about something Hannah had found. "It looks like something's been chewing it."

"No, seriously," Hannah insisted. "Look at it. This is a good find. They're mystery novels. This one's an Agatha Christie."

Callie handed the book back and wiped her hands ostentatiously on her dress.

But Hannah knew she was right about the value of her discovery. She selected five paperbacks while Callie removed the last leg from a chair that was already missing three. They surveyed the room before withdrawing, saw nothing amiss. The mirror cracked their faces, proposed unfamiliar new versions of themselves. How strange, they thought, that they hadn't seen their own reflections for over a week. They would have liked to drag the mirror with them but could think of nowhere to hide it. They turned off the light and pulled the door shut; let the dust settle and the cobwebs, lacy strands of disrupted time, fall still.

Hannah stuffed the books beneath her mattress. "Like he'd never look there," said Callie, mocking. But he didn't need to. They were sitting at the kitchen table playing Gin Rummy when he returned. "Find anything interesting?" The sharp edge they had noticed that morning seemed to have softened. He was himself again. "I haven't been in that room for ages. The attic, we used to call it."

We? The hunting lodge was family property after all. A clue.

"I figured at the very least you could use a new supply of books." He opened a kitchen cabinet, rummaged; he had climbed a small mountain, following unmarked trails, and a light, airy peace had crept into his limbs, his mind.

Callie and Hannah searched him for some sign of disappointment, if not anger. But no, it seemed they had done exactly what he expected them to do. Their relief was shadowed by something else: a sense of anticlimax, perhaps. Callie drew a five of clubs, slid it into the run she was building, discarded a jack of diamonds. Hannah followed her lead, resumed play, thought eagerly of the books she wouldn't have to hide.

Spending the day curled in some corner with a novel was nothing new for Hannah; it was what she would have done at home to pass the long, school-free summer days. No one had ever minded her habit of burying her nose in a book for hours on end. But Callie became jealous when Hannah tried vanishing into the musty pages of the storeroom cache; she sighed, pouted, broadcast her boredom with exaggerated drama. Hannah offered another book from the box, but Callie argued that it would make more sense if they read the same thing, and Hannah couldn't help seeing her point. Hannah suggested that Callie could read the book whenever she herself wasn't, but that was impractical. They both wanted to read at the same time, during the long days when they weren't permitted to go outside lest some hiker wander by and catch a glimpse of their (surely?) well-publicized faces. Cool mountain breezes drifted through the screens, and the pine trees swayed above the lodge like gaunt giants, keeping it cool and dim. Zed tended to sit on the porch, sometimes reading, sometimes staring off into the woods or up at the just-visible peaks in the distance. Even when he was reading, a long shiny gun rested across his lap. A different gun from the one Callie had told Hannah about, the one he'd kept in the glove compartment of the car. When it wasn't on his lap he propped it beside him. It was never far from his reach. They imagined he slept with it.

"Do you ever hunt?" Hannah asked him one afternoon. He was

reading on the couch that day, the gun propped against his leg. It looked like a hunting rifle to Hannah, though her knowledge of such things was limited.

Absently, he ran a finger down the barrel of the gun. "Why do you ask?" He got this way sometimes: blank, distant. Elsewhere, almost.

With the gun at his side, it had seemed a logical enough question to Hannah.

"Oh," he said, as if the touch of the gun had brought him back to himself. "No, I don't enjoy hunting."

"Why?" pursued Callie, who had come up alongside Hannah. "What don't you like about it?"

"Pulling the trigger, among other things," he said, rising from the couch. "Don't you two have something better to do?" His face had gone dark. He grabbed his keys and left; they heard tires crunch on the driveway a moment later.

When they could no longer hear the car, they ventured onto the porch. They perched daringly on the Adirondack chairs, squinting into the sunlight. Through the trees, they could make out a bit of the road at the end of the long driveway; it wasn't likely that anyone would see them even if a car should happen to pass. Still, they made no effort to conceal themselves. They tempted fate; they weren't sure why. But their hearts beat faster. "What would you do if someone pulled in the driveway?" Hannah said, as if she were simply making idle conversation.

"Why the hell would someone pull in the driveway?" Callie had adopted the habit of sprinkling her speech with mild profanities when she and Hannah were alone, in contrast with the demure persona she had crafted in the first days and still adopted at times; at other times she seemed to have cast herself as some worldly creature twice her own age, as if she should have a cigarette dangling from painted lips and a bit too much cleavage to be altogether tasteful. As if she had stepped out of the pages of one of the seamier detective novels from the attic.

"To ask directions, maybe."

Callie squinted down the driveway. "Well, we couldn't give them directions, could we? Seeing as how we don't know where the hell we are. So there wouldn't be much to say, would there?"

"Wouldn't that sound suspicious? Besides, they might recognize us, don't you think?"

"True," Callie said thoughtfully. "Our pictures must be everywhere. I bet he checks the news when he goes into town." She brought her feet firmly to the weather-worn floorboards. "We really shouldn't be out here," she said, and rose to go back inside. Hannah followed, unprotesting.

They did not venture out in the daytime again. On a dark, almost-rainy afternoon that offered barely enough light, they chose a tattered novel from their stash of musty storage-room mysteries and settled on the long stiff couch in the main room, bare feet folded under them, toenails beginning to need cutting. (Certain things Zed had not thought of.) Hannah began, reading in her best English-class style. She had just announced the discovery of a body when Callie reached out and grabbed the book. "My turn," she said, and picked up the narrative. She read with considerable drama, throwing herself into the dialogue. "Teachers always ask me to read," she said smugly when she finally came to a chapter break and passed the book back.

The plot unfolded quickly, enlivened by quirky villagers and curious domestic details. Hannah had half expected Callie to toss the book aside in scorn and boredom after a while, but she was surprisingly engrossed. A few chapters in, Hannah realized that he was watching them. Zed. Standing in the doorway, face inscrutable, he managed to give the impression that he had been there for a long time. She couldn't imagine how he had entered the room so quietly that they hadn't been aware of it; her skin tingled at the idea of being watched so surreptitiously. When Callie next looked up—after reading a great sentence in which someone remarked upon how unpleasant it was to have a body in the house—Hannah nudged Callie's shin with her knee and cocked her head ever so slightly in the direction of the door; Callie glanced sideways and saw him too.

She snapped the book shut. "Take a picture," she said, "it'll—"

"Last longer," he said. "I know." He waved his hand. "Don't stop on my account. The novel is trash, of course—but agreeable trash, and it beats playing cards all day. Carry on. But don't spook yourselves to the point where you start seeing villains lurking behind every curtain and you're afraid to go upstairs at night." He crossed to the kitchen and began poking around in the cupboards.

The girls resumed reading, but now they were self-conscious. Zed returned a few minutes later with a plate of saltine crackers and cheese: a rare between-meal indulgence. He pulled up a rocking chair and placed the plate on the couch between them. "I'll share if you let me play," he said.

"We're not *playing*," said Callie. "We're reading." She handed him the book and grabbed a cracker.

"What's the difference?" His tone suggested he was half joking but that the joke was with himself or perhaps with people in his head; it did not concern the girls at all. They knew that flicker of distant amusement by then. He flipped through the pages, found exactly the place where they had stopped, and began reading.

He sounded like a movie voice-over. As if he had written the book himself, or belonged to its world. He made it seem as if they were *in* that world, all three of them. *The body was upstairs. The murderer lurked nearby. They were all suspects. Everyone had a motive.* They could have listened to him forever.

• • •

Storms were rare that summer. Mostly the weather seemed to be toying with them. Thunder grumbled low in the distance, never coming nearer; or mute lightning flickered above the mountains, unanswered by thunder. Or the air would become bloated with rain, heavy and oppressive, even inside the lodge, and they would all listen, tense, for the first drops to spatter across the roof. *Needing* them to. And they would not.

Like them, the sky at those times seemed to be waiting. Straining toward something not yet within reach.

Callie was braver than Hannah with Zed. Hannah loved to listen to him—liked his low voice—and his slow, steady movements often soothed her, like wind in the trees. But she waited for him to come to them: to begin a conversation, propose an activity, make a request. Callie asked questions. She even provoked him, sometimes, as if to see what he would do; to see if there were limits, and what lay beyond them. Hannah could only admire Callie's courage from a safe distance while she herself hung back, watchful and wary, wishing she were bolder, more reckless: that was the kind of girl she would have liked to have been.

Sometimes Hannah worried that Callie would go too far, though she couldn't help wondering what "too far" was, and what might cause it to happen. And one evening as they finished up their macaroni and cheese by the glow of an old oil lantern and lightning bugs flickered outside the window, Callie pushed him as far as she could.

"So have you ever been married?" she asked, without preface, after gulping the last of her milk.

"No," he said shortly, rising from the table.

"Why not?" she pressed.

"Clear the table, Hannah, if you're done eating. You can wash the dishes, Callie." His voice seemed steady and unperturbed, but Hannah, watchful, was sure she saw a shadow cross his face.

"Okay," Callie agreed, "but why won't you answer? I'm just curious. I mean, here we are, after all. And you know everything about us. It only seems fair for us to know something about you, right?"

Hannah stacked plates and silverware, balanced glasses on top, carried them to the sink. Her nerves jangled with alarm. *Careful, Callie.*

They never mentioned the strange truth at the center of everything: that the three of them were not, in fact, a happy, normal family summering at a cabin in the woods. That he had kidnapped them—not even randomly, on a whim, but deliberately, efficiently, after much planning. That they were all participants in an inexplicable crime, that here was not where they were supposed to be.

Zed crumpled his napkin into a tiny ball, rose from the table. "Careful, my little friend." His voice was calm, but Hannah sensed that his heart had sped up; she felt her own heart respond, keeping pace, and a drop of sweat trickled down the back of her neck. *Now,* she thought. *Now is when something will finally happen.* She set the dishes on the counter beside the sink, turned the water on, held a finger under the faucet so she'd know when it was hot. Callie stayed put.

"Is that what we are? Your little friends? Like your pets or something? You don't tell us anything. Maybe we could understand you better if we knew more about your life." Callie stood up and the lantern lit her hair in a fiery halo. She looked outrageously beautiful. Hannah, awed and envious, wondered how he could refuse to tell Callie anything.

He seemed to soften. "Let us just say that women have always disappointed me, one way or another. Don't push it."

"Are women more disappointing than men, do you think?"

Callie still stood beside the table, making no move toward the dishes. Hannah noticed that the water had begun to scald her hand. She plugged the drain, squirted detergent, turned the water down low so she could hear the answer.

"Of course they are," Zed said, his composure more alarming than open anger. "They're more corrupt." Hannah turned the faucet on full blast, hoping to discourage Callie from persisting. Goosebumps had sprung up on Hannah's clammy arms. The danger in the room seemed to be bouncing off the walls.

"What do you mean by that? Corrupt how?" Callie moved slowly toward Zed, her eyes flashing.

Zed stood his ground, shadows shifting on his face as the lantern flickered. "Someday you may know what I mean. Or Hannah might be able to tell you." Generally pleased to be drawn into Callie and Zed's exchanges, in this case Hannah sensed an unearned insult. Why would she, now or ever, have more access than Callie to knowledge about corruption? Female corruption, specifically? *We aren't even women, after all. Just girls.*

Was she corrupt already, or merely destined for corruption? How did he know? What did he know about her that he wasn't telling her?

Hannah rinsed the dishes, one by one, and slid them into the soapy water. She wanted to throw off the balance in the room, somehow, but felt powerless. By this time Callie seemed driven—possessed, almost; Hannah wasn't sure she could have stopped if she had wanted to. "What about your mother? Was she disappointing? Is she corrupt?" Callie demanded. Startled by the violence of the questions, Hannah allowed a plate to slip, strike the edge of the hard porcelain sink. The clatter jarred her nerves, but the others didn't seem to hear. Callie was generating a tangible field of intensity. The room hardly felt big enough to contain her. Hannah turned from the sink, wiped her wet hands on her dress, let the lip of the sink dig into her back. Waited to see what would happen.

"Or your sister," Callie added. "You have a sister, don't you?" At last, his anger surfaced, flared. Hannah saw a vein pulsing in his forehead. He took a step forward; it hardly seemed voluntary. Callie had her eyes fixed on his, as if she were drawing him to her, exercising some mysterious power. It crossed Hannah's mind in an unwelcome flash that Callie might, in some bizarre way, be trying to seduce him. A sickness coursed through her. They had excluded her, forged some electrical connection of which she was not a part.

But his face closed abruptly, breaking the spell. "My mother is not your concern, and I have no interest in discussing her with you," he said coldly, and left them.

"So he does have a sister," Callie said thoughtfully, pretending to be perfectly unruffled though her flushed cheeks betrayed her.

Hannah was thinking the same thing: he had given them a rare clue. She filed it away.

At such dark, tense moments they remembered to be afraid, remembered that they were the complicit prisoners of a man about whom they knew nothing, a man whose motives and intentions were inscrutable. At such moments they wondered what was going to happen to them. But mostly they did not. Mostly they lived from moment to enchanted moment, competing for Zed's attention, slipping into the strange and intriguing territory of each other's minds. They drove out thoughts of their distraught parents, their real lives, their grim knowledge of what bad men do to little girls. They fell into a regular habit of reading mysteries out loud; they sometimes even acted out scenes. They ate salty, preservative-laden comfort food from cans and mixes. Every night seemed oddly festive, like a party. They sat together at the kitchen table, picking happily at Kraft macaroni and hot dogs or whatever dubious concoction was on the menu. Zed was almost always at his best then, talkative and benevolent. The girls waited impatiently for it to get dark so that they could light the candles and the lantern and—if they were lucky, and he was in a good mood—maybe venture outside. The world they only ever encountered by starlight seemed unreal, like some magical realm to which they had been lucky enough to discover the key: Oz, Narnia, Wonderland. There were raspberry bushes at the edge of the woods behind the lodge, and they learned to pick berries in the dark. When they went back inside they could see the red berry juice mixing on their fingers with blood from the thorns. Some nights Callie and Hannah danced on the lawn to music that was only in their heads, whirling in circles until they collapsed.

Always, there was Zed, barely visible in the darkness. Watching.

Hannah slept neatly: on her back, arms at her sides, like a doll. Or a corpse. Neatly and lightly—the slightest sound or motion woke her, not abruptly but smoothly; she glided easily from one world to the other. For this reason she became aware of Zed's nocturnal visits sooner than Callie, who slept like a fish on a dock, flipping wildly from side to side, gasping and muttering. When Hannah first heard their doorknob turn—or did she only sense it?—she lay perfectly still and opened her eyes the merest slit. She had long ago mastered the art of pretending to be asleep; she liked her mother to wake her for school in the morning, even if she had been fully conscious for hours. Her mother would come in after she had made breakfast, smelling of coffee and bacon. From this childish habit she had acquired the idea that people's best selves might be revealed in such moments: moments when they thought themselves unobserved. A wave of cooler air told her that the door had opened. The hallway beyond was unlit, and she couldn't make him out right away; but after a minute, a dark shape emerged in precisely the space where she knew he must be, the spot from which her too-keen senses had felt the air being gently displaced. He didn't move into the room but remained framed in the doorway, his gaze moving back and forth from Callie's bed to Hannah's. The moon lit a single glint in his eye. Hannah lay rigid with anticipation, every muscle painfully tensed, wondering what was next. Perhaps now was the moment, the unspoken *something* they had been waiting for; perhaps he had come to murder or molest them. Hannah didn't believe this, not really, but her body, relying on more primitive instincts, feared it nevertheless. She could hardly hear anything but the blood pounding in her ears. Still, she heard him sigh. A faint sigh, nothing more than a gentle expulsion of softly held breath. As if in sympathy, a light gust of wind stirred the curtains, crept across her skin, blew a single strand of hair across her nose, tickling. She thought she would burst.

Then he retreated. Without another sound, he pulled the door shut behind him.

Hannah relaxed her muscles, one by one, beginning at her toes and climbing toward her face.

It took a long time to let the tension go.

After that, Zed appeared in the doorway most nights. His behavior was exactly the same on each occasion. Hannah didn't tell Callie until after the third time. By then, the pleasure of having a secret had worn off; this new development required analysis and discussion. Hannah felt less threatened than puzzled, and longed for Callie's unsparing take on Zed's behavior. Callie, however, didn't believe her: "There's no way I would sleep through that," she said. "Your imagination is twisted, that's all." Nevertheless, she promised to stay awake that night in order to verify Hannah's account. She lasted only a couple of hours before Hannah heard the telltale shift in her breathing, and once again she slept solidly through Zed's appearance. This strange knowledge remained Hannah's alone. *He* was Hannah's, in a way, for the first time. And there was something to be said for that.

Although Callie professed skepticism about Hannah's story, it wasn't long after Hannah told her about Zed's visits that she announced her escape plan: not a plan to escape, but a plan for its own sake. A scheme, a plot, elaborate and labor-intensive. Late at night, in the dark, when he was on the porch: that was when Hannah and Callie talked, quietly, both of them looking straight up toward the slanting ceiling they couldn't see.

Hannah tried to talk her out of it. It wasn't necessary to make some crazy plan, she said. If they really wanted to leave, they could waltz out the front door—when he was out, or while he slept. Perhaps even right in front of him. Would he stop them? Really? He had never laid a hand on them. Impossible to imagine that he would grab their arms, their waists, haul them back. Tie them up, lock them in. He wasn't like that. Besides, where would they go if they *did* escape? As far as they knew, there was nothing for miles around.

"I just want to make a point," Callie insisted. "To show him that we could if we wanted. Even if he locked us up. Obviously we aren't really going to *do* it."

"What if it makes him mad? I mean, what if . . ." Hannah couldn't find words for what she meant. What if acting as if they were in danger somehow made it true?

"He won't know about it unless we want him to," Callie pointed out. "And that would only be if . . . if we felt like we needed to make a statement or something." She sounded defiant and a little shifty, as if even she knew that her logic didn't really hold up. *What are you thinking, Callie?* For once Hannah couldn't tell.

"He has a car and a gun," Hannah pointed out. "Well, more than one gun. He's twice our size. He knows where we are. On a map, I mean. I don't really see what kind of meaningful *statement* we can make. Or why we would want to. Unless you know something I don't."

"You don't understand anything," Callie said. Sometimes it seemed to Hannah that they exaggerated their personality differences to make sure that they didn't turn into each other. Sometimes it seemed to be happening anyway: Hannah becoming Callie; Callie becoming Hannah. It was what Hannah wanted: to be like Callie, to be brash and bold, to get her way.

So Callie, part-Hannah herself, knew all along that Hannah would help with her plan, even if neither of them was able to be honest about what it was that they were doing and why.

Anyone who's ever watched a movie or read a book knows how to make a rope out of bedsheets if it becomes necessary to plot an escape. Typically you use your own sheets because that's all you have, but Hannah and Callie were lucky enough to find old threadbare sheets in the storage room. They prepared their materials when he went out, ears alert for the sound of his car approaching. The sheets tore easily; teeth worked as well as scissors. Adding each ragged ribbon to their growing pile, they shredded until all of the sheets had been reduced to perfect tatters. The repetitive shriek of splitting fabric was strangely gratifying, the dusty afternoon hush of the cabin heavier than ever, afterward. They stashed the evidence of their labor under Callie's bed. From then on, the noisy part of the project behind them, they dared to work in the dark, on the floor of their room, when they were supposed to be sleeping. At intervals they paused, ears straining, to make sure he hadn't slipped quietly in from the porch, wasn't mounting the stairs, listening outside their door. Later it chilled them to realize that he must have done one or all of those things, unbeknownst to them; they were never in nearly as much control as they imagined. But at the time they thought they were working in absolute secrecy. Speaking only in whispers, they tied the bed-length strips together, end to end, to make triple-length ropes. Once they'd made three of these they braided them tightly. Then they made another just like it and tied the lengths together as firmly as they could. The rope they ended up with was longer than it needed to be. They knew that because they tested it one night, saw it puddle on the ground as they let it out. It didn't even look all that strong. But then it wasn't as if they needed to escape from a tower. Their rope needed to do no more than lower them from the second floor of a rather squat hunting lodge. They probably could have *jumped* from their window without serious damage, had it come to that. But that was never the point. Especially, they told themselves, since they never actually planned to escape.

The likelihood that their rope would never be put to use didn't stop them from crouching on the cool floor for three nights running, ghostly pale in their storybook nightgowns, working as efficiently as they could. They'd both start if they heard an owl or a bat. Every now and then they would whisper about strategy or argue about the design. "Pull harder," Hannah would hiss, as they tested two sheets they had fastened together. "Tie one more knot if you're worried," Callie would whisper back. The old sheets they had found all had patterns—flowers, stripes, birds—and they were every color imaginable. Had they seen their creation in the daylight, it would have been garish, absurd: a rope fit for a circus. But in the dark, the colors faded to indistinct shades of gray, as if they had braided gloomy shadows into it, or dipped each section in blood. In the dark it looked serious: serious enough to satisfy them, and to make them uneasy.

When they had tied the last knot, tested it as well as they could, and declared it complete, they coiled up the rope and hid it under Callie's bed, which was the one nearer to the window. They tied one end around one of the metal legs as securely as they could.

It was ready to go. "Just in case," Callie said—for the first time—and Hannah nodded, solemnly. *In case of what?*

In the days that followed they conferred sometimes about what to do with the rope—how to make their statement, whatever that statement was to be: That they could have left whenever they wanted, but had chosen not to? That he could trust them? They couldn't decide, and so they postponed any action, growing accustomed to its presence, curled beneath Callie's bed. Secretly they were relieved to have absolved themselves, at least for the time being, of the need to act.

A week or so later, they heard something thud against their window late one night. They were already asleep, but both sprang awake. "What was that?" Callie demanded, sitting up.

"Something hit our window," Hannah said, her voice unsteady. "It sounded like someone threw it."

Callie swung her bare feet to the floor, ran for the window. "Be careful," Hannah said lamely, and then followed her.

They stood looking down onto the dark grass for a minute before they noticed anything. Then, as they watched, a tiny pinpoint of light they had disregarded at first—dew catching the moonlight, they had thought, if they thought anything at all—suddenly flared up and began to spread in a widening spiral, growing taller and angrier as it raced. At last it burst into a bonfire and burned furiously for a few minutes more. *He must have used gasoline or something*, Hannah thought, as blue and green flames flashed out from the hot core. *To make it burn so fast and so bright.*

And then it died, leaving a big glowing spiral on the lawn.

They checked the leg of Callie's bed where the end of the rope had been tied. They weren't at all surprised to find that it was gone.

They never spoke of what they had seen, not to Zed, and he didn't mention it the following day or ever. They had made their statement; he had made his. One more indecipherable clue.

What they liked best were the nights when he allowed them to go outside in the dark—not only because they craved fresh air and the chance to stretch their legs, run at full speed, touch the grass, but because this reckless permissiveness struck them as evidence that he knew them, that he understood that they would find magic in the woods despite the mosquitoes and the damp, that he trusted them to see what he saw, love what he loved. And not to run. One night they lay outside on the mossy ground and looked up at the sky. The stars were outrageously thick and deep. This impressed Hannah more than it did Callie, who claimed that they were pretty much the same in Arrow, Nebraska, and had never done anybody much good. "Who ever said the stars were supposed to *do* anything?" Hannah demanded.

"Girls," Zed said softly, lying between them—not very close. Not touching or even close to touching. The three were well spaced out on the grass, each laying claim to a private territory. "Shush. Don't fight. Just look." It wasn't like a movie; he didn't name constellations for them or offer pseudophilosophical pronouncements about life or human irrelevance. They just looked and drifted.

For a while they were quiet. The stars got deeper the longer they looked. But even with Zed's body disturbingly between them, Hannah could eventually feel Callie getting bored and restless, so although Zed jumped a little when she next spoke, Hannah was expecting it.

"Zed, do you have any kids?" she asked abruptly.

Hannah thought she could feel him almost vibrating; he was furious, she thought, or else very sad, grief-ridden. She would have bet on anger.

After a minute he peeled himself neatly off the ground and went inside without saying a word, without brushing the sticky wet pine needles from his back.

"What did you do that for?" Hannah asked Callie, already missing the moment they had lost.

Callie tossed a fistful of pine needles in the air, let them fall back on both her and Hannah. She missed him already. "I just wanted to know." They stayed on the ground, hoping to wait out his mood. "Don't you get sick of not knowing anything?"

"Well, you're not going to find out anything important just by *asking*." Hannah was annoyed that Callie could think even for a minute that it could be so simple, that the truth would yield so easily.

Callie didn't think it was simple; she believed certain risks were worth taking. "Why the hell not?" she said. "You want everything to be so *complicated*."

This was true, Hannah supposed. Then again, everything *was* complicated. Even Callie would have had to admit that.

Once they heard a dog bark. They were at the kitchen table eating Cheerios when they all heard it. They were accustomed to coyotes, owls, bats, loons, other animals the girls couldn't even identify by their calls. Not dogs. It took them a minute to realize why this was significant, why Zed's coffee sloshed over the rim of his mug as he shoved his chair back from the table.

Then they got it. Dogs mean people.

Zed was on his feet in no time, pulling the blinds aside to check out the invasion. Callie and Hannah sat frozen, spoons halfway to their mouths. The dog sounded happy, Hannah thought. Playful. Not lost, not angry, not afraid, but as if it were having a good time. Hikers? Picnickers? *Search dogs?*

Zed turned away from the window. Somehow his rifle was now in his hands, knuckles sharp and bloodless. "Upstairs," he said. "In your room. Don't make a sound. Don't go near the window."

They left their cereal bowls on the table and raced upstairs.

Hannah and Callie lay corpse-still on their beds for perhaps an hour, only daring to whisper, long after they had stopped being able to hear the dog. They were half-afraid, half-excited, though they could hardly have explained why.

But they never heard the dog again—that one or any other. Mystery unsolved. There's really no such thing as the middle of nowhere, they were reminded. They were still in the world. A dog could wander onto their front porch and change everything. The world was looking for them. It had to be.

For the first couple of weeks or so Zed was always clean-shaven, and then gradually, as weeks stretched into a month, a dark shadow began to assume the definite contours of a full-fledged beard.

"Why are you growing a beard all of a sudden?" Callie asked (though she liked it), and he stroked it curiously with his fine, bony hands, as if half surprised to find it there.

"I don't know," he said. "Does there have to be a reason for everything?" His first words offered a nonanswer to Callie's question, but when he posed his own question he turned to look at Hannah as if responding to some challenge she had not even dared to voice.

Yes, she thought. *There does.*

They noticed other changes, too, as the summer wore on. He left the house less often. He spent more time sitting on the porch with his gun. He asked fewer questions. Every now and then, when one of the girls appeared unexpectedly, he'd look at her blankly, as if just for one unbearable instant he no longer recognized her.

The change was gradual, though; gradual enough so that they didn't think about it much. Besides, there was always the chance that *this* was normal, and the early weeks had been an aberration. How could they know?

They had been working their way through the detective novels from the storage room for weeks when he tossed a book at them one day, one of the old, serious-looking, plainly bound hardcovers from the shelves in the main room. He'd been reading it himself for a day or two, but he was clearly not the first to crack its spine; it was a much-read volume, worn and dog-eared. "You read too many novels," he said, as the book landed on the couch between them. "It's lazy. You should mix in some poetry. This might appeal to your ghoulish tastes."

It was a volume of Robert Browning's poems, and for the most part he was wrong: they were not ready for Browning's dark, driven dramatic monologues, the voices of renaissance dukes and painters and dissolute priests. They struggled through a few of them because they didn't want to let him down. But they were bored, and a little confused, and resentful. They missed their gloomy country houses, genteel suspects, politely but relentlessly mounting body counts.

But one poem did please them; one poem was short and straightforward enough to capture their imaginations: "Porphyria's Lover," in which the speaker's beloved ventures through rain and wind to pay an illicit nighttime visit to his cottage; puzzled as to how he might keep her, preserve her, possess her most perfectly, he settles upon the only action possible. While she rests her pretty head against his shoulder, he takes her yellow hair and wraps it around her pretty neck—and yes, strangles her, and there they sit, in perfect companionship, as the night wears on.

"Oh my God," said Callie. She was truly shocked, for once—Callie, who prided herself on keeping her cool, her languid aura of boredom. The last line, which she had just read aloud, still hung in the air, the one about how God had not said a word—not as the murderer sat with the dead woman all through the night. "That's seriously messed up."

"He's a madman," Hannah remarked uneasily. She felt a need to counter the narrator's strange confidence in his own logic—not just in her own mind but aloud, on the record in some way.

"Crazy. Obviously," Callie agreed.

Only then did they see Zed in the doorway. Leaning against the door frame, arms crossed in front of his chest. "Don't stop on my account," he said when he realized that they had turned their attention to him. And then retreated, began tidying the immaculate kitchen.

That was the night he touched Callie's hair.

Her yellow hair. Like Porphyria's.

Always Callie. Hannah suffered. Full of nameless sorrow, she thought she might die of longing that night—of the candlelight, soft and beautiful and full of all the things she could not have or be. Or of something darker, something she didn't understand.

Callie's fault. Callie wanted to dress up; she was obsessed with the femmes fatales in the detective novels and wanted to try the role for herself. She wrapped her top sheet strategically around herself like a kind of demented Grecian evening gown, and she constructed an elaborate updo out of her golden curls with an old rubber band, a safety pin, a scrap of ribbon, and a couple of sticks. She stuck some daisies in it to complete the effect. (He brought little bouquets of wildflowers in sometimes, to make up for their not being able to go outside. He put them in drinking glasses on the kitchen table. It was sweet, they thought.) She rigged up some jewelry out of the shiniest objects she could find in the storage room. Inclined to be critical, Hannah forced herself to be fair: Callie was just playing, really. Dressing up was her favorite form of play; she loved to decorate herself. She was a tremendous narcissist, even for a twelve-year-old. But she was also a born actress. She required costume changes.

Although Callie should have looked completely ridiculous, Hannah had to concede that somehow she made the makeshift ensemble work. She adopted a sultry accent and a languid way of moving, and it was as if she had cast a spell on herself, Cinderella-like, transforming rags to finery. Maybe it was the candlelight. To Hannah it seemed like magic, and not white magic, either. She was dizzy with jealousy.

And Zed was furious. All the vague humor and improbable kindness drained from his after-dinner face as Callie descended the stairs, staging a grand entrance. Hannah put down the dish towel and moved away from him instinctively, away from the charged field that suddenly rearranged the air around him. As Callie swayed past him, batting her eyelashes, his arm shot out as if it had a life of its own. He grasped the twisted nest of curls that was falling from the top of her head where she had tried to pin it. He pulled it all down, and not gently. The pins and sticks and daisies fell to the floor. He twisted the long coil of Callie's beautiful hair around his hand and wrist, almost absently. His eyes were dark and strange, and Hannah couldn't really look at them; she hardly even breathed. Callie raised her eyes to his, and some current seemed to dart between them. He pulled her hair. Just a little, then a little more.

"*Stop it!*" Hannah was half-dismayed to hear her own voice; she had hardly known that she was going to speak, hadn't realized she was crying. Zed dropped Callie's hair as if it were on fire, and Hannah turned and ran, wrenching the door open and fleeing into the cool dark night, knowing he would follow, knowing it was up to her to break the spell.

That was near the end.

"I imagine you girls would like to go swimming," he said after dinner one night, entirely out of the blue. It was a particularly warm, muggy night and very still. Moths flung themselves at the lantern that hissed on the table.

It was true: swimming had always been a part of summer, for both of them, and they had missed it, all those hot days at the lodge. But by way of idle conversation the remark seemed uncharacteristically pointless, even a little mean. It wasn't as if he could conjure a lake or a pool in the backyard. They said nothing, waiting to see where he was going with this. They were wary; they were on their guard by then.

But he was serious. He looked from one of them to the other, blue eyes frowning. "I'm not wrong, am I? I warn you, I will think you are very strange children if you don't want to go swimming. Hurry up and get your things if you want to go. It's a perfect night for it."

"Things?" Callie said suspiciously. "What things? It's not like we have bathing suits."

"You'll think of something," he said, unperturbed. "It'll be dark, after all. Just grab towels, then."

Still baffled, they did as he said, and stood waiting. Wordlessly he led them out the door, into the night—straight to the car. They hadn't been in it since their arrival. It was saturated with the memory of the road trip. Their abduction.

"Get in the back," he said. "And lie down until I tell you otherwise."

After ten minutes or so the car turned off the comparatively smooth road they'd been winding along and headed sharply downhill on a pitted dirt surface. Losing her balance, Hannah tumbled from the seat to the floor of the car, and Callie barely avoided following her. Hannah crouched where she was, rather than attempting to scramble back up, clenching her teeth to make sure she wouldn't bite her tongue when they hit the potholes.

Then, quite suddenly, they stopped.

"Follow me," he said. "Watch your step."

They followed the bobbing white circle his flashlight threw across the rough ground, everything else black. At first they could only smell the water and hear its gentle lapping, and then the light splashed across it.

"Here," he said magnanimously, as if he'd created this body of water just for them. "This is a good place to swim."

They kicked off their sneakers, and he averted his eyes as they turned their backs on him in the dark and pulled their dresses over their heads. Along with towels they had also each brought an extra pair of panties. This was Callie's idea. They used them to improvise bikini tops, thrusting their arms and shoulders through the leg holes, smoothing the seats across their chests—Hannah's entirely, boyishly flat, Callie's boasting two tiny swollen buds—and attempting to hook the hips over their bony shoulders enough to anchor them a little. It wasn't especially successful, but it served its purpose, more or less. Meanwhile Zed shone the flashlight away from them, across the water, elaborately respecting their modesty. When the girls were ready, he aimed the light at the water near their feet to guide them in.

The air was chilly, and they shivered a little in their underwear. When they ventured to dip toes in the water, though, they found it surprisingly warm. Even then they edged forward cautiously, their feet settling into the silty lakeshore bottom with each step. Hannah pictured dozens of tiny fish swarming around their unexpected ankles and was glad she could not see them. All they could see was the small disk of light that lay before them—nothing else, not each other, not their own outstretched arms, not the shore, not the dimensions of the lake or the woods that must have surrounded it, not the mountains that surely rose in the distance. Not the man himself, who directed the light and controlled what they saw, who could never have been far away. Nothing but the pale circle of light that beckoned them deeper into the lake, and in it, the faint waves they made themselves. That must have been what he meant when he said it was a perfect night: there was no moon, no stars. The sky was blank.

Callie was the first to plunge, naturally, when the water had reached their waists, and after that Hannah had no choice but to throw herself forward. They splashed into deeper water, flipped on their backs, and floated, eyes unfocused. They flung water toward each other and attempted blind, dizzying somersaults. They looked in his direction, sometimes, wondering if he could see them, if he was watching, but they saw nothing outside the halo of the flashlight. The water was soft and warm and seemed to hold them gently. They could hear fish jumping not far away and no longer minded; they were fish, too. They flickered through the water like mermaids, inventing strokes they'd never learned in swimming lessons. Sometimes they brushed against each other, inadvertently—their bare arms and legs soft and similar. Their unruly imaginations tried to conjure up a sense of what the man's limbs would feel like in the water, hard and male and unclothed. They felt embarrassed, as if their thoughts could travel through the air, as if he could intercept them.

But he did not join them. Did they expect him to? They weren't sure; the episode seemed so very strange, so unscripted, that it was nearly impossible to form expectations.

It is possible, though, that they had formed a hope—collectively, echoed silently between them. In any case, they let it go, gave themselves up to the pure pleasure of being enveloped by the water. He did not speak, and that was fine. He simply held the light. He gave them the lake, piece by piece.

And then suddenly he turned off the light. They heard the click of the plastic switch. They lifted their heads from the water, opened their eyes and closed them again, and saw no difference. Instinctively, they fell silent, treaded water. They could pinpoint each other's location because they could hear each other's breath, but Zed seemed to have vanished. "Where are you?" Callie asked after a moment, her voice harsh but also vulnerable. Hannah could tell that her mood had changed: Callie was angry now.

After a few seconds his calm voice carried across the water. "Why does it matter?" He was as blind as they were.

"How can you say that?" Callie demanded. Outrage vibrated in her voice.

Because it doesn't, Hannah thought, not even knowing what she meant. *It doesn't matter, not anymore.* This time Zed didn't answer. Would it be a happy ending, Hannah wondered, if he just left them there? They would huddle all night beside the lake, shivering and mosquito bitten. When dawn came they would make their way back to the road, bedraggled. Eventually someone would find them, and it would all be over. Zed would escape, perhaps. He would never be found.

No, of course he won't leave us, she thought peacefully. He still needs us. *For what?* asked a treacherous voice in her mind. *How can you be so sure? What if he brought his gun? What if he slips into the water, places his hand on your head and presses it down, down beneath the surface, and eventually you don't struggle anymore, and—* Appalled, she silenced the voice, flipped onto her back, and stretched her arms out to the sides, scissoring her feet slightly to keep her balance, feeling her peace return. As she stared up at the blank sky she saw that, as her eyes adjusted, it became less perfectly dark. Low clouds captured stray light from below—maybe from towns miles away, she thought, or houses they couldn't see—and reflected it back to the water. She could discern the outlines of the clouds, the place where the lake met the trees, a shape a few feet away that must be Callie. She had the irrational thought that the light was coming from her own gaze, that if she looked long and hard enough she could light up the woods. She sensed that Callie, out of sync with her mood, had stopped floating and righted herself, anchored her feet on the bottom of the lake, waiting impatiently. She tried to project her strange sense of calm in Callie's direction, wanting to share it, but she could tell that Callie had become unreceptive. She tried to turn her attention inward, blocking Callie out, but her awareness of Callie's unhappiness created a tension she couldn't ignore, and she felt drawn in two directions: it was as if she had to be two people, herself and Callie. She grew conscious, meanwhile, that the part of her that was exposed to the air was getting chilled. But she didn't want to stop floating.

Finally Zed said, quietly, "Enough." His voice had moved. They turned in its direction. Hannah, obedient, swam toward him, but she felt Callie's resentment collect itself and tremble though the water. "What if we're not done?" Callie called out, defiant, though she was more than done with this invisible lake. As usual, Hannah admired Callie's courage at the same time that she was annoyed by it. *Why does she have to try to ruin everything?*

"Then stay," Zed said, as if it were the most reasonable thing in the world. "Hannah and I will go."

Hannah heard Callie behind her, plowing through the water toward the shore. She wondered if he had meant it; she suspected not. He had simply known that Callie would come. Somehow this knowledge made her feel both safe and sad.

As they emerged from the water onto the chilly shore, clutching their towels around themselves, teeth chattering, they saw that there was an extra light, hovering precisely where his face should be, and they smelled his familiar pipe. Wordlessly he tapped the base, tipped out the glowing ember, and ground it out beneath his heel, turning as he did so and shining the flashlight at the car. Dripping and shivering, they piled in. No one spoke.

They couldn't have been far from the lodge when a car appeared behind them, its headlights boring into the backseat, bouncing off the rearview mirror. "Stay down," Zed ordered, straining to make out a shape, a face behind the dark windshield. He didn't alter his speed, but they could feel his sudden alertness, as if something newly rigid in his body communicated itself to them through the car itself, entering their own bodies through the rough fabric of the backseat, against which they had pressed their cheeks. They lay still and quiet, the tension between them suddenly gone. The other car kept up with them, pressing. Someone who knew the roads, perhaps, and wanted to go faster. Someone in a hurry, late for something they couldn't even imagine. *Someone looking for two missing girls, traced to this area.* Zed kept driving, long enough that they were sure they must have gone well past the turnoff to the lodge. At last they came to a stop, and the girls listened breathlessly to the tick-tock of the turn signal, the headlights bearing down on them. They veered right. The lights swept along the left side of Zed's car, picking up speed, and vanished.

They had turned, and the other car had stayed straight.

Silence returned. They drove on for another minute before Zed swung an efficient U-turn and headed back the way they had come. He killed the lights as they rolled down the long driveway, approaching the lodge in utter darkness.

No one had been following them. But people were looking, surely. They had to be.

Back at the lodge, he sent them off to bed as if nothing out of the ordinary had happened. But he was unusually quiet, and they couldn't help feeling that something had shifted, that things were not quite the same. It made them nervous.

The next day was cloudy, humid, oppressive, and Hannah and Callie's sense of unease held on. Hannah walked softly, looked over her shoulder, startled at trifles: a branch striking the roof, the hiss of the water heater, the squawk of an unfamiliar bird. Callie, on the other hand, grew reckless, restless, couldn't be still. While Zed circled the perimeter of the clearing in which the cabin was set—head down, round and round, unreachable—Callie played pageant: tried to entertain Hannah by reenacting bits of her routine, spoofing imaginary competitors. As she demonstrated her pageant walk, Hannah played judge, pretending to scribble seriously in her notebook. Callie crossed the room with strong, graceful strides, her head angled in Hannah's direction, her lips shaping a huge smile. Pausing in front of the window she turned slightly, hand on hip, flashing her imaginary audience another dazzling grin. Even without stage makeup and a fancy dress, she conveyed something of the bewitching presence that had already won her so many crowns.

They didn't know he was in the doorway until he had lunged across the room, almost catlike, grabbing the arm perched on Callie's hip and wrenching it around in front of her. Hannah had been lounging on the couch, laughing; when she saw him—or sensed him, really—she curled into a ball, clasping her hands around her knees. Callie turned red, and Hannah saw, for the first time, tears in her eyes. But she didn't struggle—she looked him right in the face, anger blazing, and her tears didn't fall.

The first fat raindrops spattered against the windows, like the ticking of a mad clock. Zed held on to Callie's arm. Every muscle in his body seemed tensed, his face stretched taut across bone and sinew. "*Don't do that here.* Not here. Do you understand me?" He pulled her a little closer and repeated: "You understand? You've left that behind. It's over." He pushed her away, gently enough, but with such visible control that it suggested a tremendous current of power flowing beneath the surface. Callie reeled a little—more from her sense of that power than from the push itself. "Never. You hear? Never. You won't be that girl anymore." Then he turned and strode out of the lodge, closing the door hard behind him.

"Well." Callie dropped onto the couch beside Hannah and crossed her legs gracefully. "So I guess he doesn't approve of pageants."

"But why—" Hannah sat up straight, folded her legs beneath her. She was afraid Callie would be offended, but she had to go on: "Why did he pick you, then?"

Callie twisted a long golden curl around her index finger. "That's the question, isn't it?" She tugged sharply at the coiled hair—once, twice; Hannah felt the twinge in her own follicles. "Maybe he meant to save me," Callie said. She made her voice sound flippant, but Hannah knew Callie was serious. And perhaps she was also right.

Later that night Hannah awoke with a pressing feeling that something was wrong. The rain had ended almost as soon as it began, and the sky was clear again; a glimmer of moonlight revealed Callie's bedding, twisted into its customary nest. Empty. She told herself that Callie must simply have gotten up to go to the bathroom. Unconvinced, she bolted upright, trying to ward off panic. Only then did she realize that she could hear voices downstairs, quiet and serious.

Hannah slipped out of the room and crept to the head of the stairs. Crouching on the first step, she eased her head forward until she could just see them, sitting across from each other at the kitchen table. At first, blood pulsed so hard in her ears that it was all she could hear, but their conversation became intelligible as she listened.

"I don't understand," Callie was saying, a sulky edge in her voice. "I thought you picked us because of who we are." Hannah caught her breath. This was what they never spoke of, not to him.

"Not exactly," he said.

"Well, then?"

He leaned forward, and Hannah drew her head sharply back, afraid he might be able to glimpse her. She could hear just as well without seeing—better, if she concentrated.

"It's a waste." He sounded very calm; there was no trace of the latent violence that had shocked the girls earlier. "A perversion. That's why you needed me. Maybe you'll understand someday. But listen," he began.

"I'm listening," Callie said. A rare subdued note had crept into her voice.

"I want you to promise me that you won't do it anymore. The pageants. Cheapening yourself like that."

A mosquito buzzed in Hannah's ear, and she raised a hand to crush it. Missed. She could feel the tension in the air like a sudden chill, or a storm coming. Callie felt it too, on the other side of the wall.

When Callie finally spoke, her voice was low and steady. "Are we going home, then?" They had lived each day, as much as they could, without speaking of *later*. They might sketch fantasies of glamorous adulthood, but they avoided talk of their actual lives: starting a new school year, buying new clothes, listening to the newest songs on the radio, meeting new people. *Later* had become a hazy concept; *back* was unmentionable. But Callie was asking, as if it were the most normal question in the world, "Are we going back?" Hannah grabbed the railing; Callie gripped the edge of the table.

"Do you promise?" Zed said.

A strange, growing pressure inside Hannah's head produced surges of dark, muddy colors before her eyes, and a band of sharp pain locked around her forehead.

The whole house waited.

"I promise," Callie said, her voice oddly robotic, and so low Hannah hardly heard it.

"Say it again."

"I promise," Callie whispered. Hannah wasn't even sure she had really heard it, but she *felt* it, as clearly as if Callie's voice were coming from somewhere inside her own body. She felt it under her skin, in the pit of her stomach.

Did that mean they were going home? Callie believed she had made a deal, that was clear to Hannah. But had she?

Instinctively Hannah believed that if Zed had made a promise, he would not break it. But he had been careful, it seemed to her, not to promise. Not in so many words.

Hannah released her sweaty palm from the railing, straightened her cramped legs, glided swiftly back into the bedroom. Slipping between her sheets, she curled up on her side and began to breathe the long, even breaths of sleep. Callie returned, tiptoeing across the room to her bed to avoid waking Hannah.

For once, Hannah noticed, Callie didn't drop off to sleep immediately. Lulled by the deceptive calm of her own steady breathing, she listened to Callie, whose unaccustomed stillness meant she was lying awake. If they were really to go home, how soon it would be? Had Callie meant what she said? Was Callie a girl who kept her promises? She had been willing Callie to promise, willing Zed to reciprocate. But in the back of Hannah's mind, an unacknowledged voice was asking another question: Did she want to go home? And if she didn't yet, what did that mean?

When she finally slipped from feigned sleep to real, she dreamed of Zed turned into a tree outside her window, while she cried because he could never come in. There was a word she could say, a magic word that would free him, but she didn't know what it was. In the dream this was because she wasn't good enough.

The next day and afterward, she kept waiting for Callie to tell her what had happened, since ostensibly she knew nothing. Hannah wanted to talk about it, to examine what he had said and what he had implied. *You needed me,* he had told Callie. Did he think Hannah needed him too?

But Callie said nothing.

The next night he allowed them to go outside, and they played hide-and-seek. By this time he seldom joined their games. He was outside, too, but they weren't sure where. They had already discovered that playing two-person hide-and-seek outside in the dark was a tricky undertaking: there was really no excuse for being found unless you wanted to be, because the person who was It could only blunder in the darkness. The real contest was with yourself: to see how long you could bear to stay hidden. It was challenging: first you started to get bored; then cold; and finally the silence grew eerie, and you began to fight off the temptation to give yourself up. The silence in the woods was actually full of sounds: even raccoons and opossums snapped small twigs under their shuffling feet, and there were bigger animals, too. If you ventured into the woods even a little way, a tree could easily hide the cabin and its reassuring lights, if only for a moment.

Hannah was It; Callie was hiding. Hannah heard Callie run off while she counted—and Callie ran too loudly, too obviously; Hannah listened hard to confirm her suspicion that she then doubled back stealthily and headed off in another direction. It's what she herself would have done. She thought she did hear Callie creeping back, in fact, though she wouldn't have sworn it. After intoning "ready or not," Hannah set off in the direction from which she thought she'd heard a telltale rustle. The best you could hope for by way of guidance in this game was an occasional shiver of branches, a quick intake of breath. A sneeze, if you were very lucky. Once she was moving, Hannah heard nothing. She skirted the edge of the woods, her steps graceful and nearly silent; she listened intently. She heard an owl, another bird she didn't recognize, crickets, frogs. She heard the wind rush through the upper branches of the trees, though the air was perfectly still down below. She crept along and didn't hear Callie. She circled the house, returned to her original spot, moved off in the other direction, listening. Once she heard a distinct crackle of branches a little way into the woods, farther than they ordinarily went. "*Callie!*" she whispered triumphantly; this was about as close as you could get to catching the hider. But no one answered, and somehow in the silence that followed she knew it wasn't Callie but something else: a deer, maybe. She leaned against a tree for a while, listening. If Callie were in motion, Hannah reasoned, she would have a better chance of intercepting her if she stayed still.

Nothing. The owl again. Bats. She was chilled; her feet were damp; her legs scratched and stinging. The house no longer looked comforting; it was far enough away that it was cold, instead, and impenetrable. She felt somehow that it didn't want her back, not without Callie. She had never, ever been more alone, more lonely. She felt tears at the back of her eyes, willed them away.

Hannah abandoned her spot beneath the tree and closed in on the house, wanting suddenly to touch it and make sure that it was real. She tried not to look at the glowing windows because they blinded her even more when she looked back toward the woods. She closed her eyes, reasoning that depriving herself of sight (which was useless anyway) might sharpen her hearing, and she circled the house slowly, trailing one hand along the rough wood to orient herself. Every now and then she would stop. She wasn't even trying to be especially quiet anymore. Who would hear her? Everyone had vanished.

Soft, insinuating tendrils of panic crept into her mind, her veins. She picked up speed. Halfway down the fourth and final side of the house she walked straight into an obstacle. Warm, cotton, breathing, flat up against her entire body, since she'd had no warning. "Callie?" she gasped—absurdly happy, not even hiding it. But even in the split second before her eyes flew open she knew that it could not be Callie. Didn't smell right; was too tall. She had walked smack into Zed. He put his arms around her as she burst into tears. She sobbed as if the world were coming to an end. She thought maybe it was. He hugged her tightly and stroked her hair. *My hair too*, she thought. Not just Callie's. No one had ever hugged her so tightly. It's okay, he kept saying. It's okay, little Hannah. My poor little Hannah, it's okay. Over and over he chanted it, until it became true. And even in the perfect darkness she felt wholly *seen*, as if her mind were inside out and all of her deepest secrets glittered like fireflies. Seen and understood, wanted in the only ways that mattered. Loved.

But in the morning he hardly looked at them and didn't speak at all.

"Something's wrong," Hannah said. She and Callie were in their beds, whispering even though they knew he had not come upstairs, in fact seldom came upstairs anymore. They did not think he slept much at this point.

"I know."

"Do you think there's anything we can do?"

"I can't think of anything," Callie said grudgingly. It was true; Hannah couldn't either. She had tried. He was drifting away from them. Not physically—they were still all cooped up in a hunting lodge together—but in his mind; they were sure of it. They couldn't follow him, and he didn't want them to.

"What do you think is the matter?" Callie asked. "You always have a theory."

Hannah thought for a minute, flattered that Callie wanted to know what she thought, wanting to be sure her answer was as clear and true as she could make it. A mosquito had gotten in the room, and she heard it buzz. "I think . . ." she began quietly. "I think he thought we would make him happy."

"And? So?"

"We don't." She swatted at the mosquito in the dark.

"Did you get him?"

"Her," Hannah corrected, having learned somewhere that only female mosquitoes bite. "Not him. No, I didn't." She could already hear it buzzing again.

"What do we *do*?" She could hear a panicky edge in Callie's voice, not even disguised. This was significant. Hannah and Callie obsessively hid their weaknesses from each other. It was pointless, because by then they knew each other's flaws as well as they knew their own; but it was a matter of pride. Their pride was one of the things they had in common.

Hannah didn't know what to say. She was thinking.

They weren't exactly afraid, even then, but they did feel uneasy. They felt decidedly uneasy, and they couldn't reason themselves—or each other—out of it.

On the last full day the sky was a strange color: a sick yellowish gray with a hint of green, not grass green but bile green, swamp green. A swamp sky hanging low and deathly heavy over the mountains. A tornado sky, said Callie, adding that her entire town had once been wiped out by a tornado—before she was born, she added, as if this didn't interest her much. She was mopey that day, restless and bored. She wanted to go outside. "Certainly not," Zed said, adding that in fact he would appreciate it if they stayed away from the windows. They wondered if he knew something they didn't. In retrospect, they thought he must have; perhaps he had heard or seen something in town. At the very least, he'd had a premonition. He prowled from window to window. Callie and Hannah sprawled on the couch, sweaty skin sticking to the cracked leather, trying to finish *No More Dying Then*, the Ruth Rendell mystery they were reading.

They had spaghetti and jarred sauce for dinner and still it didn't rain, although the air felt as if it might explode. After dinner, when the sun had set, he let them sit on the porch with him, though he forbade them the yard. He turned off the lights, and they sat in pure darkness, looking at the now-familiar patterns of stars emerging above them. Bats swooped and dove. There was no wind at all. Hannah imagined that they were ghosts, visible only to others of their kind; that they belonged somehow to the darkness. He sat in his usual

Adirondack chair, and Callie and Hannah shared the other, quietly tolerating each other's sharp angles—jutting elbows, hipbones. An opossum came out of the woods and stared at them, or seemed to. Then it turned and plodded away, neither disturbed by nor interested in their presence. Thunder rumbled all around them, too far away to give them much hope, and every now and then heat lightning flickered in the distance. Every now and then, too, he said something. Hannah understood for the first time the phrase "breaking the silence," as the quiet seemed to fall in shards around him when he spoke: his voice like a rock hurled through a window. He said there was no such thing as heat lightning. He said some people will tell you that opossums are blind, but that it isn't true. He said they should never let anyone stand in their way if there was something they really wanted to do. He said the cabin wasn't his, that it belonged to an uncle who only used it in the winter, that he had visited it a few times as a boy. They tried to picture him as a boy. He said that they should learn to shoot, because you never knew. He said his older sister had run away to New York City when she was sixteen. He said her life was unspeakable. He told them that he was sorry. "You know that, right, Hannah, Callie?"

They didn't know. How could they have known? Sorry for what? But they said they did, because it was what he wanted to hear.

He came to their doorway that night. For the last time. Hannah was awake, and for once she stared right back at him, her eyes wide in the dark. She didn't know if he could tell; he gave no sign of it. He stood there for a moment, as always, then moved softly away.

On the last morning he didn't sit down to breakfast with them. From the start, the day felt wrong. He was out on the porch early, sitting there, staring into space. He wandered in while the girls were clearing their dishes and crossed straight to the other side of the house, moving the curtains aside and peering out. They wanted to ask what was up but sensed that it would be better if they pretended not to notice anything.

"We should probably do laundry today," said Callie, grumbling a little, and Hannah could tell she wanted her to say no, let's wait till tomorrow.

He spoke up instead, surprising them, turning almost cheerfully to the room. "Don't bother," he said. "Do something fun today. Build a fort in the storage room, turn one of your books into a play. Or something." For just a second he put a hand on each of their heads, and they stood still, as if some kind of paralyzing force had shot through the palms of his hands into their skulls and through their bodies, rooting them to the floor, to the earth beneath it. As if they were extensions of him somehow. Then he removed his hands and headed back to the door. "Stay away from the windows," he warned again, as he had the day before. But they thought they heard him humming something lilting and unfamiliar under his breath as he stepped outside.

They left their dishes in the sink; it felt like the kind of day when that was acceptable. They went upstairs and raided the storage room for new costumes. They found an old trench coat, some ugly hats. They tried to style themselves as detectives and began cooking up a mystery. Hannah tossed out ideas for the murder plot, and Callie, even though she was playing a detective for once and not a femme fatale, tried to figure out what she could use for lipstick. Something food-related? Tomato paste? Grape juice? They would be rival detectives. Callie would be connected to the household in which there had been a murder—a family friend, perhaps. "We'll make it seem like you're the murderer," Hannah proposed. "And you won't be, but I won't realize that until it's too late. And by then you'll be dead." Hannah scribbled this down, conscious that it wasn't her best effort;

Callie nodded listlessly. "Look, why don't you dig through the boxes and see if you can find—"

"Shh," Callie said. "I thought I heard something."

Hannah stopped, and then she heard it too—though it was more as if she had felt something, somehow. As if the ground had shifted a little. They listened. There was a strangely loaded silence and then a gunshot. There was no doubting that it was a gunshot. Not in the distance—not somewhere off in the woods, not someone hunting out of season. Nearby. *Home.* It cracked through the humid air and ricocheted off the mountains. Hannah and Callie kept hearing it long after it had stopped.

They flew downstairs, their feet hardly touching the floorboards. Hannah paused when they got to the bottom and then veered toward one of the front windows, but Callie kept going, across the room, straight out the door, knowing something but not knowing yet what it was that she knew.

"Callie, *no!*" Hannah heard herself scream as Callie wrenched the door open. But she went anyway, unheeding. So Hannah followed. And there he was in his Adirondack chair, as always, except that he wasn't, because of all the blood, and the part of him that mostly was *not* there, which was his head . . . Callie was on her knees, mindless, trying to hold on to him, kicking the gun away from where it had fallen at his feet, ignoring the police surrounding the house even though someone was yelling through a loudspeaker, something about stepping back.

Hannah crossed the porch in slow motion, staring out at the police like a zombie. Their guns were still raised, she realized. At them, at her and Callie. As if they were criminals. They must be, Hannah reasoned, not realizing then how they must look, decked out in their detective gear, like little flashers, pint-sized perverts in bare feet and drooping hats. Without thinking, Hannah raised her hands. Like a criminal, surrendering. "Callie," she said, though her ears were pounding and she couldn't even hear her own voice, didn't know if she had really said it or just thought she had. But Callie looked up. She looked long at Hannah, then turned a hate-drenched stare on the police. Eventually she put her hands up too, and Hannah saw that they were bloody.

Finally they stepped off the porch and surrendered.

Part Three

Lois

A spring-smelling wind batters the house, grinds tree branches against the windows, rattles the panes, swells my curtains. On my computer screen, I have proof. *Lanky, solemn* . . . The evidence was a few keyboard taps away. Outrageously coincidental, absurd, perfect.

Student: Sean Michael McDougal University ID: 722455982
Status: Sophomore GPA 2.7 Credit Hours: 54
Previous Institution: Utica Upstate Community College (UUCC)
Transfer GPA: 3.0

Utica. It's not that far away; I'm sure we have plenty of students from that area. I understand that it's not the kind of evidence that would stand up in court. I feel the pieces falling into place, though; I practically hear them click, lock down. This explains so much.

Sean is the son. Zed's son. No wonder Gary has been a recalcitrant protagonist: I misimagined him from the start. I made him a grizzled woodsman instead of a sullen undergrad. It's not only the manuscript that demands revision—that much I already knew—but my relationship with Sean. I need to alter the balance of power between us. I need to find out what he knows.

What he thinks he has over me is the threat of exposure. For too long—and for no good reason—I have allowed this threat to be an effective weapon. I see how to seize the upper hand: I have what he wants, which is information. Memories. Truth. Or reasonable approximations thereof.

I have an idea.

Once again, my dilemma boils down to a straightforward and impossible question: what do I really want, anyway? You'd think that at twenty-nine I'd be better equipped to answer that question than when I was twelve, but it doesn't seem to have gotten any easier.

I will have to consider my next move very carefully.

I think back to the period during which I wrote the first novel. I had no business doing it; I did not tell my PhD adviser, who would have been outraged. I was supposed to be writing my dissertation—a three-hundred-page scholarly monstrosity—and dissertations require *all* of your attention and stamina and intellectual energy, or so we were encouraged to believe. But my characters seemed to leap from the margins of my dissertation and demand their own space. How could I concentrate on *Pamela* or *The Mysteries of Udolpho* or *Evelina*, on the serial abductions of Pamela et al., when little fleshly versions of Carly and of me danced in the margins? They, too, had been abducted; they, too, had a story.

The novel began as a strategy. I would sit at my battered secondhand desk to work on my dissertation, fortified with coffee and a little (very little) sleep, and I would open another document, a blank page, where I would allow what became the novel—the dissertation demon, I took to calling it—to spill out. After an hour or so the demon would be quieted, and I could return to my real work in peace. It felt almost as though the books were writing each other. The novel—urgent, greedy—took on a life of its own, and I ended up finishing it first. The dissertation was patient, willing to wait for my attention. The novel might have had more to offer me: writing what became *Deep in the Woods* allowed me to live again with Carly May and Zed—and to refashion them, occasionally, as I pleased.

With Sean and his stooped posture, stringy hair, tortured complexion, I have invoked a different kind of demon. How cruel fate was, making him the son of someone as handsome and intelligent as Zed.

What is Sean looking for? *Revenge*. What else could he want? I remember Delia's reaction to Sean and wonder again if there's something I should know. Is he more dangerous than I suspect? There are degrees of danger and—I hope—limits to my recklessness.

Still, I am glad that this time *I* am first, not Carly.

This demon will help me write my sequel.

Chloe

I have a couple more jobs before I can leave town. Jobs Zed would despise. Today, I'm arriving on the set of a TV crime drama called *Criminal Exploits*. It's not one of the big shows everyone's heard of, although the name is supposed to remind you of them. I'm sure the producers hope people might watch it by accident, thinking it's something else. It's a second-tier crime drama that might or might not survive into its third season. I'd say not, if I had to guess—but maybe that's my cheap desire for vengeance, based on the fact that they're about to kill me off. My fourth appearance on the show will be my fucking last. A mistake on their part, if you ask me. I have a recurring role as a psychic detective who gets called in on occasion by the supermanly Detective LaRock, the star of the show. For him, psychic ability is like an extreme version of feminine intuition, and every now and then he decides it's what's called for. Naturally this leads to lots of hilarious, sexually charged banter, where he spouts sexist crap and I try to make him see the (mildly) feminist light, while looking as sexy as it's possible for a psychic detective to look.

"Hey, Chloe!" I hear as I approach. "Dressed for your funeral, I see."

What I'm actually wearing is a short black skirt, a very cute black T-shirt, and black heels. I'd rather die than wear my psychic detective outfit in public, even though it comes with a slight chance of being recognized. (Generally I'm grateful to be recognized as any character I've ever played, though more often people are, like, *Wow, you look so familiar; haven't I seen you in something?*) Anyway, New Age sexpot is hardly my thing. I do, however, honestly think the psychic chick is a great character. "Yeah, I just hope it isn't your funeral, too," I say darkly. Tomm Marks, the director, is stocky, about five foot four with crazy red hair, and fully believes he will one day be David fucking Chase.

"Nah," he says. "I seriously doubt it. We'll get a lot of mileage out of this episode. Sorry to say it, babe, but you're worth way more dead than alive." He raises his cheek for a kiss, which I stoop to deliver. We go way back, Tomm and I. "But then, that's what it says on your résumé, right?"

I bare my teeth at him, half-joking, half-serious, tired of that particular quip.

"Jesus, you look like a vampire." He pulls back in mock fear. "Speaking of which, why the hell haven't you done vampires? Seems like you'd be a natural."

"I was in a vampire movie once," I say. "Like seven years ago, before they were all the rage. Who knew? I did get to die twice: a human death and a vampire death."

"Stake through the heart?"

"Followed by decapitation. They were taking no chances."

"Nice," he says appreciatively. "Still, we have an excellent death to add to your repertoire today."

"Bring it. Soon I'll have much bigger fish to fry."

"So I hear," he says, eying me speculatively, "so I hear." And suddenly he's moving away, shouting instructions to the crew. And I head off to change into my hipster-hippie-seductress clothes. A real triumph for wardrobe, that look.

Later, when I'm snooping around the apparently abandoned house on the outskirts of town where my psychic powers have led me, I'm wearing thigh-high suede boots and a flowery, fringy dress that manages to be both shapeless and totally revealing as I peer under the about-to-collapse front porch and through a little crack in the foundation that gives me a peephole into the cellar, where I have reason to believe the missing little girl is being held. Just as I glimpse a makeshift bed and a telltale pair of Mary Janes (and push aside a sudden vision of the little room where my twin bed and Lois's stood side by side), I hear the snap of a twig behind me. Before I can extricate my heels from the soft ground and run away, someone wraps a burly tattooed arm around my neck and presses a knife to my throat. "Well, if it ain't Glinda the good witch," drawls a cruel voice, obviously the voice of someone capable of doing really terrible things to little girls and probably sexy psychics, too. "I had a feeling you might be stopping by."

I wrench my head around to confront him. I'm afraid, but also defiant. The murderer is played with excessive gusto by an old character actor who's been kind of a pain in the ass to work with because he thinks he's above this show. Maybe he's bitter. All I know is he's pressing the dull blade of the prop knife into my tender, defenseless neck a little harder than he really needs to. "You won't get away with it, you know," I protest. "You should let me help you." Meanwhile, with one hand I'm trying to sneak my little revolver from my boot. With one swift motion of his wrist, he slashes the blade across my throat, practically from ear to ear. It's his trademark. It happens very quickly—it's meant to catch the viewer off guard; you're supposed to be expecting me to get a few more sentences in, for him to get trapped in conversation and maybe reveal something, for him to throw me in the cellar with the girl and take care of me later. But no, he means business, he doesn't waste time. You can't appeal to his better nature because he doesn't have one.

That's not it for me, though. For the rest of the show I play dead as he drags the psychic's body around. He lines his trunk with plastic and then stuffs me in it; he drives to Detective LaRock's house and arranges me artistically in the yard. Later I hang out in the morgue, freezing my ass off, lying naked on the table while I am discussed. Aside from my neck, which keeps needing touch-ups from makeup (they're worried that it looks more like a jelly doughnut than a slit throat, so they keep tweaking it), I think I look pretty good.

I'm a good corpse. I'm a pro, if nothing else. Everyone knows it.

That's what Tomm tells me later. He and Detective LaRock and I go out for a celebratory drink after we wrap. "You're a pro, Chloe. There'll always be work for a girl like you."

We're sharing a platter of oysters and a very nice bottle of wine. "God, who ever said there wouldn't?" I ask, annoyed. It's as if he's got Glinda the good witch's death confused with the death of my career. I slurp another oyster from its jagged shell. It's brilliantly cold and briny, and it helps convince me that I really am invincible. "You realize I have a movie coming up, right? Just because your stupid writers couldn't think of anything more creative to do with me than kill me doesn't mean I'm screwed, for fuck's sake. No offense, but—"

"Of course not," says LaRock, whose name is actually Murphy. "Touchy! Although I was kind of thinking they might bring you on as a regular. Oh well. You'll make a good cop, won't she,

Tomm? Like Charlize Theron in—what the hell—*Monster,* was it? They'll make you all ugly and shit, and then you'll win an Oscar." He douses an oyster with hot sauce, tips it back. I see his attention shift back to himself. That's how it is with Murphy. "That'll never happen to me, unfortunately. I'm too pretty to play ugly. Joke!" he adds quickly, checking to make sure we didn't take him seriously. Tonight I'm okay with changing the subject to him. It makes it easier to shake off the weird sense that Murphy and Tomm both feel a kind of pity for me.

Tomm has to meet someone else, so he leaves after a bit, but Murphy talks me into another bottle of wine and gets sentimental. "I'll miss the witty banter," he says wistfully. He leans forward and touches my knee. His eyes are a pale, clear blue, like a swimming pool in the morning, reflecting nothing at all. I'm pretty sure that on some level he's playing Detective LaRock, although he does manage to use my actual name. "Seriously, Chloe. How come you and I never—"

I gently remove his hand from my knee and pat his very nicely sculpted cheek. "Because I'm almost thirty," I say, mock-sadly. "The same age as you. If we'd met when I was eighteen, who knows?"

"Chloe Savage at eighteen," he says. "Hmmm. No, let's make you seventeen. Oh, man!" Murphy is regularly seen in the company of a never-ending succession of girls who are very young and very pretty. This doesn't make him unusual, in this world, although from my perspective it does make him a little boring.

"You're sweet when you're drunk," I tell him. "Sweet like a maraschino cherry, though: a little fake, my darling. I'm sure you were seducing sixth graders when you were eighteen."

And then I make a point of showing that I'm ready to go, because I realize suddenly that I have been alone for long enough that Murphy (à la Detective LaRock) actually seems strangely appealing, and even if I'm old, by his standards, I'm pretty sure I could make him love me for a few hours a night . . . But no. Bad idea. We get the check. Murphy pays, thank God. Out into the summer night. Still hot. The air is thick, as thick as air can be. I kiss him chastely and go home, a little tipsy but not very, congratulating myself on a well-managed evening.

Lois

I make a deal with Sean—or rather, I pretend to make a deal with him. He is under the impression that we made a deal, that he has me scared, that I am scrambling for a compromise.

What I've realized is that I don't have to compromise. I have promised to tell him what he wants to know in return for silence and good behavior—but what good is a promise like that? Surely I am justified, at this point, in taking reasonable precautions to protect myself. To protect myself is to protect my story. My stories, really—and the boundaries between them.

In other words, I have decided to lie. To invent. Oddly enough, I find myself looking forward to it. I invented one version of the story when I wrote the book, obviously. I welcome the chance to craft another. I think I know how to tell the tale in a way that will satisfy him.

I haven't yet told Sean that I know who he is, but I am almost certain he realizes that I've put the pieces together. Surely he wanted me to guess. But I sense that we have tacitly agreed not to speak of it—not yet, at least. He has been more subdued, less antagonistic. Not deferential, quite, but something almost approaching it. It's a pleasant change.

• • •

I meet Sean at the bowling alley. I peeked in a few days ago to make sure it was suitable, and in fact the setting is ideal. Adjacent to the lanes is a slightly grungy bar and restaurant; respectable enough for kids' birthday parties in the afternoon but sufficiently seedy to drown your sorrows without fear of judgment. The patrons aren't all bowlers; the place clearly has regulars, people who not only don't mind but maybe even perversely appreciate the faded carpet, the long sticky bar, the stridently unpretentious selection of beer. They mustn't mind the constant drone of balls, the intermittent smack of contact, falling pins. Maybe it drowns out something they don't want to hear, or don't want to think. They look like people who might have a thing or two to forget.

Which is perfect. I arrive early in the evening, postchildren but well before things are likely to get really depressing. I get there first, by design; I order a Coke and select a table in a corner. I angle my chair so that I have a clear view of the room, but with my chair poised to swing toward the corner when Sean has taken his seat. I'm wearing jeans, a black sweater; my sharp dark bob falls loosely around my face. At a glance I don't think most people would even recognize me. But it's a chance I'd prefer not to take; with my back to the room, my secret rendezvous with a male student is less likely to be observed.

Sean slouches in a few minutes late, sporting his usual trench coat, grimy locks, and ashtray aura. He mumbles "Professor" as he drops into his chair and orders a Coke from the waitress, though judging from the way his hands are shaking he seems to be sufficiently caffeinated already.

"Come here much?" he asks, looking past me. He's twining his straw, still in its paper wrapper, around his fingers.

"Never. I'm expanding my horizons. So tell me: What is it that you want to know? Why are you so interested in my life?" I've decided to play along, for now, with the pretense that I accept his account of his motives, that I don't yet know who he really is.

He starts winding his straw in the other direction. "I want to know what it was like. Being abducted and all. The real story. Not the one in the papers. Not like you told it in your book. Which I read, but I don't believe it. I want the real story."

"Two things," I begin. I intend to keep this businesslike. "First: The book isn't supposed to be true, obviously. It's fiction, with a little bit of a foundation in the truth. You know how movies will sometimes say at the beginning, *adapted from a true* story? Which isn't quite the same as saying *based on*? Well, that's what the book is. And second: Why do you want to know? What is it to you? How do you plan to use this information?" His straw wrapper is disintegrating already, plastic elbows poking through the flimsy paper. He's folding it into a clumsy sort of accordion.

"Okay. Number one? Of course I know the book is supposed to be fiction. Though I think it's kind of interesting that you thought you could get away with telling the truth if it was, you know, *packaged* as a lie. I mean, as fiction. But I don't believe what you guys told the cops, either. What it says in all the newspaper articles about him, like, never doing anything to you, about nothing happening. I think it has to be more complicated than you told it. Otherwise it just doesn't make sense. A middle-aged dude kidnaps two girls and keeps them in the woods for six weeks? You made it sound like freakin' summer camp or something. I don't buy it. And question two: I already told you. Material. It's for this book I'm writing. Research."

"Right. You never told me what kind of book, though. And he wasn't middle-aged, by the way."

"Whatever. Close enough. And what do you mean, what kind of book? Like your book. A book book. Like we read in class, only better."

"Fiction, then."

"Yeah. Like a novel."

"But what does that have to do with me?"

"I need to know what it was really like to have that happen. I mean, I can make it up, but how do I know I have it right? I don't want it to be lame or, like—candy-assed. It has to be believable." He takes a drink of his Coke, then wipes his mouth on the back of his hand. "I'll change stuff, obviously," he reassures me. "Like you did. No one will guess where I got it. I just want it to be realistic. Unlike yours."

"As I already pointed out, my book wasn't meant to be believed," I remind him. "It was fiction. Genre fiction, at that. It was intended to be suspenseful, chilling. The narrative obeys certain conventions."

"Yeah, but how can it be chilling if it isn't believable? Even in the eighteenth century people thought fiction had to be—what?—plausible, right, like you said in class."

His reference to the eighteenth century catches me off guard, and I find myself laughing. "You're thinking of Henry Fielding's argument that fiction should adhere to a standard of probability, rather than possibility. He was mostly objecting to the supernatural, and divine intervention. But even if we stick with your word, how do we determine what's *plausible,* anyway? What's plausible to me might not be plausible to you. What you're willing to believe depends on how you see the world, to a certain extent, doesn't it?"

He hoists his coat up around his shoulders, suddenly restless. "Whatever. I feel like I'm in class. So are you gonna tell me the real story, or are you gonna pretend there isn't one? Because I thought we had an arrangement, and if we don't, then I've got better stuff to do."

"Fine." I reach out and gingerly pick up his tortured straw with the tips of two fingers and place it on the table behind us. "Distracting," I explain. I take a deep breath.

"We weren't the only girls," I begin. "There were others. Lots of others."

I let my hair fall forward and look down at the scarred table. I haven't really planned the story; I'm testing my powers of invention. I spin it as I go. After a few minutes, I stop and say pointedly: "Do you want to take notes or something? If this is research, as you called it?" He's gazing out over my right shoulder. He looks attentive, but I can't be sure; his face is less communicative than usual.

"No," he says. There's a little contempt in his voice. "I remember everything."

Who says that? It is what *I* have always said; it's my gift and also a source of torment, that I forget nothing. I don't like the suggestion that Sean and I have something in common.

"Fine." I choose not to believe him; he's boasting, as usual. His academic performance this semester has not supported his claim to a prodigious memory.

What was his mother like? I wonder. Zed left her (or she left him, I suppose) not long after the child was born. Sean wouldn't have seen much of him, most likely. Still, the mother interests me. What kind of woman would Zed have chosen? Did he love her?

I have a story to tell, I remind myself. I sip my Coke and concentrate.

"He brought them to us. He kept them in the cellar, a dark, dank, low-ceilinged place. We went down and read to them sometimes. A lot of them were younger—seven, eight. At night they came out to play with us. They were chained, of course, so they couldn't escape, but they had plenty of room to run around. They could play hide-and-seek, dance around the fire . . . They weren't always the same girls, though; sometimes there would be a new one, and one of the others would be gone. We thought they had gone home, or so we convinced ourselves. But later I realized that they couldn't have been allowed to go home; it wouldn't have been safe. We heard him go down there, sometimes, when he thought we were sleeping. But we knew better than to ask . . ." My voice trails off as if I am lost in my memory. I put a faraway look in my eyes, as if I am back in the past, hardly aware of the room around me.

Sean looks rapt.

I tell him about the traps Zed taught us to set. The deer we killed. The mournful cries that came sometimes from the woods, sometimes from the cellar. The time I awoke, strangely groggy, as if I had been drugged, and saw Carly May sleeping peacefully in the bed beside mine, her bloodstained hands curled against her chest. I am amazed by how easily the story flows. Maybe this is what the novel *should* have been like; maybe *Deep in the Woods* was, after all, too close to the truth. I list the herbs he taught us to look for in the woods, and their various properties. I describe cooking experiments and their effects on our guests in the cellar. I tell him about the garlands of flowers we wore in our hair when we danced naked in the moonlight and worry that I have gone too far, but Sean's face shows no sign that this is the case. I tell him of the promises we made: eternal secrecy, unwavering loyalty. I say we kept them.

Sean watches me closely, warily, his hands buried in his pockets. He is not by nature a trusting person, but I can see that he is inclined to believe me. And why not? It's improbable, my story, but hardly impossible. I say the children are runaways that he picks up on the streets of New York, which is why no one misses them, why they were never part of the official story.

After half an hour or so I cut myself off abruptly. "Is there more?" Sean demands.

"Of course there's more. We were there for six weeks, you know. Storytelling is about selection: what to tell, what not to tell. If I enumerate every single detail, it's not a story, it's a list."

"I don't care. I don't need you to tell me a story; I'm not a little kid. You're not tucking me in. I'm interviewing you. I want information. I don't have enough." And it's true, I think, jabbing at the ice at the bottom of my Coke with my straw; he looks hungry, as if I have unleashed some sort of unholy appetite. I'm amused by his smug assumption that he is the one in control here.

"Well, that's all for today, anyway," I say, pretending to compromise. "We can meet again if you want."

He does want. We make a date. As we are walking out—not together, exactly, but simultaneously—I see a group of women descending on the bowling alley from the parking lot, and I am dismayed to recognize Delia among them. She is wearing a bowling jacket. She looks surprised to see me, and I think she's about to speak when her glance flickers over to Sean. I see her decide to hold back whatever she had been about to say. She breezes past without acknowledging me.

What is she thinking? I am certain that she has misconstrued the situation—how could she not?—but I can't imagine what interpretation she has settled upon.

I put her out of my mind as I drive home; the glimmer of interest I once felt in her seems to have faded, and I am no longer tempted to ask her advice about my disturbed student. I settle down at my computer with Gary, whose peculiar desires are clearer to me every day. My fingers dance happily across the keyboard. A prolific little jig. This is how it's been going, lately. Gary is on the move at last, and he's tracking down the actress first.

Chloe

When I got a real modeling contract, after a flurry of brief gigs in Omaha (which is not exactly the fashion capital of the universe, as I knew even then), I went out to the farm for the first time in months. They hadn't invited me, and I hadn't gone. I bypassed the house and set out on the four-wheeler to find Daddy in the fields. He was rounding up cattle with Henry, the hired man, when I found him. It was spring, chilly and wet, but I remember thinking how happy Daddy looked until he saw me. He waved, though, and I watched for a while until he could get away.

From his expression as he came toward me through the muck, I could tell he assumed my unexpected appearance must mean trouble. Why else would I show up? That made me sad, as sad as anything that had happened yet. Fucking Gail had poisoned him—taken away the one parent I had left, the one person who actually loved me.

I told him about Chicago, the agency that had signed me, the work I had lined up. He listened for a minute, his gaze focused on the low hills in the distance, and then held up his hand, palm facing me, like he was a traffic cop and I was an oncoming truck. And then he said the worst thing of all: "Talk to your ma about that stuff. That's her area of expertise, not mine."

"My ma?" I repeated. "My *ma*? Jesus Christ. Gail is not my mother. I'm telling *you* because I want you to know, because I actually care what you think—"

"There's no need to use that kind of language with me, young lady. And she's the only mother you've got. I don't see why you want to go to Chicago. Seems like you ought to graduate from high school first. Why else did you win all that scholarship money if you weren't going to go to college? But then, what do I know? I don't know why you want to hurt your little brothers, either, or why you want to run with those kids your grandma's been telling me about. Seems I don't know much about you anymore. But modeling? You want to talk to somebody about that, you talk to her, your ma. Now, I've got work to do. You go on back to the house." I started to correct his terminology again, but he stopped me. "She's my wife, Carly May, and she's your brothers' mother. As far as I'm concerned, that makes her your ma." Even if he hadn't already been moving away, kicking a small rock with the toe of one scuffed workboot, it would have been clear from his tone that this was final.

I stood for a minute, the chilly spring wind whipping my hair in front of my face. A hot pressure deep inside my eyes made me afraid I was about to cry. I turned away. By then I felt a little numb. Daddy didn't even watch me leave.

I drove the four-wheeler back as fast as it would go, jolting over the rough ground, flying over ruts, thinking, *This is the last time I will ever be a farm girl from Nebraska.* I abandoned the ATV behind a shed, snuck around the barn closest to the house, and ran straight to the beat-up old Mustang I had borrowed from Scott, hoping like hell no one would see me. But Gail was watching for me at the kitchen door, and she got to me before I made it into the car.

"What are you doing out here without letting us know, Carly May?" She was wearing a lavender pantsuit and had recently had her hair dyed a color she liked to call auburn. She had on full makeup, and she looked completely insane. While she was demanding what I was doing there, like it wasn't the house I had grown up in, she looked up at the windows of my little brothers' rooms, projecting fake fear. You'd have thought I was violating a restraining order.

"I just wanted to talk to Daddy," I said, politely enough. "I'm going now. See? Nothing to worry about." I held up my empty hands. No tiaras.

"There's no need to trouble your dad when he's working. You got a problem, missy, you come to me." No one else was around, so she wasn't even bothering to pretend to be nice. I got to see the true, unadulterated Gail. Lucky me. I watched the heels of her cheap pumps sinking into the mud in the yard, which cheered me up a little.

"Like that's going to happen," I said, flicking my gaze up and down her gaudy form in a way I knew made her feel old and ugly and judged. "You *are* my problem, Gail." I brushed past her, yanked the car door open, slammed it behind me. I rolled the window down as I turned the key. "Or you *were* my problem." With that I stepped on the gas hard in reverse and quickly spun around, doing my best to peel out. It was a good car for that, though it wasn't good for much else. Scott spent half his life fixing it. But I saw in the rearview mirror that the back tires had kicked up plenty of smelly spring mud, splattering Gail's hideous pants. I couldn't have planned it better.

When I moved to Chicago I sent Gail a portfolio shot I had defaced (mustache, black teeth—very mature; I'm not even sure what point I wanted to make). I left an address with Grandma Mabel, but I knew it would only be temporary. For Daddy I left nothing. I didn't know what to say, and I was hurt. He had given up on me, it seemed, which didn't feel fair.

Within a few weeks in Chicago, I moved again, into an apartment with a bunch of other girls. I didn't let my family know, but at that point they could still have tracked me down pretty easily if they had really wanted to. Which apparently they didn't. A few months after that, I left for New York, and I legally changed my name to Chloe Savage, which I'd already begun using professionally. I was done with Carly May. After a year in New York, I moved out to LA. I haven't seen anyone from Nebraska or heard from them, not one of them, since I left.

Until now. Looking out my back window at the tiny garden my neighbor planted out back, I hold the envelope like it might explode. In big, loopy, childish handwriting, the letter is addressed to Carly May "Chloe" Savage, and I wonder how Gail arrived at that particular hybrid. She wanted the letter to get to me, but she also wanted to make a point. "Fuck," I say loudly to the empty apartment. "What the fuck." It's not a thick envelope; I guess there's a single sheet of paper inside, folded into thirds.

Whatever Gail has to say, I'm pretty sure I don't want to hear it. But I can't just throw away the envelope, either. I put it on my dresser, neatly in the center.

Lois

About two weeks after the rendezvous in the bowling alley, I'm in the coffee shop grading a stack of papers when Delia swoops down on me out of nowhere. And I do mean swoops, as if I have been chosen for dinner by a powerful bird of prey. There's trippy, slightly eerie ambient music playing in the background. An appropriate soundtrack.

She wastes no time. "I've seen you three times now with that student," she says. "The one you originally told me was harassing you. What are you up to?"

I put my pen down and take a sip of my coffee. There's no pretense of friendship here. This is something else entirely. Which gives me permission to respond accordingly.

"I'm not sure that's any of your business." I keep my voice as level and neutral as I can make it. She's wearing a long Indian skirt of cheap printed cotton and lots of clunky jewelry; her face looks haggard. How could I ever have thought we would be friends?

She sits opposite me, not waiting for an invitation, and fixes her big dark bird-eyes on me. "There's something about you I don't quite get. Something that doesn't fit." Is she talking to herself? I wonder. I lower my pen to the page in front of me and scribble a note.

"You've been meeting with him alone," she continues, undeterred by my rudeness. "You have to admit that it looks very strange. If he's threatening you, you know, you have to tell someone. I mean, if you think you're in any kind of danger, it would be a huge mistake to try to deal with him on your own. But honestly, what I find myself wondering is—who's stalking who?—or should I say whom," she adds, lightening her tone ever so slightly for the first time since she plunked herself down. "Who's stalking whom."

"That's a rather offensive thing to imply." I wipe up a tiny coffee spill with my napkin.

"I'm not implying anything. I'm asking you a direct question, which you aren't answering. But I've seen a lot of crazy things in my line of work. And there's something off about this. Something that worries me. And I do know that kid, actually. I didn't want to say anything, but now I think maybe I should. A girl accused him of stalking her a few months back. Nothing ever happened—there was no proof, and eventually she said he just stopped. But he seriously creeped her out, with good reason. And I believed her, I might as well tell you. Also with good reason."

I make another mark on the essay I'm grading. It's a hint she can't possibly misinterpret, and I feel a twinge of guilt; I have nothing against Delia, after all, and I'm sure she means well. But I resent the earnestness of her tone. I am not enjoying this conversation, to the extent that it is a conversation.

Delia is undaunted. "You know, I've worked with a lot of women who've experienced some sort of trauma. Often as children. If I had to guess . . . no, never mind. You'll just get pissed off. But remember: if you want to talk—or if you decide you need help—you know where I am. And I'd stay away from that kid if I were you. Seriously. He's bad news."

She gives me another of her unnervingly penetrating looks, as if she can read something in my face that I'm not even aware of. Then she stalks out, the door jangling shut behind her. I don't like the idea that she came into the coffee shop purely to deliver this warning. And how did she see me three times with Sean? I only noticed her the first time we met, at the bowling alley.

As for the stalking bit? Sean has a skulking gait that makes him look like a stalker, and his customary attire doesn't help. But it's a small town, and girls can be paranoid; someone could easily have misconstrued multiple Sean sightings, however coincidental, as stalking. Nothing was proven, after all, as even Delia had to admit.

Am I under surveillance?

• • •

I rent *For Worse* the day it comes out on DVD and invite Brad over to watch it. We get Chinese takeout.

Brad lets himself in, and I hear him stomping up the stairs. He arrives smelling noticeably of beer. "Went out with some guys from History," he says, taking his coat off and tossing it on an antique chair. I pick it up and hang it in the closet.

"Have a seat," I say soothingly. He seems riled up—or what counts as riled up in Brad terms. Visibly ruffled, shall we say. "You smell a bit like a frat boy." I arrange the food on the table and bring him a small glass of wine. "Drink this. But not fast. You'll want your wits about you. Tonight we have the final installment in the never-before-seen, soon-to-sweep-the-country, exhaustive Chloe Savage film series!"

"You know," Brad says, "you should really keep your downstairs door locked. Anyone could just waltz right in."

"Like whom? Besides, I keep the upstairs door locked. As long as my apartment is safe, the entryway is irrelevant, don't you think?"

"No," he says stubbornly. "The upstairs door is flimsy. Anyone could kick it down. You could do it yourself, I bet."

"But there's no doorbell downstairs," I point out. "And I have a hard time hearing a knock from up here. What if someone came to see me, and I wasn't expecting them?"

It's a weak argument. Brad knows he's the only one who comes to see me. The truth is impossible to explain, though. When the downstairs door is locked I feel like a recluse. I might as well live on an island. I could die, and no one would find me for days. The unlocked door is a gesture of belonging. One locked door between me and the world is enough.

Brad tears the paper wrapper from his chopsticks. He is getting exasperated. "If someone were here, they would text you to come down."

"What if they didn't have my number?" *What if Carly May showed up at my door?* Could that be what I'm waiting for?

"So install a doorbell. Better yet, ask your landlady to do it."

I spoon rice onto my plate. "What's gotten into you? Has something happened? I hardly recognize you. And you don't seem nearly excited enough about this movie."

"So maybe I'm not," he says darkly—and, as far as I can tell, absurdly. He serves himself distractedly, glopping heaps of everything on his plate. "Maybe I actually want to be serious for once. Or *maybe*"—he takes a gulp of his wine—"*maybe* I just saw that Sean kid hanging around outside when I came in. And maybe I saw him lurking out there a few nights ago, too, when I happened to be driving by."

"Okay, okay! I'll lock the door. I'll lock it right now, all right? Will that make you happy? And I'll talk to the landlady about a doorbell, I promise. Better? Jesus. And Brad, don't worry about Sean. He's a weird kid, but he's harmless, I've decided. He probably lives in the neighborhood."

Brad pokes at his rice, carves a crater down the middle, watches it fill with brown sauce. Finally he says slowly: "You're a mysterious woman, Lois Lonsdale. I hang out with you all the time, and I swear, sometimes I wonder if I know you at all."

"Of course you do." I wave my chopsticks at him. "Now eat. Watch. Prepare yourself for *La Sauvage*."

"It's *le sauvage*. It's masculine."

"Oh, shut up, I know. Don't be such a pedant." Actually, though, I'm relieved. Brad sounds more like himself. I hope his mood has passed; loner or not, I'd rather not lose my only ally.

I have been telling stories to psychiatrists and psychotherapists of various descriptions for years. Not in this town, though; it didn't strike me as advisable to acquire a shrink in a small college town, where you would have the same therapist as practically everyone you knew, and you would probably run into her at the grocery store, the coffee shop, the movies. I like to keep my life more compartmentalized than that.

Oddly enough, I haven't missed it. I relinquished long ago the idea that a psychiatrist might *help* me in any way, might cure me, improve my ability to function. I am not sick, for one thing. And I am extremely functional. A very strange thing happened to me, long, long ago, that's all. That does not constitute illness. I don't dispute that it has shaped me, helped to make me who I am. But so what? Must that process be endlessly probed, analyzed, investigated? To what end?

No one has ever suggested that Richardson's Pamela was traumatized, despite the amount of time she was forced to bed down with Mrs. Jewkes and suffer her master's peculiar assaults, despite the current trendiness of trauma theory in literary studies. No, Pamela just gets on with her life. As have I.

The truth is, I only kept up the therapy as long as I did because I enjoyed the audience: a weekly storytelling forum, an open mic at which I was always the featured performer and the audience was small, rapt, and sworn to secrecy. I liked to talk it over: how we spent our days, Carly and Zed and I, what we read, what we ate. I stuck to the truth, but I didn't dig too deep. I have no idea whether it did me any good, therapeutically speaking, but it gave me pleasure. If anything, that's what I miss.

And now I have Sean. I can't imagine that this book he plans to write will ever materialize—and if it did, who would read it? The boy can hardly string two coherent sentences together. I'm safe. I can tell him whatever I want, blend fact and fiction with abandon. This is a closed circle. No stories escape.

Sean's own story remains something of a mystery; he's extremely guarded. But the more I see of him, the better sense I have of what it must have been like to be Zed's son. To lose him so dramatically: first to his parents' breakup, then to me and Carly, finally to a bullet; to grow up with horror stories instead of a father. Sean is permanently damaged; something is awry in that boy. I'm lying when I tell Brad he's harmless. But he will not hurt me. He needs me; I can feed him stories until he explodes. And

I think he is on some sort of threshold. I can't say how I know this, but I am convinced that I do. I think he will find that it is time to take the next step.

As Gary is doing now.

Should I be afraid? Am I unleashing some kind of monster? Should I warn Carly? Chloe, I mean?

If I am honest, I think that what I want most is to find out what happens next. How long will mere words be enough—for Gary or for Sean? Their trajectories are coming into alignment.

For Worse is a good movie—Chloe's best, maybe. Brad enjoys it in spite of himself. We polish off a couple of bottles of wine and an obscene amount of Chinese food—I can't remember when I last ate so much. He hugs me before he leaves, and I feel dangerously close to crying. "See, I'm not a monster," I hear myself saying into Brad's shoulder.

"No one ever said you were a monster," he says, sounding surprised. He smooths my hair, gives my back a couple of staccato thumps intended to be reassuring.

But I feel as if someone has said precisely that. The question is who, and why.

Chloe

I haven't taken every role I've ever been offered; I don't mean to give the impression that I am a complete whore, career-wise. I've turned down plenty of parts—one, for instance, in an unbelievably stupid romantic-comedy-slash-art-heist pic that actually went on to make a ridiculous amount of money. I don't do nudity—or

I haven't; I would, for the right role—but that movie would have required me to cavort naked around a museum for absolutely no good reason. Essential to the plot? Um, no. Essential to the development of the character? Only if it was essential that the character be a dimwit exhibitionist floozy. Which apparently it was. (The actress who did take the part has played pretty much nothing but dimwit-exhibitionist-floozy roles since then. Sure, she's a household name, but so is Velveeta.)

I do have standards—I really do—though I also take plenty of jobs purely for a paycheck. I'm not ashamed. I need my paychecks. And that's why this afternoon finds me posing with a shampoo bottle, gently shaking my golden curls while smiling seductively at the camera. "Try it again," orders the director. "I want your dress to swirl more when you make that turn." Next, he complains that a strand of my hair has slipped behind my back due to overenthusiastic twirling. The hair people rush in and smooth my outrageously silken locks. (Whatever they've done to my hair has nothing to do with Sauvage shampoo, just so you know. It's all a big fat lie.) Somebody tweaks an eyelash that has apparently gotten stuck to its neighbor. Then we do it again. And again. "Honey, stop acting," Sebastian yells at one point, and I know that *honey* is not what he means. "For fuck's sake. This is about pretty. Be pretty. Be sexy. Don't act. Be. It's about your fucking hair. Don't upstage the hair." By *act,* I think he means *look human*. Humanity is not the point. Personality is not the point. I get it. "Am I crazy," he asks the room, "or did we have this conversation last time? Is it too much to ask her to remember that *one . . . little . . . thing?*" His voice rises as he gestures dramatically at his largely imaginary audience. I flip him off. I know exactly what I can get away with.

This is all to be expected. We shoot a new ad every few months, and he's always like this. At first I thought it meant he would ditch me, but no, it's just how he operates. At least with women; I've heard he's different with men. Most of the other people on the set are ignoring him. Occasionally someone snickers.

We're shooting blue screen. Later I will appear in front of footage of wild animals I have never seen. Lions, mostly, with flowing manes. Originally there was talk of shooting on location—jetting off to Africa or wherever to frolic with actual lions. But in the end they scaled back the budget, and I stuck with them anyway. I am well paid to put up with Sebastian's abuse. "Send me a goddamned model," he keeps muttering. "Fucking actresses. You take a model, she knows it's all about the product. Even third-rate actresses cherish the misguided notion that they matter."

"Fuck you," I say sweetly, smiling vacantly at my shampoo bottle. "Sauvage," I whisper at the end, as my swishing hair settles back into place. I whisper "sauvage" dozens of times. Savage shampoo? It doesn't even fucking make sense. I don't knock it, though; if it helps people remember who I am, it's okay with me. They pulse my name at the bottom of the screen toward the end of the spot; the assumption is that your average viewer might think I look kind of vaguely familiar but will need help remembering my name. Savage, Sauvage. *Get it?*

Sometimes this is what being an actress is like.

"Prick," I say, when I finally stalk off the set, and he smacks me on the ass with his clipboard. He likes me well enough, when all is said and done.

"Pervert," I add, and he lets me have the last word.

Lois

Brad persuades me to attend the end-of-the-semester English department faculty party as we're walking to the parking lot after work one evening. I would have been happy to skip it, but he says that isn't an option. "We're new faculty. Parties are like meetings—they're mandatory."

"Which makes them, by definition, not fun. And therefore not really parties." My defeat is a foregone conclusion, but I can't help putting up a bit of a fight. I don't see the logic of coerced socialization with my colleagues. Surely we see one another quite enough.

"They've hired a bartender," Brad points out as we reach my car. "At least there'll be real drinks."

"Oh, good. Now it sounds like a frat party."

"Oh, come on. You know you love a good frat party as much as the next girl."

I scowl at Brad. Our relationship hasn't changed, at least not on the surface. But there's been a dark undercurrent ever since the night we watched *For Worse*. We might have established a truce by the end of the evening, but Brad had already thrown down a sort of gauntlet, and there it still lies. The gauntlet, that is—which is, of course, a glove. We are ignoring it, but we know it's there; how could we fail to? *Gauntlet: gaucherie, gesneriad, gemmule, gendarmerie.*

I ignore the gauntlet, rehearse G words, and agree to go to the party.

It's true that Sean has taken to loitering in this part of town. I'd noticed his shadowy lurking before Brad brought it up, and I tried to intuit his motivation. The better I come to understand Gary (who is currently stalking a lovely actress who is, as yet, unaware of his presence), the more insight I think I have into Sean, and vice versa. Sean's behavior worries me a little more than I am willing to admit. Still, I believe that I can keep unfurling stories for him for as long as he needs them, and I do not think he would risk jeopardizing the stories. They're all he has—all he will ever have—of *him.*

A few days ago I sat with Sean in a Pizza Hut on the outskirts of town. The restaurant seemed old and faded, and it was almost empty; a couple of families squeezed into booths could not have been less interested in us, and they made enough noise to cover anything odd that we might have said. Both of us were mashing our Cokes, choked with crushed ice, with our straws.

"Sometimes he invited us to sleep in his bed," I told him, keeping my voice low. Sean crossed his arms over his chest and slouched into the corner of the booth, listening without comment. "We wore long, old-fashioned white nightgowns. He gave us knives with which to defend ourselves. He said he wouldn't touch us, not in a bad way, but that if we felt threatened it was only right that we should protect ourselves. We curled up on either side of him like kittens. He took showers all the time, several times a day, and always smelled like soap and shampoo, but the bed itself was a little musty. We liked it, though. He slept flat on his back and never snored, although sometimes he talked in his sleep. I used to lie awake listening to him, trying to make sense of his ramblings. 'The wolves are here,' he would say. 'The squirrels in the attic are dead. Soon we'll ride the ferris wheel—we have tickets.' I always meant to write down his words, but in the morning I would forget.

"One night I heard something different from the usual sounds and jolted awake. Carly was sitting up, and she had her knife in her hand. She was holding it out in front of her. He was awake, too, still lying down, and their eyes sparkled at each other. I wondered if my eyes sparkled too, if my eyes were as pretty as theirs. Carly stretched out her arm and brought the point of the knife to his chest. Although it was dark, the moon shone into the room that night, and so I could see his flesh yield to the blade. She pressed harder and drew the blade downward. Blood sprang gently from his chest, amid the sparse curling dark hairs. Just the slightest trickle. After a while Carly lay down again and as far as I know they went back to sleep, but I was still awake, listening to their breathing. I've never slept well."

I don't plan these stories in advance; I tell them as they come to me. They come with such startling ease that they almost feel true. They frighten me, and I wonder which of us gets more pleasure from them.

Sean suddenly reached into his pocket, startling me, as if a spell had been broken. He opened his hand to reveal a knife—not a jackknife, exactly, though similarly constructed. It looked meaner; less . . . domestic. "Was it this kind of knife?" he asked.

"No," I said sternly, taken aback. This was not in the script. "It wasn't like that."

"I wish I could see what kind of knife it was," he said, wistfully.

"We'll see." *Maybe I can find a plausible picture,* I thought. I don't know very much about knives.

"I'd really like to see it," he repeated.

"The knife doesn't really matter. That's not the point. A knife is a knife. What matters is that he gave them to us. What matters is what she did with hers."

"A knife is a knife?" he scoffed, as if no one had ever said anything more ridiculous. "Spoken by someone who knows *nothing* about knives."

Most likely he was posturing. But I didn't like this talk of knives. Even though, arguably, I was the one who started it.

There's a knife store in town. Guns and Knives. It's next door to a shoe repair shop and across from a bakery. The next day I went for a walk and made a point of cruising past the window of Guns and Knives. I glanced at the displays, feeling too exposed to enter. This would require a field trip. I was thinking of Gary; Gary would have a knife, and I would need to find an appropriate knife for him. I considered doing my research on the Internet, but I didn't want to trigger offers from crazy white supremacist militia groups or get myself on an FBI list.

Which is why, the Saturday after Pizza Hut, I find myself in a huge sporting goods store in Binghamton, an hour's drive from campus. It's possible to shop for perfectly harmless things here—

tents and sleeping bags, baseball gloves, fishing tackle, camouflage outerwear—but the deadly weapons section dominates the store. There's one wall of guns, another of bows and arrows, and several cases full of knives. Neatly dressed young men stand behind the counters, looking comically incongruous. As I approach a knife case, one of them offers to help me. He calls me ma'am. "Just looking," I mutter, as if I'm perusing a display of watches or cupcakes rather than assessing the merits of five-inch blades as opposed to four inches, serrated versus straight, fixed or folding. I'm attracted to a set of throwing knives, which look a lot like daggers and seem to belong more to the world of ornate costume dramas than a contemporary world in which people actually find things to *do* with these malevolent objects. I might have been inclined to argue, until now, that an object in itself cannot be malevolent. Looking at the weapons before me, though, I am convinced otherwise. These aren't neutral instruments, equally useful in the service of good or evil depending upon the disposition of their possessors. No. Despite their neat classifications—camping, tactical, hunting, military, the vague "outdoors"—these are designed to rip, pierce, skin, sever, disembowel. These are cruel instruments. I force myself to inspect them all. What disturbs me most is their aesthetic pretension: their graceful curves, sleek handles, tooled sheaths.

Eventually I withdraw my phone from my purse, pretend I am texting someone, and surreptitiously take a picture of a sleek black bowie knife that costs over two hundred dollars. In the back of my mind is the comforting thought that Sean would be unable to afford such a knife. I can visualize it tucked in Gary's back pocket. It is perfect.

The nice young man at the register is watching me, frankly curious. I replace my phone in my purse and drift out of the store.

From there I drive to the nearby mall, feeling as though I have earned some form of indulgence. It's not the world's most impressive mall, but today I don't care. I wander aimlessly through the

Gap, Bath & Body Works, Victoria's Secret, awash in colors and textures and mall smells and piped-in music, thinking desperately about nothing at all. Trying to shut down the part of my mind that insists that this behavior is alarmingly irrational, that perhaps Delia is right to be concerned. *I know what I'm doing,* I argue, trying on dresses. *I'm a writer; it's research.* The dresses are all too big.

Brad comes to pick me up the night of the party. I invite him in for a pre-party drink, an absolutely necessary preliminary for departmental social gatherings. He comes in, removes his jacket, and drapes it across the back of my plum-colored sofa. He accepts my offer of a gin and tonic and then looks around, clearly disconcerted. "Looks like you've had your nose to the grindstone," he remarks, and I detect an odd note of caution in his voice. "Grading? Some new research project?"

"What do you mean?"

"Ah . . . the clutter? Disarray? I've never seen so much as a decorative pillow out of place here. I always feel like I should take my shoes off and be careful not to touch anything. But this is—a slightly different aesthetic."

I glance around my apartment, my eyes registering all of the familiar shapes and colors, the imperfections in the woodwork, the soft lamplight. For a moment I don't even know what he means. Then, for a flash—not more—I see the room as he sees it: stacks of papers, books facedown on the floor, mugs here and there with tea bag strings drooping from their mouths, a sweatshirt on one chair. Crooked paintings. Dust. General untidiness.

"I've been busy." Since when is it acceptable to walk into someone's house and criticize her housekeeping? I imagine my mother's disapproval. (My mother, whom I haven't called in—how long?) "I've been working on all sorts of things," I say. "If you must know." My moment of clarity has passed; the apartment looks fine to me again. "How do I look? You haven't complimented me yet." I'm wearing a new dress, courtesy of my visit to the mall, and heels, which elevate me to Brad's shoulder. I've made an effort, in other words.

Brad stands back and surveys me mock-critically. "Stunning," he pronounces. "Except . . . just a second. Stand still." With an index finger he gently brushes the skin beneath one eye, then smudges it a little harder. I can feel his breath on my face. Finally I can't help taking a step backward. "What?" I hear the sharpness in my voice.

He shows me the blackened tip of his finger. "Just a little mascara," he explains apologetically. "You're good now."

I go into the bathroom to make sure, and touch up my face while I'm at it. "Let's get going," I call, dabbing my nose with powder, wondering if it's a trick of the light or if my face really does look sharper than usual, almost gaunt. Surely not. "The sooner we get there, the sooner we can leave."

"You have such a positive attitude," Brad grumbles. "It's what I love about you, of course."

We down our half-drunk drinks and go.

Although Brad's tone has been gently mocking, his eyes are worried; I resolve to behave so impeccably at the party that he will stop looking at me that way. Fortified with cocktails, I work the periphery of the gathering, holding intense conversations about the relevance of eighteenth-century literature to present-day undergraduates, the danger of regarding students as consumers and education as a product like any other, the evils of the Greek system, and the delights of camping in the Catskills (which I have not done and have no intention of doing). I converse animatedly with Will Duncan, the fiery chair of the department, a Miltonist; Allan Pearson, a hippie throwback who so worships Melville that he talks of little else; Jonathan Meredith, our lone African American prof, who is so wary of being regarded as a token hire that he will talk about absolutely anything but race, politics, or black writers; and Ellen Van Alstyne, a doddering romanticist and the first woman to be tenured at this institution. I drift out to the back patio (the house is a suburban monstrosity belonging to the chair), where the smokers have congregated. I don't smoke, but I gulp the cool spring night air and try to relax a little.

And that's when Kate sidles up to me. I love the word *sidles*, but you don't often see it in action. She sidles up alongside me and exclaims with surprise that she hasn't seen me for the longest time, that she's so sorry she hasn't had a chance to congratulate me on my book contract. This is ridiculous, since her office is down the hall from mine and we teach on the same days, but I respond pleasantly anyway. This is what it must be like to be Chloe: managing people so gracefully, moving effortlessly from one sparkling conversation to the next, distributing dazzling smiles like candy . . . but what is Kate saying? "I'm so pleased that you've resolved your difficulties with Sean McDougal," she remarks. "I saw you two downtown, deep in conversation. At first I couldn't believe it, but then I realized that you must have taken my comment about his needing extra help quite seriously, which is wonderful. In fact, I want to ask if you'd be willing to speak at one of our lunchtime faculty colloquia. I thought you might do an interesting presentation on the 'difficult' student. You could talk a little, for instance, about strategies for adapting your pedagogy to a particular student's needs—in this case, being willing to take it off campus . . . I really think it would be a fascinating discussion. And of course as a new faculty member it would be a smart move for you. We do value research here, of course, so we're all very pleased about—what is it, *Abduction in the British Novel*?—but at a school like this we're even more interested in things like innovative teaching methods, so you could see this as an opportunity to demonstrate that you're not so wrapped up in your research that you have no time for your students, which of course is a perception you really want to avoid."

She could *almost* have been sincere. An objective listener might have thought that she really was glad to have a chance to chat with me, that she was offering a few generous pointers to a junior colleague whose success she genuinely desired. I hear a dog bark in the distance. I notice the cigarette smell in the air. A burst of laughter tinkles from the house.

Then she delivers the final blow. "Of course, there's another angle you might consider, too," she continues, brushing an errant lock of brown hair back with a thin hand heavy with silver rings. "You could look at it as preempting potential criticism that might result from meeting with a student off campus, and a male student at that. This would be your chance to, you know, seize control of the discussion, to offer a constructive reading of the situation before a less constructive one gains any sort of ground. Which of course I'm sure you'd do a great job of."

If she says *of course* one more time—that insidiously coercive phrase—I might actually hit her. My ability to sparkle has well and truly deserted me. "What a fabulous idea," I mutter. "*Of course* I can't possibly do it before the beginning of the fall semester, since this one's practically over, which detracts somewhat from its value as a preemptive strategy. But sure, put me on the schedule. I'd love to do it."

"Oh good. And as for preemption—well, better late than never," she smiles, and I storm into the house, heading for the bar. *Bitch: bouillabaisse, bacchanal, bulbil, bibelot.* Wine. *Weigela, welkin, wittol.* Stop. I sip my wine and try to reel in my word-spinning mind. I try to look perfectly at ease even though I am standing alone in a room full of chattering pairs and groups. I glance around for Brad and don't see him.

But then there he is, suddenly beside me, looking concerned, divining somehow that I am not all right. "I need to get out of here," I whisper, and within minutes we're gone.

• • •

I recover swiftly enough. I don't care what Kate thinks, really; I imagine she was exaggerating my danger. But the sheer dislike in her sharp eyes unnerved me. "She's just jealous," Brad soothes me in the car, reminding me of my mother. He offers to come up, but I refuse. "I just need to sleep," I tell him. Instead I layer sweaters over my pretty dress and text Sean: "It's time to wrap this up. I am willing to meet with you once more." Then I settle myself at the computer with Gary, whose mind seems particularly dark tonight. Even the screen looks a little off. Somehow my font size has shrunk, and my margins have narrowed slightly. Odd. I adjust the settings and try to concentrate.

Gary appears almost immediately; I don't have to coax him onto the page. What Gary wants these days is answers, and the actress doesn't have any. She is in the trunk of his car. If she had answers, she would have given them up by now. She has actually been quite pleasant, considering. Gary finds this confusing because another thing he thinks he might want is revenge. He is feeling that possibility out, testing what it might be like to inflict suffering on the girls his father preferred to him, the girls his father died for. He wonders what kind of gratification that might offer. He is growing less certain, not more. Soon he will have both of them—both girls. He thinks of them as girls, just as he thinks of himself as something less than an adult, though he is old enough to drink, and they are nearly thirty.

Chloe

My progress north is not impressive. A long line of RVs crawls up the 101, stopping at every scenic vista, losing speed on the way up hills, and braking, for no apparent reason, on the way down.

There's no point in getting impatient, so I just chug along, flipping through stations on the radio, even stopping at a few "vistas" myself. I love the big weird rocks that jut out of the water on the West Coast. They make so little sense. Even if you try to think of some far-out geological explanation involving glaciers or volcanoes or meteorites, it's impossible to imagine how they got there. At one of the stops, I'm watching the waves smash against the rocks—and half keeping an eye on the crazy bastards in wet suits down below, who seem to be trying to find waves worth surfing on—when the woman beside me in head-to-toe turquoise pipes up.

"You wouldn't catch me out there, that's for sure," she says, waving her bangled wrist toward the ocean as if to include the whole damned thing. Just for a second I picture her surfing among the rocks, turquoise tracksuit and all.

"Me neither," I say agreeably. "Where are you headed?" I don't know why I feel compelled to make polite conversation; it's not my usual thing. I can't be *that* lonely.

"Our daughter lives up the coast," she says. "In Oregon." She pronounces *Oregon* the way East Coast people do: Or-e-*gahn*. "You know, dear, you really remind me of someone. I just can't put my finger on it . . ." She's racking her brain. I prepare to admit graciously to whatever she's about to figure out. Maybe she and her husband (currently walking a tiny dog) watch a lot of action movies. It's nice to be recognized every now and then, to tell you the truth. It's not exactly swarms of paparazzi wanting to know what I eat for breakfast, but still.

"I know!" she says finally. "You look like that girl from the shampoo commercial! Just like her, only your hair's a little different, but . . . *Clyde!* I'll ask Clyde if he thinks you look like anybody. He'll be so tickled. What is it, anyway—the one with the wild animals—Savage something—Clyde!"

It doesn't occur to her that I could actually *be* the girl from the shampoo commercial.

Back in my little silver-blue Prius, creeping up the coast, I sing along with an old Stevie Nicks song, belting out the words with gusto. But what I really want to do is tell someone the story of how I was mistaken by a crazy lady in a turquoise jogging suit for someone who looks like the person I, in fact, really am. And weirdly enough, the person I want to tell is Lois.

I stop in Arcata to get gas, and although there's plenty of daytime left I decide to stay here for the night. It looks like a pretty town. I'm practically faint with hunger and want to find something decent to eat. I also have a craving for company of some kind—even a crowd of strangers. I need to hear the sound of people laughing and talking, even fighting.

He liked us to be quiet. Zed. Not a problem for Lois, who was one of those watchful, not-talking girls. It was easy for her to drift around for hours without saying a word. But quiet made me nervous. Makes me nervous—I play music, I turn on the TV in hotel rooms even if I don't want to watch it. I like traffic, footsteps overhead, dogs barking. In the cabin I would hum some stupid song when I washed the dishes, tap my foot while I was reading, click my pen if I was writing or drawing. I drove him crazy. I would ask him questions just to hear the vibration of my own voice and then his. Lois would make lip-zipping signals behind his back, twisting her face crazily at me. Or neck-chopping signals. Either way, it meant shut the hell up before you get us killed. But I couldn't take the silence. His silence, the silence of the cabin, the trees.

Although I'm not exactly in the woods, my solitary trip up the coast is starting to feel very—well—solitary. So I drive straight to the heart of the so-called historic downtown and check into a nice little hotel, nice enough that I'll be willing to let the carpeting come into contact with my bare feet and the pillows won't feel like cheap flotation devices. I'll deal with the credit cards later.

Gail used to make a big performance of being a very discriminating customer. When we arrived at a hotel for a pageant, the first thing she'd do was go over the room with her sharp, greedy eyes, looking for something to complain about. Usually she'd find it. If she didn't, she'd make something up. Then she'd call the front desk and complain that the heat vent was too close to the bed or the room had a weird smell or there was a hair in the tub or something, and she'd try to make them give us a better room or comp us something or at least do some serious groveling. This made her feel extremely classy, like a woman of the world who knew what was what and what she had a right to expect. In reality she just sounded like an asshole and embarrassed the hell out of me. Thanks to her influence I will put up with almost any inconvenience rather than complain—in hotels, restaurants, whatever. (She's also very big on sending her food back at restaurants, although that's harder for her because she's such a greedy bitch, and always hungry. If there's bread to fill up on beforehand, though, you can count on it: back her food will go.)

She must have convinced Daddy that she was a totally different kind of person from the Gail I saw when we traveled together. In her own way I guess she's an actress, too.

But there is nothing in my Arcata room to complain about. Why am I thinking of Gail?

It's the letter, of course. The one in the glove compartment.

I stick it in my handbag when I head out an hour or so later. I'm wearing a short cranberry-colored sundress that makes me feel happy and light, and flats that will let me walk anywhere I like for as long as I like. I'm pretty sure Mandy the small-town policewoman would never wear this dress, but I try to reserve a little space for her in my head anyway: a little place where she can peek out, scanning these unfamiliar streets and people with the eye of a cop, specifically a detective. Here's a weird mental trick, one I've gotten good at: it's possible to be two people at once. I can be Chloe, having a perfectly good time, enjoying this strange freedom and thinking about what I'm going to order to drink when I find myself a bar that strikes my fancy, and also Mandy, who looks at everybody with suspicion—wondering what they've done, what their story is, what's *really* going on. Trusting no one.

A couple of hours later, Mandy definitely doesn't trust the guy I agree to have dinner with, even when we're sitting cozily in a tiny farm-to-table restaurant with a nice bottle of wine, surrounded by totally normal-looking people.

But I don't think Mandy approves of me at the moment, either. It wasn't exactly an accident that I got myself sort of respectably picked up, after all. I know women who would never go to a bar alone, who hate to eat alone, would rather starve. They feel conspicuous or vulnerable or bored or unloved or just embarrassed. I've never minded, because I figured out pretty early on that I could control the impression I made, which in turn controls how people respond to me. If you want, you can close off your face and put on a look that says "don't fuck with me if you value your life," though you have to take it down a little notch for bartenders and waitresses and such. And then you can just eat or drink in peace. At the other extreme you can easily convey the message that you're hoping for company. Keep an empty chair next to you, look around, meet people's eyes, smile if they look back.

Or you can do what I did tonight. The happy medium. I sat at a little outdoor bar, sipped my wine, chatted with the bartender but kept my barstool ever so slightly angled toward the rest of the patio so I could keep an eye on people. When Mr. Not-tweedy-but-close got up from the table where he was sitting with what looked like a bunch of college students and moved toward the bar as the rest of them prepared to go, I sent him the most casual of friendly smiles, almost as though we knew each other from somewhere and needed no introduction. "Students?" I asked, glancing toward the now-empty table, and he agreed that they were. "Creative writing workshop," he said a little sheepishly. "Every now and then I like to hold it off campus. They're all seniors, so it's legal. More or less." *Another writer,* I thought, almost discouraged. But he was really quite handsome, with a nice lean build, interesting grayish eyes, a smile that managed to be both disarmingly intelligent and boyishly charming. We fell into an easy conversation—food, movies, the kinds of things normal people must talk about on dates—and now here we are, at a restaurant, eating steaks and heirloom tomatoes and artichokes and having a fine time, even though I never went to college and he apparently doesn't watch the kinds of movies I have tended to be in.

I mock him for this, only half in earnest. "So you watch serious movies, then, right? Films with a capital *F*? Not people running around shooting each other."

He laughs, thank God. "You make me sound like such an ass. This is a trick question, isn't it? You know, I like a lot of older films, too. Screwball comedies. Those films were so brilliantly written. I'm sorry, but there's just nothing like that today."

"So tell me what you write," I say finally, half afraid that it will be all downhill from here. "Have you written a screenplay? Why don't you write a screwball comedy?"

He tells me that he *has* written screenplays, that he almost had one produced, though mostly he writes short fiction. That his screenplay still might be produced, who knows? That he could write a screwball comedy and I could star in it. Opposite George Clooney, maybe. We build up a beautiful sparkly dream with words, words, words. He comes back to the hotel with me so we can live in it a little longer. Some of which takes place, I am very happy to admit, in my bed. (Mandy has disappeared by then. Maybe he finally won her over.)

It's pretty far into the evening when Jake (yes, that's his name) asks me what I'm working on at the moment. Not because he's the kind of person so busy talking about himself that he forgets to ask questions; actually I think he just doesn't want to make a big deal out of my being an actress. Which is nice. Anyway, I'm expecting him to be polite about my movie because it doesn't sound like it's quite his thing, and I'm fine with that. But when I tell him about *Deep in the Woods,* he gets all excited. "So let me get this straight," he says, propping himself up on an elbow. "The girls are abducted from separate towns, he hides them in a hunting lodge in the Adirondack Mountains for a month and a half, and then they are rescued completely unharmed? Meanwhile the kidnapper shoots himself?"

"Yeah, that's pretty much it." I wonder about the need for a recap of the plot.

"Don't you remember—well, maybe not, you're probably a couple years younger than I am. But there was an actual case in the midnineties that was exactly like this. It could be a coincidence, but the details are awfully similar." I'm still trying to figure out how to handle this, but he plunges ahead, not noticing that he's thrown me for a bit of a loop. "And the reason I happen to remember is not just that it was on the news so much, although it was, but because one of the girls involved was from Connecticut, which is where I grew up, and then the next year she actually showed up at the school I went to. It was a private boarding school," he adds, sort of apologetically. "And she became a celebrity, in a weird kind of way, because everyone knew she was the abducted girl, although she was very discreet about it. She had a reputation for being brilliant and a little strange."

I am trying very hard to picture this without letting my face reveal that this story affects me at all. But in my mind I see a New Englandy private school that I think I must have gotten from some movie: posh red brick, grassy quads, preppy kids. And there's Lois, a little older than she would have been when I knew her, and Jake, a couple of years older than that. "Did you know this girl at all?"

I ask, trying to sound casually curious while gathering enough details to fill in my picture.

"Not well," he says. "But it was a small school; I knew her a little. I actually had a slight crush on her for a while. Practically everyone did, though. She was dramatic looking, and she had a kind of mysterious quality, and she kept very much to herself. Yeah, we were all fascinated by her, in a way." I can picture this Lois, but I feel pretty sure that I know one thing he doesn't: if people knew who she was, it was because she wanted them to. There are all kinds of ways she could have kept her past secret if she had chosen—which I know better than anyone. Leaking her identity was part of her game, part of the role she had designed for reasons of her own, Lois-reasons. I understand her motivations the way I would a character I was playing—intuitively and beyond doubt.

Of all the gin joints. Coincidence is a funny thing. I decide that I'm okay with this one. But it does make this Jake guy seem like yet another puzzle piece, somehow—not completely random. Is that a problem? Could it be a problem? Would Lois remember him? What did she think of him? I don't consider telling him my story; that's just a little too much weirdness for a one-night stand, if that's what this is. I'm *tempted* to tell him—dying to, really. But it would take so long, and it might change everything. I don't want to risk it. *Sorry, Lois,* I think, and push her away.

In the morning, after he has left and I've had a cup of black coffee and a bowl of fruit in the restaurant downstairs, smiling crazily because I feel really happy for the first time in a long time, and actually sort of half wishing I could take Jake on the road with me, I suddenly feel strong enough to open the letter. How could Gail possibly hurt me now? Fat, stupid old witch. I get the letter from the glove compartment and sit on the little balcony outside my room, the sun beating happily down on my recklessly SPF-75-free skin, pretty Arcata spread out below me.

And that's when I learn that my father has died. I have killed him, says Gail. But I would bet that's her work.

Lois

Brad calls and invites me to Nicoletti's. Classes have ended and exams are about to begin, and he wants to talk about summer, wants to talk me into going on some kind of trip with him—for my own good, he says.

"I can't do it tonight," I tell him with genuine regret. I could use a real night out, though I don't want to encourage him to think we could be traveling companions. "I have plans." I hit the backspace key, erasing the last few words I typed. I hope Brad can't hear the keyboard. Gary is approaching a crossroad.

"You have *plans*? Since when do you have plans? Do you have a *date*?"

I note the tiny pause that precedes my reply, and I realize that he'll notice it too and probably misconstrue it. Oh well. "No—just plans. Something I have to do. Look, it's not that interesting, okay? Do I really have to tell you every little thing I do? I don't need a big brother, for God's sake."

"No, of course not," he says, his voice suddenly stuffy. "Forgive me for worrying about you when you act like a complete lunatic. Which is what you've been doing lately, if you haven't noticed."

I type a restless row of asterisks. "Listen, can we do it tomorrow night instead?" I use my most conciliatory voice. I don't want Brad breathing down my neck, but I don't want him to abandon me, either.

"Sorry, I have plans," he says, and hangs up.

Not like Brad. This exchange leaves me shaken. I am, to be

honest, often a little shaken these days. I've been lying low since the department party, slipping in and out of my office like the ghost I sometimes think I am. Meanwhile, Sean has stepped up his textual assault. Every day he sends newspaper clippings or file photographs or neatly typed passages from the library books I brought with me to the cabin (*The Once and Future King, Dracula, Wuthering Heights*). Like the reporters at the time, he has mined these books for resonant material, lines that might be reframed or twisted to apply to the abduction, the so-called rescue. But he has been more thorough, and his selections are more disturbing. They appear in plain white envelopes in my mailbox at school, the mail slot at my house. I don't see him in my neighborhood these days, but I know he's there, lurking. Tonight is our final meeting. I will tell him one last story, and I will demand a story in return. *Tell me about him. Tell me what you know. What did your mother tell you, your grandmother?*

That, I truly hope, will be the end of it. I have been funneling the energy from this perverse dalliance into Gary, and Gary is almost ready to make it on his own. It's exhausting, this game I have been playing. And it's hard thinking so much about Zed, being confronted so regularly with the past. This is not a relationship I want to preserve; I want to take from it what I need and then package it up neatly and move on. If that means one of us has to leave, fine; I'm guessing it will be Sean, who doesn't seem firmly anchored here. His presence at this school, in this town, seems wispy to me, like a sinister fog that has no choice but to lift when the sun is high. It may be absurd to assume that Sean will disappear when I no longer need him, but that's exactly what I expect.

Tonight, at any rate, is the payoff. Tonight I find out what he can tell me: how he can help to flesh out a portrait that's imperfect, damaged, but haunting nevertheless; that refuses to dim or age or cease to matter. I think of the eerie Victorian practice of photographing the dead, often propped up and posed with the living. Maybe I am after something like that: the illusion of resurrection, an image solid enough to bear the weight of my regret, my longing. Only Sean, of all people, can help me.

On the far side of town there's a footbridge that crosses the railroad tracks. It's charming enough in the daytime in spite of the decrepit factories along the river, but at night it's a place I'd ordinarily avoid. It was his idea, and he insisted. I finally gave in when he asked if I was afraid of him, to which I could only say no. I am the one in control here; I have nothing to fear. He said he had something to show me, something I would want to see.

I am curious in spite of myself. I park my car under a streetlight on the most populous side of the bridge and make my way across. There are a few white Christmas lights strung from the suspension wires—a bright idea on someone's part—but most of them have burned out, and the others cast a pale bluish glow that's almost worse than nothing.

He's late, and I am both impatient and irrationally angry when he finally appears at the opposite end of the bridge, slouching along as he always does, apparently in no hurry. There is no one around. The swollen river below us drowns out what little traffic there is on the streets at either end of the bridge.

"I was about to leave," I say as he approaches. It's both untrue and unwise; he's always less pleasant to deal with if he is on the defensive. "It's your turn to tell me a thing or two," I announce, before he can speak. "I've given you more material than you could possibly use. Now I want to ask some questions."

"Material?" he repeats. "Spare me, *Professor*. How stupid do you really think I am? Do you think I don't know you made that shit up? The runaways in the basement and all that? You really thought I bought that? I mean, I can use it, sure. It's pretty good stuff—more of a real thriller than what you actually wrote. But I believe, like, two words of what you told me, just so you know."

I'm surprised by his tone. It's been a while since he sounded so contemptuous, so hostile. There have been moments, I admit, when I thought we'd developed something almost like a friendship—and I liked that, in a way. For Zed's sake. I'm also surprised by his disbelief. He hid it well. For the first time I feel a hint of fear stir, like a cold wind on the back of my neck. Fear of what? It's not a question I can afford to explore just now. I make my voice indifferent, casual, trying to put us back on our usual footing: "Fine. Believe what you like. I gave you what you asked for." Why is my voice unsteady and pitched too high? "And now it's your turn."

"Go ahead, ask me whatever you want," he says, and I don't like the touch of amusement I detect in his voice. It seems entirely inappropriate to the occasion, as I understand it. The possibility that he might understand the occasion differently sets up an unpleasant kind of dissonance. It sets my nerves more on edge than they already were, if that's possible.

"Tell me about him," I say. "Tell me . . . what you know. What you heard. You were too little to remember, but . . . there would have been stories. Your grandmother's memories . . ." My voice sounds more tentative than I would like. For the first time it occurs to me that he might know nothing at all. He was only two, after all. The family might never have spoken of his father, might have wanted to protect him from that knowledge. He might know his father only as an absence.

He laughs unpleasantly. "Yeah, I figured we'd get around to that eventually. I knew that was your real game. I bet you did a little background check, right? Found out I'd gone to school in Utica? And then everything just fell into place?" He thrusts his hands in his pockets, pulls his coat tighter. "You started looking at me different around the time you came up with that theory. I could tell what you were thinking. I knew what articles you'd been reading. I could see how it would make sense to someone as crazy as you."

He thinks *I'm* the crazy one? No, it's obviously an act. I expected him to deny it at first. Doubt is his only weapon. All the same, I place a hand on the cool steel railing, steadying myself.

At that he takes a sudden step toward me. "Did you tell anyone you were coming here? I'm just curious."

It's colder out than I realized. And we are far from anyone who might hear—say, if I called out. This is not going as I planned. "Of course," I say lightly. "Professor Drake knows I'm here."

"Lying again." His face is in shadow; I can't read it. "Anyway, whatever. You want me to tell you what I remember? Little personal details about the nutjob who kidnapped you when you were a kid? That's kind of fucked-up, Professor Lonsdale. More fucked-up than you know. Hey, can I show you something first? Do you mind? I said I had something to show you, remember?"

What could it be? I think quickly, trying to catalog possibilities. A photograph, another article, some artifact. It could be the very thing that will answer all my questions. It could be something unspeakable. A stray beam of light from somewhere behind me flickers across his pale, not-quite-handsome face, his unsmiling eyes. I realize that I am afraid to see what he has brought.

He reaches into the deep pocket of his loose, flapping coat. "Here," he says. "It's just like the one you told me about."

It's a knife. My knife, the one I took the picture of. It lies casually enough across his palm, but his thumb loops loosely around the handle. He's not gripping it now, but he could be with the slightest adjustment. "Yes," I agree. I'm surprised to hear my voice, apparently calm, utterly rational. "That's it, all right."

His fingers curl around it and he speaks slowly. "I'm not who you think I am, Professor Lonsdale. I've just been going along with your crazy fantasy. I had my reasons. But I'm not that kid. I kind of wish I was, though. That would be pretty fucking interesting." At some point he has taken another step toward me. A wall goes up in my mind. This can't be true; I won't consider it. I have put the pieces together so very carefully. Everything fits. I have to be right.

But if I'm not . . . A small voice whispers a warning. If I'm not, I should be running.

I don't run.

"I'm sorry I couldn't be who you wanted me to be," he says almost gently. "But I can still help you. See, I'm not as dumb as you think. I know a way to help you. And you've taught me so much that I really *want* to help you, believe it or not."

There is something dark and unfamiliar in his face. I do not know him, I don't know myself, I don't know anything. "I don't think I'm the one who needs help here," I say. I try to infuse my voice with my usual scorn, but I don't hear it. I hear someone else's voice, almost childlike, defiant in defeat. I try to summon my strength, send urgent messages to my strangely paralyzed limbs. *Flee*, I think. *Run*. But he's too close. I feel as trapped as if I were chained to the bridge.

"Oh yes you are," he says. "Because this isn't *Pamela*, with its stupid happy ending. You definitely need help." He looms ever closer. His eyes are cold and ugly, dark and deep—so unlike Zed, who was beautiful and kind, among other things. "See, you're not the only one here with a theory," he continues, standing so close he could easily grab me. He's half a foot taller than I am, and then some. His shadow swallows me. "And my theory is that your kidnapper guy—not, I should remind you, my dear dad, sorry to say—was severely fucked-up. He had you guys, everything went according to plan, and then he lost his nerve. He couldn't, like, act. Something was wrong with him. The whole thing was a total failure. But once he had you, what could he do? He had to keep you, right? There was no going back. Hey"—he interrupts himself suddenly—"are you listening? Do you get what I'm saying? You know I'm right, don't you?"

"No," I manage to say. "You're sick. You have no way of knowing what he intended. He never meant to *do* anything. The plan was perfect." I am trying to think ahead, to figure out where he's going with this. I have no idea. I don't believe Zed lost his nerve, but at the same time a bolt of curiosity cuts through my fear.

"No, you have to know better than that." He has never sounded so confident, so self-assured. I keep my eye on the knife; he continues to hold it lightly, grubby nails visible in the bluish light. "But here's my other theory. You'll like this one even better. I actually got the idea from one of your bullshit stories. See, you're also fucked-up, Professor Lonsdale. I bet that actress is, too. And here's what I think: it's all *because* he didn't do anything. Because he was a crappy kidnapper. You know what you really needed?" I hear frogs in the shallow river down below. A car, too far away. A barking dog on the other side of town. I can't see his eyes, just two black holes in his face, but I can't stop trying to find them. He leans forward, his face way too close to mine. "To be marked," he whispers. "You got away too easy, too clean. The mark is only in your fucked-up head. Like when you told me the other girl had carved his chest with a knife one night, that was a good idea, except you should have made him carve her, too. Otherwise, it's like—unbalanced. You guys needed something to show for all that weirdness, something permanent. Something real, something to hold on to. That's my theory. And that's why I brought you this. It's not too late. You can do it yourself." He holds the knife out. Offering it to me.

I want to say I have no idea what he's talking about, but I do. A crazy vision of what he's thinking flashes through my mind: I see myself taking the knife firmly in my hand and slashing it across—what? My thigh, perhaps, through my jeans. I see him watching while the blood gushes forth; I feel the pain, perfect and blinding.

Am I reaching out my hand?

Light flits across his body again, brighter this time, too bright to be headlights belonging to a car on the nearest street, and I realize that what's actually blinding is a flashlight shining in my face. It can't be far away. That's when I finally scream, my voice surprisingly clear and strong, echoing off the banks of the river. I clasp my hands together and bring them up sharply under Sean's, knocking the knife away. It lands near my feet and I kick it; it goes skittering across the bridge and then sails into the dark. I don't even hear a splash. My leg actually hurts from the imaginary gash. Sean is reaching for me, I'm sure he is, when a deep voice calls out: "Hey! You little bastard! Get away from her!" I see Sean's eyes widen, and then within a second he turns and flees across the footbridge, away from the voice. He runs awkwardly, but he's surprisingly fleet. "You're a fucking nutcase, Professor Lonsdale! And you know I'm right!" he yells, not looking back.

I spin around, and a dark shape moves swiftly toward me. "Lois!" The shape is calling to me in Brad's voice, is wearing Brad's jacket, brandishing a large flashlight. "Lois! Are you all right?" No, I'm not. But I am outrageously relieved to see him. Habit compels me to conceal my gladness, though, to show no weakness. It's annoying, after all, to need rescuing. *Again.*

"I'm fine," I say, and although my voice sounds reasonably calm my knees buckle, and I reach out and clutch the guardrail, bracing myself against cold, hard metal. I reassemble my scattered mind, my wits. I'm Dr. Lois Lonsdale, perfectly reasonable woman, respectable professional, successful author. *Not crazy.* I reach in my mind for a soothing string of C words, and they don't come. There's blank space where my words are supposed to be, like the distance between the swaying footbridge and the cold river below. A space you could fall through.

"That was Sean, right? Was that a *knife* he was holding?" Brad sounds both incredulous and angry. "Have you lost your fucking mind?" I don't say anything. That tone of voice, I tell myself, grasping at indignation, doesn't deserve an answer. *Not crazy.*

"Come on," he orders, reaching for my arm and pulling me along. I go readily enough. He passes my car and guides me to his, not very gently. "You can pick yours up tomorrow." He's not asking, and I don't bother to object. Suddenly I feel as if something inside of me has collapsed, some elaborate, delicate structure has come crashing down. "Fucking nutcase is right," he says, starting the car. "I won't argue with that." And he doesn't say much else until he escorts me into my apartment, makes me a drink, and sends me to bed. "We'll call the cops tomorrow," he says, and I save my arguments for later, though of course that can't be allowed to happen. This is between me and Sean—and Zed, and Carly May.

I don't even thank him.

Chloe

I veer east and head for Nebraska. I don't think about why I'm going or what I expect to find or what I plan to do when I get there. I don't even think about Daddy, and I sure as hell don't let myself think about Gail. I stop only for gas and cheap truck-stop food and feel like Carly May again, like the passing miles are erasing time, year by year, dragging me backward. It's not a feeling I like much. But I have to go. There's never any question of not going.

Lois

One day that summer, Zed burst into our room with a big dictionary open in his arms. "I have a good one for you, Lois," he announced. I had already learned to be wary; I knew he did not approve of my spelling. It was pure memorization, requiring no critical thought or creativity, he charged—nothing more than a game. A waste of time, like Carly's pageants. But now the ground seemed to have shifted; he was full of a strange energy. Still, I expected a trap. "*Syzygy.* Can you spell that, my little monkey? Come on, spell it like you're on stage."

"Syzygy," I said, and I could hear the trepidation in my own voice, although I knew the word. "*S-y-z-y-g-y. Syzygy.*" The word had pleased me when I found it, its oddity curiously balanced by its symmetry, its visual spikiness counteracted by its lilting rhythm. But it is also a word all serious spellers know, a spelling-bee staple.

"And what," he asked quietly, "does this word *syzygy* mean?"

I shook my head, looked down, ashamed because it was clear that I should be.

"Who cares?" Carly interrupted, in a brash attempt to draw his attention away from me. He shot her one of his rare scathing glances. Even though she was defending me, something in me was glad to see that she, too, could lose his favor.

He slammed the dictionary shut and tossed it at me; it landed on the floor beside me with a thud. "Look it up," he said, and strode from the room.

Syzygy is a complicated word. It can refer to the alignment of three celestial bodies: the sun, the earth, and the moon, for instance. Or it can refer to any two points in the orbit of any celestial body (planet, moon, whatever) where the object is *either* in opposition to or in conjunction with the sun. Or it can refer to any *two* related things—and these things may be either alike or opposite; each thing retains its own individual characteristics within this relationship. Or, in poetry, it can refer to two feet in a single metrical unit. All of these possibilities taxed my very limited, sixth-grade understanding of both astronomy and prosody. Etymologically, I noted that *syzygy* comes from a Greek word referring to the yoking of two oxen; this at least I could visualize. The definitions seemed not so much simply disparate as downright contradictory. *Syzygy* is a relationship between two things or a relationship between three things. It implies things that are alike or things that are opposite. It involves the solar system or poetry or oxen.

Zed returned later for a report, as I had known he would. I was more nervous than I had ever been at school, but there was no need, in the end: his mood had softened. "We'll concern ourselves only with the astronomical application," he began, sounding teacherly. "Let's say that I am the sun." He positioned himself in the middle of the floor of our room and signaled us to rise. "You are the earth, Carly, and Lois, you're the moon. Now you know of course that the earth revolves around the sun. Revolve," he commanded Carly. "And the moon of course revolves around the earth. That's you, Lois."

We revolved. The room was really too small for three celestial bodies; we tended to collide, and soon we were laughing. "Pay attention," he admonished. "Stop, both of you, when you find that all three of us are in a straight line." Within a few seconds this more or less occurred, and we halted abruptly. I had ended up in the middle, with the sun on one side and the earth on the other. "Syzygy," he proclaimed. "And since the sun and moon are on the same side of the earth, they are considered to be in conjunction. Now, resume orbiting."

He stopped us again when Carly, the earth, was in the middle, and he stood on one side of her and I, the moon, on the other. "Syzygy again. But this time the sun and the moon are in opposition. This is the full moon. During conjunction, the moon is new. Either way, this is when the tides are strongest; the gravitational pull of the sun and moon work together. Understand?" We nodded.

"Well, then," he said to me, nodding as if he felt that something had been settled. And he left. We tumbled to the floor from our orbits and regarded each other in silence for a moment as our laughter died away. It was Carly who spoke first, looking at the door through which he had vanished. "He's crazy, isn't he," she said slowly.

"Bats in the belfry," I agreed. It was an expression I had heard my father use. "But . . . not in a bad way, exactly?"

Carly looked thoughtful.

I imagine the word *syzygy* has never been used so much in conversation as it was in our odd little household that summer. To me, it had acquired yet another level of resonance from our performance of it, and it had less to do with the alignment of celestial bodies than with the shifting relationship between the three of us—sometimes aligned and sometimes not; in conjunction or opposition. Both of us orbiting him; me circling Carly circling him. Eclipses, tides. They could all be understood in terms of syzygy—or its absence.

Later, we became two related objects, not three. Locked in some sort of orbit, I am tempted to say. Or yoked: forever bound, against our will. There is an explanation I came across once, written by someone who was attempting to resolve the seeming contradictions in the word's meaning, the apparent confusion between two objects and three. In science, he said, the identification of two aligned objects necessarily implies a third: the investigator or observer. This, too, seems rife with interpretive possibilities. Who's the observer here? Then or now?

One morning near the end of the semester I awake with the cabin fresh in my mind; I dreamed it again. I pad into the kitchen in my L. L. Bean slipper socks, last year's Christmas present from my parents. I make strong coffee; I empty the dishwasher. But really I am walking barefoot across the rough wooden floors of an Adirondack hunting lodge. The floorboards are warmer in the places where the speckled sun has forced itself through the overhanging branches of the trees that surround us. I am afraid.

My dreams have always insisted upon the fear I don't remember feeling at the time.

I call Brad and belatedly thank him for rescuing me, if that's what he did. I cannot think about the night on the bridge. Sean sent me a copy of a document purporting to be his birth certificate, indicating that he was born in Greene, New York, to Patsy and William McDougal. Which proves what, exactly? I recycled it. Brad is angry with me for refusing to go to the police. He demanded an explanation, and I refused. My desire to confess to him has vanished. For now I'll keep my story to myself. My stories. There's strength in that, and safety.

Nutcase: Nameko, neginoth, norgestrel, nagami, ninjutsu. Nacreous, nobelium, nonuple. Nilpotent. Niqab. Nemesis.

My words are back.

Part Four

Chloe

You could say I treated my father badly. You could say it was shitty to go off and leave him like that, never bother to write or call. Maybe it's fucked-up that I call him Daddy in one breath and then in the next admit that I haven't seen him in over ten years. All I can say is this: he abandoned me first. I was just a kid. And if he had ever wanted to find me, it wouldn't have been that fucking hard.

I'm driving. Trying to think and trying not to think.

Lois

He only meant to help me. It was an offering. Misguided but genuine. Not a threat. He knew I wouldn't take his suggestion—wouldn't mark myself, as he called it. It was a test, and I passed. I believe this, mostly. It was my fault. It doesn't matter. He is not who I thought he was. Just a troubled student. I never want to see him again. *I'm not crazy*. I'm moving on. I find it hard to leave my apartment, though, and I can't face going to campus. Brad administers my final exams for me and brings me stacks of papers to grade; he is reluctant to leave me alone. I grow accustomed to his watchful presence. I am not good company, but he doesn't seem to mind.

One evening we are sitting side by side on my couch, grading papers in what I think is companionable silence, when I notice that it's been a while since I heard the steady scratch of Brad's pen. I glance sideways, wondering if he's dozed off midessay, and am startled to catch him watching me intently. Surprised into looking directly back at him, I realize how seldom I really do look straight at Brad. His dark blue eyes are too serious, too intense. I turn my attention back to the paper in my lap, but it's too late. Brad reaches out and touches my hair—terribly gently, like the slightest of breezes. Then his hand moves from my hair to my chin, pulling my face back to meet his. "Lois," he begins, the very word a blow. I brace myself for what I know is next. "I'm so worried about you. You have no idea how much I care about you. Let's just get out of here, let me take you somewhere, let's . . ."

I wrench my face from his too-tender grasp with none of his gentleness. "I do plan to get out of here," I say. I can hear the chill in my voice. "As soon as I submit my grades. But I'm going alone." Part of me wants to fly at him, pummel his stupid plaid flannel shirt, demand why he crossed the line—the friendship line, so carefully drawn and defended; why he is ruining everything. But that's not the part of me I allow to speak. "I'm grateful for everything, I really am. But I think I need to be alone now. I don't expect you to understand."

He looks confused, and I realize he's wondering whether I am simply repeating my intention of going away on my own at some point, or whether I actually mean that I need to be alone this very minute. I stand up and move toward the door so that there can be no doubt. I pull my old cardigan tightly around my chest, holding myself in.

Awkwardly, he begins to gather his papers. "I don't understand you. I really don't. Not your bizarre involvement with Sean, not your treatment of me. And I wish to hell I didn't care." His words seem far away, addressed to someone else; I don't let them in. "I think you're making a mistake," he says as he leaves, his words sad and heavy with reproach. He closes my apartment door quietly behind him, but somehow I'm relieved to hear the downstairs door slam so hard the whole house shakes.

When he's gone the air in my apartment seems to settle, and I feel as if some important balance has been restored. *Lois, you're the moon.*

I go to my computer and act on the plan I hinted at to Brad: I buy a plane ticket to Vancouver, leaving a week from today. I will arrive well before I am scheduled to meet with Chloe, before shooting on the film begins. It seems like a good idea, for reasons I can't altogether explain. Alone, I don't have to.

Then, with a curious kind of relief, I decide to abandon my grading and turn to Gary. He's there waiting, but he is floundering a bit. He still can't decide what to do with the actress. He doesn't know how to find the writer or what he'll do with her when he does. The actress pounds on the trunk from the inside, but no one hears her. I wonder how much air she has. I wonder how I could calculate this. I Google it, idly, and am shocked to discover that I am one of countless people who have inquired how long a person can survive in the trunk of a car. A scan of several discussion threads reveals that there are no easy answers: there are too many variables, weather chief among them. The actress is in no immediate danger, I conclude, as long as it's not too hot and Gary is providing her with water. Of course he is, I decide. He brings her food and water and he asks her questions through a crack in the trunk, though there is nothing she can say that will make him happy. He keeps his hand on his knife in case she tries anything stupid. He prefers knives to guns—because of his father's death, of course. He was only a child, but he's heard stories all his life, even if they weren't intended for his ears—and usually they were not. He's read the newspaper reports. He wants nothing to do with guns. He's building a small arsenal of sharp objects.

I learn, too, that cars manufactured after 2002 are equipped with an escape mechanism: an internal latch that will release the trunk. This doesn't strike me as a problem for my plot; naturally Gary drives an old junker. (What kind, exactly? I make a note to myself: I'll need to figure this out.) I remind myself to check my own car to see whether it has an escape lever. How would you know to look for it, if you found yourself in a trunk? Before quitting for the night I make sure the actress has a bottle of water and a snack. I wonder briefly how she can eat and drink if she's gagged, how Gary can ensure her silence if she isn't. But these are the kinds of problems I can solve.

I don't think about the knife that lies at the bottom of the shallow river on the other side of town, though Gary's newest knife is very much like it.

Chloe

At first, Arrow seems unchanged. The same businesses line Main Street, the same wide spaces separate the houses. The kids riding bikes up and down the side streets might as well be the same kids, with the same dogs at their heels.

But when I knock at the door of the farmhouse, a stranger answers. "Can I help you?" asks a middle-aged woman in an old-fashioned housedress. A dress Gail wouldn't be caught dead in. There's a bulldozer in the yard, some kind of construction going on in the back of the house. An addition. Bad idea.

For a very uncomfortable second I can't think what the hell to say. Then I manage to stammer, "My father—my family—used to live here."

"The Smiths?" the woman says, helpfully enough. She looks vaguely familiar. Very vaguely. "That was a while back. They moved into town years ago, before . . . you know. When they sold the farm." Not being clear on who I am, exactly, she isn't going to give much away.

No point in asking her questions, but I ask one anyway. "Where in town?" Daddy would never have sold the farm. I'm confused. There's something going on here that I don't know about. I don't know how he died, of course. Gail's note was skimpy on details. Had he become sick years ago?

She tells me the way to my grandmother's house, and I get back in the car.

Grandma Mabel's house has been torn down and replaced with some horrible modern thing that looks totally out of place on the street, which is lined with respectable mid-twentieth-century white houses, like in some John Mellencamp song. This one is big, square, plastered in pale pink faux adobe. Gail comes to the door in tight jeans and a low-cut, sleeveless blouse. Somehow she's already heard that I'm here—my Prius hasn't gone unnoticed, here in the land of big American cars. Or maybe the woman at the old farm called. Gail's makeup looks freshly applied, in my honor. She isn't smiling.

"You've had some work done," I say, following her into the kitchen.

"You mean the house?" She looks around proudly, like a cat that just ate a goddamned German shepherd. But meaner than a cat.

"No, I mean you." I don't bother to keep the nastiness out of my voice. It's already clear that there is going to be no pretending.

There's been extensive lipo, I speculate, and some work on the face and neck. Lots of work on the boob region.

"Where's Grandma Mabel?" I ask, seeing no signs of her furniture, her taste, her presence. The pastels and gold accents look like they might be at home in a Barbie penthouse. Or Florida. This could only have happened over Grandma Mabel's dead body. Which would make a certain amount of sense, I suppose. I brace myself for the news.

"She's out at Ravenswood."

That's a nursing home twenty miles away. Could be worse. "I'll go see her," I say, before I remember that I should tell Gail nothing, nothing at all.

"She won't know you," Gail says, smiling for the first time. "Too late for that, too. I promised your father I would write, but I didn't think you'd show up. I told him you wouldn't," she says with satisfaction, letting the implications of those words sink in.

"You're a bitch, Gail. As always." I will ask her nothing, tell her nothing, give her nothing that her meanness can feed on.

Just then a young man shuffles into the kitchen. He's wearing boxers and a dirty T-shirt, and his gut is trying to find a way to poke out of the place where the two meet. He smells like cigarettes and dirty sleep. He pats Gail sort of half on the ass, half on the hip, and asks what's for dinner.

She brushes his hand away. "Look who's here," Gail says. "It's your long-lost sister."

He looks up and shakes his floppy bangs out of his eyes. "Carly May?" He sounds doubtful. "Jesus."

"Get dressed," I say. "I'll take you out for something to eat."

He looks at Gail. For permission? A mama's boy and a loser, it looks like. Way to go, Gail. "I won't stand in your way," she says.

His eyes slide back to me. "All right," he agrees. "I'm down with that. Gimme five minutes." He retreats.

"He'll tell you anything you need to know," says Gail, then

she disappears to the back of the house, too. She sort of flounces away, like she thinks she's making some kind of dramatic exit.

Eddy's calls itself a bar and grill, but it's not really much of either. It sells cheap beer but would probably frown upon anyone who drank more than two or three in a sitting, and practically all the food on the menu is fried. I take Jaden there because there's nowhere else to go but the diner, and that would be less private. At Eddy's we slide into a dark booth. I wipe a few crumbs off the table. Hardly anyone else is here. I remove my sunglasses and suddenly laugh at myself, feeling like an asshole. As if anyone would recognize me—or give a shit—after more than a decade.

"I've seen you in the movies," Jaden says, surprising me. "Braden and I used to watch you all the time."

I try to get my head around this. "You knew, then? Did Daddy know?" All these years I've thought I was a mystery to them. I assumed my new life as Chloe Savage was a secret, and not a very hard one to keep.

"Yeah," says Jaden. "I guess we've known for a while. Not in the beginning, I mean, when you first left, and Ma wrote that book. At that point it really was like you had just totally disappeared. But then after—I don't know, a few years—we started seeing you sometimes. We do have TV in Nebraska, you know. Movies, even." He sounds slightly reproachful that this has not occurred to me. "Dad made Ma promise not to spill the beans to the media," he adds. "Otherwise she would have outed you forever ago." Had it been arrogant to assume that my planet was so far from theirs that I could remain undetected even if my face were splashed across millions of screens? *Not Carly's face*, I defend myself. *Chloe's. Which is different. Carly doesn't exist.* How did I ever persuade myself to believe they wouldn't find out? Suddenly my confidence in my anonymity seems downright delusional.

Jaden doesn't look accusing; in fact I revise my impression of him slightly now that he is fully dressed and seems to have brushed his teeth and at least splashed water on his head. He used to be a pretty cute kid. I can see traces of that early promise in the parts of his face that aren't puffy and sprouting tufts of half-assed facial hair. Maybe he's not as much of a lunk as I first thought. *But.* I didn't come here for some sentimental guilt trip.

"Tell me about Daddy," I order.

Between bites of his hamburger, he does.

First it was just depression, he explains. Then a series of little things. Dizzy spells, memory lapses. Then they sold the farm ("Why?" I demand, and Jaden says, "Because Ma said they didn't need it anymore"). Soon afterward he was diagnosed with Alzheimers. "Early something—"

"Onset?" I suggest.

"Yeah. Early onset."

He also had arthritis, weird nerve issues, chronic colds—he was always a little sick, said Jaden, though not enough to be really worried about. Minor things. Without the farm he sat around and read all day, became more and more withdrawn. He would try to start little projects around the house and then abandon them. His memory got worse and worse. He was on all kinds of drugs, Jaden said, for a million different things. And that was what had happened: A million different drugs. An accidental overdose. A miscalculation on someone's part, probably his, definitely not Gail's.

"Could he have done it on purpose?" I ask, trying to sound completely neutral, like it makes no difference.

Jaden looks shocked. "Of course not," he says, flushing, looking a little pissed off for the first time. "Jesus. Why would he do that?"

Because Gail took his farm away. Because he was bored to death. Because I deserted him. Because he felt like hell. Because he was lonely. Because he lived in a fucking pink house on the same plot of land where the house he grew up in used to be, after his mother was shipped off to the old folks' home. "Have dessert," I tell Jaden, as if buying him a shitload of cheap, crappy food will make up for something I haven't done. Or for the tiara incident, maybe. I watch him devour his chocolate brownie sundae, vaguely grossed out.

I learn that he graduated from high school, doesn't have a job yet. That Braden went to Iraq and came back in one piece except for the fact that his brain was shaken loose by a roadside bomb that left him otherwise intact, apparently unharmed. "He's totally fucked-up," says Jaden with feeling. I can't tell what feeling exactly. Braden lives with his equally fucked-up girlfriend in a trailer outside of town. Grandma Mabel doesn't know her own name, much less anybody else's. You can go see her, but she's rude to visitors. She likes two of her nurses and no one else. She talks to people no one else can see, and doesn't seem to like them much, either. I decide not to go see her after all. Gail is "writing" another book. He starts to tell me what it's about, but I don't even want to know.

Lois

I turn my head to the window and look down. Clouds bulge and billow miles below us. I open my laptop and try to write, but Gary won't cooperate. I'm almost relieved. I have no choice but to read the novel I bought at the airport, dozing on and off. My mind is strangely quiet.

I like being nowhere. I wish I could stay longer.

In Seattle, where I have a brief layover, a text from Sean intrudes upon my unfamiliar sense of peace: *You're getting closer, aren't you.* I shiver, wishing I had never given him my number. Could he possibly know where I am, what I'm doing? I imagine him lurking near my house, watching me load my luggage into my trunk early this morning, drawing conclusions. But even if he saw me go, how could he know where? Closer to what? It's a bluff, surely. I delete the message, push it from my mind.

I rent a car in Vancouver and make my way to the tiny town where I've decided I can hide out for a few days. Carly-Chloe and the other cast members will be staying at a lovely inn ten miles outside of town; even if it weren't booked solid, it wouldn't suit my purposes. In a week or so I'll check into the charming bed-and-breakfast the movie people have secured for me, but for now I'm here and not here. I get a room in a decent-looking but decidedly unassuming motel just off the mountain highway that runs through the middle of town. At first I feel oddly conspicuous, worried that people will suspect me of some illicit purpose; I invent a plausible story about my vacation plans in case anyone is suspicious enough to ask what I am doing here. At the same time, I realize that I'm being absurd; why would anyone notice or care? *You're not the center of the universe, Lois,* I hear someone reminding me. My mother? No. It's *him*. Zed. But he had gone to such trouble to find me. His messages were mixed, to say the least. We *were* the center of the universe, Carly May and I. For a summer.

Chloe

I drive to Omaha, leave my car in long-term parking, and book a flight to BC. I'm sick of driving, sick of watching the stupid fields go by. I'll figure out later what to do with the car. A germ of a plan occurs to me: I could pay Jaden to pick it up and drive it out to LA. If I want a brother. Do I want a brother? I'm not sure, and in no mood to think more about it. At the airport I sit in a sports bar and drink wine and read magazines. On the plane I sleep. It feels like it's been a while.

Lois

I'm pleased to find an old-fashioned diner within easy walking distance of my motel. I go there for an early dinner. (I plan to leave the evenings free for writing.) I order a grilled cheese sandwich with fries, though I haven't had much of an appetite lately. Brad asked if I had lost weight and I denied it, but later I stepped on the scale and found that it was true. I didn't have much to spare, to be honest; I never have. I suspect that if I were so inclined, I could live on pizza and macaroni and cheese, and I would still be a wisp of a person. I nibble a french fry, thinking maybe I should try to gain some weight, maybe even attempt to exercise regularly.

And then I catch myself, surprised that such mundane thoughts have overtaken me, momentarily driving aside the worries that have preoccupied me for—how long? Sean. Gary. My sequel. The movie. And Carly May, above all. Or Chloe. What if Chloe Savage is an utter stranger—someone I don't know at all? What if she has eliminated every trace of the scrappily arrogant, willful, precocious Carly May? What if I am absolutely the last person in the world she wants to see?

No, I remind myself, my peace shattered. Chloe Savage requested this meeting. She chose to do the movie. She hasn't forgotten, no matter how hard she has tried. She's curious. I can feel it. That might not be *all* she is, but at least there is that. Which is a place to start.

Start what? What if she hates you? My mind spits this possibility at me without warning. *What if she has always hated you?* Not true, I fire back. Way too simple. *But she could hate you for the book*. I know her better than that.

Hate: Hetaera, houghmagandy, halieutics. Hebetate. Hadeharia (constant use of the word *hell;* who requires a word for this?). *Hyalopterous*.

I eat too slowly; my grilled cheese ungrills and reconstitutes itself as a solid slab. I push my plate away and dig in my handbag for my wallet. It's too bright in here. That's the worst thing about diners everywhere: they drench everything in a glaring light.

Back at the motel I sit at my little desk, open up my laptop, and tap it awake. The only source of light in the room is the computer; I keep the room dark enough that the window gives me a view of the parking lot rather than throwing my own reflection back at me. The last thing I need to see is my own pale, tired face, thinner than usual. On the screen is a list of files in the folder in which I keep the novel. The files include earlier versions of the beginning, a rough outline that stops well before the end, lists of ideas, characters, sections I cut but couldn't bring myself to get rid of—and, of course, my working draft. Why my eyes stray to the right, past the file names to cryptic columns of information about KBs and dates last modified, I'm not sure. But what I notice suddenly, as the cursor hovers over the draft icon, is the time signature:

Date modified: 6/25/2012 2:50 PM

June 25 is . . . today? Yes. I haven't been paying much attention, but that much I know. At 2:50 I was on the runway in Seattle, about to take off. My electronic devices were appropriately turned off and stowed.

And yet. My file was accessed—and not just accessed but modified—at precisely that moment.

My laptop never left my bag. My bag was under the seat in front of me.

Which means it was accessed remotely.

Now I remember the text message from Sean that hinted at a disturbing awareness of my activities. Now I remember that day I opened my draft and found that the font and the margins had been altered. I had blamed the changes on some sort of computer glitch. My Gmail calendar charts my itinerary. E-mail records correspondence with my agent. How much could Sean have seen? I know nothing about computer hacking. My vague notions of what is possible are informed by movies and TV shows in which bespectacled computer geeks can hack into anything they put their minds to, from the Pentagon to the secret ravings of would-be serial killers. Sean doesn't strike me as that clever, but who's to say? I have underestimated him before.

So let's just say it's possible. What does it *mean*?

I have no idea. I find myself strangely at a loss to speculate.

I change all my passwords, though I have no idea if that will make a difference. I disable the calendar function. I shut down my Facebook account for good measure, though I seldom use it.

I sit in the dark and think.

Chloe

I feel like hell by the time I land in Vancouver. Rinsing my face in the ladies', I give myself a good hard look in the mirror. There are shadows under my eyes, which isn't exactly shocking. There's a fine line just above my left eyebrow and the faintest echo of another just above that. My left is the eyebrow I raise. I'm being punished with wrinkles for all the snotty, skeptical looks I've ever given anybody. I don't think a casual observer would see the lines. The cameras are the first to notice when you start to fall apart.

I haven't gone down the Botox road, but my time will come. I've already held out longer than most people I know. Sometimes I wonder what the hell I'm trying to prove. No one's going to be impressed by my virtuous attachment to aging naturally. I'm not Helen fucking Mirren. Chloe Savage can't afford much in the way of professional virtue. And no one would expect it of her.

I smear concealer on the shadows and scowl at myself in the mirror. Some people practice their prettiest looks in the mirror, and I won't pretend I'm above that, but these days I prefer my grim face, my pissed-off face. Since no one else is in the bathroom I bare my teeth at myself, just for a second. As I turn away, I think I see a shadow of a dark wig in the mirror—stiff and cheap, not one of the many wigs I've stuck on my head as an actress, but the original wig, the abduction wig. I remember trying to charm myself in the ugly gas station restroom mirror, dark fake bangs cutting sharply across my forehead. Everything has changed since that day, every single fucking thing I can think of. One of my hands goes up to my head, and I almost expect to feel plasticky doll-hair. But it's my own, soft and fine and needing a wash.

I'm a cop now, I remember. I scrape my hair back into a ponytail and replace the lipstick in my purse, unapplied. I stump through the airport toward baggage claim like someone who has a complicated relationship with her authority, her power, the gun in her holster. Well, no gun in the airport, obviously, but generally, in her everyday life. I look warily from side to side; I make my face half-cocky, and then I let it slide back to shrinking insecurity. I need to believe in this cop.

My designer luggage doesn't help.

Who the hell would want to be a cop?

I could have had someone pick me up, but I rented a car instead. I want to be operating under my own steam here.

I also want a drink, cop or no cop.

• • •

The inn where most of the cast is staying is pretty far out of town. Deep in the woods, for obvious reasons. I start to panic when I first see it, but then I notice that it has a pub on the first floor. Smart innkeeper-in-the-middle-of-nowhere. I'm staying in a private guesthouse behind the main inn. It looks rustic from the outside, but it's actually nicely appointed. I run a bath, stuff my clothes in drawers, scatter my possessions reassuringly around the room, turn on the TV for company.

I treat myself to a tiny bottle of whiskey from the minibar and slip into the tub. Lulled by the voice of a female news anchor in the background, I try to think of nothing. I have a feeling this will get harder and harder from here on out.

Beside the tub is a large window that looks out on the dark woods behind the inn. There's a shade, but it isn't drawn. Stupid place for a window. Not that there's any reason for anyone to be back there, but it doesn't look like there's anything to stop them, either. I imagine a face appearing there—suddenly, out of the trees, peering in at my naked self in the bath. It's a good setting for a horror movie. I yank the shade down. Then I take a swig of whiskey. *Don't start getting jumpy,* I tell myself. *God knows you're annoying enough already.* I dunk myself beneath the water so that for a minute I can't see a damned thing and all I can hear is the rush of water drowning out my thoughts. Drowning out whatever makes me *me.* I wish to hell there were easier ways to do it.

Later I head over to the bar. I am half Chloe, half Mandy the cop; it's a necessary compromise. Mandy has such god-awful taste (in clothes, hair, everything) that I can't bring myself to risk meeting my fellow cast members (who aren't even here yet, I'm hoping, but you never know) as a fashion-challenged small-town policewoman. That's not a first impression you could recover from. Inside, though, I'm still playing Mandy, which is why I sit, not at the long, curving wooden bar, but at a small table in the corner of the low room, all dark wood and pale stone and exposed beams. From here I can see everyone, but it's hard for them to see me.

I'm here to watch, not to be watched; to see, not to be seen. What a weird feeling.

I drink wine, which is another compromise: I intend to limit my Canadian martini consumption but can't fully embrace Mandy's beer-swigging ways unless I want to spend half my life on the treadmill. (I assume there's a treadmill here. I picture hiking through the actual woods, and my blood runs cold. My revulsion is so strong that it surprises me.)

I'm on my second glass of sauvignon blanc when I notice a man across the room situated, like me, in a corner, his back to me. He's wearing jeans and a flannel shirt that has a distinctly designer look, and he's in the process of growing out a really expensive haircut. He has set himself apart from the other patrons—cheery vacationers, mostly well-heeled Canadians who look as though golf and tennis courses are their native realm.

An actor. Suddenly I'm convinced, without even seeing his face, that I know who this is. *Turn around,* I tell him in my head. Not because I want him to see me, because for once I don't. I want to get a look at him.

He doesn't. He's reading a newspaper. After a while—I am now on my third glass of wine and have scored a little bowl of bar snacks—he folds the paper, puts it neatly aside, and starts texting maniacally. He doesn't turn. I swear to God: he never fucking turns. Something about his movements practically hypnotizes me: the way he sits, the way he lifts his hands to brush his hair back every now and then, the way he tilts a pint of beer to lips I can't even see—it's an impressive economy of movement, I think, analyzing him like an actor would (an actor who has drunk nearly a bottle of wine, granted). He's only using the absolutely necessary muscles for each small action; his overall stillness isn't disturbed. Finally he gets up, stuffs his phone in his pocket, leaves the paper behind, tosses money on the table, and walks out. He stands up with his back to me, turning ever so slightly sideways to give a polite wave in the direction of the bar, turns his back again, and strides out.

Still, I know what I know.

The man I've just seen is no other than Billy Pearson. He's playing *him*. He is Zed.

Lois

I create a new file and title it *Ideas for Conclusion*. If Sean has indeed been hacking into my computer and spying on the developments of my sequel, I don't think he will be able to resist that bait. I assume that he badly wants to know what happens to Gary: what course of action he chooses, and how it turns out. What he gets away with. If I have been using Sean as a template for Gary, has Sean been doing the reverse? It's almost too appalling to contemplate.

What the document really contains is one cryptic sentence: *It's over, Sean.*

Surely what he's done is illegal. It must be; it's like trespassing, or home invasion. But what more can I do? *You have to call the police*, Brad told me after the night on the footbridge. *And tell them what, exactly? How much and starting when? No, thank you.* I imagine he would have the same advice now, but only I can make sure that this ends well. I've made my move; now I wait for his.

Hacker: Hyssop, hajib, hydrangea. Howadji. I've forgotten how much I like *H* words. *Hapaxanthous, hygrophanous. Hwyl*. (Yes, really. It's Welsh.) *Hymenopterous. Haecceity.*

Haecceity? I can see it clearly, but it's just a collection of letters, with no sense attached. Zed wouldn't approve. I type it into my computer, wondering whether such searches can be tracked. My computer is haunted: that's what it feels like.

Haecceity means *thisness, hereness*. Being present. Interesting. What reassures me is that I am here, and he is there. Whatever Sean wants from me, I am far enough away to be safe.

In the meantime, I have come a long way. I'm in this beige-and-brown motel room for a reason. From my window I see the outskirts of a tiny town—gas stations and fast food—and, in the distance, mountains. In the other direction, I know, lie the woods. And that's where I'm headed. Into the woods, deep in the woods. Like a fairy tale. Or a horror movie. I'm here, and so is Chloe. I breathe. I sip my bitter, cooling coffee. I plan. I turn my phone off.

In town I buy a notebook—just a plain ruled spiral affair, with a black cover. This is where Gary's final moves will have to play out. I feel an odd thrill at the prospect of composing longhand, as if it might allow me somehow to claim kinship with my long-dead eighteenth- and nineteenth-century novelists. It's like going back in time and attending a masked ball.

Haecceity. Thisness. Here-and-nowness.

Chloe

What would Mandy do the morning after she had made the mistake of following a minibottle of whiskey with an entire bottle of wine?

Mandy would eat breakfast. I don't, usually, so this is a huge treat. Mandy is supposed to be pretty fit, but she should still look like a small-town cop—not the doughnut variety, but not like a walking clothes hanger, either. I've been advised to eat like a slightly more normal person. In the morning I order eggs and fruit and a whole slice of wheat toast in the same little pub where I drank the night before. (Maybe what Mandy would eat is a stack of pancakes and a couple slabs of bacon, but there are limits.) I go back to the bar each evening for one discreet nightcap and retire to my room. I have not seen Billy Pearson again—not in the bar, not in the main lodge, not on the grounds. It's as if I imagined him, though I know I haven't quite reached *that* level of crazy. He's here somewhere.

I picture him out in the woods—hunting, maybe?—which is ridiculous, but I can't shake the image.

On the fourth day it rains. It starts the night before and by morning shows no sign of stopping. It's misty and gray and colder, and the rain beats down like radio static you can't turn off. I eat breakfast in my room, read for an hour, and head to the fitness center. (Because there are, of course, treadmills, not to mention a full gym.) Mandy has been running every day, doing weight training (which I, Chloe, hate more than most things, but it seems like a police sort of thing to do, so I'm trying it), and going to yoga and Pilates classes. There isn't a whole hell of a lot else to do, after all. I also read a lot; there's a great collection of left-behind pulp fiction in the main inn, and I'm working my way through the romantic thrillers and mysteries. There's some serious stuff, too, but I haven't been in the mood. I justify it by telling myself this is what Mandy would read in her spare time, to escape from the world of actual crime and dull, stupid police work. (*Screw you*, Mandy says in my head. She doesn't say *fuck* much. She's no prude, but gratuitous vulgarity isn't exactly her thing, either. *I read Dickens and—and classic detective novels.* I try to soothe her: *Of course you do. But you might like these, really. Try one!* Like I'm offering her candy, or drugs. She'll come around.)

Today I've been on the treadmill for almost half an hour and am seriously dying for a walking break (I don't like running much more than I like lifting weights) when a familiar tall, dark not-quite-stranger strolls in and hops up on the treadmill next to mine. Which seems a little too neighborly, if you ask me, since the machines that are *not* next to me are unoccupied. But I'm also curious. And caught off guard, which leaves me with an awkward-teenager feeling that I haven't had for years—which, in fact, I hardly ever felt even when I was a teenager. So maybe it's Mandy's influence. He gives me a polite nod and has begun to set his machine when he turns his gaze sharply back my way, like he's just figured something out. I'm looking straight ahead, of course, not wanting to get caught checking him out. So he doesn't catch my eye. Instead he starts running, picking up speed swiftly, cranking his music up so loud I can hear it through my own headphones. Ridiculously, I find myself embarrassed to switch into walk mode, so I keep running even though by now I really do want to die. I even step up my pace a little. *You ass*, I tell myself, *who the hell are you trying to impress*? But it doesn't help.

I finally quit when my legs are so weak that I think I might actually fall off the stupid treadmill. I don't mess around with a cool-down period, just turn the thing off, balance my feet on the sides, and wait for the belt to stop.

Surprisingly, he stops too.

"Hey there," he says as I mop the sweat from my face. "You're Chloe Savage, aren't you? The lady police detective?"

"Police detective," I say, pulling my headphones from my ears. "She's no lady." (Although, I think, she actually *is* sort of a lady.) I smile a little lewdly to take any possible obnoxiously feminist sting out of my smart-assed words. At the same time, I think: *Poor Mandy would hear that shit all the time. No wonder she's a little uptight*.

"Right, of course not. Hence her crush on the kidnapper?" He twinkles his eyes at me.

Nice trick, I think, glad that my face is no doubt so purple from exhaustion that a little girlish blush is unlikely to make much difference.

Don't get the wrong idea. Billy Pearson, as everyone knows, has a gorgeous wife (not in the business, miraculously) and an insanely cute kid. He is not hitting on me, and I am not developing a crush on him. Whatever heart I have is still hanging out with the English prof back in California, strangely enough. It really is.

But the fact that Mandy is drawn to the kidnapper—not to say obsessed with him—is fucking with my head a little. As is the fact that Billy Pearson looks so much like the real kidnapper that I keep blinking to clear my vision and make sure I'm seeing straight.

Or at least I think he does. Can I really trust my memory? I was twelve, and I was traumatized. Maybe I'm just pouring Zed into this guy's shell, this actor with a slight physical resemblance to him—this actor who is looking at me like he can read my fucking mind, which annoys the hell out of me.

"Did you just get here?" I ask casually, like I couldn't care less. Like I didn't see him in the bar almost a week ago.

"Nope. Usually I run outside, but the rain . . ." He grimaces charmingly and gestures toward the streaky, spattered windows. "There are great trails out in the woods, you know. Miles of them. I hate treadmills—running and running and getting nowhere." *How original*. Another disarming smile, like he has a whole arsenal of expressions guaranteed to win you over. Which I find off-putting, though Mandy is kind of taken in. "No offense, of course, if that's your thing."

"Running in any form isn't exactly my *thing*."

"But you do it anyway," he remarks cheerfully—and also, I think, kind of ambiguously: What's that supposed to mean? Is it good or bad?

"Also," he says, leaning over a little as though he's telling me a secret, "I've been hunting."

Hunting? Did he really just say that? "*Hunting?*" I repeat skeptically, remembering my imagined scenarios. "Seriously?" *But he didn't hunt, the kidnapper. You would have expected him to, but he didn't. You've guessed wrong.*

"Seriously. Well, I didn't actually shoot anything. But I carried a gun, and I wore the whole hunting get-up, and I looked for animals to shoot. I even aimed at them: I just didn't pull the trigger."

"Because you didn't want to, or because you couldn't?" I don't know him well enough to ask him probing questions or adopt such a mocking, familiar tone. (I think that's how it would be described in one of the novels I've been reading.) I feel almost embarrassed by my rudeness. Embarrassment is not usually a problem for me.

He doesn't seem to mind. "It was never part of the plan. I mean, what the hell would I do with a dead rabbit? No, I was just trying to get into the guy's head. The kidnapper. I'm having sort of a tough time with him."

His surprising willingness to confide in me—because that's what it seems like he's doing—loosens some key link between me and sanity. In fact, that chain must have been weaker than I ever guessed, because what I blurt is this: "Well, you look a lot like him!"

I am immediately appalled. *Since when are you such an idiot?* I ask myself in horror. Mandy joins in: *Do you really have to tell everybody everything? You'll never find out anything that way, you know. Some things are best kept to yourself.*

Meanwhile, I try to recover. "I mean—what I imagine—"

"I know," Billy interrupts, "I've actually been doing some research. You know this script is based on a novel that's based on a true story, don't you? I mean really loosely based. It was a real case back in the nineties. I've seen some photos of the guy: school pictures, Boy Scouts, stuff like that. We have the same coloring and build, pretty much. But I'm trying to get a better sense of what the hell he was thinking. I mean, I don't think he was just nuts. Sure, that was part of it, but I feel like he must have wanted something, something that made sense, at least to him. He wasn't a stupid guy. And he never did hurt the girls, as far as anyone knows. If you believe what the girls said, anyway. It's just such a mystery." He scratches his handsome head, then smiles, a big self-deprecating grin that, finally, charms me in spite of myself. "So yeah, I'm going all method and shit."

How many people could say that and not sound like complete assholes? *My guard is up*, I tell myself.

We agree to meet for dinner.

Lois

It's hard to believe that this is the landscape in which they have chosen to cinematically reconstruct our summer in the cabin. Everything is on a different scale here: the mountains are grander, the clouds are stacked higher in the sky, the woods to the east look like they go on forever. So far I haven't ventured much beyond my motel. I've established a routine that involves breakfast and an early dinner at my diner, a long afternoon walk along the quiet, windy highway, and many hours in my room, scribbling in my notebook, which is already almost full. The day divides so neatly, so willingly, so gracefully; it's like coaxing a well-creased map to refold along the old lines, reducing a floppy, unwieldy square to a slim, tuckable rectangle. I find this quiet sense of order bracing.

I seldom look at my phone. When I do, I delete Sean's texts unread. I should be curious about his response to my computer-file decoy, but for now I prefer not to think about him. He's thousands of miles away. I'm pretty sure he doesn't have a car. I don't think he has the kind of friends who might loan him a car or money for an expensive plane ticket. He's still drifting around town in his trench coat, no doubt, surly but essentially harmless. Even his threat to disclose my secrets seems less powerful from a distance; what would it matter, really, if everyone knew my past? Or that I am Lucy Ledger, of whom they probably haven't heard? This is how I think by day. At night I dream of the woods: my woods, the woods I half remember. They are a looming, peripheral presence; I was almost never *in* them, really, just surrounded by them. Pine, spruce, maple . . . but the pine dominates, and it's the pine that becomes loquacious when the wind rises. I remember the shadows cast by trees on the walls of the lodge, the squeak of a branch as its tips brushed against our bedroom window. Its fingers, rather: I understand why branches are called limbs, active extensions of living bodies, with wills of their own, things to say. In my dreams the trees are alive, the sun never shines, and Zed is far more sinister, more threatening, than he ever seemed in reality. I awake disturbed and also guilty, as if I have betrayed us by imagining such malevolence.

Sometimes Gary is there, too: or at least I think he is. Hiding in a closet or a bathroom, lurking in the woods. He looks a lot like Sean.

Dream: Dulcimer, desiccate. Denouement. Too easy. *Daguerreotype, deleterious, doppelgänger. Debauchee, décolletage, deshabille.* Is there a theme emerging? *Dacoity. Dacquoise*, which is a cake. Let them eat cake, have your cake and eat it too. Is that what I'm trying to do on some level? No, no theme. You can make meaning out of anything. Random scraps. *Dystopic.* Enough! *Dashiki.* Better. But the words won't stop. *Dactylomegaly,* which involves having exceptionally large fingers or toes, though you could figure that out without being at all familiar with the word. *Dactyl + megaly*: all the clues you need. The best *D* word of them all: *dziggetai.* A Mongolian wild ass, which has absolutely nothing to do with anything.

Double entendre: deliquesce, dressage, dreidel, dirndl. I am stuck, it would seem, on the *D* words. *Drunken, drama, depression, desperation, doom, dwindle, dire.* Far too easy. *Doggerel.* Better.

You're getting close, aren't you? I think I am.

Chloe

Charming Billy calls my room the next morning and invites me to go for a drive. "Have you gone to check out the set yet?" he asks, and something in my stomach lurches.

"No," I admit. "Is it finished?"

"I hear they're putting the finishing touches on the cabin. I'd love to see it before it's completely overrun with people and equipment, just to get a feel for it. Wouldn't you? I mean, I know your relationship to it isn't as intense as mine, but I think it could be useful for you. Come on, it'll be more fun if you come with me."

My feelings are violently mixed. Yes, I want to see it. Of course I do. Also it scares the hell out of me. On top of that, I'm weirded out by Billy's habit of saying *me* and *you* when he means *the kidnapper* and *the police detective.* I find myself thinking, *Your relationship to it isn't as intense as mine? Are you high?* And then biting my tongue, which I don't trust anymore after yesterday's moronic slip.

In any case, *fun* isn't exactly the word I would use to describe my expectations. But I agree to go. What else am I here for, anyway? Why did I make such a point of arriving early? Why put this off? Part of me hopes that this hunting lodge bears no resemblance whatsoever to the one I remember; that it's a Hollywood, fairytale idea of a hunting lodge, all picturesque, not a real one. And some irrational part of me, I realize, expects (and hopes?) to pull up to an exact replica of the cabin where I spent the summer of my twelfth year.

• • •

Billy has rented a Range Rover, which makes me wonder if he isn't a little bit of an asshole after all.

Here's the story with Billy: He is without a doubt the name in this movie—the only one, really; they got the rest of us cheap. He isn't quite A-list, but he's close. He could be, eventually, if he makes some smart choices. He hasn't done much serious stuff—mostly rom-coms and some pretty tame action pics. Whether he can really open a big film remains uncertain; most often he's the best friend, the ex-boyfriend, the brother. This has worked well for him, as he usually manages to steal the show. He oozes charisma and likability on the screen (as, I must admit, he does in person).

Obviously that makes him an interesting choice to play a psycho-kidnapper; you won't be able to help sympathizing with him. I'm actually surprised they have the guts to play it that way. Even in Lois's book, he's a pretty ambiguous figure—compelling and genuine, sometimes charming, sometimes sinister. If charming Billy can capture *that,* he'll go a long way toward proving he's the real thing. I assume that's his plan. *All method and shit*. Please.

Riding in the passenger seat beside him, I'm struck again by his slightly freakish resemblance to Zed. He's wearing jeans and an untucked T-shirt, his face a little stubbly, his hair just outgrowing its pretty-boy neatness. He's intent on the road, which is winding and narrow, and he isn't talking, which is rare. If I close my eyes I could almost be twelve again, driving across the country, maybe somewhere in the woods of Pennsylvania. Full of—what?—hope? Excitement? Yeah—but fear, too. A kind of fear that's mixed with pleasure, though; like fear of the dark, or ghosts, or roller coasters. A thrilling kind of fear.

"God, would you stop staring at me, Chloe?" He laughes self-consciously. He's one of those people who says your name all the time, practically every time he addresses you. Most people don't; in fact lots of people almost never call you by your name at all. It feels weirdly personal when someone does, like your name is a cozy secret you share, or a little pat on the ass.

"Sorry. I didn't mean to. I was just spacing out, I guess," I say.

"Oh, so you weren't actually admiring my chiseled beauty?" He pretends to be crestfallen, breaking the spell. Zed didn't laugh much. His emotions were almost as dramatic and visible as Billy's, but they occupied a much lower, darker register. When Billy laughs and sparkles, he bears only a ghost of a resemblance to *him*. A manageable ghost. Endearing, even.

"Chiseled is what you call that look, is it? I'd say more like craggy-mountain-man, myself." I'm chattering to cover up my stare and whatever inappropriate expression might have accompanied it; I hardly know what I'm saying.

"I was just thinking," he interrupts, to my relief. He's turned serious again. "Seriously, I was just thinking: imagine what it would have been like to be those girls. Especially the first one, the Nebraska one. I mean, she rode across the whole freaking country with this guy. What could that have been like? What would they have talked about? Or would he have, like, played the radio? She could have been gagged or something, I guess, but I doubt it. They must've stopped for fast food, had hamburgers together. I mean, that's fucked-up, right? But it's also just fascinating. God, I love this part!" He strikes his fist against the steering wheel and then, without warning, slams on the brakes. "Damn! Sorry. Almost missed the turn. Getting carried away." Generally I find his self-deprecating reversals endearing, but I'm still too busy grappling with his little flight of fancy to appreciate this one. I'm still gripping the door handle as he takes a ridiculously sharp turn—and then, with no warning, there it is.

There it fucking is.

And then again, there it isn't.

It's set well back from the road in a small clearing in the woods, but you have a good view of it from the driveway. It's roughly the same size as Zed's lodge, maybe a little smaller. The line of the roof is subtly different—the angle isn't as sharp, maybe. I realize as I study the building that the truth is I almost never saw Zed's lodge from the outside, not in daylight, anyway. Its outlines are pretty vague in my memory. This cabin can easily step in and become *the* cabin; almost any cabin could.

Yes, that's me, Miss Rationality. Forget that my hands are shaking, my breath has gone shallow, and a viselike pain has locked around my forehead. This is just a cabin. A fake. A movie set. In western Canada. It should have no emotional value whatsoever. That would be ridiculous.

Right.

I find that I have something to say to Billy, even though technically the moment when it would have been natural and appropriate to respond to his remark about the Nebraska girl passed a few seconds ago. "I think she would have felt—I mean, even if he was being nice to her, treating her well—she never would have known what was next, right? Even if they were having a fine old time and eating hamburgers one minute, for all she knew, the next minute he could chop her up and throw her in the woods, right? Because what else do psychos do? I think that even if they felt safe, the girls, there always would have been this doubt—this fear that just around the corner . . . you know?" My garbled words sound strangely urgent, even to me. Billy gives me a quick look with a little bit of surprise in it, and then he nods slowly.

Thank God he hasn't picked up on anything; he just thinks I've used my actorly intuition to get inside Nebraska-girl's head. Callie, she's called in the movie and in the book. I imagine Lois choosing a name so close to mine, imagine what she would have been thinking. She changed her own name completely, made herself a Hannah. It's like the name Lois in the sense that it's a little old-fashioned, a little plain—but it's also becoming popular again, which Lois isn't; there's a slight connection but not an obvious one. Me, on the other hand? Carly, Callie. *Please.* She was keeping me close.

We get out of the Range Rover, walk around. The ground is damp and soft with pine needles. My heels sink in. There are a few workmen around, but no one bothers us.

The Adirondack chairs on the porch are wrong, I'm glad to see. They look old and worn. The real ones were freshly painted. Dark green. Zed must have painted them when he was getting the place ready for us.

Everything is different here. And I am not Callie or Carly May. Or Chloe, even. I am Mandy, the police detective. I should look at this place with the eye of a cop—looking for places to hide, unlocked windows, places the kidnapper could be watching me from. I'm wearing sensible shoes—cross trainers—not heels. I'm out of uniform, plainclothes, jeans and a T-shirt. I have a light jacket back in my car, which is a little Toyota, not a Range Rover.

I'm working. There are no ghosts. And before long (I check my watch) it'll be time for a drink.

Lois

One evening at the diner, a conversation at the bar catches my attention, breaking through the cloud of dark thoughts that usually preserves my solitude even when the diner is at its busiest. "Upstate New York, this time," a man is saying, eliciting a few laughs from other patrons. "Maybe British Columbia will win an Oscar one of these days," says the woman behind the counter, refilling the first man's coffee. "We're so versatile, aren't we? We can be anyplace you want us to be—New York, California, Ireland for God's sake." This sounds like a conversation they've had before, I think; a curious fact of their existence, now that BC is such a popular filming location.

"There's only one big-name actor in this one," another man remarks. "That Billy Pearson, you know him? Looks like a movie star, that's for sure, but I never thought much of him as an actor." Someone else starts listing Billy Pearson films, and they all contribute.

Billy Pearson is playing Zed, of course. I have focused so intently on Chloe Savage that I've spared little thought for him. I try to conjure up his face, transposing it gingerly onto the one I remember. It might work—physically, at least, it might work. I have just begun trying to frame my doubts, to explain to myself what it is that I think Billy Pearson might have trouble capturing, when I hear the woman behind the counter pipe up again. She's wiping the counter down with a rag. Her thin dark hair lies limply against her neck, her jaw. I try to imagine a more flattering cut. "He's here already, you know. I heard it this morning. He's been seen driving around with a blond woman. One of the actresses, most likely."

"He's married, isn't he?" This from the man who seems to be the best informed. He must watch entertainment shows or read some celebrity magazine. "Could be the wife."

"Nope," says the thin-haired waitress. "The wife has red hair. This was definitely not the wife." Her news hangs in the air, generating suspicion. I wonder why it would please them to know that Billy Pearson was up to no good.

But I'm also thinking: *Some blond woman? One of the actresses?*

Chloe has arrived. It could be anyone, but it's not. It's Chloe.

Chloe

The actresses playing the little girls are complete unknowns. I approve of that decision. I've met a lot of child actors, and most of them seem too knowing, too old-before-their-time. No wonder. But it taints them a little bit. Lois and I were precocious in our own ways, no doubt about it, but we were still essentially children, and sheltered ones at that. To start out with. We were different by the time we got back.

When I first see them, though, I'm not so sure. I'm having breakfast in the pub, where a faint cocktail-y aroma seems to me to linger teasingly even in the daylight. Billy has joined me—this has become our routine on the days when I don't slink off to the local diner I've become attached to, though he says his wife and kid arrive next week, so that'll be that, I assume. Neither of us is very chatty in the morning, which is the only reason I'm willing to share a table with him at that time of day. Especially because I'm not stupid, and I know it looks bad. Stories will get back to the wife, and suddenly sitting at a table drinking coffee and reading random Canadian newspapers will seem like evidence of a torrid affair. Which we are definitely not having.

Anyway, I hear the girls before I see them. They sail into the quiet room with their entourage: Parents, small siblings, God knows who else. Coaches? Nannies? Shrinks? The girls' clear high voices rise above everyone else's. They may not be seasoned professionals, but they sure as hell aren't lacking in confidence or presence. *Strike one against them*, I think, since Lois and I were just stupid small-town kids. I had hoped they would have a little of that quality, just a glimmer, even, and now I'm doubtful.

Billy raises his head, too, and puts his paper down. "It's the girls!" he says, with a little too much excitement in his voice, as if he's been getting bored and welcomes a new form of stimulation.

"Looks like it. Noisy little wenches, aren't they?" I sip my coffee. I don't put my newspaper down, though I haven't really read a word of it the entire time; it mostly seems concerned with various environmental measures in western Canada and minor crimes committed in the area, and I think it might be the most boring paper I've read since I left Nebraska.

"Be nice," says Billy. "Let's go introduce ourselves."

"You go. I'm not ready."

He gives me a funny look—a well-deserved one, I guess. "You're very strange sometimes, Chloe Savage," he says, standing up. "But *I* am going to go introduce my charming self to the lovely young actresses we're going to be working with in the middle of the woods all summer, with you or without you." He pauses, as if he assumes I'll change my mind.

"Without," I say, pretending to be absorbed in the sports section.

And then he is preening (really, there's no other word for it) before the girls and their clucking companions: They are so excited to meet a real movie star! They want his autograph! They can't believe this! He's even cuter in person!

Meanwhile, I slip out. I'll meet the lovely young "actresses" (*my ass!*) on my own terms.

From then on Billy tends to spend his days with the girls—doing God knows what, hiking in the woods or something. He joins me in the pub in the evening, sparing me the awkwardness of drinking alone.

I don't mean to imply that I've been completely antisocial. The movie people have been arriving throughout the week; I've met the director, some cast members, and the costume designer, who apologizes in advance for what she's going to make me wear. "You're going to fucking hate me," she says. "Seriously, you'll be lucky if you ever work again." She's joking, but I wonder how funny that really is.

"Maybe you'll get an award," I suggest. "If the clothes are so ugly."

"Nah." She scowls. She's tall, cadaverous, zombie-esque. The slightest twist of genetic fate would have made her a model. Instead she's practically hideous. Her mouth is fouler than mine, which I appreciate. "For awards you've got to do period. Doublets and hose–type shit."

"Well, the nineties must be damned near 'period' by now, right?"

"Depends on the film. We're not really working the period angle here; it's a pretty shitty decade, style-wise. Which means," she says, flashing a rare and terrifying smile, "no baggy jeans. No gigantic shoes. At least you have that to thank me for."

Then she wanders off. I like that about her. She comes and goes downright stealthily, which is kind of a relief when you're surrounded by so many people who have made an art form of entering and exiting rooms.

I still spend a lot of time reading; the detective novels and gothic romances continue to distract me. I hang out at my little diner downtown sometimes. It's a bit of a drive, but there are never any film people there, and I can sit in a booth and try to think Mandy-thoughts. I don't tell anyone at the diner who I am, but I'm pretty sure they know I'm from the cast. Whenever I walk in I feel like the conversation that slams to a halt was probably way more interesting than anything they're willing to say while I'm there. I keep hoping they'll get used to me and go back to acting naturally when I'm around, but I guess that would take longer than a few days. But maybe people wouldn't talk freely in front of someone like Mandy, either. She's a cop, after all, and also a woman. Maybe you would have a harder time trusting her than you would some local good old boy. Maybe you wouldn't want her poking her nose into your business. The script makes it clear that when Mandy is trying to dig up information about the quiet man living alone at the old hunting lodge, the locals aren't much help. She's not from the area—not from the point of view of the locals. She's from Albany. It's not much of a drive, but it's *the city.*

I'm having coffee and eggs at the diner when this hits me. I've been thinking of Mandy as a hick, more or less (and my childhood in Arrow earns me the right to use the word). But she's a city girl, relatively speaking, and an outsider herself. The novel gives her more backstory than the movie has time for; you know that her grandparents are from the Adirondacks, and that her father returned to the mountains after he left her mother. She has one foot in the world of small towns like this one and another in Albany, an anxious, self-important city midway between New York City and the rural wilderness called the North Country.

I wonder again what Lois was thinking when she invented Mandy. Did she just want to distinguish her book from the real story in a few concrete ways? Did she think the story needed an adult female character in order to attract the right kind of readers? (Which would have been smart, I admit.) Or is it more than that: does Mandy have some significance of her own, some coded meaning, at least in Lois's (obviously) fucked-up mind?

I can ask her, if I really want to know. She'll be here in three days. I find it really hard to imagine this meeting—for some reason I haven't allowed myself to think about it much—but I do believe it will happen. Lois. In three days.

Suddenly my plate blurs, and I think for a second that I might actually be sick. But no, it's just emotion, real and raw and weirdly anonymous. There's anger in it, and loss, but that's not all. Its intensity reminds me of the kind of feelings you have when you're a kid, so powerful they really can knock you out, make you puke, cause you to see red. It's been a long, long time, I realize, since I've felt anything like that. Am I not a cold-hearted, unfeeling bitch after all? Or is it a question of repression?

Shut up, Chloe, I tell myself.

I throw money on the table, and the queasy feeling passes. The regulars nod formally to me as I go, their curiosity politely suppressed.

Only one of us can be batshit crazy, I tell myself. I have a sneaking sort of feeling that Lois—rational, orderly Lois—might have claimed that role. That means I need to keep it together.

You too, Carly May. My old self seems nearer than usual. *As if she wants something.* But that thought has a distinct scent of crazy, which I have just sworn to avoid.

When I get back to the guesthouse, one of the girls is sitting on my doorstep. By now I've met them, but only in passing. They don't seem all that interested in me, and I don't blame them. We don't even have that much screen time together, naturally, since I spend most of the movie trying to find them and then figure out how to rescue them.

The one on my porch is the dark-haired one—the Lois girl, Natasha in real life and Hannah in the movie.

I raise my eyebrows at her and then lower them quickly, thinking of wrinkles. I wait for her to say something, since I assume that's what she's here for. She's sitting on my little step, pulling the red petals off a perfectly good flower from the garden. (My father would have known the name of it.) The woods stretch out behind the little row of carefully spaced guesthouses, so thick that they're dead dark even in the middle of the day. I haven't so much as set foot in the forest.

"Sorry," Natasha says when she sees me, looking up but not getting up. "You don't really like us much, do you."

I find myself laughing. "If that's your idea of small talk, maybe I do. But no, seriously, why would you say that? I don't like you or not like you. I don't know you, do I? It's not personal."

"Really?" She narrows her pretty blue eyes at me, and I feel as if she's trying to look inside my head. "It feels kind of personal. I see you watching us sometimes with a really weird look on your face. Like you can't stand us."

God, is she right? I hope not. "Seriously, kid, that's just my normal expression. Ask Billy, he'll tell you. Get used to it."

"Actually it's Billy that told me maybe I should come talk to you," she says. Then, on a totally different note: "Did you just call me *kid*? That's, like, so old-fashioned, isn't it? Like from some old movie? You know, like"—she scrunches up her face and drops her voice, becoming a weird cross-dressing caricature of some old male movie star—"See ya around, kid." She winks. "Or, you know, 'Here's looking at you, kid.'"

"God, please, stop. I did say it. I don't know why. So what do you want, anyway?" Conceited little monster.

"Acting advice."

My heart warms ever so slightly. "Is this your first film?"

She lifts her sharp little shoulders in a show of modesty. "I've done some made-for-TV stuff and commercials. But yeah, pretty much. How old were you when you started acting?"

"Older than you," I say, and my heart is cold again. "So? What is it?"

"I don't get it," says Natasha. (Hannah. Not Lois.) "I mean I don't get the story, exactly. I don't see why we *like* the kidnapper guy. Why don't we think he's a pervert? Why don't we run away? And why does he want us, anyway? Since he doesn't seem to want to—you know—molest us or anything. Honestly. I just don't get it." She looks genuinely glum.

How to answer? I sit down on the porch beside her. "People are complicated," I say slowly. "You like him because he likes you. Because he's handsome and intelligent and mysterious. Because you're bored. Because he thinks you're special, he thinks you're incredibly smart and pretty, and you're vain and shallow enough to be a total sucker for that. Which isn't your fault, because you're twelve, and you can't help it." I ignore the look of protest on her face. "Because it's an adventure, and he's in charge. Because you're so lonely at home you could die. Because being kidnapped is like being in a book, and you've always wanted to be in a book, because you're the kind of nerdy shy little girl that reads all the time." She looks thoughtful, though also skeptical. I can see that she's a skeptical girl. Good for her, I guess.

"Besides," I say, standing up again. "He's Billy, remember. If Billy kidnapped you, would you run away?"

Natasha giggles in spite of herself.

"I didn't think so," I say, and pointedly turn to unlock my door.

Lois

I find the film location easily enough, following the map some lowly production assistant sent me. I drive past the dirt road turn-off and park by the side of the road a few yards down. Shooting hasn't begun yet, but there are people around, and I don't want to draw attention to myself. I stroll along the road like a local woods-dweller taking a constitutional, glancing innocently around, and then I turn down the narrow road as if by chance, as if nothing but idle curiosity guides me.

Just for a second, my heart stops.

They have done a good job, I think, straining for objectivity, for distance. The cabin is nearly a perfect replica of the one I described in my novel, and it's eerily similar to the original, at least as I remember it. I focus on the differences—the angle of the second-story roof, the cars in the driveway, the carefully weathered Adirondack chairs—in order to ground myself in the present.

I can hear hammering from within the cabin and reassure myself that the people belonging to the cars are most likely inside, putting the finishing touches on the sets. I venture a little farther down the driveway, the trees stretching endlessly above me, blocking the sun. I hear birds and the breeze that politely disturbs the treetops without bothering to descend to the ground. I could be in my little bedroom, mine and Carly's, and those could be our trees, our birds, the ones outside our window, the ones that reminded us where we were, told us we were all right. Without warning, three figures emerge from behind the house, running: a man in a plaid flannel shirt and two young girls—one dark-haired, one fair. They are chasing him, grabbing at the tail of his shirt, his belt loops. *Why is it light? It was always dark when we were outside. The ground was cool and damp at night when we stretched our sequestered limbs. Mosquitoes feasted on us, and we tried not to mind. Only at night were the mountains our own.*

The girls are shrieking with glee, which Carly and I would not have dared. They are more forward than we were, more confident, a little in love with themselves. And he is permitting them to catch him, to drag him down, which Zed would never have done; he would have made us catch him for real. Everything was for real with him.

They've seen me. They stop playing and turn curious gazes my way. I feel like a ghost; I'm irrationally surprised that I am visible to them. I feel as if we exist on separate planes, and only I am privileged (or cursed) to see across the misty distance that separates us. *You're doing it wrong,* I want to cry. *Let me explain.*

Instead I wave casually and turn back, retracing my steps. I feel as if I'm fleeing.

Chloe

Two nights before the shoot begins, Billy doesn't show up for happy hour in the pub, so I'm back to drinking alone. Everyone's here now, from the director on down, but I haven't connected with anyone except maybe the wardrobe woman, and she seems to be staying somewhere else. I'm sitting at my usual corner table, reading a book—another detective novel, with a lurid blood-smeared knife on the cover; it reminds me of the books Lois and I used to read, and feels like a connection. A shadow moves briskly across my table and I look up, bracing myself to be pleasant, which is not really what I feel. My mood has been getting darker.

The thrower of the shadow is a tall, striking, strong-featured woman with outrageous red hair, long and wild and curly. She sticks out one handsome, man-sized hand. "Hi!" she says, her green eyes springing at me like stalking cats while her mouth smiles broadly. "Chloe Savage? Fiona Pearson. I hear you've been keeping my husband out of trouble. So sweet of you. Someone has to do it. You'll be glad to know I'm here to relieve you of your duties." Under her gaze I feel almost guilty. I remind myself that my dealings with Billy have been shockingly sexless. This crazed warrior queen has no business staring at me that way.

I force myself to return the pressure of her hand, lowering my book partway to the table to make it clear that she offers only the mildest of distractions from my reading. "You're welcome," I say. "But the girls have pretty much taken him off my hands since they arrived." I nod my head toward the doorway, where Natasha and Justine (the Carly-actress, the me-actress) are making their entrance. "They adore him already," I add. "They've been doing a lot of bonding. So important for their performances, don't you think?" The girls are actually thirteen, not twelve, and they're both looking particularly lovely tonight, in the awkward, kittenish, fetching way of thirteen-year-olds, just on the verge of everything. Fiona's eyes follow mine. "Pretty, aren't they? God, I wouldn't be that age again for anything in the world." I feel strangely torn between the impulse to intensify her jealousy by transferring it to Natasha and Justine, and actually trying to be pleasant to her; there's something sort of compelling about her.

But the Fionas of the world have never liked me much. She suggests with glaring insincerity that I should stop by their table for a drink later, and sails across the room toward the young actresses just as Billy enters, a small boy trundling along with him, his cherubic mini-Billy face framed by Fiona's wild red curls.

Poor Billy doesn't even glance my way.

I have a salad and another glass of wine; more and more people have stopped by my table. The whole scene seems to be getting much more social suddenly. But I'm not in the mood; I feel vaguely pissed off at everyone. I slip out when I think no one's looking, an extra bottle of wine under my arm recklessly charged to my room. Before I get to my guesthouse, I hear multiple feet pattering behind me and a breathless chorus of "wait up!" I'm surprised to see Natasha and Justine running after me, dragging the little Pearson child between them.

"We're babysitting," Natasha explains when I let them catch up to me.

"*Fiona* asked us to," Justine adds darkly.

"She didn't ask, really. She *ordered*." I can't help smiling at their undisguised bitterness. "She said, 'Why don't the *children* run and play.'" Natasha scowls at the boy.

"What's the kid's name?" I ask. I'm sure Billy mentioned it a thousand times, but it's not the kind of thing I tend to remember.

"Liam," Justine says, grudgingly. I find myself fascinated by the intense expressions that flit quickly across her face. Love, vengefulness, despair. Was I like that once? There's something familiar about her, a kind of echo. It's there with Natasha, too, but not as strong.

The truth is I can't stand girls their age, as a rule. Maybe it's because of the echo; I couldn't really stand myself at thirteen, either.

"Liam!" says Liam, enthusiastically. I look at him critically. "Is he about two, do you think?"

"Probably," says Justine. "Terrible two."

"Two!" says Liam.

We all contemplate him in silence. Condensation from my bottle of sauvignon blanc soaks through my thin dress. "He really is a cute little fucker, isn't he?" I don't mean to say this. It just comes out. But it's true.

The girls giggle and agree, suddenly my conspirators. They grab his fat little hands and swing him back and forth between them a couple of times, a little more cheerfully, while he sputters inanely, "Liam whee!"

"So why did you follow me?" I ask finally. "Fiona didn't make me an honorary child, did she?"

They laugh again, as I knew they would. They're so vulnerable! So manipulable! I have a weird impulse to hug them. Protect them? I shrug it off. I think of my bottle of wine, warming.

They shrug in sync. "We're bored," says Natasha.

"You seem kind of cool," Justine adds. "By comparison." I admire the way she undermines her compliment. I'm almost flattered. "The other adults are acting kind of like assholes."

"Language," says Natasha, as if she can't really help it, and I think of Lois, trying so hard not to be prim.

"Screw that," says Justine.

"You guys want to come back to my cottage for a bit? You can talk shit about everybody, if you want. I don't care."

"Sure," they say, carefully nonchalant.

"Juice?" says Liam hopefully.

"Juice," I agree, hoping there's some in the minibar. Diet Coke for the girls. Sauvignon Blanc for me. We'll sit on the porch and watch for lightning bugs. I've been told it's rare to see them out here, but we can hope.

Later, after Fiona has fetched the kids (with a *very* unconvincing show of gratitude, I might add), my phone rings. Not my iPhone, which wouldn't be all that surprising, but the landline in my room. Billy, calling to apologize for his wife? But he has my cell number. Lucy Ledger's agent, confirming our meeting? Not likely; everything's arranged. The front desk? I pick it up out of pure curiosity and am unsurprised when there's nobody there at first. "Hello," I say. "Hello, hello! Who is it?" I hear breathing. Someone *is* there. "Hey, asshole," I say, pretty cheerfully; it's the wine, I guess. "You're boring me," I say. "I'm going to hang up now." And I'm about to when the breather finally says something. It's hard to understand because he's obviously trying to make his voice sound weird.

"I know who you are," the voice croaks.

"Well, congratulations! I guess you've got the right number then."

"No, I mean I know who you *really* are," says the fake voice. "I know everything."

He sounds youngish. He must want something. What could it possibly be? For a few seconds I have no idea what to say to him. I run through various possibilities. Jaden sold me out? Could it be someone from back home? Some enterprising tabloid reporter? Surely not. Who else knows?

Lois? Someone Lois knows? But who would she tell, and why, Lois who loved secrets more than life?

"You have no idea what you're talking about," I drawl pleasantly while my mind continues to race.

"I can tell everyone," he says, the hoarseness wavering. "Everyone will know. There's only one way to stop me."

"Oh, spare me," I say, with an indifference I don't feel. "I'm sure it'll be great publicity for the film. It's a wonder I didn't think of it myself." And I hang up. I look blankly out the back window into the black woods. Strange. Very strange.

But honestly: who cares? It's an interesting question, I decide, upending the last of the bottle into my almost-empty glass.

I care. I've built up my world too carefully, for whatever it's worth. My fake history is well established; no one has ever questioned it—my Connecticut upbringing and all the rest. I can't stand the thought that it could all come crashing down.

And how on earth could he have gotten my room number, whoever he is? I check the door to my cottage, reassuring myself that it's locked. I find myself staring out the back window. Instead of the dark woods, I see my own face looking back at me. Some trick of the light makes me look old and anxious. *Fuck it,* I say to myself, and toss back the rest of my wine. A pathetic show of bravado, I have to admit.

Lois

At the diner I learn that the actress tends to arrive around ten, on the days she comes at all. The employees now know who she is, but their interest in her is mild and polite. I decide to stake out the diner. The first day she doesn't show, and I worry; there's only one more day before we are actually scheduled to meet. I want to catch her off guard. I want the upper hand, at least to begin with. I fear her professional artifice; I want to startle her into being real, if she is not in the habit of it. Which I don't know, of course; I have constructed an imaginary Chloe in my mind, draped a rather terrifying personality around the long delicate bones of her half-famous physical self.

But when I see her on the second day, framed in the doorway of the diner, dark glasses concealing half of her face as she scopes the place out, fear is not what I feel. I feel—what? Lost, helpless, lonely, worried. Safe, strong, loved. I feel twelve. I smell warm pine, pipe smoke. I feel jagged mountains all around us.

She is walking in my direction, as if she has a regular table and is making her way directly to it. She passes me, in jeans and ballet flats and a silky, floating white blouse, wavy blond hair loosely pulled back. She slides into the booth directly behind me, her back facing mine. I can sense the practiced gesture with which she removes her sunglasses. I imagine her glancing at the menu—but not needing to study it, knowing already what she wants, because she orders the same thing every time, as I do. It is one of the things I know about her. One of the things that cannot have changed.

"Carly," I say quietly, not turning my head, not knowing that I am going to say it until I hear myself, hear the quiet word jolt heavily against the bright, unsuspecting air of the diner.

Behind me all is still. The booth does not so much as tremble. I know that the slightest of movements, even vibrations, would be communicated to me through the taut vinyl. But there is nothing: suspension, the refusal of somethingness, the eye of some storm.

"Lois," she says, her tone of voice echoing mine precisely, carving through the air, which has become thick with strangeness. "Or Lucy, should I say."

"Chloe."

"You're here early." A stranger's voice, almost.

"I wanted to see . . . everything." I feel as if my words are far away; I am spearing them one by one through dark, rushing water, clumsily, not quite finding the ones I need.

"See your little puppet show, you mean? Your fucked-up reenactment?"

Anger was always a possibility. We are still back to back. I wish I could see her, trace the bits of Carly May still visible in her face.

The waitress appears. "Coffee," Chloe barks. (Carly? Chloe? Even in my mind, I hardly know what to call her.) The woman looks taken aback; clearly she's accustomed to the actress being more pleasant. Her eyes drift my way, checking on me, and I shake my head and wave her away.

"Our meeting is tomorrow," Chloe points out coldly when the waitress is out of earshot. "No one even fucking knows I'm here. What are you doing, stalking me?"

I feel myself turn red. I suppose this is a form of stalking, this staking out of the diner. I think of my *Carly/Chloe* file, the Web sites I bookmarked. *Stalking.*

"It's just a diner," I say, keeping my voice level. "It happens to be near my motel." *Guilty!* If I weren't guilty I wouldn't be defending myself.

"It's *my* diner," Chloe says, and I now hear more than a glimmer of Carly May, petulant and possessive.

I feel myself rising, leaving my breakfast half eaten. I'll pay at the counter. I don't know what will happen if I stay. I think I might cry. This has been a mistake.

"Your book is full of lies," Chloe/Carly says calmly. "We'll talk about it tomorrow. I'm looking forward to it."

The waitress returns with Chloe's coffee and I slip away, not trusting myself to speak, letting Carly have the last word, as always.

I don't think she looked at me. Not once.

Chloe

When Lois is gone I pick up my coffee and promptly spill it all over the fucking table. I'm shaking. I sop up the spilled coffee with tiny paper napkins from the dispenser next to the ketchup and try to figure out why I'm so upset. I consider a range of emotions, and what I settle on is something between scared shitless and pissed as hell.

Which makes no sense. What am I afraid of? What am I pissed off about? I feel a stirring of guilt, deep, deep down in some emotional abyss I tend to steer clear of. Poor Lois; that's hardly the welcome she deserved, stalker or no. And for a minute I feel wounded, almost sick, and even though it's been almost two decades since it last happened, I remember this feeling all too well. I'm slipping into Lois mode. And it's like I just stuck a fork in my own heart.

Maybe some people always know exactly what they're thinking or feeling. Maybe most people, even. I wouldn't know. If I really want to know the truth about myself—my emotions, motives, whatever—I need to take a very cold, hard look within. Because in general, I lie—to myself, I'm pretty sure, along with everyone else. Call it acting if you want. It's falsification. The opposite of truth. I'm very, very good at it.

Turning my attention inward, I'm half afraid of what I might find. It's like scanning for a tumor, something malignant and spreading and undeniable, a threat that must be faced. Wrenched out, maybe. Thrust into the light. Put under a fucking microscope.

And what comes up is a memory—not repressed, quite, but filed away, locked up, dusty but not faded:

It was near the end. We had maybe a week left, though of course we didn't know it. God, I can smell the room, see the shadows on the walls . . . It was late, the middle of the night, and Lois thought I was sleeping. I was awake, though, because my period had started, and I had miserable cramps and no idea what to do about them. I was curled up clutching my abdomen, counting the waves of pain. (Lois had said I should ask Zed for Advil or something, but I would not.) I heard Lois get out of bed and move to the dresser. I opened my eyes just a slit, and as they adjusted to the darkness I could see that she was brushing her hair. When she looked toward me, I closed my eyes and pretended to be asleep. I'm not sure why, looking back. I could have said something. Anything. I should have stopped her. Not that I knew exactly what she was up to—how could I?—but then again I *did*, somehow. If I'm totally honest, I have to admit that I had a sense of what she was up to.

She put the brush back down on the dresser, straightened her white nightgown, and drifted out the door.

He didn't sleep in his room anymore, we knew that. So I wasn't surprised to hear the stairs creak softly in the places where they always did. Although I couldn't see her, I could almost feel each careful footstep. I knew when her hand brushed over the raised knot in the unvarnished wooden railing halfway down, the one your dress would catch on if you weren't careful, and I knew exactly when she reached the bottom. And then I couldn't hear her anymore, but I knew where she had gone. Five minutes, maybe. Ten at the absolute most. I heard a door slam. A minute later Lois was on the stairs again, moving quickly this time. She burst into the room, bringing cold night air with her. She thrust her tiny self into her bed—quietly, but I could feel the violence of her movements. She curled into a ball—don't ask me how I knew—just in time to contain the first huge sob that shook her. I've cried like that once or twice. I know how much it hurts, really hurts, like someone is punching you in the gut. I almost forgot my own pain, I was so focused on hers. But Lois's willpower was even stronger than her misery; she swallowed each sob before it escaped. All I could hear was a sharp little hiccough each time, and the sound of the sheets brushing against her skin as she shook.

It was a long time before the number of seconds between sobs started to stretch out and her breathing got smoother.

I didn't have to ask what had happened. I knew, as surely as if I'd been there myself. Lois never mentioned what had happened that night, never suspected me of having seen anything, and I never brought it up. I felt guilty, as if I had been spying. But I also felt like I had something on her. Lois had a weakness, and I knew what it was.

And there was another emotion, one I didn't recognize at the time, or wouldn't: rage. By the next morning, I was blindingly, dizzyingly furious with her.

Because she broke the rules. Because she offered herself up, more completely than I ever had. Because she wasn't supposed to be the brave one, the reckless one. Because it should have been me.

Because she kept a secret from me, or thought she did.

Because she brought on the end, somehow. She fucked up the balance, crossed the line.

Something like that.

Lois

So much for the upper hand.

I return to my motel and burrow into the cool darkness of my room like some tiny pointy-nosed mammal. Tomorrow I am supposed to check into my B&B, but for now I prefer the anonymity of this nondescript roadside pit stop. I try to sleep, so that I won't have to face my own mind or submit to the torture of memory (*your book is full of lies*), but I can't quite manage to leave consciousness behind. After a while I pull my notebook into bed with me, squinting at the scribbled pages, retracing Gary's recent steps.

Gary is frustrated. He had known the abductees would be adults now, but their maturity disturbs him: the women he has captured (he has them both, finally) are not exactly who he needs them to be. He feels thwarted. They are too old, too fucked-up, too *different*. They are not the pretty, flat-chested, bratty twelve-year-olds he imagined. He's not sure what they have to offer him. He begins to think about children. Maybe what he requires is a more perfect reenactment of his father's crime. But how would that satisfy his desire for revenge? Who would suffer? Who would understand? More than frustrated, he's confused. And growing desperate. He has bought another knife, and he's scoping out pretty twelve-year-old girls. He's as lost as I am. *Stay in character, Gary,* I admonish him. *Don't stop making sense.* But I don't feel as if he listens to me anymore. I have a sudden urge to get him out of this elaborate mess I've entangled him in. Could he toss the knives off some bridge, free his captives, go back to his trailer and resume chopping wood? Would that be in character?

I don't manage to solve Gary's problems, but, for the moment, he solves mine; I drift mercifully into a long sleep while squinting in the dark at my own wild handwriting. My unused laptop hums quietly in the corner of the room, endlessly charging. I feel as if Sean is watching me from it. This sense follows me into uneasy sleep.

Chloe

I spy Lois through the curtains in my sitting room tripping down the path to my guesthouse and am surprised by another stabbing thrust of guilt. She's dressed very professionally, in a neat little suit and heels, and I understand this to mean that she is extremely hurt. That I have hurt her. Well, she caught me off guard; my claws shot out; I feel like shit. What else can I do? I'm wearing jeans and a T-shirt, and I realize that I've chosen the opposite strategy: I'm showing her my exposed belly; she's in full battle armor.

She raps sharply at the door.

And there she is: little Lois, twelve. Her body language says don't fuck with me, but her big eyes are as sad and vulnerable as ever.

"I'm sorry," I blurt out as she pauses on the threshold. It's what I had planned to say, but in the end it comes out spontaneously: I don't have to act.

And then, to my great relief, she reaches out her arms and hugs me; a short, sharp Lois hug, but real nevertheless. "I know," she says, her voice muffled by my shoulder, then withdraws and steps past me into the room. She accepts a glass of wine and plunks herself down on my sofa. "So what did you mean, *exactly*," she asks, "when you said my book was full of lies?"

I was going to suggest that we go out on the porch, but suddenly it seems right that this part of the conversation take place in a small, enclosed space, where no one else can happen by, where it's just Lois and me. And Zed. I arrange myself at the other end of the sofa.

"Is it because of Mandy?" she continues, pressing, her poise slipping ever so slightly. "Because that's—"

"Nope. Not Mandy. I get Mandy, more or less. You needed someone outside, that makes sense to me." She has stayed small, Lois; she can't be more than five-three or -four. She's thin, as always—too thin, maybe, though in my world there's no such thing. Delicate. Her hands are clasped neatly in her lap. She used to sit just that way when he read to us.

"It's a bit of a time warp, isn't it?" Lois breaks in. Psychic, as always. "I keep flashing back there, too. So. Full of lies, you said?"

"I was awake that night," I say. I keep my voice neutral. Not accusing, not judging. "That night toward the end. I heard you go to him. I heard you crying afterward."

Her head jerks up.

"You went to him. And you never told me. And you didn't put it in the book. It would have changed everything, if you had. It would have made Hannah a more interesting character in a way. Less innocent. It would have made Zed more complicated too. More sympathetic, maybe."

She reaches for her wine. I see her turn inward, as if her eyes have flipped around to examine the past, not the present. I tip my own wine back. I can wait. I can tell that she's remembering—not stalling, not making shit up. It surprises me, how much I want to know what she's going to say.

"He was changing," she says, leaning forward. "Things were different. I was . . . afraid. I hadn't been afraid before, but I started to be afraid." A sudden breeze sweeps through the little house, rustling curtains and magazines, smelling like rain, raising goosebumps despite the heat. A rumble of thunder follows. British Columbian thunder or Adirondack thunder? Both. Lois goes on. "I didn't know what he wanted. *We* didn't know what he wanted. Remember, Carly May?"

It's strange to hear that name. I wonder if that's why she's saying it. She is speaking to the ceiling, but I nod. Of course I remember.

She tilts her head down, looks right at me without a warning. "I wanted him to be happy," she says simply. "So that everything would be okay." She takes another great gulp of wine, and somehow I know to stay silent and still.

"And I wanted him to love me," she adds, her voice very small but surprisingly steady and clear. "Didn't you?" She glances toward the window. "But I couldn't bring myself to put it in the book. I thought about having Callie do it instead, but that felt wrong. So in the book I made Mandy love him, in her own way. It's not a lie, it's more like . . . a translation."

She pauses, and I see her face tighten slightly. Like she's shifting from defense to offense. I wait.

"And besides—" she begins quietly, not looking at me.

"Besides what?" I think I know what's coming.

"Well, I'm not the only one hiding something, am I? You've read the book, I assume? So you know I heard you that night in the kitchen. I heard you promise."

"So? What was I supposed to say? I felt like he was saying that if I didn't promise, he'd never let us go. So yeah, I promised. So what." I'm surprised by how angry this makes me. This was the other thing that pissed me off about the book, I realize. That she gave me away and not herself.

"Of course you had to promise," Lois agrees. "But you could have kept it, and you didn't. You betrayed him."

"Bullshit. He was dead by then. And besides . . ." Here's the part she doesn't know, the part I've tried to forget. "Besides, he didn't believe me anyway," I say flatly. I remember the way he looked at me. His eyes were so sad. So disappointed. He knew I was lying, and he was kind enough not to call me on it. "He knew I didn't mean it, even at the time."

"We both let him down, then?" Lois's voice sounds very small, almost childlike.

"I guess we did. But not—"

"Not overall. Not in the grand scheme of things. No, I think you're right."

And there we sit for a long time. The storm rolls in and the shutters rattle and the lights flicker, and rain blows through the screens.

Lois

"You have to stay here with me," Carly says later. "I won't let you go back to that shitty little motel." I explain about the bed-and-breakfast, but she talks me down. "That's ridiculous. You can sleep on the sofa; it pulls out. Or I could. We could flip for it. I have more space than I need. You can meet everyone; they'll love to meet the writer. You have to come. You'll get a kick out of it. Besides, you're a part of it. You should be here." So I agree, finally, partly because that feels true, partly because I am not keen on drinking and driving and she is clearly not keen on sobriety. We drink more wine. We tell our lives. That part is strange: reduced to words, my life seems very small and far away (except for the Sean part, which I omit). As though it belongs to someone else. It gives me pause; should it be so easy to cast my life aside, shed it like old skin, reduce it to a tidy little blurb? Or might that in fact be the best way to extricate myself from the mess I've created?

We move out to the porch in the aftermath of the storm and sit in the dark, the woods behind us full of night noises. We listen for a while. "It's not the same, though, is it?" I know that she will know what I mean. "Similar, but . . . definitely not the same."

"Thank God," she says, with fervor.

Later: "Would I have read anything from the eighteenth century?" she asks languidly, trying to understand what I do for a living. "Keep in mind I didn't graduate from high school."

"Maybe *Gulliver's Travels*?" I venture.

"Little people, right? Didn't they make a movie of that?"

"Lots of movies. What about *The Rape of the Lock*? *Robinson Crusoe*?"

"Very faint bells might be ringing," she says. "Or they might not. Dude on an island, that last one? What a funny century to pick."

I don't bother to explain why that isn't true; it doesn't seem to matter. "Read *Moll Flanders* sometime," I suggest, half-seriously. "She's kind of an actress, in her own way. You might like it."

"Maybe I will," she says. "Just to surprise you."

I tell her I've seen all of her movies. I tell her Brad watched them with me, and answer her unspoken question: "Brad? No, nothing like that."

Gradually it emerges that we are both perpetually single, unloved, unloving. I tell her about the teacher I seduced in college and then passionately avoided for three years, and the string of awkward, unrepeated dates that followed. She sketches her serial loveless flings. We contemplate each other for a while. "No," she says eventually, although I have not spoken. "I don't want to hear any crazy shrink shit about that. Don't even start." I'm glad enough not to start, because I don't want to hear it either. However appropriate it might be to blame Zed for our romantic haplessness, I fail to see how it could be useful.

At last Carly lurches to her feet, heads inside to find me a nightgown and sheets for the sofa. (She seems to have forgotten the bit about flipping for the bed.)

Before trying to sleep, I check my phone for messages: There are several texts from Sean, which I uneasily ignore. A missed call from Brad, which surprises me a little, but no message. I can't tell whether I'm relieved or oddly disappointed. And a call from a number that's unfamiliar but from my area code. I hesitate for a moment, then play the message.

"Lois. Delia here," says a faraway voice. "I don't know if you're even in town, but there's something I thought you should know. That kid, that student of yours, Sean McDougal—the cops are looking for him. It's the stalking thing again, but worse this time. Apparently he showed up outside some high school girl's bedroom window and showed her a knife—that's what she says, he just showed it to her. She screamed, and he ran. This was two nights ago, and no one's been able to find him since. The cops are thinking he might have split, somehow. So—well, he's out there. Somewhere." A pause. "Anyway. I thought you should know." Click, and silence.

Stalking? A knife? A high school girl? *He's out there.* For a moment I am utterly disoriented: it's Gary who's stalking high school girls, right? Against my better judgment? The connection between the two plots eludes me for one confused moment. *Sean isn't a character in a story,* Delia points out scornfully in my mind. And Brad stands beside her, shaking his head, disappointed.

I check the time. If it's 2:00 a.m. here, it's 5:00 a.m. there. I'm not sure whether the wine is sharpening my senses or dulling them; my very uncertainty suggests the latter. *There's nothing to be done now,* I tell myself sternly, and sink into the sofa for another night of troubled dreams.

Chloe

It takes me a minute, when I wake up, to remember Lois, and all that happened yesterday. My first instinct shocks me a little. *Nice to see you, Lois! Good-bye, Lois!* Slam the door. Leave it all behind, again. But when I stalk out of my bedroom to make coffee, I see Lois curled up on the sofa, absurdly enveloped in my nightgown, looking tiny and strangely peaceful. Too late to slam this door even if I wanted to. It feels weird, tiptoeing around so as not to wake her; I'm not used to bothering about anyone else. Not a judgment; just a thing I notice.

I'm waiting for the coffee to start spurting from the machine, already feeling guilty about the noise it will make, when the phone rings again. The landline. This time I don't hesitate before I grab it. "Yeah," I say aggressively, sticking a coffee mug under the spout, and I listen for a few seconds to the expected silence. "Hey, asswipe. You called me; I answered. Say what you have to say, or I hang up, and then I make sure you can't get through again. So if you have something to say, now's your chance."

"She's there, isn't she?" The voice sounds like it's underwater, and there's a fairly obvious attempt at disguise. It sounds a lot like the percolating coffee.

"You're going to have to be a little more specific," I say, glancing over at Lois. She's flipping over; I can't tell whether she's awake.

"She's there. You can't trust her, you know. Tell her I fucked up, and it's her fault."

"Tell who? Who the fuck are you, is my question."

"She knows. Tell her I read the book she's writing. Tell her it's over."

"What's over? Listen, if you're going to talk in riddles—" He hangs up. I stare at the phone, trying to piece things together. What did he say last time? It was about me: *I know who you are.* Maybe I should have paid more attention.

Lois has pulled herself into a sitting position, clutching the sheet around herself, her face and hair peculiarly unruffled. Her voice sounds urgent, though. "Who was that, Carly?"

"You're going to have to call me Chloe." I meant to say it last night. I can't handle this Carly business.

"I know, sorry. I'll practice today. Nothing but Chloe, I swear. But—who was on the phone?" She's looking at me with her funny little Lois-expression, like a very pretty and terrifyingly smart fox. She already had it when she was twelve. Her head tips slightly to one side and she looks as if she's reading my mind. "It was a prank caller, wasn't it? How many times has he called before? What did he say?"

"Why don't you tell me, if you know so much about it? Sounds to me like you know exactly who it is." Hard to believe anything remains unconfessed after last night, but trust Lois to hold something back. I mentally replay the anonymous voice's words in this new context, thinking they might make more sense. And they do, a little, but it's a disturbing kind of sense. Lois's expression is worrying me. It's just a prank call, right? But she looks almost afraid.

"It sounds like someone is taking a little too much of an interest in your life," I suggest, which is putting it mildly. "And since he seems to have tracked me down somehow, which the front desk is definitely going to hear about, maybe you'd better tell me what's going on."

And so she does. I remember my earlier sense that maybe Lois was losing it, that I was going to have to be the sane one at this crazy party. My suspicions are well and truly confirmed.

Lois

With some difficulty, I persuade Carly—Chloe—to let me return alone to my motel and collect my things. She has conjured up absurd visions of Sean appearing magically in the middle of British Columbia with a small arsenal and a heart full of violence. I try to explain that Sean lacks the wherewithal (money, transportation, sheer energy) to carry out such a plan even if he wanted to, and why would he? I ignore the nagging voice at the back of my own mind that is no longer so sure. She insists on accompanying me until I tell her that I have some errands to run and business to take care of, the prospect of which visibly bores her.

And I do, though not the kind I lead her to imagine.

For one thing, I need to confront Chloe's revelation that she witnessed my humiliation on the night I have tried very hard to forget, and I need to do it alone. Carly, the soundest sleeper on the planet; I never for a moment considered the possibility that she was awake. Odder still is that she didn't say anything to me the next day—or even at the time; why wait? Was it discretion, or patience, or something darker? It seems out of character.

Of course focusing on Carly's unsuspected witnessing allows

me to avoid facing the really disturbing thing, which is my own behavior, long ago, shocking and uncharacteristic in its own right. Driving toward town, I carefully unwrap this memory, loosen its bindings. Freed, it springs back to its original size and shape with remarkable ease.

Yes. I went to him. This I have never told anyone, not even through the filter of fiction. This I have not even told myself.

It was one night near the end, after a strange tense day. I brushed my dark hair to make it smooth and shiny. I unbuttoned the top two buttons of my long white nightgown, I steeled myself (for what I did not exactly know; I was not, for once, narrating my actions to myself), and I prowled downstairs to the leather couch on which he sprawled. A few splashes of moonlight provided just enough illumination for me to discern his outline, to tell that he was lying on his back, face tilted upward, head cradled in the crook of the arm flung over his head. Every few seconds the kitchen faucet dripped. His breathing was slow and regular. I stood by his side and watched him—my eyes, I imagine, boring into him. My breathing gradually fell into sync with his. I stood there with no plan, no intention, no trepidation, even. I knew somehow that he would wake up, I never doubted it, and at last he did. I say *at last*, but it was probably only a matter of two or three minutes; it seemed like a long time.

And then his eyelids flew open—I felt this as much as I saw it—and his right arm shot out, groping beside him for his gun, until he saw that it was me and not some intruder and his hand grasped my wrist instead. Hard, heavy. And the air, too, was suddenly heavy, weighted with darkness and quiet. *Lois?* he rasped, in a voice not entirely his own.

Giving in to the weight of his hand and some other impulse, unarticulated, I sank to my knees. I reached out my free hand slowly, practically in slow motion—I watched its ghostly form stretching away from me—until it reached his face. I touched with tentative fingertips a heavy eyebrow, a scratchy unshaven cheek.

His face had always fascinated me—its hard, sharp lines, broken by occasional softness. But when my fingers grazed a lip, his other hand appeared suddenly and seized my wrist. Hard. He had both wrists now. *Get out,* he said, rising from the couch and thrusting me away, wrists aching. *You've made a mistake. I don't want you. Go!* His voice was low, cold, a growl that wouldn't carry more than a few feet. It was too heavy; it would sink to the ground, collapse through the floor the way it sank into my mind. *Go. I don't want you.* I don't know how many times he said those things.

I rose to my feet, turned, and fled, wanting more than anything to undo myself, erase my presence. Shame is what I felt. It was like bleeding from every cell. Uncontained, vile, horrible. *Corrupt,* as he had said once. Now I thought I knew what he had meant.

I threw myself in my bed, curled up with my shame, tried to smother it, bury it, snuff it out. It escaped in the form of hot, hot tears and flooded the world.

I had only wanted to help. I had only wanted to keep him. I was only trying to hold at bay the horrors I sensed in the wings. Something had to be done, of that I was sure. I had made the purest offer I could conceive of: *Here. Take me. Do with me what you will. Here's my entire person, my skinny virginal body, my pointy little face, my sharp and darting mind, my fierce love. It's what I have.*

I had guessed wrong, I had done the wrong thing, the wrongest thing. *I want to die,* I thought over and over, and I think I very nearly meant it.

Shame, I find, can survive long periods of dormancy. Given the proper stimulus, it reawakens as strong as ever. Mine suffuses me, hot and blinding, with a power that has only intensified with time. I have to pull off the road, rest my forehead on the steering wheel while my mind goes red. I relive again and again my unspeakable offering, his unbearable rejection. I feel again that I am rotten inside. Unwanted and unwantable.

By the time I reach the motel I feel a little sick. Part hangover, I imagine, and part memory-sickness. I pack up my things and toss them in the car. Out of habit, I stop at my diner. I'm not ready to see Chloe again—I need to repair the damaged edges of myself, to refortify.

And there is something else, too. Over coffee I text Sean: *Where are you? I need to speak to you. It's important.*

He writes back almost immediately: *No talking just writing. Safer wouldn't you say?*

The diner isn't crowded; there's just a low hum of chattering voices around the bar, more private and somehow more comfortable than silence. I recognize all the regulars now, and I am familiar and unremarkable to them, too. Is writing safer, really? I'm no longer so sure. But it's easier, in a way; I have been dreading the sound of Sean's voice, the weight of his unfathomable expectations.

I text back: *Maybe, maybe not. Anyway: I hear you're in serious trouble. Tell me what's happened.* My knowledge of Sean's disturbing recent behavior should kill any scrap of sympathy I might have had; I am shocked to realize that it seems to have had the opposite effect. I feel almost motherly; surely this is not a tone I've adopted with him before. But his crimes are mine too. I am responsible.

What's up with gary why did you stop writing?

Gary has been confined to my notebook, safe from Sean. He's done nothing at all since it occurred to me that he hadn't gone too far to turn back, that he could release his captives and simply go home. Easier said than done; that's not exactly how novels tend to work. So far, I have been unable to figure out how to save both Gary and the novel. Now I picture Sean impatiently awaiting Gary's next move, reading untold layers of significance into each stage of his vengeful (and confused) pursuit of the actress and the professor.

It's too late, now, to berate him for breaking into my computer, reading my novel. It's not what matters anymore.

Gary has gone back home to chop wood, I text. *He's finished. It's over.* Is this true? It feels true, suddenly.

Why????? Its not over what a cop out.

It was all a mistake.

But i have proof . . .

Proof of what? Fiction isn't proof. I'm not finishing the book. It was a mistake. I sit up straight, take a look around, gulp my coffee before hitting SEND. I'm lying; no such thing has crossed my mind. But this, too, feels true. Do I mean it? When did I decide? Yes, I think I do. I've been chasing shadows. The book is a self-indulgent romp. It's dangerous. It's caused enough trouble. Contract be damned. I'll write something else. SEND.

Silence. I try again: *So what has happened?*

Some stupid shit its nothing and none of your business.

I think for a minute. I risk it: *Gary let the women go, you know. He got rid of his knives. He's not going through with any of it.*

Nice try. Youre the one whose nuts professor. You can't erase it, it still exists. You can't just create gary then uncreate him.

Sure I can. It's all lies. Just like you always said. It's true: I don't want Gary to be real. I don't want to go back inside his head. I've been there too long. It seems like a dream, the sequel, weirdly vivid but unreal. The kind of dream you try to banish when you wake up, though it resurfaces throughout the day, coloring everything.

At the bar, a man laughs loudly. Sun glints off the cars in the parking lot.

Do you need any help, Sean?

You mean gary.

This is my crime, the thing I must undo.

No. I mean Sean, my student, a kid who's in trouble. He may not be Zed's son, but he must once have been a little boy, sweet and imaginative and needy. I try to imagine that.

Spare me the teacher stuff. I know too much.

I don't text back for a while. I can't think of what to say. I feel like Dr. Frankenstein when his monster runs off. Sean is a mystery, finally. And his fate, unlike Gary's, isn't mine to write. I can't send him home and write *The End*.

Before I can compose a reply, he texts again: *Say hi to Chloe Savage for me :-/*

I drain the chilly dregs of my coffee and think. I think very hard, and I figure out nothing at all.

Where are you? I text back on an impulse. But he doesn't answer.

Chloe

Lois wants to be all incognito and just present herself as an old friend from my New York days. I flat-out refuse. "No fun in that," I tell her. "No way. It's Lucy Ledger time, my dear. You owe me one." Why does she owe me one? I'm not sure, really, but it feels true, and she seems to buy it. Anyway, I like the idea of showing up unexpectedly with the writer, of all people; we're due for a little drama around here. Also—less pleasantly, I know—I sort of like the idea of watching Lois squirm a little. She'll be on the spot; people will ask her awkward questions about where she got the idea for the novel, what the kidnapper's true motives are, what Mandy could possibly see in him. I'm pretty curious to hear what she'll have to say.

Conveniently enough, there's a cast party this evening: a captive audience! We're all here now; shooting begins tomorrow. Lois is less thrilled than I am about this staging opportunity. "You're as nervous as a girl getting ready for the fucking prom," I mock her as we're getting ready. Lois looks completely stunning in a red silk cocktail dress—sleek, tiny, and elegant, like a very expensive cat. I feel vulgar and overblown beside her, all flesh and hair. I have to keep checking the mirror to remind myself that I am more than holding my own.

"I never went to my prom," Lois says. "I wouldn't know. Did you go?"

"I dropped out, remember? What's your excuse?"

"Boredom? Also, no one asked me," Lois says very matter-of-factly, slipping her feet into shoes that give her an extra four inches.

"Really?" I take a minute to try to imagine Lois's high school life, adding to the mix the prep school stories my Arcata friend told me, a dash of my own tragic past in small-town Nebraska, and every teen movie I've ever seen. "They were probably scared to death of you," I decide, and Lois laughs.

"Wise of them," she says without a trace of bitterness. Side by side, we check ourselves out in my full-length mirror.

"No wonder he picked us," Lois says, joking. But also not really joking. Then her voice turns serious. "What would he think if he could see us now? Can you imagine?"

What else do I try to imagine, ever? "No, I can't, and I don't want to. That's the twisted road to crazytown, my girl, and that ain't where we're going tonight. Come on. Let's go conquer the fucking world. And get a drink, for God's sake." Because the truth is I'm not just thinking about Zed, I'm thinking about Daddy, too, and wishing he could see me. I could prove that I haven't done so badly. Which might or might not be true.

I drag Lois to the door, and we trip across the lawn. And she's a huge hit, and everyone loves her. You'd think she'd been going to Hollywood parties all her life. She stands slightly apart with this little mysterious smile, and the world comes to her. It throws itself at her feet. Billy is totally smitten. The girls adore her and keep sweeping her away, interrogating her in corners, touching her hair, shining their pretty eyes into hers. I'm conflicted: I'm proud of her, like she's my protégée or something, which of course she isn't, though I *am* responsible for bringing her here; she's mine. *She's mine,* I want to tell them. But I also feel the old jealousy surfacing. I remember when Zed's eyes would follow her, wondering what she thought, how she would react, what went on in her little head. Leaving me behind. "So enigmatic, our Lois," he said to me once, and I swear to God I wanted to cut her throat. So I was the obvious one, was I? Fuck that, now and then.

Endless champagne takes the edge off, reminds me that I am Lois too, that all admiration is shared: we're in this together. And I wonder suddenly if her fucked-up proposition to Zed makes more sense if I think about it like that. Sure, it was her idea, her body: but maybe it was purely *us* she was offering up. *Us,* contained in her. Maybe it wasn't about her. Maybe I should believe she only wanted to save us all, like she says. That makes a fucked-up kind of sense. I don't want to believe it, but I kind of do, almost as if Lois has invaded my mind. *She did the only thing she could think of. It was fucking brave. It didn't work. But it wasn't for her. It was for us. For us and for him.*

There's only one really awkward moment all night: Lois and I, after being separated for a while, find ourselves face-to-face. I think I see a touch of weariness in her eyes, maybe even a hint of panic, and I admit I am glad. I always like it when Lois's feelings are forced to the surface—or I always did, anyway. I have no patience with this enigmatic crap.

Suddenly Fiona swoops down on us, dwarfing Lois and making even me feel a little smaller. After a couple of minutes of random chatter, she looks at us more intently, sweeping her gaze from me to Lois, Lois to me. "So," she says, so abruptly it's borderline rude, her crazy red hair lit up by the torches that surround the lawn. "How is it that you two know each other?"

It's a harmless enough question, I guess. But somehow nothing Fiona says ever manages to sound quite harmless. It sounds pointed, like a cheerful little arrow.

Lois looks down at my feet, sips her wine; she's passing this to me. We both understand Fiona's words as an attack, though her motive is hazy. A calling-out of some kind.

Lois is right: it's my place to answer; I know Fiona better. "We don't, really." Lois's glance darts back to my face. "I mean, just from the movie and all that."

"Our agents put us in touch," Lois interjects, which isn't exactly true but sounds true and is very vague in terms of details like time and place.

"Really!" says Fiona, raising her majestic eyebrows. "Somehow I got the impression you two went way back. I don't know what it is, exactly, that gave me that idea." She studies us quite openly, as if she's trying to figure it out. "You're sure you're not hiding something?" It's a joke, of course. She means to unsettle us. But it's creepy.

I raise one shoulder, an exaggerated gesture of dismissal. "Who knows? Maybe we knew each other in another life." I didn't mean to say this, didn't intend to sound flippant. Lois looks a little alarmed. Exit Chloe Savage! I raise my empty glass and wave it in the direction of the bar. "Time for another splash, I think! Anyone else?" I saunter off without really waiting for an answer; both of their glasses are pretty much half-full, though I've learned in the past week that Fiona is no lightweight in that respect. As I move away, I hear Fiona change the subject. "So my husband is absolutely *fascinated* by his character, this charming madman, this tragic kidnapper," she begins. "And I was wondering how . . ."

I move faster, block her out. I don't even want to hear it. I feel a twinge of guilt, ever so slight, for ditching Lois. *She can handle it,* I tell myself, cruising barward. And I'm sure she does.

Lois

I don't even know I'm asleep until I hear a phone ring and realize that it has woken me up. The room is dark; it could be any time of night. I am nested in soft cushions on the floor, half-covered by a cashmere throw; I can hear Carly breathing on the sofa just feet away. It is her phone that's ringing. "Carly," I say. "Chloe?" She stirs. She drank quite a bit more than I did; she seems to be dragging herself up from some deep place. I reach for the phone, convey it into her groping hand, am relieved when she finally mutters, "Yeah? Do you realize what time it is?" (Which is sort of funny, because she can't have any more of an idea than I do what time it is. I wonder if we fell asleep midsentence; I can't remember a line between talk and sleep. I dreamed that our conversation continued.) "Billy! What the fuck? Slow down. Repeat yourself." She listens for a minute, then swings her feet to the ground with surprising alertness. "I'll be there. Wait . . . fuck, no, never mind. We're there. Two minutes. Tops."

She jumps to her feet, slides her shoes on in the dark. "The girls are missing," she says, and it takes a minute for me to understand what she means. (We are the girls; we are both missing and not missing, depending on how you look at it.) "The actresses," she says impatiently. "Natasha and Justine. They've disappeared. They aren't in their room. Someone went to check on them and found them gone. They're forming a search party. That was Billy Pearson on the phone—he was just coming in from the pub, and one of the mothers told him. Get up. Don't change, just put on shoes. Grab us a couple of bottles of water; I think I might still be drunk. Let's go." Practically passed out no more than a minute ago, suddenly Chloe is alarmingly functional.

"To join the search party?" I say stupidly. I look down at myself. We fell asleep in our party clothes. I can feel makeup crusted on my eyes.

"There's no time to change," she says urgently. "Just put on shoes you can walk in. Did you fucking hear what I said? The girls are *missing*. What the *fuck* does that mean?" she says, but to herself, like this is some kind of riddle she has to solve.

I am thinking *missing*. Taken, by someone. Someone who knows they're here. Someone who knows the story. I shake my head and run my fingers through my tangled hair, trying to clear my mind. I take two bottles of water from the minibar and shove my feet in my sneakers, vaguely aware of how ridiculous they will look with my dress, vaguely aware that this is absolutely beside the point. My last text to Sean appears before my eyes. *Where are you?* No answer . . .

Perhaps two dozen people have assembled on the patio behind the main inn, their faces garish and strained in the powerful security lights that have replaced the festive torches that burned here just hours ago. Chloe and I are among the most ridiculous, but the competition is stiff. Fiona is wearing a trench coat belted over a slinky nightgown; the director's gray hair is standing straight up, and his shoes are untied; other cast members still sport ravaged party makeup and suggestively disheveled clothes. The girls' respective parents are wearing their hotel bathrobes and look oddly interchangeable and seriously befuddled; one of the mothers weeps quietly and steadily. Only Billy Pearson looks wide awake and as crisply dressed as ever, and he seems to be in charge. *He's throwing himself into the role*, I find myself thinking, then reproach myself for the uncharitable thought. He can't help acting; it doesn't mean he isn't sincere. He continues, his voice at once commanding and full of emotion. "We need to know if anyone else has any information that might help us: anything you saw or heard or noticed, even if it seemed totally irrelevant at the time." No one says anything. *Where are you?* No answer.

"Have the police been called?" I ask, eying the bleary-eyed rescue party dubiously.

"They have not," Billy tells me. "The parents want to wait until we are certain they're actually missing. And chances are the police would consider it too early to act, anyway." Everyone has seen enough cop shows to know that missing persons aren't taken seriously for at least twenty-four hours, although this situation seems enough out of the ordinary to me to warrant bending the rules. I'm surprised at the parents; you'd think they would want the police involved right away. *Why are they hesitating?* I wonder. *What are they thinking? What did my parents think when they noticed I was missing? How long did it take them to call the police? When did they start to be afraid?* It seems odd that I never asked them. I suppose I still could. In the shadows, Billy looks more like Zed than ever. That he is coordinating the search, not necessitating it, sets off a strange series of ripples in my mind. Currents are clashing, roiling the surface. I wrench my gaze away from him before I can get sucked in, drawn down; this feels dangerous. *Think*, I order myself. *Be rational. You're known for it, Lois, deservedly or not.* Calm, collected, sensible Lois.

"Has everyone been accounted for?" I ask, perhaps too loudly. "All of the hotel staff, for instance?"

"We can't be sure," Billy answers, sounding a little sheepish at having to admit a gap in his detective work. "We have the manager looking into it. But in the meantime . . ."

"I have a dreadful sense about this," Fiona pipes up, her voice deep and vibrating. "How many people know what this movie is about? Plenty, I imagine. This could be someone's idea of a macabre joke, abducting the actresses playing the abductees, or it could be something even more twisted, more diabolical—"

"For God's sake, Fiona, don't," says Billy. Chloe has grabbed my arm, and in fact I, too, find Fiona's words disturbing, though not for the same reasons as Billy. "Don't be so melodramatic. There's nothing to suggest anything of the kind. Their room is neat, there's no sign of struggle, no sign of a break-in, no reports of strangers. We have no reason to suspect anything violent. All we know is that the girls aren't in their rooms. And that their beds haven't been slept in."

I picture the girls at the reception, doll-like in party frocks and age-appropriate flats, flitting in and out of the crowd, alternately descending on someone temporarily deserving of their attention and retreating to the periphery, whispering together, laughing at everything. I caught them guzzling champagne dregs once or twice. They had been very sweet to me: *"Chloe didn't tell us you were coming! She never said you were so pretty! Why didn't you ask for a part in the movie? Because that would have been so awesome!"* They looked happy, vibrant; they glowed with life. Could something really have happened to them? Surely not. But I glance toward the woods, a dark blank wall looming behind the bright lights of the inn, and shiver violently. *Where are you?*

"We've already checked every room in the inn, and we have someone going back over it and double-checking right now. What the rest of us are going to do is spread out and form a line and sweep the property," Billy is saying. "Just like, you know, in the movies." A few people laugh a little at this; the others shoot them disapproving glances. "If you don't have a flashlight, make sure you stand between two people who do. This is how far apart we should be." He uses the people closest to him to demonstrate. "If they are here, we will find them. And after we've done the grounds, we'll move into the woods." Here his voice trails off, and there's an uncomfortable silence. Sweeping the well-kept grounds is one thing, but those dense woods are not going to give up their secrets easily—not to amateur detectives in plush white bathrobes, armed with nothing more than incipient hangovers and cell phones.

We are swept forward with the search party. Automatically, my eyes scan the ground in front of us, as if the girls could possibly be crouching nearby in the midst of this racket. I'm using my phone as a flashlight but thinking that what I should really do is text Sean again. If only I could be sure that he was still in New York. Could I have underestimated him so badly? Is he really capable of such a terrible game? As yet he has done nothing violent, not that anyone knows of. He's interested in pursuit, in information; he's interested in control. He's disturbing and disturbed; he's decidedly creepy. But is he dangerous? Should I say something? *Do* something? My mind spins as we stumble along. There's a bit of low chatter along the line, but most of us are searching in silence, straining our ears as well as our eyes. *Don't be missing, don't be missing* . . . I picture the girls arranged on the forest floor, blood drying on their neatly sliced throats; they look like the cover of one of the novels we read that summer. A knife glistening with red rests nearby, no doubt wiped clean of fingerprints.

We have covered a broad swath of lawn when I feel Chloe tugging at my arm, pulling me back out of the light, away from the crowd. As the others surge forward, Chloe neatly separates us from them. No one appears to notice. "This is ridiculous," she hisses. "I have a better idea. Follow me; I'll explain when we get to your car."

I finally have to give voice to what I'm thinking, even though it can't be true, if only because it's very possible that Chloe is thinking it too. "It's not Gary—not Sean, I mean," I say, as much to myself as to Chloe, horrified by my slip. "It couldn't be Sean, I just heard from him yesterday." *But where was he? He could have been anywhere.* "It's not him, if that's what you're thinking." I hear something like panic in my voice. But I'm right, I know I am. Sean isn't in this story anymore; he's shaping his own plot. He may do dreadful things; it wouldn't surprise me at all. But not this one. History wouldn't fold back on itself so neatly, so perversely. Life isn't like that.

Chloe, walking fast, turns and shoots me a strange look. "I don't know who the hell Gary is, but you better hope this isn't your little stalker friend. I think you should definitely fucking call him, though, don't you? Just to see what he has to say? Anyway, I told you, I have an idea. I just don't want to say anything yet. In case . . ." She sounds shaken. It's rare for Carly—for Chloe. In a flash I remember standing in the rain, agreeing to climb in the backseat of Zed's car, Carly May smiling mysteriously from the front seat. These girls would never do what we did. They're wary; they know the world is dangerous. Which doesn't mean . . . but I won't put my fear into words. I won't.

I fumble with my phone as we hurry toward the parking lot. I jab a finger at Sean's most recent text and press CALL. I lift the phone to my ear as it begins to ring. I already know he won't answer, no matter where he is. He'll see that it's me, and he won't answer. I end the call before I get transferred to voice mail.

Chloe gives me directions without saying where we're headed, but I recognize the way to the hunting lodge replica, where shooting is scheduled to begin tomorrow. I don't ask questions; I just drive. Suddenly, without permission, Gary rears his head, and a new section of plot unfurls:

> *Gary gets a job on the set of the movie the actress would be starring in if he weren't holding her captive. He encounters two impossibly pretty young actresses and realizes that they are a better prize than the actual girls, now grown up, though of course he can't release the actress and the professor because they can't be trusted to keep quiet, and besides, shouldn't they pay for what they've done? For robbing him of a father? But he wants the young girls too, so pretty, so sure of themselves. He makes a point of meeting them on the set, and they can barely conceal their indifference. As a random member of the crew, he ranks low in their world, it's clear; who do they think they are? Someone needs to show them . . .*

"What are you thinking?" Chloe asks suddenly, breaking the spell. I shut Gary down, remind him he's done, finished.

"Oh . . . I thought for a minute I had an idea for my novel."

For an irrational instant, I fear that Chloe can see inside my head, watch me spinning stories out of this crisis. I blunder on: "It's nothing. It won't work; I just remembered something else. Never mind." I have abandoned the novel, written it off, left it behind. Gary released his prisoners and went home, fizzled into nothingness. The fact that this slipped my mind so easily disturbs me. Carly is gazing at me with peculiar intensity, I realize. The road is so dark that I am reluctant to take my eyes from it, but I glance quickly at her, wanting to read her. She is giving me a hard, hard look, so hard it feels like a blow.

"You're using this, aren't you?"

Using what, I don't say. I know what she means. It is always a mistake to underestimate Chloe. "Not exactly," I say. I want to say more, to excuse myself, to explain that I changed my mind, stopped just in time—but I don't. I let my answer hang in the air. This is, after all, the thing that lies between us: my telling of the story. Our story. Making it mine.

"It's a sequel," she says. "Right? Isn't that what you told me yesterday?"

"Yes, in a way. It picks up the story years later, though. Or it was going to, but I—"

She interrupts. "So it's just lies, then. Since there is no real story years later, right?"

"Well, fiction," I say, but not defensively. If she is punishing me, I have a strange feeling that I deserve it. *Guilty.* "Not lies, really. Just fiction."

"Except for the bits that are true."

"Yes. There are also some true bits. And . . . some sort of true bits," I add, thinking uncomfortably of Sean and the period during which I cast him as the son, the period when I created Gary. It's a dim and disturbing memory, as if it's someone else's: a dream sequence in a movie.

"That's fucked-up," says Chloe. "People say actors are fucked-up, but that's *really* fucked-up. You *use* people." Something horrid drips from her voice.

"Maybe," I say. "That's one way to look at it, I guess. But . . . it doesn't hurt them, does it?"

I have slowed down by now, looking for the little dirt road, easy to miss in the dark, though the construction crew has erected posts with reflectors on either side. "Kill the lights," hisses Chloe, ignoring my question. "Drive past." I obey, parking a little way down, as I did on my first visit. It's very different in the dark. "Get out quietly," she says. "My theory, if you haven't guessed, is that the girls are here. *If* your little friend hasn't taken a road trip, that is." Surely she wouldn't speak so flippantly if she thought it might be true. Surely it isn't true. *But the knife incident was more than forty-eight hours ago. He's been on the run since then. That's more than enough time to* . . . to get anywhere, really.

The girls, Chloe keeps saying. Not my girls or Gary's girls; not Callie and Hannah, not Lois and Carly May. Real girls, getting paid to pretend to be Carly and me at twelve. Real girls who have—impossibly or inevitably—gone missing in the middle of the night. In this strange place, surrounded by woods.

We use our flashlight apps to provide illumination as we double back along the road, make our way down the driveway, and approach the cabin. The pine needles and soft ground muffle our footsteps; we don't have to try to be quiet. Only our breathing seems loud. All around us swell the nighttime woods noises. Our lights catch eerily green patches of grass, slivers of rough bark, tiny bright eyes deep in the trees. I steal a look upward, needing to check the present against my memory, to see which is more real. The stars are thick and deep here, as they are in the Adirondacks.

"I don't see a car anywhere, do you?" Chloe whispers.

"Maybe around back. But . . . who do you think has them? I mean, who brought them here?" I'm not sure now whether Chloe thinks they're here of their own volition or not. Her mind is dark to me. I feel very Lois, and very alone.

"They're thirteen and resourceful. They're pissed off because Billy Pearson has been paying less attention to them since his wife and kid got here. I can think of lots of ways they could get their hands on a car if they really wanted. That's what I hope, anyway. Otherwise . . ."

She doesn't have to say what otherwise is. Otherwise is unspeakable.

"Shh!" she says suddenly. "Listen." I listen. I hear nothing and everything: wind and insects and small hidden animals. Breath. My breath and Carly's. And . . . just maybe . . .

I am considering the possibility that I hear more human breath than two people can account for when someone grabs us from behind, arms locking around our waists with a suddenness that stops my breath cold. And then for a second I *am* back there, in the Adirondacks, and I have been hiding, and Carly has found me, and Zed is waiting for us on the porch . . . And at the same time it's Sean, I can smell him, and he has a knife, I can feel the blade pressing—

I am about to yell, I think, when I hear a giggle, and then another giggle, and then two dimly outlined forms are running in circles around us, their voices joining in a giddy chorus: "Did you hear us? Did we scare you? What were you thinking when we came up behind you? How did you find us? What are you *wearing*? Are you pissed off? Does anyone else know? Are they worried? Are we in trouble? We just wanted to see it at night . . . to be alone here, without a million people around, and lights . . . because that's what it's like for our characters, right? We felt like we needed to know what it was really like . . . We thought it would help us understand . . ." Our phone beams carve them into fragments, flickers of long hair, pale skin, triumphant smiles, tight jeans. For a second I see them as girls in a kaleidoscope, geometrically fractured, beautiful in every new configuration. I'm dizzy with anger and relief. *They're just pretty girls. Just pretty, pretty girls, sure the world is theirs to command, never dreaming that danger is real, that . . .*

"Well, did it?" Chloe finally asks when their voices trail off. "Help you understand?"

"It did," one of them says, her voice suddenly serious and subdued. "It's actually really amazing out here, in this totally weird kind of way."

"And kind of beautiful," says the other one. Natasha, the me-girl. "I mean, have you looked up at the stars? I've never seen so many. I swear I didn't know there even *were* so many."

Their city-girl stupidity about the stars grates on my frayed-to-the-limit nerves. Their laughter feels like a dismissal of what happened to Carly and me; it cancels out the pure gladness I should be feeling. I find myself looking past them, peering hopelessly into the darkness, and realize with a start that I am looking for Zed, waiting for him to emerge from the shadows and announce that the game is up. *"Time for bed,"* he'll say. *"Inside, quick. Brush your teeth before you turn into pumpkins."* As if we're children. The past is collapsing into the present. Of course we're not children. Of course Zed is not here. *You are the earth, Carly, and Lois, you're the moon.* But only if the sun is there to anchor us in space, to preserve our delicate alignment. Otherwise, what are we, what can we hope to be?

Now that Justine and Natasha's chattering has quieted, replaced by a curiously reverent stillness, I find myself impressed almost in spite of myself by their uneasy grasp of the mystery around us. Their sense of wonder. Maybe there is hope that they will take my lies and make them true, take my truths and turn them into lovely fictions. We all stand in the dark for a moment, looking upward, before Carly clicks her phone back on. "All right, girls," she says. "Next thing you know, we'll be lying in the grass and discussing the goddamned constellations, and this isn't that kind of movie. I need to call Billy and your parents and try to get your little asses out of trouble. Whose car did you take?" Chloe has turned matter-of-fact and practical all of a sudden, and it strikes me that she is essentially playing Mandy, though a version of Mandy infused with a bit of her own worldly vulgarity. It occurs to me, too, that in playing Mandy she gets a chance to love Zed one more time, safely and from a distance—and to lose him again, too. Zed, embodied by Billy, no doubt closely observed by a vigilant Fiona . . . I wonder if I want to stay. I wonder if I can bear to watch.

The girls confess at last that they bribed one of the prep cooks to let them use his car. "Will he get in trouble?" they demand anxiously, and I'm glad that they can think of someone other than themselves. "It wasn't his fault, really. We were very persuasive." They look at each other conspiratorially, reveling in the strangeness of their ability to make men do their bidding.

Chloe

Now that the girls are safe, I'm cold, damp, exhausted, and free to be pissed off at them. Shooting starts tomorrow, and no one will have slept. At their age it won't matter, but I'll wake up with an extra decade carved in my face if I don't get the minimum hours of unconsciousness. They're laughing now, oblivious to the fact that they have actually scared the absolute shit out of everyone. I want to knock their pretty heads together.

I've had enough stargazing. I hold my hand out. "Give me the damned keys," I say. Justine is reaching into her pocket when, over her shoulder, I see a shadow detach itself from a tree and slouch toward the cabin. I blink. My eyes are caked with mascara and interrupted sleep, after all. They make their own shadows.

Is that a shadow?

"Lois." My hand has already shot out, grasped her tiny wrist. *"Lois!"* I lower my voice. The girls stop chattering, lean into each other. Lois turns slowly, follows my gaze. I see the shadow again, slinking along the side of the house. Moving in our direction. *Zed*, I think for one crazy moment. *Looking for us*.

Then Lois screams. Long and shrill, like someone else's voice has invaded her throat, and someone else's fear, because the Lois I know has never been afraid of *anything*, much less some stupid shadow. Lois's scream slices through skin, veins, echoes through my heart. The girls, clutching each other, eyes wide and baffled, duck behind me. The shadow freezes.

When Lois stops screaming, the air still rings. Metal on metal, as if the night is sharp. She wrenches her arm free and steps away from me, toward the cabin. "Sean," she says, her voice shaky but restored to its usual octave.

Not Zed, not a shadow. Lois's fucking stalker. And she's walking toward him, red dress and smeared makeup garish in the moonlight, like she belongs on a movie set. *Which this is.*

What the hell is she doing?

I lean down to Justine and Natasha, whose faces are pale with fright. "Go to the car." My voice comes out a low growl. "Call Billy, call your parents. Run. *Now.*" They go, arm in arm, long legs flying behind them.

I start across the lawn after Lois, who is moving like a sleepwalker, slowly and steadily. "I didn't think you'd make it," she says to the shadow, as if this is a perfectly normal conversation in the middle of the day. "How did you do it?" She sounds almost impressed.

"Got your credit card number off your computer. And your whole itinerary. And I followed those stupid girls. Wasn't exactly challenging." It's a young man's voice, tight and peevish and smug. "I could tell you didn't take me seriously. I was sick of it."

"That's not true," Lois begins, and then in the distance I hear a car door shut. The stalker hears it too; he jumps and emerges swiftly from the heavy darkness around the lodge. To me he looks slight, unremarkable. Something glitters, though, in his hand.

"Sean!" says Lois, her voice sharp. "They're not part of this."

The girls. I dart forward to intercept him, place myself squarely in Sean's path. *I'll keep them safe*, says some crazy voice in my head. I can't quite make out his face, but I can see that he's nothing like Zed. I can still feel the shiver of senseless hope that shot through me. Sorrow and loss, hardly faded after eighteen years. But there's no echo of Zed here, no trace. How could Lois ever have thought so?

Sean pulls up short when he sees me. "Yeah, but *she* is," he says. "Carly May Smith!" Shockingly, he sticks out a hand—not the one that glitters—as if we're going to be fucking properly introduced. I back away, and he laughs, dark and unhinged, arm returning to his side. "I can see Professor Lonsdale has told you all about me."

"The police are looking for you, Sean," Lois says calmly. "If you turn yourself in, you won't be in much trouble. But they know where you are. And the knife isn't going to help your cause, believe me."

What if we had fled when Lois screamed? Could we have gotten away? Too late. For a second I think I hear something behind me. A voice? A rustle of clothing? But no, nothing. Wishful thinking. Escape and rescue seem equally unlikely.

"Maybe we should go sit down," Lois proposes. "On the porch, maybe? We've all had a long day." Her matter-of-factness should be reassuring, but it's having the opposite effect. Now *I* want to scream. I've watched enough crime shows to know what she's doing: she wants to keep him talking until someone comes. Fictional psychopaths always want to stand around and tell you their goddamned story before they shoot you or stab you or slice parts of you off or whatever. Right now my faith in fictional psychopaths is a little shaky. Besides, there are always exceptions, even on TV: the guy in *Criminal Exploits* just slit my throat with no warning, for instance. It can happen. And I can discern the contours of Sean's knife now: it's long, curved, cruel-looking. It's not an ordinary knife. It's a very, very serious knife.

But Lois is already putting her suggestion in motion. She's stepping up onto the porch. She finds the outside light next to the front door, lowers herself into an Adirondack chair, stretches her legs out. "Just like your book," Sean says, and they exchange a look. I feel strangely excluded, as if they're in on this together. *Has she lost it?* I wonder suddenly. All this time I've been thinking that Lois was mildly off-kilter but basically sane. Maybe she's actually out of her fucking mind.

Sean follows Lois onto the porch and produces a roll of duct tape from the deep pocket of what I can see now is an extremely shabby trench coat. My first thought is that wardrobe could have come up with something a little more original. Then I think I must be as goddamned crazy as Lois.

But he's not going to tie her up, and he's sure as hell not getting me in one of those chairs, fancy knife or no. "Jesus," I hear myself explode. "You're going to tape her to a freaking Adirondack chair? I don't think so." I lurch forward. I have no plan, but I have my eye on the knife. Isn't this what Mandy would do? I'm taller than he is and very possibly stronger. I can see his face now; it's sprinkled with acne, fine-boned, sun-deprived. And scared to death: I see fear cross his features like an eclipse and marvel at his reaction to my attack. Then I am being shoved aside, hands grabbing my waist, digging into my ribs—and now it's my turn to scream, unthinking, until I see that it's Billy pushing past me, grabbing Sean, wresting the knife from his grip, forcing his hands behind his back. "Tear me a piece," he orders, tossing the duct tape to Lois. She pulls out a length of tape, tears it with her teeth, hands it to Billy, who looks more Zed-like than ever. After a few repetitions Sean's wrists are secured behind his back and his ankles looped together.

"I heard him coming," Lois explains to me, squeezing Billy's hand. "In case you were thinking I was completely insane." She grips the broad arms of her chair and pushes herself up to standing. "These are wrong, aren't they?" she says, looking down at the chairs. "It's not like my book at all. Ours were nicer."

Lois

It feels like forever until we're in my rental car and I'm driving back to the inn, after the police and the parents and the endless questions. In the rearview mirror I see the faintest glow in the sky behind us—not the sunrise but its promise.

"The police will be coming for us," I'd said as I stepped off the porch, like stepping off that other porch so long ago. "For Sean," I corrected myself, though no one seemed to have been listening to me. They hauled Sean away, and I was glad. But what would he do with the scripts I'd so recklessly fed him, blindly driven by my own inarticulate ghosts? *Ghosts: Grafology, gemelliparous, galanty. Gegenschein, gilderoy, gorsoon.*

Beside me, Carly leans back, lets her head roll to the side, mouth hanging slightly open. Chloe, I mean. She would hate to be seen this way, but I am reassured by her vulnerability, by her unprettiness, however fleeting. (*Unprettiness: Not a word. Ughten, uvelloid, unberufen. Upaithric.*)

You are the sun . . . We've been orbiting an absence, a mystery, an unnamed threat, Chloe and I. I don't think it's a mistake, the movie that begins filming tomorrow—this oblique, fictional reenactment of our past. Once we've collapsed the past and the present, the truth and the fictions, we will peel the layers apart, organize the pieces, and put ourselves back together. More or less.

Chloe stirs. She isn't sleeping, after all. She turns her head away from me, toward the window, and in the still dark car, lit only by the dashboard controls, I already feel the weight of whatever she's about to say.

"Would he have hurt us eventually?" she asks quietly, her voice almost without inflection, making the words as neutral as words can ever be. "Do you think? Killed us, I mean?"

Although she could mean Sean, I know she doesn't. She means Zed. It has taken us a long time to ask that question aloud; almost twenty years. But I find that I don't even have to think about the answer.

"He would have had to, wouldn't he? Because what he wanted was impossible. He would have had to kill us to keep us. Like 'Porphyria's Lover.' He gave that to us to read, remember? The man who strangles his lover with her own hair?" I shiver. "'*And all night long we have not stirred . . .*'"

"What did he want? I'm guessing you think you have that figured out?"

I don't like the bitterness that has crept into her voice, but I understand it.

"He was lonely? He was bored? The world disappointed him? He feared female sexuality? He wanted to save his sister; he wanted to keep us pure because he couldn't protect her. He loved—"

"No, God, stop," Chloe says. "I take it back. I don't want to put it into words. It's better without words. I don't mean you're wrong, it's just—"

"I know. Exactly. Better not to say." I know that is what she wants to hear. But I'll never believe it. I think the words are necessary. Why else did I write the book, after all?

"I still don't think he *meant* to hurt us, though," Chloe pushes on, not able to let it drop.

"Well, not in the way that he did." I slow for a small dark animal crossing the road. A raccoon; the headlights catch its eyes. "I don't think he had really thought very much about how *we* would feel. He was thinking about himself. He was quite selfish, in a way." We've never criticized him before, not out loud. We both laugh uncomfortably at the absurdity of suggesting that a kidnapper of young girls might—just might—have been a little selfish.

"Yeah," Chloe echoes, "just a little selfish. He never *meant* to break our hearts."

"Never." Because we didn't escape injury, after all: we were far from unscathed. Our frail, ridiculous, twelve-year-old hearts. Some things you can't put back together again, ever.

The woods rise darkly on either side of the road. I remind myself yet again that they are not our woods. Their secrets have nothing to do with us. The stars are the same, but as morning nears, they're fading. *Stars: sacring, scelestic, scialytic, scintillescent, scripturient, soliform, somniate.*

Yes, Zed, I know what these words mean. *Sacring:* consecration. *Scelestic:* wicked. *Scialytic:* banishing shadows. *Scintillescent:* twinkling, obviously. Like stars. *Scripturient,* a good one: possessing a violent urge to write. *Soliform:* like a sun, sunlike. *Somniate:* to dream. *Syzygy.*

It's not hard to wrest meaning from those words.

ACKNOWLEDGMENTS

I am tremendously grateful to Barbara Jones for being the kind of editor people say no longer exists; this book owes much to her sharp eye and narrative insight. I also want to thank everyone behind the scenes at Henry Holt, especially Lucy Kim for the striking jacket art and Stella Tan for her handling of the details. A profound thanks to Kimberly Witherspoon at Inkwell Management for making it all happen, to Monika Woods for being an amazing reader and providing endless support, and to Alexis Hurley for ensuring that the novel will find readers beyond these shores. I'm grateful to the Vermont Studio Center for the fellowship that allowed me to see the book through its final stages in beautiful surroundings and excellent company.

There aren't enough words to thank Gina Barreca—friend, mentor, reader, all-around fairy godmother. Her generosity is unparalleled, her influence immeasurable. Alison Umminger has been a generous, thoughtful, and magically perceptive reader from the start, as well as the very best of friends. Other brilliant friends have also provided invaluable readerly and writerly support—Aaron Bremyer and Dionne Irving Bremyer, Greg Fraser, Chad and Gwen Davidson, Meg Pearson. The English Department at the University of West Georgia has been wonderfully supportive all along, despite having hired me as a Victorianist. I offer love and endless gratitude to my family, my fiercest supporters: Homer Mitchell, Wendy Mitchell Starkweather, Homer David Mitchell, and Kim Marie.